Calling All Dentists

by

Tara Ford

Is ignorance really bliss? Never take it for granted

Copyright © 2014 Tara Ford
All rights reserved.
ISBN-13: 978-1496190468
ISBN-10: 1496190467

Other titles by Tara Ford

Calling All Services

Acknowledgements

Thank you to every single person who has supported me throughout my writing journey, once again. A special thank-you goes to my family and friends who attended the launch party for my first book (Calling All Services) – Mum S, Brian, Nigel, Liam, Zak, Abbie, Luke, Mum F, Sharen, Lewis, Chloe, Annalise, Benita, Clair, Angie, Reid, Paula, Rosie, David, Jo, Sarah C, Dawn, Jane H, John H, Michelle, Jane F, Sarah N, Katt, Suzi, Stevie-Eve, Will, Sarah F, Tasha, Nicola, Debbie Warford (Yay!) – she will be smiling now and Basil Kupersamy who I need to say a big thank-you to, for all of his support from day one and for always managing to make me look half decent in a photograph. Amazing feat.

I would also like to thank everyone (past and present) at EJS for their continued support – they are like a second family to me. Thanks to Sarah Boyce for her enthusiastic, positive appraisal of my first book and for passing it around to the neighbours. Thanks to Tilli Stevens for her keen interest in the release of this book and for downsizing me at an appropriate time in my life. Thank-you to Colin, Karen, Lynda and two members of the fishy crew – Caroline and Debbie L. for their continued support and last but by no means least, thanks to the world for giving us beautiful people like Sarah Bennett (Mini-Me).

A big thank-you to Jane Hessey for all of her valuable help and expertise even though it caused her tears, screaming and torment, but here's to the next one if she can bear it.

Thank you to all my Twitter followers and Facebook friends – I appreciate every one of you for your kind support.

The biggest thank-you goes to you for taking the time to read this book and if it is the second one of mine that you are reading – thank you even more so.

Tara Ford
http://taraford.weebly.com/
Twitter: @rata2e
Facebook: Tara Ford-Author

For Pat

Chapter 1

"I would rather give birth to an elephant," said Emma with a devilish glint in her eye.

"Oh that's ridiculous Em, you must do something about it," replied Ruby, chewing her fingernails vigorously and looking rather nervously at her friend.

"No – actually I would rather give Pete oral sex."

"That's not very nice at all Emma."

"That's exactly my point – it's a dreadful thought isn't it?" Emma let out a huff and turned back to stare intently into the bathroom mirror.

"No, I mean that's cruel of you to say that about Pete and rather rude, if I might add." Ruby looked hurt in an odd sort of way.

"Well, would you?" asked Emma, intent on getting the required response. Ruby shrugged her shoulders, said nothing, then sloped off to her bedroom and closed the door quietly behind her.

"What's the matter? Have I upset you?" asked Emma as she opened the door and peeped in to the room, feeling somewhat guilty.

Ruby was perched on the end of her single bed, clutching her latest *Mills & Boon* novel tightly in her hands.
"No not really," she said half heartedly, "You always make fun of Pete though and he's one of the kindest people I know and

I'm sure he's madly in love with you. It's just not fair to say horrible things about him."

"I think you like him more than you let on Ruby Winters," said Emma, joining Ruby on the end of the bed.

"Oh don't be silly. Besides, he would never be interested in anyone like me anyway." She sighed deeply and fingered the pages of her book.

"You fancy him don't you?" screeched Emma as she threw herself back on the bed and crossed her hands behind her head.

"No, I... I just think you're unkind sometimes. He would do anything for you. You could click your fingers and he'd come running at a moment's notice."

"You do fancy him – I knew it," squealed Emma, excited at the thought of her secret plan to fix up her flat-mate, work colleague and best friend with Pete, the office wimp, who she had no interest in herself – whatsoever.

"Oh please, stop trying to change the subject Emma, you do need to get that..." she pointed to Emma's mouth, "sorted out."

"Hmm," replied Emma, deep in thought. "Maybe I will one day."

Pushing her glasses up her nose, Ruby opened her book and pulled the leather bookmark out. "I'll make the appointment for you if you like," she said as she flicked the pages backwards and forwards and finally settled for the page just before her bookmarked place.

"No, I'll sort it out soon, don't hassle me," huffed Emma as she got up and left the room.

Back in the bathroom, Emma smiled and pouted in the mirror. Then she spoke in an exaggerated way to open her mouth wider, exposing her beautifully white teeth. "Heelllooooo... mmmyyy... naaameeee... is Emmmaaa..."

Tutting to herself, she knew Ruby was right. She had to see a dentist and pretty soon.

At twenty six years old she'd built up a deep-set fear of dentists. Hearing horror stories, from practically everyone she knew, just made the matter worse. Emma hadn't seen one for at least eight years and until now hadn't had any plans of ever seeing one again – well not while she was conscious at least.

The last time Emma plucked up the courage to visit a dentist, it had been a horrific experience and she barely tolerated the root canal surgery she had needed for her gum disease, but thanks to her mum, who was in attendance, she scraped through. She then had a dodgy filling which caused the same tooth to break in half a week later, right in the middle of a fancy dress party. At first Emma thought the sausage rolls on the buffet were exceptionally crunchy until she discovered she was chewing part of her own tooth. She had spent the rest of that evening worrying that the half tooth could be seen and desperately trying to talk through gritted teeth as the searing pain of sensitivity from the exposed nerves was constantly triggered by the air she breathed. It was then that Emma vowed she would never see a dentist again.

Now, she feared she'd left it all too late. Most of her perfectly aligned teeth were wobbly, four of them felt like they were hanging by threads and her gums had receded so far that there were gaps forming between each tooth. She couldn't eat crusty bread or apples anymore, in fact there were many things she could no longer munch her way through, and being an avid food lover, it was a pretty miserable existence. She'd noticed that everyone seemed to talk to her teeth now and Emma knew she had to do something about it quickly before they all started to drop out. Reaching for her baby toothbrush, she tentatively began the painstaking task of brushing them like they were ancient artifacts being discovered on an excavation site.

Ruby peered around the bathroom door and smiled, "Sorry Em, I don't mean to go on at you all of the time. I... I just get worried about you."

Emma shot a cursory glance at her toothpaste grin in the mirror and then spat out the contents of her mouth. "I know you aren't mean Rue. I just need to do this in my own time. I know it needs to be sooner rather than later but I get so anti when I think about it." Emma turned to the mirror again and grinned widely.

"Your teeth are so perfect Em, I'm sure the dentist could do something to your gums to stop them receding."

"Yeah – probably give me more of that root surgery stuff or something even worse."

"Um," replied Ruby, "well you've got to save your teeth whatever it takes, haven't you?"

"Suppose," said Emma and began to brush them again rather obsessively.

It was the weekend and both Ruby and Emma usually spent one day shopping (usually together) and the other one cleaning their small flat and doing the washing and ironing in preparation for the busy working week ahead. Today was shopping day and as there were only two weeks left before Christmas, Emma realised that she really needed to start buying some presents for her family and of course, the secret Santa present, which was always an embarrassing episode at work.

The office staff equated to just six people, two of whom were Ruby and herself, the rest were men. Sadly, the men had no idea what to buy for each other, let alone the girls if they had the misfortune of picking their names out of the hat. So the whole idea of an office secret Santa was a bit silly and pointless – but they all took part in it just the same.

"Who did you get for your secret Santa?" called Emma as she went past Ruby's room to her own.

"I'm not supposed to tell you Em, it's a secret."

"Oh come on Rue – no one will know will they."

"Ok." Ruby paused and then added, "It's Dave."

"Oh no," laughed Emma, "What are you going to get him? Maybe a pink tutu would be nice for the works party."

Giggling into her book, Ruby replied, "I couldn't do that, I'd be too embarrassed."

"Why? He wouldn't know it was from you would he?"

"No, I can't. I'll get him some aftershave or something like that."

"Ah, you've got to have a laugh Rue – go on buy him something funny. I'll help you choose it."

"Who have you got?" Trying to change the subject, Ruby put her book down and went to the bathroom.

"Pete," laughed Emma.

"Ah don't be horrible, get him something nice," said Ruby, sensing the mischief in Emma's laugh.

"Yeah, I was thinking of getting him a nice blow up doll so he can have a really fun time at Christmas." The bathroom door closed quietly and Emma knew that Ruby was going to sulk in the shower.

Although the two friends were both work colleagues and flat mates, they were completely opposite in their personalities but they got on together surprisingly well. Emma was the dominant one in their home while Ruby was the quiet, unassuming geek who plodded along aimlessly. Ruby dreamed of white weddings, white Christmases and white fluffy clouds and anything else that she could dream about that might be white or fluffy – or both.

Her appearance matched her geeky personality well, as Ruby's wardrobe consisted of a selection of sloppy plain jumpers, five blouses (one for each day of the working week) several pairs of cheap jeans and 3 pairs of black, straight-legged trousers (three identical pairs, for work). She had never had a real boyfriend, unless you could include her school-crush, Justin. She had kissed him on the lips once, when she was fourteen, behind the communal wheelie bins of the block of flats where her parents lived. When Justin returned for a second round, a few days later, his chapped lips parted and they kissed momentarily, but then Ruby put a halt to it and ran home disgusted by his attempt to put his tongue in her mouth. She didn't see him ever again.

Emma, on the other hand, was the complete opposite to Ruby in every single way imaginable.

"Come on are you ready?" called Emma, pulling her heavy coat on.

"Coming," replied Ruby as she tiptoed through the hall, stopped short of Emma and gave a geeky grin. Dressed in her usual grey rain coat, grey *Ugg* boots, grey knitted hat with a pink pompom on the top and grey mittens, Ruby looked her usual, unfashionable self. Drab, was a more appropriate description.

"Right, presents first and then we'll go to *New Look* and have a look at their party dresses," said Emma as she linked arms with her little 'book-geek' and pulled her out of the front door.

The shopping arcade was heaving with frantic Christmas shoppers, weaving in and out of the countless shop doorways. Bright red 'Sale' signs dominated almost every window, showing the percentage reductions of the products within. The main café, in the centre of the enclosed shopping arcade was full to overflowing with hungry bargain hunters, tired mums and miserable dads.

"Where do you want to go first?" asked Emma, scanning the expanse of the retail centre, as they descended on the escalator from the multi-storey car park above.

"I don't mind. Shall we just walk along each side and then we could pop in all of them?" suggested Ruby (which was unusual because she never suggested anything outright and was far too timid to voice any opinions of her own).

"Fine by me," chirped Emma as they stepped off the escalator and began to move slowly through the crowds of people, pushchairs and over-sized carrier bags.

Laden with countless bags, wads of receipts and aching feet, Emma grabbed the two dresses and shoved Ruby towards the changing rooms. "You are going to look totally awesome in this Ruby." She smiled reassuringly, realising her geeky friend was already panicking about looking anything like 'totally awesome'.

Knowing exactly what she had been looking for, Emma slipped the black, ruched dress over her head and pulled it on. Peering in the mirror, she turned from side to side, admiring her slim figure and then turned back to face the mirror full on. As long as she didn't open her mouth too wide, she decided that she looked pretty good. Scooping up her long brown hair which tumbled down over her shoulders, Emma tied it up in a rough high bun and liked the look even more. "Have you got it on yet?" she called over the cubicle's partition wall.

"Yes," replied Ruby quietly.

"Let me see then."

Stepping out of their cubicles at the same time, they stared at each other.

"Wow... I mean a big wow. You look gorgeous Rue," said Emma, transfixed by her friends' voluptuous figure, barely contained within the sleek red material of the dress. With a plunge neck line and a crossover knot tied centrally above the waste, the dress accentuated Ruby's ample bust while the length highlighted her long, slender legs from just above the knees. "*Bridget Nielsen*, eat your heart out," said Emma, trying to plump up Ruby's cropped blonde mop. "You should spike your hair up a bit – you'd look like a super model."

"Um... not sure," said Ruby as she shyly glanced at the long mirror opposite the cubicles. "Who's *Bridget Nielsen* anyway?"

"Just some glamorous supermodel, from my mum's era. You have got to get it Rue – you look stunning. It's about time you made a change from those 'special black trousers' that you always wear when you go out."

"I don't know Em." Removing her purple rimmed glasses, Ruby squinted in the mirror.

"Oh my God – you have got to buy it and you have got to wear your contact lenses that you never bother with." Emma couldn't take her eyes off this new image of Ruby. "Please buy it Rue, I'm not kidding; you could have Pete falling at your feet looking like that. I know you like him." Emma had already decided that they would actually make a perfect couple – two wimpy geeks together in happy geeky-wonderland, which would no doubt be very white and fluffy.

"He should like me as I am, shouldn't he?" she replied only slightly huffily.

"He's probably never noticed you. In fact no one notices you Ruby because you hide behind your baggy blouses and sloppy jumpers." Emma held her breath anxiously waiting for the tears but thankfully they didn't come.

"Oh nobody is interested in me, I know that Em. I'm not boyfriend material," she sighed.

"Yes but you could be, if only you put yourself out there a bit more. You're like a wilting wallflower. I hope I'm not upsetting you Ruby but you need to find your own *Mills & Boon* sweetheart and live in the real world." Slinging an arm around Ruby's shoulder, Emma empathised with her. "Actually, don't buy it." Grinning slyly, she winked at Ruby. "I'm going to buy it for you, for Christmas."

"No you can't do that Em. Please it's far too expensive," said Ruby with a panic stricken look on her face.

"Yes I can, come on hurry up and get it off."

Slithering back in to her cubicle like a sand snake, Ruby continued to reason with Emma about the possibilities of not having the dress, over the partition wall, while they changed back in to their clothes.

"I'm buying it and that's that, you can have it as an early Christmas present. All you need to get now are some shoes to go with it and maybe a handbag too. I refuse to allow you to wear your lace up *Hush Puppies* with that dress and you're not taking your rucksack to the party!" Emma burst into raucous laughter and then she heard a sigh coming from the other side of the wall.

"Ok," replied Ruby, faintly.

The bookshop was filled with old age pensioners, middle aged couples, bookworms of all descriptions and a few younger women who were checking out the latest Chick Lit novels.

Heading straight for the fictional romance section, Emma assumed Ruby would be directly behind her. "What are you buying this week?" asked Emma as she turned around to see an elderly lady peering strangely at her. "Oh sorry, I thought my friend was behind me."

The small woman raised her bushy grey eyebrows and smiled an oddly familiar semi-toothed grin. Emma managed to smile back but with lips tightly closed as she scanned the book aisles for Ruby. Across the central aisle, Emma could just make out the almost fluorescent pink pompom on the top of Ruby's hat, sticking up above the shelves. Strangely, she was in the reference section.

"There you are I've been looking for you. Thought you were behind me," said Emma as she stood alongside her friend. "What are you doing here?" she asked, surveying the animal reference books.

"I just thought you could get Pete a nice book about dogs for his secret Santa present."

"Seriously?" said Emma, amazed by Ruby's thoughtfulness over a cheap, jokey office gift. "You really do like him don't you – admit it."

"I feel sorry for him when you all tease him in the office, that's all."

"He loves it Ruby. He gives as good as he gets, you know that."

"Um," replied Ruby, picking up a large hardback book called 'The Dog Dictionary'. "This is nice, he'd like this..."

"Fifteen pounds! I'm not spending that much, even if it is at a reduced price." Taking the book from Ruby, Emma awkwardly placed it back on the shelf while trying to balance six carrier bags in her other hand. "Come on, hurry up and get your new book, then we can get home. My feet are killing me."

"Maybe you shouldn't wear high heels then, they are supposed to be bad for your back," said Ruby bravely, as she headed off to the fiction/romance section. Carrying two bags in each hand and her rucksack on her back, Ruby's little pink pompom wobbled about like a jelly on a plate as she toddled off.

"Right, last shop. If we can't find anything in here, let's forget it," sighed Emma.

Looking across the expansive shop floor, littered with shelves, boxes, display cabinets and swirly card racks, Ruby spotted another department and began to head off in the direction of... yet more books.

"Not more books Rue, surely."

"Only having a quick look," she replied as she tottered away.

"I'll be over there then," called Emma, pointing in the opposite direction to the novelty gifts and party-time department.

Nodding her pompom profusely, Ruby smiled sweetly and gave a tiny wave with her delicate fingers.

"I've found a brilliant present you could get for Dave." Emma grinned as she approached Ruby, who had managed to find a seat and was almost buried under a pile of books.

"That's funny because I've found the perfect one for Pete." She laughed, holding up a small reference book on dog breeds. "This one is only four ninety nine." Noticing the item in Emma's hand, Ruby's eyes widened in horror, "I'm not buying that for Dave!" she screeched and then worriedly, looked around the shop to make sure no one had heard her.

"He won't know who it's from Rue. Come on it'll be a real laugh." Emma held out the adult sized, fancy dress outfit. "It's only six quid, he could wear it in the office, it would be so funny," said Emma, desperately trying to convince her naïve friend.

"I'm not buying a fairy tutu and wand for Dave, it's not fair," said Ruby, still clutching the dog book and beginning to turn pale.

"I've got an idea then. Why don't we swap secret Santa names? I'll have Dave and you can buy a nice little dog book for Pete. How about that?" Breathing a sigh of relief, Ruby nodded and smiled as she stood up and clutched the book tightly to her chest.

"I don't know why you get so worried Rue, Dave will probably wear this all over Christmas."

"Um," replied Ruby as they headed for the checkout. "It might not be appropriate. He has only just got married and his husband might not like that sort of thing."

"It'll be fine. Dave is the feminine one after all. I expect Josh would be quite happy to see his... err... husband, dancing around in a pink, sparkly tutu," laughed Emma, raucously.

"Um," muttered Ruby and handed her treasured dog book to the young girl at the checkout.

Chapter 2

Sunday morning at ten o'clock sharp, the phone began to ring. Aware that Ruby was up already, Emma lay in bed and waited for her to answer it. Emma knew who it was and she really didn't want to go today. Her raging toothache along with a new throbbing abscess was making her feel quite unwell. A quiet rap on the door indicated Ruby was on the other side, and then it opened slightly.

"Emma? Pete's on the phone," she whispered, poking her head through the opening of the door.

"Tell him I'm not going today, I don't feel very well. Say sorry for me." Emma sighed and turned over.

"I'm sorry Pete but Emma really doesn't feel very well today, she said maybe next week? She's ever so sorry." Emma could hear Ruby talking in her sweet little voice. "Yes ok, thank you. Goodbye"

"What did he say?" called Emma from her room.

"He just said it was ok and hoped that you get better soon. He doesn't really talk to me much when he phones up for you," said Ruby, poking her head around the door again. "Do you want me to get you anything?"

"No, I'm getting up now. Thanks anyway."

"Is it your teeth again?"

"Yes, but I'll get over it, before you start." Emma smiled, "You should have gone with Pete, kept him company."

"Oh no, he wouldn't want me dragging along with him. He always seems in a rush to get off the phone quickly when I talk to him."

"He doesn't talk to you much Rue because you hardly ever speak to him," said Emma, pulling her dressing gown around her and slipping her fluffy booties on.

"I don't know what to talk to him about…"

"Books! You could probably write a book between you about books." Passing Ruby at the doorway, Emma headed for the bathroom, "You could make up a story about a doggie romance or something like that," she laughed, before closing the bathroom door behind her.

"Do you want a coffee?" called Ruby.

"Yes please," replied Emma, realising she may have just upset her dearest friend again. She didn't ever mean to hurt Ruby but sometimes she felt very frustrated by Ruby's inability to socialize or even make herself look or sound attractive in any way to entice members of the opposite sex. Emma couldn't understand how Ruby loved her romance books so much, to the point of constantly daydreaming about her perfect man (and Emma had always had a sneaky suspicion that the perfect man in Ruby's dreams, was in fact Pete) and yet she didn't seem to want to put any romantic gestures in to practice.

Shuffling into the kitchen, Emma reached up in to the cupboard for the *Paracetamol* and took two out. "Pete will need a replacement companion soon anyway. I don't intend on doing it for much longer," said Emma huffily. "It just gives him the wrong idea and I'm sure it's giving both of our parents the wrong idea too."

"But it's just an innocent walk surely..."

"Yes, in your eyes and mine but certainly not in Pete's."

It had been going on for over a year. At least twice a month Pete called Emma to arrange a doggie-duo trek. Emma really wasn't sure how it came to be a regular Sunday morning activity. Emma's parents, along with Pete, both owned dogs, in fact the same breed of dog – Boxers. It had come up in a conversation one day and Pete had suggested that they take the dogs out together on a Sunday morning. It wasn't a problem at first for Emma to collect her parents' dog, Misty, and take her out for a long stroll with Pete and his identical bitch, appropriately called Woof (Emma wouldn't have expected any other name for Pete's dog). Emma's parents were both out every Sunday morning at the wholesalers, buying stock for her mum's shop. So the fact that Misty got a nice long walk was very helpful to them.

"That's a shame if you don't take Misty out anymore," said Ruby, pouring hot water in to the coffee cups.

"Well I'm not doing it after Christmas and that's final. He'll just have to find another partner."

"What about your parents, won't they be disappointed?"

"No not at all and I think it'll do my dad some good to take the dog out for longer walks, before he ends up vegetating in his reclining chair." Emma laughed, and then held on to her jaw as it ached from her swollen gum.

***

Motionless in the Monday morning traffic, Emma and Ruby sat silently as the engine of Emma's worn out car ticked over noisily. "Two more weeks Rue..."

"Yes, it's gone very quick this year."

"Hopefully these last two weeks will go even quicker," said Emma, pulling away as the traffic began to ease, "I cannot wait for the Christmas work do, sounds like it'll be the best one yet."

"Um," muttered Ruby, staring out of the passenger window in another one of her daydreams, "It's expensive though."

"Yes I know, but we've never had a do like this one before so it should be good. And there are so many people going from *Webb's*."

"Um." Ruby's lack of enthusiasm wasn't unusual if the activity didn't contain a book in it somewhere, but Emma was determined it was going to be a good night – for both of them.

The fact that Emma had her eye on someone of the male kind, made her more hell-bent on going all out to make sure that both her and Ruby looked their best. Emma wanted to have a good night and she really didn't want Ruby to be tagging along behind her, no matter how much she loved her, hence the premeditated 'set-up' with Pete.

Arriving in the car park of *Webb's DIY Store*, the girls jumped out and shuffled across to the staff entrance at the rear, as an icy wind blew across the concrete expanse from the nearby fields.

"Morning!" called Colin Roberts as they entered the huge store and headed for the wooden staircase up to the office.

"Good morning," said Ruby politely, as they passed him. He was the 'Big Boss' as Ruby always referred to him, but to Emma, he was just Colin. She had the utmost respect for him and his position but in her eyes he was still – just Colin. Emma said nothing as she gritted her teeth together to dampen the pain, spurred on by the raw wind outside. Nodding and smiling, she rushed past him and clomped up the creaky, wooden stairs.

The office was warm and always peaceful early in the morning, before the shop opened. Emma walked over to her desk (seven o'clock spot), next to Colin's (five o'clock spot) and plonked her bag on top of the piles of paperwork, invoices and delivery notes.

"Morning girlies," said the familiar high pitched voice of Dave as he skipped in to the office. "Which of you two lovely young ladies is going to make me a nice cup of coffee?"

"Count me out!" mumbled Emma, through her teeth.

"Ooh... get out of the wrong side of the bed did we Ems?"

"I'll make the drinks," said Ruby. Her coat was already hung up on the hooks by the door and her bag neatly stored away under her immaculate (one o'clock spot) desk.

"Good girl Rubes," replied Dave rather patronisingly, thought Emma, "What's wrong with you today Em?"

"Nothing really, just don't feel too well, I'll get over it though."

"Sorry sweetie, last thing you need is for me to come in bouncing about, eh?" he said, genuinely apologetic, "I'm just so excited – 2 weeks to go and then it's Christmas!" Dancing around the room like a fairy, Dave whistled a cheery tune of *Dance of the Sugar Plum Fairy* and Emma was then completely convinced that the secret Santa present she had bought was absolutely the perfect gift for him.

"Good morning! Oh you're here... are you feeling better Emma?" asked Pete, politely, as he walked in to the room wrapped up in his maroon scarf, gloves and hat which were all (very sadly) matching. Emma could never quite understand why Pete wrapped himself up like he was about to go on a hike across Antarctica, when he had just got out of his car and walked the few steps across the car park and in to the building.

"I've dosed myself up to the eyeballs on *Paracetamol* so I should be able to get through the day. Sorry I couldn't make it yesterday."

"Coffee anyone?" asked Ruby quietly, but no one heard.

"Don't worry about it. Maybe we could do it next week?" replied Pete.

"Maybe," said Emma half-heartedly. She had no intention of going next week either or any other week again for that matter.

Strolling into the office, Colin was deep in discussion with Jeff Carnell about the Customer Service training, scheduled for the approaching New Year. "Sure, that's not a problem at all. I'm very happy to organise the team."

"Good... good," said Colin, accepting a mug of coffee from Ruby as he passed by.

"Morning," said Jeff, looking around at everyone and then sitting down in his (three o'clock spot) executive style, reclining office chair.

The office housed six desks, each one kitted out with its own set of filling cabinets behind. There were two large windows at one end of the room, where Emma and Colin sat, facing the door. The other four desks were situated two on either side of the room. Emma had been the one who'd decided one Friday afternoon, when they were all bored and tired, that they should all have allotted times, instead of names, as the layout of the office and although not particularly circular, looked like the numerals on a clock face. The doorway was 'twelve o'clock' and if anyone turned up at the office door, one of them would say either 'midday' or 'midnight', depending on whether the visitor brought good news or bad or indeed, whether the caller was liked or not. It was the office secret code and in hindsight, Emma thought it was slightly ridiculous, but it had stuck ever since.

Gazing at her desk full of papers, Emma sighed. She had to get everything tied up before the Christmas break. Her high ranking position in the company as the Finance Officer meant she had a lot of responsibility and sometimes, an awful lot of headaches. Juggling the funds, paying bills and worst of all, the payroll, Emma couldn't afford to let things slip... but they had. Preoccupied with her teeth of late, Emma hadn't kept things organised and now she faced a massive sort-out session.

Suffering from Monday morning blues at the best of times, today was no different, in fact it was worse. Her aching jaw and general feeling of being under the weather only hindered her further as she turned on her swivel chair and stared out of the window behind her, absent mindedly.

"You alright there?" asked Colin as he plonked himself down at his desk beside her and rubbed the top of his balding head.

"Yeah, I'll be fine. Feel a bit yucky, that's all."

"You should have stayed at home."

"I've got too much to do Colin. I'll be ok," she said, turning back round to her desk as a tall figure entered the doorway at 'midday'.

Striding over to Pete's desk (at eleven o'clock), Darren leaned over and spoke quietly to him as Emma watched intently. Trying to catch Ruby's eye, she attempted to wave her hand but Ruby, as always, had her nose buried in paperwork, ready for the filing cabinet, unaware that a rather sexy and muscular, pert bottom was bending over directly opposite her.

Darren often came to the office to talk to Pete, the Purchasing Manager, about deliveries or the latest sales pitch. He was 'Mr. Popular' with the ladies on the shop floor and rumour had it that he was the best floor manager they'd ever had.

Darren had been with the company just five months and he'd successfully turned the shop floor around, from its days of an uninspired workforce and lacklustre sales performance. He was vibrant, conscientious and totally gorgeous in Emma's eyes. He was going through a difficult divorce which sadly, involved the little lives of his two young boys but Darren always managed to keep a stiff upper lip when things really weren't going his way. Both of his sons were going to live with their mother and Darren had been heard to say that it was 'not fair how women always seem to get the kids'. At 31 years old, he had quite a lot of baggage but that didn't lessen his appeal in the slightest. Unknowingly, he was Emma's prime target at the Christmas work do, once she'd somehow set Ruby up with Pete.

Watching the curve of his bottom undulate as he talked and gesticulated, Emma was mesmerised until suddenly, he turned his head to look directly at her while Pete searched through a ream of paper. Gulping her way back to consciousness, Emma smiled gently and then almost crumpled in her chair as he smiled back and slowly winked a sexy, long-lashed eye at her.

"Here they are," said Pete, handing several sheets of paper to Darren. Nodding his head, Darren smiled and then turned around and left, while Emma sat with her hand propped under her chin and gazed dreamily at his buttocks exiting the room and disappearing down the stairs.

Once the men had left the office, to collect their daily quota of bacon rolls for lunch from the local café, Emma rushed across the room to Ruby's 'perfect place of production'.

Nibbling on a meal of pre-prepared, cold root vegetables and a mug of chicken soup, Ruby looked up.

"Did you see Darren come in earlier?" asked Emma, excitedly.

"No... why?" mumbled Ruby chewing a lump of soggy swede.

"He smiled at me – I mean he really looked at me! And guess what else he did..."

"What?"

"He winked at me Rue. I think he might like me."

Pulling Jeff's chair across the room, from behind his desk, Emma sat down next to Ruby and opened her oat snack bar. "I can't wait till the Christmas do; it's going to be so much better this year," she said excitedly, as she sank her teeth in to the oat bar and wished she hadn't as the pain returned and began to throb in her gums.

"Um," replied Ruby and straightened the pencil on her desk. Glancing back at her own desk, Emma took a quick look at the mess and the scattered bits of paper laying everywhere, and then she weighed up the unsurprising neatness, order and precision of Ruby's desk. Her pen pot sparkled, a spare pencil, rubber and lime green sharpener, lay in a perfect row by the side of the letter rack and there was one solitary sheet of paper in her 'In' tray.

"Gosh, I really need to get my paperwork sorted out don't I?" said Emma, cringing at the thought of what lay ahead.

"I could help you this afternoon," smiled Ruby through her chicken soup lips.

"Oh fab-u-lous-oh! If you could do my filing that would be so helpful. I owe you one Rue."

"No you don't. Remember that expensive dress you bought for me, I owe you."

"No, that's a Christmas present Rue. And the key to your future."

Ruby stopped chewing for a moment and stared worriedly at Emma's big grin, but said nothing.

The roar of Dave's laughter could be heard well before the men reached the bottom of the stairs. Bumping up them, two at a time, Dave was the first to appear in the office, "Doughnut?" he called, holding out a bag full of them. Shaking their heads, Emma and Ruby declined his offer.

Emma had to make sure her dress fitted perfectly for the party and Ruby only ate healthy foods really, but her dress would fit perfectly even if she ate doughnuts for the next two weeks. She possessed a metabolic rate that infuriated Emma – she could probably eat anything and everything and not gain an ounce. Ruby had 3 big meals a day and sometimes nibbled healthy snack bars in-between, yet her slight frame just had to conceal a mammoth metabolism as Emma knew that if she ate as much as Ruby, she would end up looking like a Sumo wrestler.

"Right, Emma you still need to pay for your meal love," said Colin, grabbing a check list from his table. "I'm paying the final installment for the work do on Wednesday."

"Oh sorry, I completely forgot. I'll go to the cash point tonight and then pay you tomorrow."

"While we're on the subject of money, you still owe twelve pounds for the coffee club Em," said Jeff, overhearing Colin.

"Yes, I'll get that too." Emma smiled sarcastically.

Jeff picked up the ringing phone on his desk, "Good afternoon, *Webb's DIY*," he said, politely and then raised his eyebrows and rolled his eyes to the ceiling.

As the company's Customer Service Manager, his patient, calm personality was perfect for the job, particularly when Mr Kibble was on the phone. Everyone knew when Mr Kibble was on the phone by Jeff's contorted and anguished facial expressions. Jeff had had many years of experience in dealing with tricky customers – who were *always* right. He usually liked to keep himself to himself, get on with his work and then rush home to his lovely family at the end of the day but when Mr Kibble was on the phone, Jeff was prepared to bare all and share the experience with everybody. Mr Kibble had of late truly tested Jeff's patience and it seemed that poor old Mr Kibble was actually going completely insane.

"Ok, well there are only three more people to pay up, apart from you," said Colin, smiling at Emma as he left the office to find the other non-paying culprits.

The Christmas do this year was an unprecedented occasion. Normally the staff of *Webb's DIY Store* went out for meals in little 'clicks'. The office crew went to the local pub/restaurant, usually at lunch time on the last day. The checkout girls would go nightclubbing and grab a take away on the way home. The rest of the staff on the shop floor usually went for a meal at a restaurant of their choice, one evening in the last week before the Christmas break. And poor old Bill, who lovingly swept the floors all day long, in between helping to make up pots of specifically prescribed colours of paint, always declined any offers of a night out and much rather preferred to go home to his dear wife.

This year was different and Darren had been the one to suggest to Colin that the company should 'gel' a bit more, by having a Christmas do which involved the whole team. When Colin approached Emma about subsidizing part of the costs for the staff, she thought it was a brilliant idea and quite affordable within the store's budget.

"That'll get the team-building spirit going." Colin had said, realising that Darren's idea was just what the company and all of the staff needed.

"It shouldn't be a problem at all," Emma had said, "Looking at the latest figures – the forecast is good."

The staff had been given the option to pay in installments and with two months notice, the lower paid members of *Webb's* could easily afford it.

The venue was underneath a multi nightclub complex, by the southern coast. A total of thirty four companies would be attending the dinner/dance/disco, in a giant sized conference hall. Some twenty nine staff from *Webb's* had signed up for the Christmas party, excluding Bill, which reconfirmed the popularity of Darren's idea.

Emma was always the last to pay up for anything, not through lack of cash but lack of a memory. In contrast, Ruby was the very first to pay her dues, always efficient, responsible and highly predictable.

Raising his eyebrows and rolling his eyes towards Emma, Jeff listened to the person on the other end of the phone. "No, sorry we don't Mr Kibble." As soon as he'd said the name, everyone (except Ruby) stopped what they were doing and looked at Jeff. "I'm not sure that would stop them anyway sir." Looking around the room, shaking his head from side to side slowly, Jeff rolled his eyes again and grinned as he continued to listen to the voice on the phone. "Would it be better to shut the door at night sir?" he said despondently. "Well if you came down to the store I'm really not sure that we would have anything that would meet your needs Mr Kibble." Resting back in his chair, Jeff rubbed his balding head while staring up at the ceiling. "You might try a pet store sir?"

Dave tried to suppress a giggle and Pete's ears pricked up when Jeff mentioned a pet store. Ruby continued to systematically file away some of Emma's paperwork, oblivious of Jeff's phone call and his patiently waiting audience.

"Yes... ok... sorry we can't help you today Mr Kibble... Goodbye." Placing the phone back onto its base with a thump, he sighed and then laughed out loud.

"Well, what did he want this time?" asked Dave, impatiently.

"A Christmas tree protector!" laughed Jeff.

"A what?" enquired Emma, passing some more papers to Ruby, who was busy behind her.

"His kittens are attacking the Christmas tree," sighed Jeff, trying to be serious for a moment, "They've pulled it down twice." The phone rang again, "Good afternoon, *Webb's DIY.*" Again Jeff rolled his eyes and shook his head in despair. "No, sorry Mr Kibble, we don't sell self-supporting fence panels. Wouldn't they just climb a fence anyway?" Jeff paused, "Yes but..." Rubbing his fingers across his brow, Jeff scrunched up his eyes as if in pain. "Err... no and how would you see your Christmas tree anyway if it were fenced off sir?"

Dave jumped up from his chair and shot out of the office just in time, before he screamed a high pitched squeal of hilarity, and then bumped straight into Colin who was returning from his debt collection expedition.

"What's going on?" asked Colin, stepping casually over the now crumpled heap of Dave's contorted body at the top of the stairs, before he could stroll into the room.

"Mr Kibble," whispered Pete, pursing his lips to contain the laughter.

"Say no more," Colin replied and walked over to his desk. "Just you now Emma," he said, waving the check list and some cash under her nose.

"I know, I know... tomorrow Colin," replied Emma, straining to hear Jeff's one-sided conversation with the ever-intriguing and totally peculiar, Mr Roderick Kibble - *Webb's* very own raving lunatic and number one customer extraordinaire.

Chapter 3

Thankfully for Emma, the rest of the working week flew by as she battled with the throb of yet another, loose tooth and the ever present abscess. She scraped through every challenge with a regular dose of *Paracetamol*.

Ruby kept quiet, understanding exactly what Emma was going through and knowing that a persistent nag would only cause friction between them. Now and again, Ruby would give her a gentle look as if to say, 'Well you really should go and see a dentist, it's not going to get any better'.

The large secret Santa box was placed just outside the office, on the landing, where no one could see each present being put in.

Darren stayed down on the shop floor for the rest of the week and sadly, Emma only ever caught very brief glimpses of him as he darted about from one department to the next. When she entered or left the building, she always made a detour through the shop for one reason or another (but Ruby was fully aware of the *real* reason). Between toothaches and paperwork, Emma desperately tried to think of valid reasons why she might also need to go down to the shop during the day, but couldn't come up with anything that didn't sound totally ridiculous. So the wink from Monday became a faded memory. Emma only hoped that Ruby wasn't right and that he didn't have something in his eye.

"Shall we go shopping again tomorrow? For more Christmas presents and stuff," asked Emma as Ruby came out of the bathroom dressed in her teddy bear onesie and a towel turban. Friday evening was bath night for both of them (the rest of the week they took quick showers) – hair washed, bathed and dressed in comfy and cosy nightwear, they would usually curl up on the two sofas (they both had their favourite one) and watch a film together.

"Yes that would be nice I still need to buy a few presents."

"Don't tell me, you want to get some more books."

Ruby grinned at her and then went into her room to blow dry her hair. Most of her family received a book of some description for Christmas, whether they liked it or not. Ruby thought that you couldn't go wrong with a book as a gift, as everyone had some kind of interest and there would always be a book to cover it.

"And we should have a look for some accessories to go with your dress. I could do with some new earrings too."

Nodding happily, Ruby turned the hair dryer on and began to dry her hair flat to her head, as usual.

"It's only a week away. We'll have to do a practice run on your hair and make-up before next Saturday night," shouted Emma, over the loud hum of the dryer.

Ruby screwed up her face. She had shown her displeasure of having a make-over several times, but Emma wasn't having any of it and insisted that the Christmas do was going to be the beginning of a new and exciting life for Ruby – whether she wanted it or not. Switching off the dryer, Ruby looked up, "As long as you keep your promise to go to the dentist in the New Year, then I'll wear some make-up," she said quite adamantly.

"Deal," replied Emma, surprised by her friend's new vigour and strength of character.

***

Another Monday morning came around far too soon but Emma's spirits and enthusiasm had lifted from the previous week as she returned to her office desk. Her do-it-yourself-surgery at the weekend had eased the painful lump in her mouth but yet another poor tooth had gone numb. Assuming that her teeth were slowly dying, one by one, Emma had become accustomed to the pattern of events after each lump appeared. The effected tooth would loosen once it had been attacked by the swelling and then just seemed to die along with any pain. Emma's fear of the dentist was far greater than any fears of the detrimental implications to her own well-being and the health of her gums.

"When are we doing secret Santa?" asked Dave, returning to the office breathless, after running errands for Colin. "The box is full already," he squealed pathetically.
Emma thought he sounded like a *Dame Edna Everage* impersonator having his testicles crushed in a nut cracker. Everyone looked up (apart from Ruby) and shrugged nonchalantly.
"We'll do it Friday lunch time," said Colin, handing over yet more paperwork for Dave to distribute. "And stop tearing about like a demented deer, you'll do yourself an injury," he laughed.
The stairway up to the office had two tiers and most of the men ran up the steps, two at a time. The sound of their heavy footsteps, pounding on the rickety, wooden steps was like a herd of elephants storming into the office.

"Are we all going to the pub Friday lunch time?" asked Colin, peering around the room questioningly.

"Yep – I'm up for that," called Dave from the top of the stairs, before thudding back down them, two or maybe even three at a time.

Pete and Jeff looked up and nodded simultaneously. Emma glanced across the room to Ruby.

"Rue, are we going for a pub lunch on Friday with this bunch of misfits?" Lifting her head in surprise, Ruby had totally missed the conversation going on around her, whilst she busily read her emails.

"Sorry?"

Friday, lunch at the pub... are we going?"

"Oh, yes, that would be nice," she replied, vacantly.

"Less of the 'misfits', Miss Frey," said Colin, eyeing Emma with a cheeky grin. Colin had a lot of respect for Emma and although he wasn't that many years older than her, he tended to play the father-figure. He was a kind and thoughtful man but he was also stringent and meticulous in his work.

"I just hope you are all going to behave yourselves, we don't want a repeat of last year do we?" giggled Emma.

"Err, let's not talk about that," said Pete, "It wasn't my fault that I got stuck under the toilet door."

"Well actually Pete, it was. Who else would be so bloody stupid," announced Jeff, looking to Colin for backup.

"You did cause a scene in there mate. It was bloody hilarious though," Colin snorted. "But at least you got a free meal out of it."

From her little world over in the corner, Ruby looked across to Pete and expressed a gentle, sympathetic smile towards him.

"Oh dear, you have to admit, looking back at it now Pete, it was a classic," said Emma, shaking her head at the thought of him lying on the floor, in the men's toilets, trapped under the cubicle door.

The previous year's Christmas pub lunch had been an embarrassing disaster for Pete, while the others had spent the afternoon rolling around the office in tears of laughter at his ill fate and getting absolutely no work done at all. Trapped in the toilet cubicle, Pete had waited for what seemed like an age for someone to come and rescue him, but no one came. In his wisdom, he had decided to crawl under the door to escape so he could inform the staff of the faulty lock. Unfortunately, Pete's watch strap had become snagged on the broken bottom door hinge and he couldn't free it. Laying half way under the door, he couldn't get his other hand back under and across his chest to reach the watch and he couldn't go back either, hence the situation began to bring on one of his panic attacks. As his chest swelled and he started to breathe rapidly, he became completely wedged under the melamine door. It was several more minutes before anyone found him and by the time everyone had been made aware of 'The trapped man in the toilets', Pete had become very flushed and faint.

There was pandemonium in the restaurant until the owner and two of his staff entered the men's toilets and gradually eased Pete back inside the cubicle, by holding his head tight to the ground, repeating to him, 'Don't panic' and 'Calm down' Once back inside the cubicle, Pete was able to unhook his watch from the metal hinge. When he'd calmed down and returned to the disposition of a normal functioning human being, the owner passed him a screwdriver under the door and thankfully Pete was able to dismantle the lock eventually, after a few tears and another panic attack.

Emma and the others had been almost unable to walk back to *Webb's* that afternoon, for fear of wetting themselves or falling down on the pavements in tears of laughter.

"Make sure you don't wear your watch this year," roared Colin and they all fell about laughing again... except for Pete... and except for Ruby (as usual).

"This week is flying by, isn't it?" said Emma. "We haven't even done your practice make-up run yet."

Slumped on the sofa, Ruby shook her head and then looked up from her book. "It'll be alright, I'm sure we could just do it on Saturday night."

"Afternoon, you mean," Emma laughed, "I'm not saying you're a mess or that you'll need a big make-over, but we need to start getting ready in the afternoon."

"Why?" asked Ruby, puzzled and inexperienced in such matters.

"Well, we've got to do our hair. Then our nails need painting and we have to let them dry. Then put make-up on, which can take a while, and then we need to put the finishing touches on our hair styles – oh and get dressed (obviously) and all sorts of other stuff too."

"Oh," said Ruby, "I didn't realise it would take that long."

"Well I've got to do it twice over haven't I?" Emma paced the living room excitedly, trying to picture what Darren would look like dressed up in a smart shirt and trousers, "So it'll take me twice as long, won't it?"

"Um," replied Ruby, before returning to the safety of her *Mills & Boon* book.

***

Scraping the icy windscreen of her car, Emma felt a rush of excitement surge through her as she thought about the dinner/dance tomorrow night.

It was the last day before the Christmas break and Friday's were usually good at work anyway. Today was even better than a normal Friday though, as they would be finishing two hours earlier and there would be no work done this afternoon, whatsoever. By the time they returned from the pub lunch and then had a laugh opening their secret Santa presents, it would be time to go home.

The white frosty morning and clear blue sky only added to Emma's already euphoric state as she jumped inside the car and turned the key in the ignition. The engine chugged and began to warm up her faithful old car.

"Are you ready yet?" called Emma, from the front door a few minutes later.

Their ground floor flat had the added bonus of having its own exterior front door, rather than a communal entrance, while the flat above was accessed from a staircase running up the side of the building. The girls hardly ever saw the couple who lived above as they commuted to London each week and seemed to go out a lot at the weekends. So Emma and Ruby's home was a peaceful place, perfectly priced and pretty – even in the middle of winter.

Hurrying back through to the kitchen, Emma stopped and stared, "Why are you making a packed lunch Rue – I've been outside waiting for you?"

"Oh gosh, I've forgotten about the pub haven't I?" she giggled, chopping up the last pieces of apple and placing them into her clip container.

"Yes you have, you plonker. Come on, stick it in the fridge for your tea – I've left the car running."

Collecting her rucksack, Ruby removed the tub of prawn salad and popped that in to the fridge too. "I'm sorry Em, I'm ready now. I don't know what I was thinking of..."

"Pete?" laughed Emma.

"No," she replied shyly, "I wasn't thinking about him at all." Lying was not one of Ruby's traits and sadly, Emma believed her.

Lunch in the Queen's Arms was an uneventful affair, in comparison to the previous year's Pete-inspired misadventure. Ruby remained on her best behaviour, as she was always and politely nibbled at a Chicken Caesar Salad while she listened to the banter between Emma and the four men. The atmosphere was relaxed and jovial as everyone began to wind down for the Christmas break ahead.

"Are you going to your mum's again this year?" asked Pete.

"Yes, on Monday. I'm only staying there until Boxing day," replied Emma, wishing he would get into more conversations with Ruby than herself. It was a shame that Ruby lacked considerably in the conversationalist department and most people were pretty stretched to try and initiate any sort of chit-chat with her. "Rue's away the same time as me, so it's handy that neither of us will be home alone – isn't it Rue?"

"Um," she muttered with a mouthful of lettuce and tomato.

"What are your plans?" asked Emma trying to continue polite conversation.

"Oh the usual – at home with Mum and Dad. My sister is coming over in the afternoon on Christmas day and then we're all at her house on Boxing Day," replied Pete, looking slightly despondent.

Emma had no empathy for Pete's lonely existence. At twenty six, the same age as herself, Pete had no life outside of his job, his parent's and his beloved dog. His infatuation with Emma was irritating and pointless as far as she was concerned and she wished he would see the possibility of a real relationship, which was sitting right under his nose, most of the time. Emma had decided that she would try to push hard to create a spark, no matter how small, to ignite in Pete's mind, hopefully generating a new interest in Ruby. That, Emma had determined, was her first mission at the Christmas do. Her second was to inject an ember of enthusiasm into Darren, which she truly believed could turn into a flame and subsequently, a roaring fire and better still... an inferno.

"Get the drinks in," shouted Dave cheekily, across the table, to Colin. As the lowest paid and least qualified member of the office team, Dave made up for his lack of status amongst the 'professionals' as he called the others, by being the audacious clown. "I'm gagging here!" Winking at Emma, he held up his glass and offered it to Colin while grasping his throat with his other hand.

Emma suddenly felt queasy at the notion of Dave 'gagging', as her corrupt mind wandered in the wrong direction and stopped just short before the full visual image took effect. Then, to everyone's surprise – except Ruby's (she hadn't noticed), Colin stood up obediently and headed towards the bar with his hands in his pockets, leaving the others to finish off their 'Christmas-special', turkey meals (apart from Ruby who had gone 'all-out' with a chicken salad).

"How the bloody hell do you get away with it every time?" asked Jeff, staring at Dave in amazement.

"I think he fancies me," laughed Dave, winking again.

Although no one said anything, the looks on their faces were one of slight disapproval at Dave's insinuating remark.

"You wish," said Emma.

"Seriously?" Shaking his head, Dave changed the subject. "So, I wonder who has got the cheesiest present this year." He smiled and looked around the table, waiting for a response.

"Well it depends who bought your present, doesn't it Dave?" said Jeff, smiling sarcastically. Jeff tolerated Dave's anomalous character but quite often he could be seen to bite his tongue when he considered a remark to be distasteful and in Dave's case, this was quite often.

"Oh very funny Jeff, I'll have you know I put a lot of thought into the present I bought this year." Pulling himself upright, Dave appeared slightly perturbed by Jeff's comment and teasingly sucked a whole baby carrot into his mouth, attempting to insinuate something far cruder.

Returning from the bar, in what must have been record time; Colin sat down, "These are on me... and so is the meal," he said, as he pointed to the drink laden tray being carried over by a young bar maid.

"Ah, cheers Colin," said Dave with a wide grin stretched across his perfectly shaved and moisturized face.

"Thank you," said Pete and Ruby, almost simultaneously.

"Yeah, cheers Colin, mate," added Jeff.

Seated next to Colin, Emma placed her arm around his shoulder. "Bless ya, thank you," she said, warmly, "Happy Christmas to you too."

Almost on a par with Colin in the *Webb's Superstores* rankings of employees, Emma's genuine appreciation was heartfelt. She still looked up to him and always would, even though her creditable position within the company made her worthy of an even standing.

At ten past two the tribe of office staff returned to their desks, much later than their normal one hour lunch break allowed, feeling full-up, lethargic and ready to go home. The shop floor would remain open until six o'clock, as was normal on a Friday however there were hardly any customers to serve, so the checkout operators were trying to look busy by tidying up the shelves around their stations. An atmosphere of merriment seeped through the store touching everyone, as the speakers in the rafters played joyous Christmas tunes.

Wearily slumping down into her seat, Emma surveyed the others who were slouched over their desks, half-heartedly clearing up their paperwork or moving things around to create an illusion of 'My desk is tidy, therefore all my work must have been completed', apart from Ruby of course, who was busily dusting and polishing surfaces in close proximity to her desk – which was absolutely immaculate (as always).

Picking up an invoice from her tray, Emma looked at the payment due date – 6th January – it could wait she decided and returned it to the growing pile. Her zealous drive had got up and left the building, she couldn't be bothered with any of it. It was about time her four day break started – before she fell asleep at her desk like a lioness after the kill.

"Secret Santa time!" screeched Dave, dancing around on the landing. Jolting back to a conscious level, Emma watched through the doorway as he carried the box of goodies in to the room. Pete and Ruby actually looked like they were almost excited to see the roughly wrapped objects, protruding from Santa's box. "Shall I dish them out?"

"Go on then, if you must," said Colin, peering over his reading glasses and scratching his bald head.

"Who's first?" asked Dave, handing out the gifts.

"We'll all open them together," said Colin, raising his eyebrows and shaking his head in despair at Dave's childlike antics.

Amongst the sounds of ripping paper, words of 'thanks secret Santa' and packages being torn apart, was the faint thumping of Emma's broken heart and gulps of grief as she desperately tried to contain the horror lurking behind a false smile. Who had bought her present?

Squeals of delight resonated around the office from Dave's desk, as he held out his fairy outfit and laughed raucously. "Oh, I love it! Who got this for me?" Nobody replied but the other men joined in with Dave's frolicking and laughter.

Ruby looked across the room to Emma and grinned as she held up a brown leather diary and pen set. Emma reciprocated the smile and nodded in acknowledgement. However, she could not show her present to Ruby for fear of bursting into tears and running out of the store. She had to pluck up the courage to laugh it off. She had to avoid revealing her gift to the others and escape from work as quickly as possible. Who was it that secretly bought and wrapped her present? Did they all know or was it only the culprit's idea? Emma quickly shoved her present in to her desk drawer, smiled at anyone that might be looking her way and then proceeded to appear 'awfully busy' as she rushed out of the office, carrying some paperwork down to the shop floor.

Half an hour of pretence drifted by very slowly before everyone began to say their goodbyes (until tomorrow night) and leave with their presents. Emma had now stuffed her gifts deep inside her oversized handbag and managed to evade any questions about what she'd received from secret Santa. She had sidestepped any questioning by rushing off down stairs to sort out a pretend problem quickly before the Christmas break, tearing away to the toilets in *urgent* need, or making phone calls to puzzled sales reps who wondered why Emma was saying that she was returning their call – when they hadn't called her in the first place.

"You're very quiet Emma, is everything ok?" asked Colin, pulling his heavy coat over his shoulders.

"Yes fine, I'm just knackered," she replied quietly. "I'll see you tomorrow night Col."

"Looking forward to it," he said, and then picked up his things and left.

Descending the stairs together, Pete, Ruby and Emma said their farewells to the staff on the shop floor and wished others, who weren't going to the dinner/dance, a very merry Christmas. As they reached the car park, Pete stopped mid-stride, "Fancy a quick drink before we go home?" he looked from Emma to Ruby and back again. Ruby's eyes lit up as bright as a pair of sparklers and she stared at Emma like a lonely, lost puppy.

"I've got a terrible headache coming on. I'll skip it if you don't mind. Why don't you go Rue, I'm sure Pete would give you a lift back, wouldn't you Pete?" Emma turned to him and smiled falsely.

"Err... sure."

"No, it's alright, I'll come home with you if you've got another migraine coming Emma," said Ruby, faithfully.

"Oh ok. Well never mind then," Pete replied quickly, and began to edge away. "We'll catch up tomorrow night, yeah?"

"Definitely," said Emma, vaguely.

Ruby smiled sweetly at him and then Pete left rather hastily.

As soon as they were in the car, Emma's defensive brick wall crumbled and she heaved a heavy sigh before a tear popped out from her eye.

"Is it that bad? Will you be able to drive home ok?" Ruby worried.

"I haven't got a headache, I'm sorry Rue. I just need to get home."

"What's the matter?"

"I'll show you when we get home," said Emma, slinging her bag onto the back seats and pulling her seat belt on.

"Shall I make you a coffee?" asked Ruby tentatively.

"Please." Clutching her oversized bag, Emma slumped on the sofa without removing her coat. Somehow the restriction of her long, woolen-mix coat wrapped around her, made her feel safe, secure and shrouded. And then the tears really began to fall.

"Oh my goodness," said Ruby, placing a cup of coffee on the table next to Emma, "What has upset you Em, is it your teeth?" she asked, innocently.

"You could say that," spluttered Emma, through the sniffs and snuffles. "Do you have any idea who bought my secret Santa present?"

"No... not at all. Why?"

"I know it wasn't you or Pete. That only leaves Dave, Jeff or Colin," she sobbed.

"How do you know it wasn't Pete? He's such a kind and caring man, he would be the type to buy anyone a touching gift to make them weep."

"No, you've got it all wrong Rue!" cried Emma, frustrated by Ruby's utterly geeky, innocence and naivety. "I'm upset because it's flipping horribly cruel – not 'touching'."

"Oh no, I'm so sorry." Reeling from Emma's angry words, Ruby sat back in the chair as if she had been pinned to the upholstery.

"Sorry Rue, I didn't mean to frighten you. I shouldn't have said that." Emma's tears were beginning to dry but the evaporation was building into a cloud of anger above her head. "I can't believe it – whoever did this has spoilt my whole bloody Christmas."

"What did you get?" asked Ruby, nervously.

Rummaging around inside her handbag, Emma found the two gifts, pulled them out and held them up for Ruby to inspect.

"Oh no." The horrified look on Ruby's face said it all. Then she too, burst into tears.

"Why are *you* crying?"

"I can't believe they could be so cruel," whispered Ruby through her hands which were covering her face, "I thought we were all friends in the office. I thought everyone cared about each other. Why would someone do that?"

"Because they thought it would be funny," said Emma, wiping the last tear from her cheek. "It must be so obvious and I hadn't realised."

"It's not Em, really it isn't."

"You're used to seeing me practically all day, every day Rue. You don't notice it anymore. Someone is trying to tell me something or maybe it's a collective message from them all."

"But it is only a joke Emma – isn't it? You bought Dave a joke present. I suppose he could have taken it badly, couldn't he?"

"No, it's not the same Rue. Dave is more than happy to express his homosexuality and the fact that he is married to a man. He just doesn't care what anyone thinks about his outspoken, provocative ways. You either love him or hate him and he's not bothered either way. But this is a personal insult," said Emma, waving the gifts in the air.

"Isn't the fairy outfit a personal insult?" questioned Ruby, patting her eyes with a tissue.

"No, he openly displays his sexuality – there's a big difference Rue. I've never discussed my problems or issues with anyone except you, so it's not a subject to joke about. Do you see what I mean?" Emma's frustration was showing as she snapped at her dearest friend.

"Um." Ruby nodded her head, turning down her mouth at the same time.

"I need you to try and find out who did this... Would you do that for me?"

"Why do you want to know who it was? Couldn't it cause more problems?" Ruby was worried now, she couldn't possibly cope with being a detective but she also didn't want to upset her very best friend.

"If I know who it is, then I can quietly talk to them and explain my problem and let them know how upset I am. I can't work with someone that secretly thinks I don't give a damn."

"I don't think I could do it Emma... I mean... how could I find out anyway?"

"All you need to do is casually drop it into a conversation and tomorrow night would be a good time, after they've had a few drinks. There are only three of them so it would just be a case of elimination." Suddenly realising just how difficult a task that would be for Ruby, as she hardly ever got into conversations with anyone, Emma said, "Look just keep your ears and eyes open for me, would you?"

"Yes I will. I'm so sorry for you Em. Would you like another coffee or maybe something stronger?"

"No, coffee is fine thanks and I'm sorry for burdening you with all my problems Rue."

After a quick 'best-friends' hug, Ruby walked through to the kitchen with sloped shoulders and her head hung low.

Emma knew that her little bookworm friend wasn't able to cope with any animosity that could potentially surround her at work. Returning the wind-up, plastic chattering teeth and the electric toothbrush to her bag, Emma vowed that she would have to do something about her gum disease now – she'd left it way too long and if the presents were anything to go by, her colleagues also thought she had left her teeth or gums unattended for far too long.

Chapter 4

Focusing on its reflection in the deep, murky lagoon, the hideous creature opened its repulsive mouth, revealing shards of decayed bone fragments randomly spaced and partially buried in bleeding, pus-filled gums. It smiled to see itself as the rancid water of the lagoon reflected an image of a long haired freak with teeth rising out from its mouth like broken gravestones in an abandoned cemetery…

Jolting awake, Emma reached for her mouth and felt her loose teeth pulsating with every beat of her racing heart. It was only a dream – another nightmare – a terrible subconscious portrayal of her inner self-image and yet she did not have rotten teeth like her dreams portrayed. Lying awake in the darkness, she feared a return to the blackness of the lagoon and the formidable mind games that played on her anxieties. Inevitably, she soon slipped back into a world of disturbed sleep, devilish dentists and terrifying tooth monsters.

Having slept intermittently, due to the shock and heart-ache of receiving such a spiteful present, Emma felt worse than she had the previous night and the constant torturous nightmares had only made matters worse. Her confidence had been stripped away by a silly joke-toy and an item of personal hygiene that millions of people used every day. She'd really taken it badly and could not see any humour in it at all. Colin, Jeff or Dave had maliciously set out to humiliate and distress her. But why? She had no idea. Considering herself to be a well-liked member of the team, she couldn't understand the motive behind the gifts. If she had to guess who it might be, her money was on Dave.

The last minute rush around the over populated shopping centre was a blur of thousands of critical eyes, staring and waiting for her to open her mouth or worse still – smile, as Emma tried to shake off the images in her mind. Unable to think straight, she wasn't sure who she'd bought Christmas presents for and who she hadn't.

Her mind wandered to the evening's grand Christmas party and Darren and her optimistic hopes of getting a date with him, as she meandered aimlessly around, led by Ruby.

"Well if I've forgotten anything it's tough, I'm not shopping anymore," said Emma, "My feet are killing me again."

"I'm finished, if you want to go home now," muttered Ruby, clutching a bag containing yet another romance novel. "I can't wait to read this one, I've wanted it for so long," she said, excitedly.

Ruby's collection of *Mills & Boon* and various other romantic novels was extensive. Her bedroom consisted of a single bed, a small chest of drawers and three large bookcases, along with a small built-in wardrobe. The town's largest book retailer knew her well and if they didn't stock particular titles that Ruby wanted, she would order them directly through the shop.

"Why don't you just buy eBooks – rather than clog up your bedroom with hundreds of paperbacks and hardbacks?" Emma had said to her one day.

"I would much rather have physical copies. They look nice in the bookcases around the room. They're like wallpaper aren't they," she'd said, smiling widely. "And they're nice and colourful."

Emma hadn't replied and had then decided it was best left at that.

"Right, let's go then, I could do with a nap before we start getting ready," said Emma, apathetically. Her heart just wasn't in it anymore.

"Ok." Ruby looked deeply at Emma for a moment, "Are you feeling better today?"

"I didn't sleep well last night. I'll be ok if I get an hour this afternoon." Linking arms with her little friend, Emma dragged her back through the arcade, filled with frantically, stressed-out Christmas shoppers and hastily headed back to the car park. If their return to the car had been commanded by Ruby it would have taken two hours to do the five minute walk back. Ruby's too kind, too thoughtful and too generous character would have let every passer-by pass by, with a guided hand to help show them the way, before she'd managed to take two steps forward. Emma's ethos however was to charge through the crowds, gently nudging everyone out of the way, to get to where she wanted to go – and fast.

After a peaceful, afternoon sleep, Emma woke feeling far more refreshed and slightly more confident than she had earlier in the day. She couldn't be that bad surely, she thought as she went to run a bubble bath.

Having read almost half of her new book in the time that Emma was asleep – which was only an hour and a half – Ruby was sat on her bed chewing her finger nails.

"I've got some false ones Rue, shall we put some on for tonight?"

"Will I be able to get them off again?" asked Ruby, looking anxious.

"Yes of course, don't worry. You might like them anyway and decide to keep them on over Christmas." Sensing Ruby's nervousness, Emma continued, "Are you really worrying about tonight?"

"I've never worn a dress like that before," she said, pointing to the luxurious red piece hanging from the wardrobe door.

"Exactly! You're going to turn everyone's head when you walk in that door and Pete will be completely gob smacked."

"I'm not sure Em, I'm shy. I don't like to stand out."

"You won't stand out as everyone will be dressed up, but you will look totally different from the usual Ruby that they're used to." Emma smiled, "Have a drink with me to calm your nerves before we go. I've got some *Baileys*. You've had one of those before, I know you liked it,"

"Um," she replied. "Alright I'll have just a very small one."

It was a logistical nightmare, trying to coordinate the bathing, hair styling, make-up, nails and accessories of one person – let alone two. Emma didn't have a plan and rushed around from one bedroom to the other, looking for this and searching for that, letting this dry while applying that, waiting for this to heat up while re-dampening that bit and so on and so forth. She desperately needed a drink – it was very hard work creating two beauties. "Fancy a *Baileys* now Rue?" she called from the kitchen.

"No thank you," said Ruby as she sat at Emma's dressing table, peering into the lit 'Diva' mirror. "When will these be dry?"

"Give it another five minutes then I can do a top coat," said Emma, returning to her room in a dressing gown and towel turban. Placing a tall glass of *Baileys* on the table she looked at Ruby's nails, "We should have started them earlier really but at least you haven't got anything to do apart from get dressed."

Studying her new nails Ruby blew on the bright red varnish and then held her hands out in front of her, "They do look nice. I feel like I'm quite grown up."

"At twenty four, I would hope that you are grown up by now," laughed Emma, switching on the hair dryer and tipping her head upside down to blow more volume into it. Flicking her head back up, Emma stood upright and looked through the mirror at Ruby, "What do you think then?"

"You're not going out like that are you?" asked Ruby, her big blue eyes widening with worry.

"Yeah, this is my new hairstyle. Don't you like it then?"

"It's a bit... big."

Laughing out loud, Emma shook her head and her mane of fluffed up mousey brown locks settled back down on her head. "Don't worry, it won't look like this by the time I've finished with it. Here have a little slurp of this," she said, sticking the large glass of *Baileys* under Ruby's nose.

"Do you want your own one this time?" called Emma from the kitchen.

"Oh, all right but just a small one please."

This time Emma carried through two large glasses of the creamy Irish whiskey and put them on the dresser. "That's not a small one," exclaimed Ruby, picking it up and sipping the contents, "It's delicious though."

"Be careful you don't get drunk before we get there."

"I wouldn't get drunk," giggled Ruby who was feeling quite relaxed and happy – or maybe slightly drunk already and after only a couple of sips.

"Keep still," whispered Emma, staring right in to the tiny, unblemished face of her friend. The little black wand hovered in close proximity to Ruby's eye-lashes.

"I can't you're tickling me. It makes my eyes water."

"Just try and keep looking up, I've nearly done the bottom." The whole process of applying professional looking eye-shadow to the outer corners of Ruby's eyelids and the eyeliner had rendered her a tearful, blubbering wreck as she squinted and squirmed, laughed and cried, moaned and blinked her way through the process. "There, just the tops to do now."

"Then I'm finished am I?" asked Ruby, sniffing and blinking away the welling tears.

"A bit more blusher, some lipstick and you're done."

"Lipstick! I'm not wearing that stuff." Ruby chuckled, already feeling the toxic effects of almost a whole, large glass of *Baileys*.

"Try it and see what you think. You can easily remove it if you don't like it." Applying the finishing touches to Ruby's surprisingly long and thick top lashes, Emma stood back and stared in amazement. "Wow! Your eyes look stunning." The colour of sea blue, stood out like never before in her eyes and the make-up had created an illusion of enormous eyes, which gave Ruby an irresistibly charming elf-like image. Her platinum blonde hair added the finishing touches to a truly magical look of innocent beauty. The expertly crafted soft peaks on the top of her head and strands of hair falling on to her forehead finished the look with an almost impish appeal. "I can't believe how fantastic you look Rue," said Emma, unable to avert her gaze from Ruby's super-size eyes, "You're truly amazing!"

The taxi had been booked for six thirty, allowing plenty of time to get to the venue and meet up with everyone before they all went to sit down for their meal.

"Rue, five minutes and the taxi will be here," called Emma, taking one last look at herself in the long mirror. She was pleased with the image in the reflection. Her black, figure-hugging dress appeared to knock a few pounds off her weight and accentuate her average sized breasts. Pre-fluffed hair had been tamed with a brush and curling tongs to create tumbling, twisted ringlets which ended just above the slopes of her chest. Emma smiled her usual closed lips smile and winked a false lash into the mirror. *Not bad*, she thought, tugging the hem of the dress down just above her stocking caressed knees. Turning around to the sound of tottering footsteps, Emma's jaw dropped as Ruby appeared. Holding onto the walls and wobbling on her high heels, Ruby was a picture of magnificent beauty.

"I can't walk in these things Em."

"Just hold on to me until you get used to them." The perfectly matched red shoes accentuated Ruby's curves and her long legs that seemed to start right up and under her armpits. "You look so lovely Rue, I'm jealous."

"You do too," she giggled, under the influence of one drink. "I don't think I should drink anymore tonight though, I'm wobbly enough now."

"You'll be fine once you've eaten."

The door bell rang, signaling the arrival of their taxi and the two gorgeous young ladies grabbed their jackets (Ruby had borrowed one of Emma's more fashionable ones) and left for the Christmas party.

Chapter 5

The stream of taxis stretched the whole length of the road and Emma and Ruby watched patiently from the back seat as each one pulled up to the complex and emptied its contents of well dressed, cheerfully babbling people. As the cab crawled along at a snail's pace, the girls scoured the pavements and the large paved frontage of the complex in the distance. "Can't see anyone we know," said Emma peering out at the people passing by.

"You wanna git out ere luv?" asked the burly unshaven driver, tapping his thick, hairy fingers on the top of the steering wheel.

"Shall we Rue?"

"Alright, hope I can walk ok," Ruby giggled. She'd been doing a lot of tittering in the cab and Emma could see that the driver had grown a little fed up with listening to a giggly girl who couldn't handle her drink, at such an early hour of the evening. Rudely, he'd turned the radio up to listen to the golden oldies, while beating the dashboard and steering wheel with his giant hands, like they were drum sticks playing on a set of drums.

"Yes please, here will be just fine. Thank you," said Emma, apologetically.

"Six quid luv," the man grunted, coarsely.

After paying the fare and a tip of one pound – not that the driver had deserved it – Emma climbed out of the cab and hobbled round to the pavement where Ruby stood waiting and wobbling, with a huge, silly grin on her face.

"Come on, it's freezing, hold on to me and we'll get through this lot," said Emma, linking arms with her friend and proceeding to drag her through the crowds, while supporting her in an upright position.

Stepping down into the huge hall, Emma and Ruby stopped and looked around in amazement. Hundreds of people milled around long dining tables, laid out in some twenty or more rows, stretching the whole length of the carpeted hall. At the far end was a long stage, set out with microphones, giant speakers, guitars and a sparkly drum set. Below the stage, a wooden dance floor lay empty of pounding feet. To the right and also to the far left of them, the girls could see two bars, both of which were lined with queues of people, waiting to be served. Music gently filtered down from the high ceiling above and countless glistening glitter balls turned slowly, creating speckles of dancing light across the entire hall. The babble of voices, laughter and shouting filled the building with merriment. An atmosphere of fun and excitement flowed out from every corner. Emma's heart skipped a beat in anticipation of the glamourous evening that lay ahead.

"Here's the table plan Rue," said Emma feeling optimistic about the work's Christmas do, "Let's see where we are first and then we can go and get a drink."

The display board showed the seating plan for every company and Emma soon found the tables designated for their superstore. "Here we are," she pointed to the centre of the diagram. "That's the twelfth row, around the middle, somewhere over there," she said, pointing in the direction of the dance floor.

"Hello Emma, where are we then?" asked Colin, appearing from behind her.

Turning sharply, Emma smiled, "Colin, hi!"

Looking decidedly smart in his grey pinstripe trousers, pink shirt and a silver tie, Colin grinned as he surveyed the grand hall.

"Bloody hell. I didn't recognise you!" he gasped, staring Ruby up and down while she was hanging on to the free standing display board like a calendar girl. Colin's mouth dropped open, "You look great!" he said and then snapped his mouth closed again.

Ruby smiled coyly, "Thank you... err... you look very smart too Colin."

Glancing at the seating plan, Colin nodded and then pointed to the bar on the left side, "Can I get you two a drink?"

"Thank you," said Emma, scooping Ruby up in an arm link and pulling her along behind Colin, to the bar.

Several groups of men were dotted around the hall, holding on to glasses of different sizes, chatting, laughing and generally eyeing all the women passing by them, as the trio made their way towards the queues.

The bar staff – and there must have been at least ten of them – busily went about their business of pouring drinks, pulling pints, talking to and serving customers. They moved swiftly and effortlessly, dodging each other in an obviously rehearsed way, in the confines of the small area behind the bar.

"What are you girls drinking?" asked Colin, still looking astonished by Ruby's dramatic change of appearance and trying desperately not to stare at her open mouthed.

"Two *Baileys* please Col," said Emma, nodding at Ruby for an agreement.

"Yes thank you," replied Ruby shyly, as she focused on Emma constantly. It meant that she didn't have to acknowledge where she was or how she was dressed. Having the blinkers on was a safe option and hopefully would carry her through the night. Either that or several more *Baileys* would aid her in conquering her fears and in-built inadequacies, at least temporarily anyway.

A throng of men and women still poured into the hall, down the steps from the complex above. After five minutes of patiently waiting, Colin was served and handed two glasses, filled with *Baileys* and ice, to the girls. Many passing admirers had smiled or eyed Emma and Ruby as they stood waiting with Colin but Ruby had remained transfixed on Emma and noticed nothing at all.

Thanking Colin, Emma turned around and looked across the hall to the area where they would be seated. "Shall we go over and see if anyone else is here yet?" she asked, as she grabbed Ruby's arm and beckoned to Colin, "Follow me."

Every table was identically laid out with white, oval shaped dinner sets on maroon coloured table cloths with white and silver patterned table runners. The cutlery was abundant and confusing, thought Emma – she always wondered which ones to use first and struggled to remember whether she should start from the inside-out or the outside-in. Alternate white and maroon candle decorations stood in the centre of each section of table, which comfortably seated six people on each side. Each set of tables had been joined together to form one long table in varying lengths to house each company's number of guests.

It was a mammoth event which qualified the one hundred or more staff of waiters, waitresses, bar staff and chefs who'd been hired for the whole month leading up to

Christmas, to pull off such a grand multi-company, multi-functioning dinner/dance event.

"It's lovely here," said Ruby, bravely viewing the hall, "Isn't it?" Her false courage supported by the alcoholic drink.

"Yes. It should be a good night Rue. Try and enjoy yourself... and relax." Emma winked at her, excited by the thought of Pete seeing how beautiful she looked.

"Where is everyone?" asked Colin, still slightly taken aback by Ruby's new look.

"I'm sure they'll be here soon," replied Emma, scanning the hall.

"Over there," pointed Ruby, "Are those the girls from the shop floor?" Colin and Emma peered through the crowds to a group of girls dressed in short dresses and skirts and bright sparkly tops. They looked like they were going to a night club rave rather than a posh dinner/dance.

"Yeah, that's Jade, Chloe and the others," said Colin, his eyeballs almost protruding on stalks as he weighed the young girls up. As soon as he had spoken, the young women turned and looked over in their direction and waved, having just worked out the seating plan between them.

Returning the friendly gesture, Emma felt slightly peeved that the five girls did indeed look highly glamourous in their sparkly outfits, as they made their way over. What with Ruby – the gorgeous nymph like creature – and the young "giggle-girls" (Emma liked to refer to them as 'air-heads' or "giggle-girls" because they were always chortling on about something or other that was usually totally pointless and they giggled a lot as well), with hem lines practically up to their waists, Emma wondered for a moment just what her chances were of pulling Darren this evening. Well, he did wink at her, she supposed, *didn't he?* And she did look pretty good herself, just slightly more mature looking, as long as she didn't smile too widely – *didn't she?*

The girls waved again and pointed in the direction of the bar on the right and then made a signal that they were getting a drink by holding an invisible glass and tipping it to their mouths. Then they were lost in the ever increasing crowds at the foot of the entrance steps.

"Ruby, Ruby, Ruby, in a red dress. Wow!" Turning round, Emma, Ruby and Colin were surprised to see Dave, Jeff and Pete standing behind them.

"Is it really you?" asked Dave, "I mean, hey girl, you look totally fab...u...lous!"

The three men stared at Ruby, open mouthed, eyeing every detail of her curves and long legs. Dave's admiration was more jealousy than wanton longing and Pete's frozen expression was unreadable but Emma assumed there would be a hint of fear in there somewhere.

"What do you think guys? Doesn't she look stunning?" said Emma, looking directly at Pete.

"Hot lady," squealed Dave doing a little jig around Ruby.

Nodding his appreciation of the effort made to get Ruby looking like a goddess, Jeff smiled warmly, "Suppose you set her up for this Em," he said.

Sipping her *Baileys* in nanosecond intervals, Ruby's cheeks had almost reached the point of closely matching the colour of her dress.

"Yes I helped her get ready, but I've just brought out the hidden inner-Ruby that we don't usually see. Isn't that right Rue?" said Emma, feeling more peeved that no one had actually commented on her own hard earned appearance.

"Um," replied Ruby through gulps and giggles.

Pete stood mesmerised and said nothing as he watched Ruby nervously resting her top lip on the rim of the glass and tilting it constantly to take yet another small sip.

"Looking good yourself Ems," shouted Dave as he tapped Jeff on the arm and signaled they head towards the left hand bar. Walking away with a wiggle of his rear, it was quite obvious to other people that Dave was gay and he didn't care what anyone thought of his overly camp persona. Dressed in an almost see-through lemon and yellow glittering, pin stripe shirt and skin-tight black chinos, his gait was light and bouncy and there was an air of opulence about him.

Watching them disappear into the crowd, Emma couldn't help but feel very suspicious about Dave's secret Santa recipient, but then she reminded herself that the other two suspects in her investigation were just as likely to find humour in someone else's misfortune. Momentarily, her heart sank as she recalled her dream and the inner self-image she had. *Just don't smile too widely*, she thought to herself as she gulped her drink down quickly, looking for some renewed courage and confidence in the bottom of the glass.

In the space of ten minutes, everyone from the store had arrived and greeted each other with squeals of delight and hugs and kisses like they hadn't seen their colleagues in months. Some of the people had been to the bar first, while others found the *Webb's* table and then did the rounds of saying hello to everyone. They all eyed and commented on 'Ruby in the red dress' and then went off again to the bars.

Ruby in the meantime continued to sip perpetually, looking up from her glass from time to time to smile at her constant flow of admirers.

Although Darren hadn't been over to the table yet, he was in the building. Emma had spotted him chatting to the group of five 'giggle-girls' at the bar. *He's old enough to be their bloody father surely*, thought Emma, wishing she had worn something a little sexier than the conventional black dress. But she was sexy, even in a plain dress, she tried to convince herself. She was mature, unlike the giggly bimbo-heads whose dress sense left nothing to the imagination and everything to the eye. Surely Darren would be interested in her once he saw her and steer away from the silly little 'giggle-girls'?

"I knew there was something very different about you tonight Ruby," said Pete, returning from the bar looking slightly inebriated at such an early stage of the evening – although Ruby was too. The alcohol had removed some of his inhibitions and he merrily attempted to chat away to anyone who would care to listen. The problem was that no one really wanted to hear him piping on about work and dogs, which were the only two things worth noting in his life.

"Oh, do you mean the dress?" asked Ruby.

"No, your glasses, I mean you're not wearing them. Can you see?" laughed Pete.

Giggling in to her hand like a little girl, Ruby then went to push her glasses up her nose but remembered she wasn't wearing them, "Oh... yes, I can see. Contact lenses, I don't wear them often."

"You look very different," he said softly and smiled at her, admiringly.

"LADIES AND GENTLEMAN, PLEASE TAKE YOUR SEATS, DINNER IS READY TO BE SERVED," announced the steward, dressed in a smart dinner suit, standing on the stage. The myriad of waiters and waitresses had gathered around the outer edges of the hall, each holding a basket filled with a selection of white, brown and wholemeal bread rolls. A gentle scuffling sound could be heard, right across the hall, as hundreds of chairs were pulled out from under the tables and the guests began to sit down.

Looking along the length of the *Webb's* table, Emma tried to guess where the best place would be to sit down. She wanted to be as close as possible, if not next to, Darren. "Rue, let's sit down there," she said, grabbing Ruby by the elbow and dragging her away from Pete.

"Where are we going?" called Pete after them. "Jeff, Dave, down this way." Beckoning to the others to follow him down to the far end of the tables, Pete followed behind Ruby and Emma.

At the same time, the rest of the staff began to take their seats and sort out who was sitting next to whom in the middle section. Keeping a watchful eye on the seating arrangements, Emma soon realised she had blown it, there were only about twelve seats left and they were split at opposite ends of the long table.

"There are enough seats for all of us here," said Colin, counting out six seats. The men quickly grabbed a chair each while Emma stood casually looking around the hall for the 'giggle-girls' and Darren. Ruby snatched the chair next to Pete on the very end of the row which left only one seat, on the end opposite Ruby and next to Dave. Looking back to the table, Emma realised her hopes of sitting near Darren had been crushed, in fact she couldn't be further away as she watched Darren and the five pathetic little air-heads saunter over and sit down at the other end. Emma's mouth turned down as she realised that he wasn't even aware that she was there at all.

After the rush of bread baskets to the buzzing tables, came bountiful bottles of bubbly champagne and wines. The black and white uniforms of the service staff were dotted around, along the lines of tables, making the hall look like a giant draughts board. Small candle-lit lanterns illuminated each table with a subtle yellow glow and bowls of party poppers and blowers sat invitingly between each lamp waiting to be pulled and bellowed.

"Are you ok?" asked Ruby quietly, leaning across the table on her elbows.

"Yeah, I suppose." Emma nodded and faked a smile but screwed up her nose at the same time. "Wish we'd sat somewhere else or at least me," she whispered, indicating with her eyes to the other end of the table.

Ruby leaned over further and looked down the length of the table to see Darren sitting on the opposite side, at the far end. He looked like he was having a fun time chatting and laughing with everyone around him, particularly with the young girls.

"Why don't you go and talk to him after the meal?" said ruby, pouring out a glass of white wine. Her alcohol consumption had taken on a new vigour as she started to become decidedly braver and a lot chattier. Grinning at Emma she too indicated with her big blue eyes, but only as far as Pete, who was laughing and talking across the table to Dave and Jeff about poor old Mr Kibble and his strange requests to the shop.

"I will," said Emma, "I'll get him up on the dance floor later." Reaching across, she took the bottle of wine from Ruby, winked at her and then poured herself a large glass.

The four course meal turned out to be money well spent as the staff of *Webb's DIY Superstore*, wined, dined and became very merry. Subtle Christmas tunes played through the ceiling speakers during the course of the meal, filling the hall with a high-spirited atmosphere, along with the babbling sound of voices, laughter, occasional shouting and the mass clattering of cutlery on ceramic plates.

Ruby bravely joined in conversations with Dave, Jeff, Colin and Pete with renewed confidence and a few hiccups here and there. Her voice had grown louder with every glass of wine and Emma began to wonder just how much she could drink before she became an unconscious heap, slumped across the table.

At least she's having a wonderful time, thought Emma as she sat quietly watching and drinking. She'd studied every one of her secret Santa suspects throughout the meal and listened in on every conversation trying to pick out any clues as to who did it, but to no avail. Now and again she would nod and smile at them so that she appeared to be taking part in their conversations. At other times she glanced along the table trying to catch a glimpse of Darren but it was difficult to see him seated on the same side as she was. By the squealing sounds of laughter resonating along the table from the 'air-heads', Emma guessed that he was the centre of attention amongst that, mainly female, end of the table.

Feeling very alone, Emma had drunk more than she should have and now considered the possibility of being unable to make it to the toilets in a straight line. Although her best friend sat opposite her, Emma much preferred to encourage Ruby to talk to the men, and in particular Pete, rather than talk to her. It also gave Emma a break from Pete's usually incessant infatuation with her and gave Ruby a chance to win him over, even if it was only for one drunken night. Emma had now decided that she should get Ruby drunk more often – that way her friend might stand more of a chance of hooking up with someone in the future and preferably that someone would be Pete.

As the dinning came to an end, members of the band entered the stage from behind heavy, black curtains and took their positions among the instruments and microphones.

Suddenly the lights dimmed and an array of brightly coloured stage lighting filled the hall with dazzling rainbows of flickering light in all shapes and sizes.

The sixties tribute band began their show with a mind-blowing fast paced song from *The Beatles*. The dance floor remained empty as people got up from their seats, headed for one of the four toilet signs or went to queue at one of the two bars.

"Do you want to go to the toilet Ruby? I'm going now," shouted Emma over the noise of the guitars and drums. Nodding her head, Ruby wore a wide grin as she stood up, adjusted her dress and then sat straight back down again.

"I feel a bit funny Em," she giggled.

"Come on, we can help each other," said Emma standing up and copying Ruby's actions with her dress. Attempting to stand up again, Ruby toppled slightly and leant right over Pete.

"Oh, sorry Pete," she laughed, holding on to his shoulders to steady herself.

"Where are you two off to?" he asked, drunkenly.

"Toilet... going for a little wee-wee." Ruby whispered in his ear and chuckled.

Looking up at Emma, slightly embarrassed, Pete smiled and rolled his eyes. Emma suddenly thought he was quite cute when he did that. *Definitely too much to drink*, she concluded instantly and shook her head to get rid of the alcohol induced notion of Pete ever looking anything like 'cute'.

Linking arms, the girls headed towards the nearest toilet sign, supporting each other every step of the way. Ruby's high heels were unstable as her drunken ankles tilted and tottered their way to the long queue of women waiting outside the ladies rooms.

Noting that Darren was still sat at the *Webb's* table with the half-dressed girls, Emma felt quite annoyed that he hadn't even noticed she was there. He hadn't even bothered to look for her.

"I'm going to talk to Darren when we get back," she said, gently pushing Ruby by the waist, along the queue.

"Ok, ask him to come to the other end of the table and he can sit on your lap."

"Err, no Rue – somehow I don't think that would be a cool chat-up line," said Emma, still tightly holding on to Ruby in case she toppled over and caused an embarrassing scene, right outside of the toilet entrance.

Ruby swayed slightly on her heeled shoes. "I like Pete you know," she said with a new coyness.

"I know you do. Tonight's your chance Rue. I can tell he likes you too." Emma wasn't sure of her last words but had to try and encourage an interest to build between the two of them. Scheming in her head, Emma decided she would point blankly ignore Pete and stay away from him for the rest of the evening, whilst pushing Ruby towards him at the same time. If she did manage to link up with Darren, that alone would speak louder than words – once she was snogging his face off anyway.

Amazed by Ruby's new personality after consuming quite a few drinks, Emma listened to her chatting away to the women in the toilets. "Oh, I like your dress. Where did you get it from?" she said to one young woman who was wearing a short leather-look, black dress with a low front and back. "I suppose you can't possibly wear a bra with a dress like that." The slim blonde smiled at Ruby and shook her head while sticking her chest out revealing a full cleavage. "Ooh... I like your shoes," she mouthed to another lady, pointing down at the pair of blue suede, three inch heels. "Oh... blue, blue, blue suede shoes... I love your blue suede shoes," she sang.

"Rue, come on you can share with me," said Emma, dragging her drunken friend by the arm into a vacant cubicle, as the puzzled but amused faces of twenty or more women stared at them in astonishment.

Expecting Ruby to shriek in disgust at the very thought of sharing a cubicle and being present at the passing of water, Emma hesitated before beginning the process of lifting her dress up and lowering her underwear to sit down. "Are you ok in here?" she whispered.

"Oh, hurry up, I need to go too. Quickly, before I pee my pants," snorted Ruby before bursting into tears of laughter and crossing her legs tightly.

Dragging Ruby out of the toilets before she could comment on anyone else's appearance or burst into another song, Emma heaved a sigh of relief as they headed towards their table.

"I'm going to sit on Pete... over there. Oops, I mean sit with Pete," Ruby said and wobbled off to the end of the table, chuckling.

As she watched Ruby totter off, Emma wondered if her little geeky friend would regret getting drunk in the morning. She also worried now that Pete might regret Ruby being drunk too.

Having just returned from the bar, Pete was sat on his own clutching a pint glass in his hand and a glum look on his face. He appeared to be studying the first brave dancers on the wooden floor, below the stage, as Ruby joined him at the table. He smiled like he was genuinely pleased to see her and Emma knew that now was the time to escape – time to track down Darren, who seemed to have disappeared. She guessed she would most likely find him somewhere in the crowd around the bars.

More women were joining the brave boogie-babes on the dance floor as the band continued to play 'Golden Oldies' and play them very well. The lead singer was a middle-aged man of extraordinarily good looks, Emma noted on her way past. *He's probably plastered in loads of thick make-up,* she mused, *you'd need it under those bright stage lights.*

"Hello, how are you?" asked one of the 'giggle-girls' as Emma approached the waves of people waiting their turn to order drinks at the bustling bar.

"Oh, hi," she replied, surprised that she hadn't noticed the scantily dressed woman before, "Gina isn't it?"

"Gemma."

"Oh, I was close, at least I got the first letter right," laughed Emma nervously, convinced that the perfect girl was talking to her teeth. "Where are your other friends?" Emma desperately searched the sea of bobbing heads that were twisting and turning and moving up and down in the motions of laughter and loud chatter.

"Oh, well Sarah is right there," said Gemma, turning and pointing to the girl directly behind her who was talking to two young men. Emma nodded and smiled casually to disguise the fact that she didn't really care where the girls were – she was only interested in Darren's whereabouts.

"Where are the other three? Err, what are their names, Jade, Mandy and Chloe?"

"Oh, don't call Amanda, Mandy, she hates it," giggled Gemma, "They're over there, in the far corner with Daz. They've just made it to the front of the queue." Rolling her eyes, Gemma tutted, "It's lovely here but they could do with some extra bar staff, don't you think?"

"Yes it's obviously a popular venue at Christmas time. Daz?" Emma smiled, "Is that what you call Darren? For a moment there, I thought you were going to tell me that they were doing their laundry over in the corner." Emma cringed immediately and bit her bottom lip – what a ridiculous comment to make and more so in her highly regarded professional position too.

"Yeah, we like Darren he's so funny – we couldn't ask for a better manager, he's really cool." Gemma suddenly burst in to a roar of laughter and cupped her hands over her mouth, "Oh... I get it!" she squealed through her fingers, "Daz – the washing powder!"

Emma rolled her eyes and looked over to the other girls and Darren who thankfully, were totally oblivious to Emma and Gemma's cheery exchange of lowbrow humour.

"Oh good, I'm so pleased that you all get along with him," lied Emma, "I don't know him that well but I'm fully aware that he has done a lot for our company to date." Emma cringed as she thought about her intentions to snatch him away from his five admirers and have him to herself and what would the girls think of her. Did she actually care? No.

"Think he's got the 'hots' for Amanda you know," Gemma said to Emma's teeth, with what looked like a slight look of antipathy.

"Hmm," Emma replied, "Well good luck to the pair of them." She hadn't given up, but Emma felt uneasy and the ugly head of 'confidence-crusher' reared up again through her drunken mind. "I'll catch up with you again later Gemma. I'm going to find Colin and the others. Bye."

"Ok, bye," said Gemma, smiling and waving a small delicate hand before she turned around to join in the flirtatious chat with Sarah and two young men from another company.

There were so many different companies in the hall and Emma began to look around at the small clusters of people, gathered together in company-clumps across the whole expanse of the hall. She tried to guess which companies some of the people belonged to. There was a rowdy rabble of young men and women to the right of her, who appeared to be overly flirtatious with each other to the point of confusion, none of them seemed too fussy about which sex their oblique suggestions were aimed at. A subdued syndicate of middle-aged gentlemen scrupulously dressed and looking decidedly stern in their motionless stance, seemed to be top-notch solicitors and barristers and surveyed some of the function's guests with, what Emma thought, was a look of distaste. She was convinced that they had just contrived to set up a new law firm, right in the middle of the hall, as she strained to listen to their constantly, abbreviated jargon. To the left was a small coterie of female friends who could only be connected to the beauty or fashion trades, Emma surmised, judging by their outlandish hairstyles, crazy, multi-coloured clothing and mad make-up. Some of the other groups remained at their tables, while others bunched together at the bars.

One brave, but obviously very drunk young man had joined the many women that had now ventured to the dance floor. He was the centre of attention and loving it, although his inebriated state must have clouded his judgement, for his admirers and onlookers were actually mocking and taunting him in a mass onslaught of ridicule. Some of the women wiggled around the pathetic man like he was the central handbag, plonked down on the floor as a focal point for their group's dance-workout. Emma was sure his bosses wouldn't think he was too cool by the way he was performing – unless he was the boss of course. She smirked and then moved closer to the bar.

Feeling quite alone once again, even though she was surrounded by hoards of people, Emma looked up at a tall man, standing right next to her in the queue to the bar. He turned around and smiling down at her with a chiselled jaw, he spoke in a low-toned voice.

"Hi, do you want to go in front of me?" Then he stepped aside, creating a small gap, "I'm not in the queue, well at least I don't think so," he laughed. His brilliant white teeth and deep brown eyes caught Emma's attention. *Oh my God, he is gorgeous*, she thought, as she politely accepted his offer and began to move in front of him. Brushing past, she noticed his solid looking, upright physique, his wide shoulders and muscular arms, which she could just make out underneath his shirt. He was smartly dressed in black trousers, a crisp white shirt and a narrow black tie. His short cropped, dark hair was slightly heavier on the top, which fell on to his forehead in random soft spikes. Emma couldn't bear to look at his handsome features another moment, for fear of her eyes popping out on stalks or an embarrassing bout of dribbling and uncontrollable blabber coming out of her mouth.

"Thank you," she muttered shyly, without opening her mouth too much. The natural instinct to keep her lips closed as tightly as possible kicked in as soon as the flush of admiration blossomed on her face. Although the gaps between her teeth were not that noticeable to others, Emma had a warped self-image which had been made worse by her constant nightmares.

"You're welcome," he replied in his deep, throaty voice. Emma's heart fluttered as she felt his breath on the back of her hair.

"Andrew – over here!" shouted a woman, across the sea of heads and then the gorgeous hunk headed to the other end of the bar as Emma watched him leave.

Spotting Dave, Jeff and Colin over in the direction that the man, she now assumed was called Andrew, was going, Emma decided to follow him to join her colleagues.

"Where've you been?" asked Dave as she joined them, whilst still watching where 'Andrew' was heading.

The hunk of a man hadn't noticed her following behind him and had met up with the woman who had called his name, just meters away from where she stood. He was obviously attached (well why wouldn't he be – a gorgeous looking man like that – even Dave would have fancied him), so Emma didn't dwell on the fact that she fancied him stupidly. And besides, there was still a chance that she may get off with Darren.

"There was a massive queue at the ladies," Emma said, diverting her gaze back to Dave, "I had to drag Ruby out of there. She was singing to everyone." The three men looked puzzled at Emma's revelation and she too, knew that it sounded ridiculous that Ruby would ever do anything like that.

"*Baileys* is it Em?" called Colin, who was standing closest to the bar.

"Yes please. Thanks Colin." Emma realised he'd already bought a couple of drinks but she thought, why shouldn't he? After all he got paid more than anyone else and he was married to a doctor so she guessed that Colin and his wife, Rosie weren't short of money. They had one child, aged six and she was an adorable little thing, well-mannered and cute. In fact, he pretty much had it all Emma had decided a long time ago, so she imagined that it wouldn't hurt his bank balance if he bought the drinks all night.

"Where is she now then?" asked Jeff, always the concerned gentleman.

"She's talking to Pete."

"He was blown away by the way she looks tonight," laughed Dave, "Well, we all were."

"Really?" said Emma, relieved that there was a possibility that she may now escape the obsessive charms of the other geek in her life... the dog-geek. *Hmm, two geeks together*, she thought, *perfectly matched*. Pete just hadn't noticed the potential of having a relationship with Ruby before.

"Come on, fancy a dance Em?" said Dave, jiggling and wiggling on the spot like a nervous jelly, as Colin carried the glasses over and began to hand them around.

"Maybe a bit later Dave," she replied and strolled back with Colin and Jeff to the table.

Pete and Ruby were deep in conversation as the rest of the office crew joined them. Looking slightly awkward, Pete turned around and smiled as Ruby continued to lean over the table on her elbows, propping her fuddled head up.

Glancing back, before sitting in the chair next to Ruby, Emma scanned the glitzy queues to see if she could see the man called Andrew but he was gone, or at least he'd been sucked up by the undulating surf of bodies. Although there were several heads that towered above the rest, she wouldn't have been able to distinguish which one belonged to him in the dim light.

Darren was still in the far corner, by the bar, with Amanda and Chloe, but Emma hoped they would soon find their way back to the tables and then she would pounce with all her charms – providing he wasn't linked up with Amanda. *She's far too young for him anyway*, thought Emma, feeling rather despondent.

At about twenty five years of age, Emma guessed, Amanda had been with the company for two years, working as a checkout operator. Her tall, sporty figure was crowned with a head of long blonde hair which she usually had tied up in a ponytail at work but tonight she wore it down and as straight as a ruler, which suited her sleekness and complimented the very short sparkly, black dress she was wearing. Emma could see why Darren might be interested in her and her long legs that seemed to end at her ears and she totally understood why Amanda would fancy him. *Hopefully*, thought Emma as she sat at the end of the table oblivious to the others, *hopefully Amanda would go off and find someone else – someone her own age with less baggage. Hopefully.*

"Are you alright there, Miss Dolly Day-dream?" called Dave. Emma jolted out of her daydream, looked up and smiled.

"Yeah, just wondering when we were going to have that dance?" she said, pulling herself upright and trying to appear cheerful and enthusiastic.

"Come on then," replied Dave, jumping to his feet. He stretched his arms out, wiggled his feet and wobbled his behind, "Just limbering up to wipe the dance floor clean with my moves."

Jeff overheard, rolled his eyes, tutted and then continued to talk to Colin about family matters.

"Coming for a dance you two?" asked Emma, butting in on Pete and Ruby's drunken conversation about the work of dog wardens.

Pete looked horrified. Although he was somewhat inebriated, Pete wasn't quite drunk enough or freed from his inhibitions to throw himself around on a dance floor like a demented baboon – and he really would have looked like some deranged primate with fleas up his arse – there was no doubt about that.

Through bleary eyes, Ruby shook her head, "My feet are aching Em, I'll stay here for now, maybe later?" she shouted over the sound of *Chubby Checker's, 'The Twist'*.

"Come on Em, I love this one!" squealed Dave as he began to twist his hips and lower himself to the floor rather awkwardly but prettily.

Emma hesitated for a moment before Dave beckoned her to follow him as he headed towards the dance floor. Suddenly Emma's eyes were drawn to the giggly gang of girls, gathered next to the stage, in the centre. The girls had formed a circle around Darren who was happily dancing in the middle and swinging his hips. His gyrating torso looked incredibly sexy, Emma thought briefly, as she was mysteriously drawn in his direction. Her heart raced and she mingled into the crowds of predominantly women, slowly edging her way towards the stage and Darren.

Following behind, Dave jigged, twisted and jived his way through, drawing attention to himself from many of the women who were impressed by his moves and outright confidence. His global presence was exhilarating, enlivening and energetic as he took control of part of the floor and gave his best performance to the doting onlookers who were decidedly reserved in comparison.

The girls and Darren were drawn to the spectacle of Dave's daring dance moves, as a larger circle began to form around him and the women started to clap and cheer. They pointed and laughed as he threw himself to the floor and spun around on his bottom. Joining the circle, Emma smiled at Darren as he looked across and saw her for the first time.

Darren pointed to Dave, then laughed and shook his head, "Crazy," he mouthed to Emma as he gently moved his hips to the music in a sexually tantalising way. A flush of heat rushed to Emma's cheeks as she began to mimic Darren's moves by rolling her hips around and pushing her chest out. This was her chance, she had to edge her way closer to him and get in between him and Amanda. The young girls swirled on tip-toes and laughed as Dave cajoled them to let go of their inhibitions and join him in the centre. Luckily for Emma, Amanda was the first to move towards Dave and the pair began to dance together, twisting until the music changed. Casually, Emma danced her way around the outside of the circle and stopped two bodies away from Darren. *Keep cool, pretend you're not bothered about seeing him*, she told herself as she began to dance to *'(Do the) Mashed Potatoes'*.

Then the band sped up with a succession of fast paced swinging sixties titles and the lively dancers heated up with their energetic movements under the multi-coloured disco lights.

Dancing her way even closer to Darren, Emma smiled as she caught his eye again. Returning the greeting, he shook his head and puffed out his cheeks.

"I'm getting too old for this," he mouthed and then proceeded to leave the dance floor.

Slowing down almost to a halt, Emma stood and watched him move away, through the crowd towards Amanda, who was still jiving with Dave. When Amanda saw him, she disentangled herself from Dave and laughed off her departure, trying to tempt the other girls to take her place. Disheartened, Emma's gaze followed the pair as they met on the outside of the dance floor. Amanda linked her arm into his and they walked away laughing and fooling around.

Emma's surroundings zoomed out of focus as she realised she was stood still, in the middle of a throng of sweaty, drunken people, breathlessly cavorting around her. The sound of the music faded away and Emma's mind strayed back to the nightmares she'd had last night, while an overwhelming feeling of loneliness and fear encompassed her. Like a grey cloud, she floated away from the heaving band and bouncing bodies and headed back to the toilets. She needed a mirror and she needed reassurance that she didn't look like the lagoon monster from her deepest, darkest dreams.

Chapter 6

Magically, Ruby and Pete had become attached at the hip as they continued to spend the evening talking incessantly about all sorts of geeky topics. The incipient escorting of each other to the bar suggested that they had become united in a geek-driven relationship – of sorts. Emma was thrilled that she had achieved her first objective, which was to get Ruby and Pete together.

Her second goal however, had not come to fruition and it had become more than apparent when she had left the toilets. There they were, in the corridor, looking into each other's eyes, whispering and giggling. Darren's hands gently held Amanda's small waist and one of her legs was wedged between both of his. Unable to bear witnessing the pending kiss between them, which was definitely on the agenda, Emma swiftly strode past them with her gaze diverted towards the exit sign, leading back into the hall. Before turning into the hall, she stole a glance back to the couple...

Emma knew she'd completed her mirror check on the terrible spectre – the lagoon monster, whose uninvited emergence had proven to be in vain. And she had to admit that she actually still looked ok and had been relieved by her own visual judgement. So why did Darren now have his tongue half way down Amanda's throat?

As she approached the empty tables, assigned to *Webb's DIY Store*, Emma scanned the surrounding area, searching for a sign of Ruby. She lifted the tablecloth, crouched down and peered under the table – just in case her friend was sprawled out unconsciously on the floor amongst the odd discarded bread roll, spent party popper casing and soggy patch of spilt alcohol – but she was nowhere to be seen and neither was Pete. Gulping down the last drops of her *Baileys*, Emma looked along the table, filled with empty bottles, glasses and burnt out lanterns, for any remaining wine. Half way along there was an almost full bottle of *Zinfandel*. Snatching it up guiltily, she walked back down to her seat and poured herself a large glass, waiting and hoping that someone would come back to the table soon, just so that she didn't look like a 'Billy-no-mates'.

No one came back and Emma drank her way quickly through the rest of the wine while passing the time of day with the odd stranger (usually a drunken man) that staggered by.

"Ello babe, wanna dance?" said a middle-aged, sad looking man with messy hair as he leaned over the table.

"No thanks, I'm just waiting for someone," she replied courteously. The stale alcoholic fumes emanating from his breath like a fire breathing dragon were causing Emma to feel nauseous.

"Wanna drink?"

"No, I've got one thanks," she replied, feeling slightly uncomfortable and fearing that she may have just made a new friend. Luckily the man hobbled off without a goodbye and headed towards his next unsuspecting victim.

Moments later, Colin and Jeff appeared, "We're off now Em," said Colin, looking rather rough and tired. Jeff looked in a worse state than the man whose salacious offers Emma had just declined.

"Oh dear Jeff, you don't look too well," she said, containing a giggle. Unable to stand still without holding on to the back of the chair, Jeff nodded and then hung his head down. "You'd better get him home Colin, he looks bloody awful."

"Yeah, I will. Have a good Christmas Emma." Bending down, Colin kissed her on the forehead, "See you next week."

"You too Col. It looks like you've drunk too much as well," she laughed, "Bye Jeff, have a good one." The good will went straight over the top of his head as Jeff turned a grey colour before her eyes. "I think you'd better get him out of here quickly," Emma added.

She watched Colin guide Jeff through the masses and then suddenly Emma caught a glimpse of a red dress flicking around on the outskirts of the dance floor at the far side, nearest the bar. Focusing through tired glazed eyes, she thought it was Ruby momentarily, but then brushed the hope aside as she could just make out the figure of a woman dancing around like a drugged up sixties hippie, waving her arms about in the air. Ruby wouldn't be dancing like that.

A second glimpse proved Emma wrong, her jaw fell open and she almost dropped her glass to the table. It *was* Ruby.

Attempting to dance alongside her by alternating his feet and lifting them straight out to the sides and back again, like the balls of a man-sized Newton's Cradle, was Pete – the dancing penguin. His arms held firmly to his sides, he looked more like he was attempting a warped version of the Irish jig, in comparison to Ruby's flailing arm thrusts and uncoordinated leg flicks.

Emma swiftly made her way towards the deranged pair of twirlers in awe of their uninhibited act of madness. Standing back, for fear of being hit by a passing arm, Emma was astonished by Ruby's dance moves – she had never seen anything like it before in her whole life.

Pete smiled pathetically when he spotted Emma behind them and then he turned back to his hot dance queen.

"Ruby. Hi," shouted Emma over the thunderous sounds of the drums. "Rue, it's me – stop a minute."

Ruby caught sight of Emma and halted abruptly, grinning through the beads of sweat permeating across her face as she puffed and panted. "Are you going to dance with us Em?" she spluttered between short breaths.

"Oh my God, Rue. I never knew you could dance – and certainly not like that." Emma raised her eyebrows and eyed Ruby's bare feet questioningly.

"Oh I love it, I've never had so much fun," she puffed, and then began to wiggle her hips again. "And I've been chatting to Pete all night, we've got so much in common and we never realised."

"I don't doubt that." Emma nodded her head and grinned, "I'll join you for a while, the others are starting to leave already but it doesn't finish until one o'clock."

"Where's Darren?"

"Don't ask, he's with that young girl Amanda." The corners of Emma's mouth dropped.

"Oh dear, are you alright?"

"I don't care," Emma lied, knowing it had knocked her confidence quite badly, "Good luck to them but I think she's a bit young for him though."

"Um," replied Ruby and turned back to Pete. "Come on Pete show Em what you can really do."

Pete laughed and then looked shyly towards Emma and began to bounce about like he was on a pogo stick. Ruby started to shimmy towards him with her ample breasts springing up and down and thrusting from side to side.

Bursting into laughter, Emma joined in the fun in a slightly more reserved manner and danced beautifully to the lively music.

Several minutes later, a sense of being watched pricked at Emma's conscience. She turned her head to see the hunky man from earlier in the evening. He was dancing with four, older women, just ten metres or so away from her and her festive-bopper friends. She hadn't noticed him before, although his height stood out in the thick of the crowd. Unable to distinguish whether he was looking at her or Ruby, who was attracting some attention by all of the men and the women on the dance floor, Emma smiled and edged away from the newly discovered disco diva and Pete.

The women surrounding the suave man were having a fun time and provocatively dancing in front of him one at a time, then stepping back to give another one a turn. The man, who Emma remembered was called Andrew, went along with the flirtatious frolics, laughing and encouraging them. Realising her small, courageous smile had gone unnoticed; Emma guessed he'd been watching Ruby's cavorting rather than hers. Trying to ignore the fact that he was totally gorgeous, Emma turned away and continued to dance on her own while Pete and the jive bunny gave it their all, close by.

"Go Ruby!" shouted Darren, strolling over with Amanda hanging off his arm and the remaining girls from the shop floor in tow, staggering behind them. The girls formed a circle with Pete, around Ruby, and squealed to Amanda and Darren to join them.

"Come on Emma, join in," said Darren before he was dragged off by his blonde attachment.

"Is that your friend?" a voice asked from behind Emma. Turning swiftly on her heels, Emma recognised the distinctive voice.

"Yes," she replied in a quivery murmur, "I think she's had too much to drink." As a rush of saliva filled her mouth, Emma realised her jaw had dropped open and snapped it shut tightly.

"Looks like she's enjoying herself," he smiled warmly, "May I join you in a dance?" Speechless, Emma could only nod her head as he took her hand and led her in a jive dance.

"Can I buy you a drink?" Andrew asked, when the tempo of the music began to change, "This is thirsty work."

"Yes… err… thank you." In a daze, Emma followed Andrew to the bar. She looked back at Ruby who was oblivious to anything – apart from Pete. The newly acquainted dance partners had joined together again and danced side by side in the expanding circle of *Webb's* staff. Emma was amazed by Ruby's stamina and her ability not to fall over in her drunken state.

Andrew introduced himself as they approached the bar queue, "My name's Andrew, what can I get you to drink?"

"Emma… I mean… *Baileys*." Andrew looked puzzled, "My name's Emma."

"Emma Bailey?" He smiled.

"No, sorry, I mean could I have a *Baileys* please. Sorry… thank you."

"Oh!" laughed Andrew, "Your name's Emma and you'd like a *Baileys*. Is that right?"

Wanting to kick herself for sounding totally foolish, Emma replied, "Yes… please… I mean… thank you."

"Follow me we'll go round that way," he said pointing in the direction of the end of the bar. Grabbing her by the hand, Andrew led the way around a large group of people who were standing around talking. Emma followed, clutching his big hand and unable to believe her luck. What this incredibly gorgeous hunk saw in her, she really didn't know, but even if there was an ulterior and probably sexual motive to his interests, it was fun just to go along with it for now.

Pulling his wallet from his back pocket, Andrew paid for the drinks and handed a large glass of *Baileys* to Emma. "Doubled it up, saves keep coming back and queuing up again," he said and then winked at her.

"Thanks again," gulped Emma before she took a sip. Her heart felt like it was in her throat and she would have liked to knock the whole drink back in one go, just to calm her nerves that had switched to high alert from the adrenaline rushing through her veins.

"Boo!" giggled Ruby, having sneaked up behind Emma. Pete tagged along beside her, breathless and red-faced.

"Oh, you made me jump," said Emma, slightly relieved to see her friend. Her pumping heart couldn't cope with the handsome man standing in front of her and she needed a distraction just long enough to down her drink, to evoke calm and courage.

After some friendly introductions, Ruby and Pete went off to the bar and Emma realised that, at long last, Pete was totally over his infatuation with her. He hadn't batted an eyelid when she introduced Andrew to him. In fact, Pete was so boss-eyed over Ruby in her red dress that Emma thought she could have been standing there naked and he wouldn't have blinked an eye. He had a new infatuation and Emma prayed it would last for both of their sakes.

The band played their final song and a rapturous applause filled the hall as the musicians waved and nodded their appreciation of the accolade and then left the stage. Just moments later, a refreshingly young DJ took to the stage and captured his audience with a cheeky grin and a raucous roar of, "ARE YOU READY?" Nodding his head to the dancers on the floor below him, the energetic man turned to his partner at the mixing deck, signaled with a nod to start and then turned back to the front, "LET'S P...A...R...T...Y!"

After copious amounts of *Baileys*, too much dancing, introductions to almost everyone who still remained from *Webb's DIY Store* and polite acknowledgement of the four women Andrew had been with previously, Emma and Andrew went to sit down at the *Webb's* table with Ruby and Pete.
Darren and Amanda had disappeared somewhere and the four other 'giggle-girls' were flirting outrageously with some very drunk men around the dance floor.
The DJ's two hour slot was coming to an end and the music had now slowed down to some classic smooches. "Come on," said Ruby, grabbing a permanently stunned Pete by the wrist and whisking him off to the dance floor again.
Emma and Andrew laughed together as they watched Ruby fling her arms over Pete's shoulders and kiss him on the cheek with a force so strong that she might as well have punched him in the face. Having spent the last couple of hours dancing with Emma and her friends, it was obvious that Andrew was becoming accustomed to his new acquaintances and Emma hoped that he wouldn't be able to help but like them.
"Do you want to dance?" asked Andrew in a, 'please-come-to-bed-with-me' voice.
Emma's alcohol addled mind had now given her the confidence to feel calm about how sexy he was, how handsome he was and how shag-able he was. She was just going to enjoy it while it lasted.
"Yes, ok," she replied, nervously but excited by the thought that she would now get some much closer contact with him.

He was good. He moved slowly and seductively to the romantic music, holding Emma tightly around the waist. His hips writhed as he pushed them into hers, and his hot breath gently caressed her face. Emma was in heaven on the dance floor. Smooching with the best looking man in the grand hall, she thought she was dreaming as he held her close. Provocative in his movements yet courteous and civilised, Andrew's demeanor swept her away into a dizzy haze of heightened emotions. Sensually stepping around the other couples on the floor, Emma briefly glanced across to see Ruby and Pete in a tight embrace, almost eating each other's faces off as they kissed awkwardly and erratically. Looking up to Andrew, she smiled as she noticed that he too was watching her friends' inexperienced display of affection.

The evening had come to an end and Emma wondered what would happen now they had all made their way out of the hall, collected their coats and were standing outside waiting for taxis with dozens of other people.

Ruby and Pete had turned into a pair of love-struck teenagers and waited at the back of a queue, holding hands and gazing into each other's bleary eyes.

Andrew had disappeared for a short while to say goodbye to his colleagues before rejoining Emma and escorting her out to the taxi queue. "I know this is going to sound really cheesy but do you want to come back to mine for a coffee?" he asked, before putting an arm around Emma's waist and pulling her in to him.

"Err... yes... ok, I mean, why not. Just for a quickie. Oh my God, I didn't mean like that. I meant a quick coffee," she replied just before he lowered his head down to hers and kissed her gently on the lips. It was like an electric shock as his firm lips pressed onto hers for what seemed like an eternity but was actually only a brief moment. "I... I need to talk to Rue... Ruby," stuttered Emma as her heart pounded in her chest and her cheeks flushed.

Emma pulled away and headed over to Ruby but just as she approached the love-birds, Ruby said, with a slur, "Do you mind if Pete comes back to ours for a coffee?" Emma struggled to recognise her friend's new extrovert personality and wondered if it would last through to the morning and in fact, how was Ruby going to feel about everything in the cold light of a new day?

"No, that's fine. You beat me to it – I was just going to tell you that I'm going back to Andrew's place for a coffee, so I'll be home later. Don't leave the key in the front door if you lock it. I won't be able to get in," said Emma, unsure whether Ruby had actually taken in anything she had just said.

Pete nodded in acknowledgement, "I'll look after her, and don't worry, you won't get locked out."

"I don't live far from here, do you want to walk?" Andrew said before he turned and smiled at Pete. "Can I give you my address and phone number, just so you know where I'm taking her?" he said directly to Pete as if he was snatching Pete's daughter away from him. Emma admired the low tone of his voice which seemed to get sexier with every word he spoke.

"No, I'm sure she'll be fine. Won't you Em?" Pete had put on his 'responsibility' voice, "Give us a call if you need us." He attempted to wink at her but ended up contorting his face in to a screwed up, silly looking mess.

Emma grinned sarcastically, pecked Ruby on the cheek (not that she noticed) and then linked arms with Andrew.

"Shall we go?" Andrew breathed on to the top of her head.

"Yes sure," she replied, excitedly, "I'll have to hold onto your arm, these shoes are killing me."

Waving goodbye to Ruby and Pete, Emma set off with Andrew. Further along the taxi queue the girly gang of gigglers and Dave were waiting at the front, where they were chatting to a new group of young men as Emma passed by them unnoticed. Darren and Amanda were nowhere to be seen.

Into the cold night air, which was already forming crystals of ice on the parked cars along the way, Emma tottered along the quiet roads with Andrew as he spoke softly about her rather unusual friends, Ruby and Pete. Emma was unsure of where she was going or who she was going with, after all she hardly knew Andrew. However, at this present moment, foolishly or not, it didn't matter and she didn't care.

Chapter 7

Just a five minute walk through the sleeping streets and Emma had arrived at the apartment block where the gorgeous man she was hanging on to, presumably lived. The frosty air sent shivers through her as she waited for Andrew to unlock the wide, front door.

"Come in, I live at the top. Sorry we've got two flights of stairs to climb," he whispered, while pointing up the stairs. Turning to Emma, he cupped her face in his cold palms and kissed her lips gently but briefly, before reaching for her hand and guiding her toward the stairs.

The foyer of the large Victorian building smelt fresh and clean. A small vase of plastic orchids and a black, mesh letter rack sat on an old, wooden table underneath an ornate, gold and green mirror. Emma's first impression was – posh, unlike the flat she shared with Ruby, which was very basic and in a very plain looking building.

"Take your shoes off if you want to. Make yourself comfortable while I get the coffee."

The freshness of the late night brisk walk had increased Emma's groggy, drunken state as she slipped her shoes off and looked around the small apartment.

Tastefully decorated, the small lounge/diner had been well thought out and it seemed that every piece of quality furniture had been made to measure. At one side of the room was a large, curved leather sofa which could comfortably seat four people. The luxurious white leather contrasted against a deep pile, black rug on the floor. A grey marble fireplace, housing an ornamental black stallion, raised up on hind legs, was a spectacular focal point. A small, unassuming television stood on a low, grey, marble table in the background, on the opposite side.

Glancing up through her blurry eyes, Emma noticed a wide mirror above the fireplace and stared at herself, checking that she still looked the best she possibly could – under the circumstances. In her alcohol induced state, she decided she looked ok and even if it was poor judgement now, she'd got this far so she couldn't look that bad.

"Do you want plain or Irish coffee?" asked Andrew, poking his head around the door.

"Oh, Irish would be nice. Thank you."

"Sit down, make yourself at home," said Andrew before disappearing again.

Settling herself down into the soft, enveloping leather of the sofa, Emma curled her legs up and snuggled into its deep richness. The warmth in the room suddenly made her feel cosy and tired. Her eyelids began to feel heavy and she struggled to keep them open. Adamant that she was not going to fall asleep or do anything that might jeopardise this potentially blossoming relationship, Emma pulled herself back up and wandered through to the kitchen where Andrew stood gazing out of a small, curtain-less, window while waiting for the kettle to boil.

"Nice place," she said, smiling tightly.

"Yeah it's not bad. Cost a small fortune though."

"Oh," said Emma, surprised, "You own it then?"

"Yes, well I own a mortgage." Andrew laughed, "Sugar?"

"Err... yes, two please, thanks," she replied, trying to keep her eyes fixed to the back of his head and not his buttocks, which were perfectly round, under his trousers.

The Irish coffees were done and Andrew picked them up, at the same time signaling with a nod of his head, to go back through to the lounge,

"You're quite small when you take your shoes off," he said with a smile, as he carried the coffee through. Emma followed, suddenly feeling 'quite small' in comparison to his height of at least six foot, she guessed.

"Well I suppose anyone would be, compared to you. How tall are you? You must be six foot at least." Emma laughed.

"Six, two."

"There you are then. I'm average height, so it's not me being small, it's you being tall." Emma smiled and then sat down next to him.

As he passed her coffee over, their fingers touched. Another electric shock, sent shivers through Emma's over-sensitive body, "But we'd be the same size in bed wouldn't we?" Emma squirmed as the realisation of what she'd said dawned on her. "I mean... err... sorry, I didn't mean to say that," she tried to giggle it off, "Ignore me, I must be drunk."

"Don't worry about it." Andrew stroked her hair away from her face, aware that she felt uncomfortable. Leaning towards her, he took the mug from her hand, placed it on the table and then kissed her coffee-moist lips softly. Slowly, his lips teased hers to open slightly, just enough for their rapid breaths to merge into one. Tingling sensations raced through Emma's body, reaching out to every erogenous zone she had, with a feather like touch. Her heart beat quickened as they remained entranced by the mutual movements of their warm lips.

In the cool darkness of the bedroom, Andrew slowly began to unzip her dress while Emma continued to kiss his mouth softly. As the dress fell to the floor, Andrew's hands cupped her small shoulders and pulled her even closer to him, before embracing her completely in his arms.

Vulnerable to his charms, wearing just her underwear and stockings, Emma began to undo the buttons of his crisp shirt – which smelt of a musky, sensuous cologne – revealing a strong and smooth muscular chest underneath.

Releasing his embrace, Andrew shook the shirt from his back, loosened his trouser belt and pulled it away, dropping it to the floor. "You're beautiful," he whispered as his mouth caressed her neck and shoulders.

Emma's heightened state of euphoria, turned her legs into quivering, useless limbs and she sat down on the bed behind her.

Pulling his trousers off, Andrew gently pushed her further back on to the bed and lay down beside her, stroking her stomach and kissing her hard on the lips. Easing her over on to one side, he unclipped her bra and teased a strap away from her shoulder. "I want you," he breathed into her ear, his gravelly voice deeper than before. He removed the other strap and pulled her bra away.

Emma's eyes rolled – her thoughts and emotions fizzed and bubbled as she began to writhe with pleasure. This gentle, naked man had straddled her with his muscular legs.

His strong arms supported his weight as he took in the beauty of her flesh in the dim light.

Disrobed and willing, Emma desperately waited in anticipation as he sensually touched her lips with his own. Breathing in the warm, sexually scented air, Emma gasped as she felt the pressure inside her and the throb of Andrew's gentle and slow advance. Then they were one, moving together rhythmically, until an explosive end.

"Actually it was all three of us if you really must know Emma," said Dave defensively, pacing up and down on the hard wearing office carpet. Emma was speechless and could only stare with her mouth slightly open.

"We didn't know what else to do. Thought you might get the hint this way," said Jeff, shuffling in his chair uncomfortably and looking to Colin for back up, as usual.

"Well, for Christ's sake Emma, how long were you going to carry this on for?" Colin moaned, "This Company has a reputation to keep."

"Yeah and we don't want manky looking birds like you letting the team down, do we?" added Dave.

Burning tears welled up in her eyes but Emma remained silent as the lump in her throat began to choke her.

"Sort yourself out for God's sake Emma," Colin groaned whilst rubbing his creased forehead, vigorously.

"Yeah, you look freaking horrendous girl." Standing directly in front of her, Dave's piercing eyes stared deep into hers as Emma began to shed many tears of shock and disbelief at the cruelness of her colleagues.

Then the office carpet began to melt away underneath Emma's feet, into the deep, dark lagoon...

Sweaty and shaken, Emma jolted awake and took a moment to adjust her eyes to the bright winter sunshine, sifting in through thin, cotton curtains. Instantly her head rattled as she tried to move it – too much alcohol the previous night. It had been just a dream. Another horrible nightmare about her teeth. She lay still in the big bed and thought about the terrifying dream for a moment, trying to make some sense of it. There were no clues and she still didn't know who had given her the secret presents. It was playing on her mind far more than she realised.

Lying under a strange duvet, naked and warm, Emma looked around the room, hazily recalling the previous night's events. Gathering all her erratic thoughts together, she remembered where she was and who she was with. Her mind spun round and round in a balmy muse and images of the erotic experience she had indulged in. And where was Andrew? Was it real? Was he really that gorgeous and hunky or had the bountiful *Baileys* tainted her judgement and vision?

A faint clattering of crockery came from the other side of the closed door and Emma guessed that Andrew must be in the kitchen. Urgently needing a coffee and some headache tablets, she got out of bed, reached for Andrew's white shirt and put it on. The shirt almost reached her knees and the thin material was teasingly revealing.

"Hi... good morning. How are you feeling?" Andrew was indeed truly handsome, just like she'd remembered.

She stuttered and spluttered her wishes, "Hi, err... would it be ok if... err, if I have a coffee?"

"Only if I can have a cuddle first," he smiled, holding out his well built arms. Instantly Emma felt relieved and more comfortable as he kissed the top of her head. The stale smell of sex seeped from his black, silk kimono, sending Emma into a heightened state of libido again. The sexual energy between them was powerfully electric like a storm's force – something she had never experienced before.

Over an hour later, unconcerned about her own commitments and responsibilities, Emma sighed happily. He was the most perfect thing in her life at this moment and probably any other moment she'd ever had in the past. At present, she didn't care about anything else apart from being with him for as long as it would last. Hardly knowing him and with so few words spoken between them, Emma decided it was really unimportant. They'd communicated through their actions, which shouted out a mutual feeling of attraction and respect and that was all she needed for now. Having just experienced yet another hour of erotically beautiful pleasure, on this bright and beautiful Sunday morning, she lay in Andrew's bed again, in a close embrace and drifted off to sleep with him once more. The two cups of morning coffee still rested in the kitchen, where they'd been made – stone cold.

"I'm starving. Do you want a bacon sandwich?" asked Andrew as he busily prepared another two coffees. His hair stuck up in tufts on the top of his head making him appear even cuter than he had before. Emma was sure it would be very difficult to make him look anything else but super sexy – unless he had a carrier bag over his head. But then he'd need a body bag to hide his whole body, as it too, was the fittest, firmest and most sexually arousing male physique she'd ever had the pleasure of getting her hands on.

"Oh yes, I could eat a scabby horse, I'm so hungry."

"I've got nothing in but I was thinking we could go to the café just around the corner. Not sure if they do horse-meat anymore though."

"Ok, but what about my dress?"

"Well I'd put it on if I were you..."

"Yes..." spluttering into chuckles of laughter, Emma tried to explain, "I mean it might look a bit odd if I turn up wearing an evening dress."

"I see what you mean. Well I can lend you a jumper or something." He smiled and passed a mug of much-needed coffee to her.

They walked the short journey to the café, hand in hand and in silence as the icy wind bit at their cheeks. Now and again, Andrew looked down at her, smiled and winked. Now and again Emma looked up at him and just simply smiled. They strode along in a haze of sexually charged energy.

The sizeable café was busy and they didn't look like the only ones who had been partying into the small hours, as Emma spotted another couple who appeared to be dressed in the same clothing they'd probably worn last night. Sitting down at one of the last vacant tables, Emma felt slightly embarrassed wearing a giant sized blue hoodie over her black dress.

"You even look beautiful in my old hoodie," said Andrew, admiring Emma with his dark eyes.

"You'll wake up soon and see me for real," she replied uneasily. How could anyone think she was beautiful this morning? Or any morning for that matter, Emma wondered as she tried to pat her hair down again.

'Medusa' had sprung to mind when she'd peered into Andrew's mirror earlier, in fact it was more like, 'Medusa on a really bad-hair day'. Her heavily made up eyes had wandered down her face during the night of intensely passionate and highly charged love making and eventually Emma had to remove most of her black make-up.

"What do you fancy?" asked Andrew, picking up the menu.

"Apart from you?" Emma's cheeks flushed as she lowered her head coyly, why did she always have to come out with really cheesy, pathetic statements when she fancied someone?

"It's crazy isn't it," he replied, "I've never done this before. I mean... you know – this." Andrew pointed a finger and waved it back and forth between them, while raising his eyebrows suggestively.

"No, neither have I, well not like this, not so full-on like this." Changing the subject before the two love birds began pledging their undying love for each other and offering marriage, although she felt that she could, Emma said, "Could I have the small Full English?"

"Sure, I'm getting this. Coffee too?" Smiling tightly, more so than usual, Emma nodded and felt a rush of excitement surge through her again as he stood up and headed towards the serving counter.

She could not believe her luck. Ruby was going to be so pleased for her – RUBY! Never for one moment, had Emma thought about Ruby and what she might have or have not, got up to last night. Vaguely recalling that Pete was going home with her, for a coffee, Emma suddenly wondered if her little friend was okay. Musing over Ruby's uncharacteristic behaviour last night, Emma smiled to herself. Was she awake? Did she have a bad head? Was she regretting anything? Was Pete still there (no probably not)? Would Ruby be worrying about where she was? Her mobile phone had been in her handbag all the time, which was back at Andrew's flat, so she couldn't check to see if she had any messages. Glancing up at the clock on the wall above the server, Emma was amazed to see that the time was twenty past two. Where had the day gone? It had been sucked up by sex and sleep – that's where it had gone.

Their mid-afternoon breakfast was a rushed affair as a dear little old lady sat opposite them and proceeded to talk to Emma and Andrew, for the duration. She was obviously very lonely and the pair of lover's couldn't help but be polite and listen to her every word. As soon as they had finished their meal, they made their excuses and left rather quickly, heading back to Andrew's flat, through the biting wind.

Three times in just over twelve hours – it was becoming outrageous in Emma's history book. Soaking wet, she lay semi-upright, staring up at the ceiling as perspiration trickled down her cleavage. She knew it would be time to leave soon and then this magical dream would come to an end, albeit temporarily, she hoped and wished desperately. Returning to the bedroom, Andrew bent over the bed and kissed her mouth softly, "Come on the shower's hot now."

It was plainly obvious that the warm water, freshly scented shower gel, two naked, lustful bodies and the mutually strong attraction would inevitably lead to love making once again. This budding relationship was undeniably intense in such a short timescale. Slower, softer and emotionally deeper, their sexual act was the most amorous and tender yet as the warm water cascaded down their highly aroused bodies.

Emma's skin tingled all over as she wrapped the towel around her, knowing that this last episode of sexual activity had been something she'd really never experienced before.

Her longest lasting relationship, with Gareth, hadn't been this good and that went on for fourteen months. There was something very different and special about Andrew. He was like some sort of gratifying, gorgeously good-looking, God sent down from Heaven to please her. With her head spinning and her heart skipping, she felt like a small child playing hop-scotch as she got dressed and combed through her wet hair.

A smell of strong coffee seeped into the bedroom, calming her dizzy mind. How could she be falling for this man so quickly or was it complete infatuation? Knowing she had to go, knowing it would be difficult to see him over the Christmas period and knowing her feelings were stronger than maybe they should have been at such an early stage, Emma felt desperately in need... in need of him.

Checking her mobile again, Emma thought it odd that Ruby hadn't replied to her earlier message. When they'd arrived back from the café, she'd texted Ruby to let her know of her whereabouts and that she was all right.

"Everything ok?" asked Andrew as he wound strands of her damp hair through his fingers.

"Yeah, just wondering why she hasn't replied," she said, holding her mobile up. "She might be in bed feeling ill. After all she was pretty drunk last night."

"What about the bloke she went home with, err...Pete?" Andrew sounded genuinely concerned for Emma's best friend, "Have you texted him?"

"No. I think I'd better get home and check everything's ok. I need to get packed too." It was almost five o'clock and Emma had to pack a weekend bag ready to go and stay at her parents' house for Christmas. "Haven't you got to pack your things too, if you're leaving tomorrow?"

"Yes I suppose so. Do you want to climb in the pocket of my holdall and I'll take you with me?" he laughed, although Emma detected a hint of truthfulness in his comment.

If she could have fitted in the pocket and if she wasn't going to spend Christmas with her family, which was how it had always been since she'd left home, she would have said 'yes, I'll jump right in'.

Pulling up outside Emma's flat, Andrew put the handbrake on and turned the ignition off. His sleek, racing green, antique *Honda Prelude* was luxurious and fast. Emma was not surprised to see that he drove a sporty looking car like this. He obviously had money and possibly a good job but they hadn't got as far as discussing each others' working lives, home lives, families or history. In fact they hadn't talked about much except the fact that they were both going away to spend Christmas with their families. The only thing Emma knew was that Andrew's family lived in Kent, some ninety miles away and he would be there for a week. He'd told her at some point in the intervals between sex, sleep or nourishment that he would be returning home for the New Year because he'd been invited to a party at his local pub – a friend of his was playing in a band there.

"You've got my number haven't you?" Andrew spoke softly and Emma's throat turned lumpy as she looked into his eyes and couldn't bear the thought of leaving him.

"Yes," she replied, unable to think of anything else to say that wouldn't take all night long.

"Wish we could stay together longer." Reaching across, Andrew slid his hand around the back of her neck and stroked her softly.

As the familiar shivers began to run down her spine, she managed to speak but with just a hint of a squeak. "Keep in touch and have a lovely Christmas." Emma smiled weakly.

"Would you come with me to the New Year's Party?" Andrew's big, brown, pleading eyes looked deep into hers.

"Yes, I'd love to." She didn't really have any plans after Christmas and usually spent each year waiting to see who came up with the most interesting offer for the New Year. Ruby always stayed with her parents 'to keep them company when the fireworks go off', as she often said, so Emma was usually left to her own devices. This year, she didn't care how many New Year invites she got – it was a cert – she would spend it with Andrew. The excitement swept across her again as he smiled his beautiful smile and leaned over to kiss her goodbye, very softly. Reluctantly, Emma climbed out of the car, closed the door and slowly walked away with her heart in her shoes.

Chapter 8

The front door was locked. Emma thought it a little strange at such a late time of day. Taking the key from her handbag, she turned around and just caught a last glimpse of Andrew as he silently drove away. The memories of their torrid, twenty hour, love affair tingled inside her as she watched the car disappear out of sight. Then he was gone.

The flat was eerily quiet as Emma removed her high heeled shoes – which had turned her toes numb, having trekked and hobbled to the café earlier, clinging on to Andrew's arm for support – and opened the living room door.

"Ruby!" Emma stopped in her tracks, threw her bag and shoes on the chair and slowly removed her jacket without taking her eyes off the two bodies lying on the sofa, under a duvet, top to toe. Rubbing her sleepy eyes, Ruby looked up and smiled.

"You're late, where have you been all this time?" said Ruby, staring at the wall clock. Looking like an electrocuted punk rocker, her hair stood on end in every conceivable direction and her old make-up looked like it had been applied by a make-up artist for a Dracula horror movie.

"Just out," said Emma, quite abruptly, she really hadn't wanted to see someone else here, not now. Emma's plans had only included a catch up girly talk with Ruby, a hot bubbly bath, a bit of packing and an early night. "Have you only just woken up Rue?"

"Um," Ruby replied, pulling herself up and gazing questioningly at the opposite end of the sofa. "Pete... is that you down there?" she giggled, "Oh, my head hurts." Still wearing her crumpled red dress, Ruby lifted the duvet and peeped underneath to see if Pete was dressed. He was.

Stirring awake, Pete opened his eyes and blearily scanned the room before closing them again. He pulled the duvet over his head and turned over. Both Emma and Ruby looked at each other and grinned awkwardly.

"I can't believe you've been asleep all day Rue, are you alright?" asked Emma as she noticed two glasses and a bottle of white wine on the table. "How much did you drink last night?"

"Lots, I think," she chuckled again.

"Are you still drunk?"

"Probably," said Pete in a muffled voice, from under the duvet.

Pete surfaced from under the quilt and rubbed his aching head as Ruby moved her legs over the side and sat up.

"I'll make some coffee," said Emma, heading for the kitchen. "What the hell has happened in here?" she shouted back. The windowsill was coated in little lumps of mud and Ruby's red, suede shoes had been carefully placed at each end – filled with soil.

"What?" called Ruby, worried at what she might have done as she struggled to remember anything from last night.

"Shoes." Pete gave her a look of despair, shook his head and wished he hadn't as the pounding set in.

"What have you done to your shoes Ruby?" Emma stood in the doorway, puzzled by the odd sight. Shrugging her shoulders, Ruby turned to Pete for some clarification.

"She took them off last night when we were queuing for the taxi." Sitting up, Pete continued, "When we got back, she decided she wasn't ever going to wear them again, so she went into the communal garden and filled them up with soil – with her bare hands! The ground was frozen but she still managed to do it. I did try and stop her Em, but she wasn't having any of it."

"Why Ruby?" asked Emma, stunned by her friend's stupidity.

"Because I thought I'd never wear them again," Ruby sat chewing her broken nails nervously and then realised that most of them weren't even her own and they were all stained black from the soil, so she stopped immediately and stared at them in disgust.

"But why fill them with mud Rue?" Emma despaired of her now, too.

"Because I thought they'd make nice flower pots," Ruby was close to tears, "I know I've been very silly. I'm sorry."

"Well they're your shoes Rue – it's just a shame to mess up such a beautiful pair."

"Think it's a bit late now," said Pete, deflated.

"I'll make that coffee," said Emma, heading back to the kitchen as her mobile began to tinkle faintly. Returning to grab her bag, Emma searched for the phone and pressed the button to read a text message.

Missing you already. Andy xx

Emma's heart skipped a beat and she felt giddy with pleasure. Unsure whether he would text her once he'd dropped her off, Emma was relieved to get the four words and two kisses.

Missing you too. I'll be thinking of you until I see you again on New Year's Eve xxx

Pressing send, Emma cheerfully popped her phone back into her bag and almost skipped past Pete and Ruby back to the kitchen. "I'm sure your shoes will look lovely with some flowers growing in them," she said with a change of tone in her voice.

"I said I'm sorry," cried Ruby, still sitting next to Pete and looking like a bedraggled, lost puppy.

"No, I mean it, what a lovely, unique idea Rue."

Coffee finished, *Paracetamol* administered and duvet folded, Pete decided it was about time he got home. His parents would be pulling their hair out with worry, even though he had sent them a drunken message last night, which, when he read the saved copy, looked rather odd.

Att emms stay here sleep wiv them luv Pt.

"Do you want me to run you home Pete?" Emma asked, half-heartedly.

"Are you sure you don't mind?"

"No that's fine, I'll just get my bag," said Emma, checking she hadn't missed any more messages. Sadly there were none and she popped her phone back in her bag, "Are you coming Rue?"

"Yes please, I need some fresh air."

More appropriately dressed on a Sunday evening in one of her usual sloppy jumpers and leggings, Ruby slid on her raincoat and stood beside Pete with a cheesy grin on her face. "We're going out for a meal after the New Year," she said quietly and shyly as she looked to Pete, "And then we're going to Hillhead View to celebrate."

"Oh that's great news. It's a shame you're not back for New Year's eve Rue," said Emma, "I'm so pleased though, you obviously got on very well last night." As the awkward moment began to set in, Emma pulled on her coat and said, "Right, let's go."

A Chinese takeaway and lashings of coffee was just what they needed, as Emma and Ruby settled down in front of the TV on their respective sofas. "So how did it go with Pete last night then? Why were you both asleep on the sofa all day?" asked Emma, stuffing a small chunk of chicken ball into her mouth. She had to be careful these days, with her loose teeth, that she didn't put too much in her mouth. She couldn't chew food very well and always feared biting down on some of her teeth in the wrong way, as it would make them even wobblier.

"We didn't go to sleep until about seven o'clock this morning," she said between spoonfuls of fried rice, "We talked all night."

"Talked? All night long?"

"Yes... why?" asked Ruby, defensively.

"What did you talk about all night? Anything else happen?"

"No, it did not! We just talked about books and things." Ruby looked guiltily at her friend, "I know what you're thinking Emma, but I can promise you we did nothing of the sort."

"I wouldn't care if you had. In fact I would have been very happy for you if you did." Emma smiled and picked up another small piece of battered chicken and nibbled at it.

"Alright, but I can assure you that we are just good friends at the moment."

"Just good friends that kiss an awful lot," laughed Emma.

"I was very drunk and feel terrible about all that kissing in public." Ruby squirmed in her seat.

"Was it good though, because that's all that matters?" Ruby didn't answer but her reddening cheeks spoke for her.

"What about you, did you have a nice time?" she asked, trying to change the subject.

"Yes I did. I'm a bit shagged out... literally!"

"Oh my goodness, did you have sex then?" Ruby's eyes widened and the next spoonful of rice stopped midway as her jaw hung partially open.

"Yes... four times," said Emma, nonchalantly, pouring more sweet and sour sauce over her chicken balls.

"Oh my God Emma... are... are you alright?" Ruby's face turned pale, "Who were they?" Moving to the edge of her seat, she placed her plate on the sofa and clasped her hands together, apprehensively. "I thought you didn't seem to be your usual self. Are you hurt?"

"You could say that." Emma grinned.

"Oh my goodness, you're in denial. Was it one of those Group-Bongs?" Ruby squeezed her hands tighter together as she began to feel sick.

Laughing out loudly, Emma squealed, "It's not a Group-Bong Rue, it's called a Gang-Bang!"

"Oh no, you've been raped haven't you? You're acting strangely Emma. I'm concerned that you're in a state of post-anguished-delusion." Ruby was close to tears, "Should I call the police?"

"No!" Emma shook her head and peered at her friend, across the room as she was almost hyperventilating, "And what the hell is post-anguish-delusion?" She laughed.

"Oh, I don't know, but you know what I mean. It happens doesn't it? I mean – women get defensive over what has happened to them, don't they? They're in denial."

"Ruby – calm yourself down for goodness sake! And don't you mean post traumatic stress?"

"Oh gosh, yes that's the one."

"Everything's fine, it was Andrew. Remember him?"

"He organised it? Oh no Emma. He seemed to be such a nice..." stopping short, Ruby took a breath as the realisation of Emma's laughter and apathy swept across her face, turning her gaze to horror. "Did you want them to do it? Is that why you don't seem to care?"

"Rue," said Emma quietly and calmly, "If you'd let me get a word in before you started panicking, I could explain." Picking up her plate of food again, Ruby sat back and listened. "It was only one man, not four."

"Andrew?"

"Yes."

"How long have you been seeing him? I never knew..."

"I only met him last night Ruby, remember?"

"But you said you had sex four times."

"Yes, with Andrew." Ruby's mouth hung open again. "Once last night and then 3 times during the day today."

"What, properly?"

"What do you mean, 'properly'?"

"Err... you know... actual sex. I mean when he goes inside."

"Yes, properly Ruby," Emma laughed again, "You can do it more than once you know."

"Oh gosh! Do you like him then?"

"Well, I would think so, wouldn't you? I don't often go around having non-stop sex with men." Emma felt a bit annoyed that her wonderful, enchanting tale was being unpicked in a very unromantic way. "We just connected in such an explosive way Rue. I've never known anything like it before."

"Is he Superman? I thought men could only do it once and then they had to have a day off," said Ruby and giggled coyly.

"Where did you get that idea from?" laughed Emma.

"I'm not sure. Don't they have to produce more sperm stuff before they can start again? You know, like fill up their testicles again?" Ruby blushed at the word 'testicles'.

Emma roared with laughter and almost choked on the piece of chicken she had held in the side of her mouth, "Look Rue, this is getting far too much like a biology lesson, you have got a lot to learn. Get a book about sex or something. I thought you would have known more about this type of thing, from all the slushy books you read." Emma took a sip of her coffee and continued, while Ruby sat across the other side of the room staring silently and rather blankly. "I've had an amazing time with Andrew. I think I've fallen in love with him at first sight."

"Really, so soon? Is that because he can do it 4 times?"

"No Ruby, that's not the reason why. He's really lovely, in *every* way."

"When are you seeing him again then?"

"New Year's Eve, so we'll both be away that night," said Emma at the same time as her phone sounded another muffled tingle from inside her bag. Jumping up, she almost knocked her plate off her lap before catching it and placing it on the table by the side of her sofa. "That might be him now," she said excitedly as she grappled around in her bag, "He's texted me once already since I've been home."

I can't stop thinking about you. It's doing my head in. Andy xx

Emma's heart galloped like a racehorse as she sent a reply, *Ditto, haven't even started packing yet xxx*

"Is it him?" asked Ruby patiently.

"Yes," purred Emma, throwing herself back on the sofa and hugging her phone to her chest as she peered up at the ceiling dreamily. "He can't stop thinking about me."

"Oh that's so sweet," whispered Ruby in her most endearing way. "Do you think he wants some more sex?"

"No Ruby, I'm sure he doesn't," Emma thought for a moment, "But even if he did – I would be up for it too."

Ruby gasped in amazement, "Again?"

"Yes – again!" Emma grinned slyly, "I think it can be safely said that we both got very lucky last night and ended up having a fantastic time at *Webb's* work do!" stated Emma, "This will be the best Christmas ever!"

"Could I ask you a question Emma?"

"Of course you can. You can ask me anything, you know that. What?"

Ruby shuffled in her seat and looked uncomfortable again. "It's just... well... did you kiss him?"

"Yes, of course I kissed him."

"Oh, ok. I just wondered, well, you know with your teeth problems..." Ruby grinned weakly.

"I know what you mean Rue but it wasn't a problem at all. He's not one of those 'deep-throat' kissers. He's a very sexy, almost teasing type. You know what I mean – the ones that don't need to stick their tongue down your throat to be sensational kissers," Emma paused briefly, "No actually, you wouldn't know what I mean, would you?"

Ruby shook her head, "No, not really."

"He's sweet and gentle Rue, and incredibly sensual in everything he does."

"Oh, I see," replied Ruby.

Although Emma knew that she probably didn't really see at all.

Chapter 9

Good morning ☺ *Just wanted to say goodbye before I leave. Have a very happy Xmas. Andy xx*
Pressing the reply button, Emma sleepily sent a message back. *Have a safe journey and a lovely Xmas with your family. Kisses Em xxx.* The dullness of her room meant it would be a cloudy and cold day outside. She shivered, turned over in her bed and tucked the quilt tightly around her before drifting back off to sleep.

"Em... Emma... What time are you going to your Mum's?" Ruby was on the other side of the bedroom door, dressed, packed and ready to leave for her family's Christmas get together.

"Going round for tea," replied Emma as she peeped out from under the quilt, "What time is it?"

"Two o'clock."

"Oh dear, better get up then," said Emma, dragging herself out of bed. Plodding to the door, she noticed her legs and groin ached like she'd run a marathon the previous day. "Gosh, I ache all over," she mumbled as she passed Ruby in the hallway, on route to the bathroom.

"I'll be going soon. Do you want a coffee?" called Ruby, merrily. "I've got time to make us one before I go."

"Yes please," said Emma, peering into the mirror at her teeth. Most days, she spent some time talking and smiling in different ways, into the mirror, to check how she looked to others. Pulling silly faces at herself, Emma was convinced she had as good a chance as any, if she entered a Gurning competition, of winning. Her teeth were always worse after a drinking session but she had particular concerns about one of the front ones, on the bottom row. It was clearly moving just by the force of her tongue rocking it backwards and forwards. The strangely pleasant feeling of the tooth's movement made her reminisce about her childhood days.

When she was losing her milk teeth, her dad pretended to chase her around the garden with a pair of pliers, saying he was going to pull them out for her so he could get the *'Tooth Fairy'* money for himself. Smiling to herself, Emma finished in the bathroom and then went through to the lounge where Ruby sat waiting with two coffees.

"I'll be going after this. Here, this is for you, but you're not allowed to open it until Christmas day," she said, passing a small, sparkly red, wrapped present to Emma. "I hope you like it Em."

"Ah, thank you Rue. I haven't wrapped yours yet," said Emma guiltily.

"I've had mine, you bought me that dress."

"No, I got you something else as well."

"Shall I wait until I get back then?"

"Unless you've got time to hang around while I wrap it now?" said Emma, eyeing the intriguing little gift in her hand.

"No, I need to get going Em, if you don't mind. It'll be nice to come back to another present after Christmas."

"Ok, thank you for this," said Emma, waving the perfectly wrapped, small and mysterious gift in the air, "I hope it's not a set of dentures or anything like that." Emma laughed out loud when she saw the horrified look on Ruby's face, "Only joking, I'm sure it will be something lovely, knowing you."

Ruby grinned, "I do hope you'll like it."

"Have you booked a taxi?"

"No Pete's dropping me off at the station. He's so sweet isn't he?"

"Yes he is. Well have a lovely Christmas won't you," said Emma, "And let me know when you arrive safely."

"And you too, Em. Yes I'll text you."

Draining the last slurps from her coffee mug, Ruby picked up her coat and headed towards her suitcase with retractable wheels (it was the trendiest thing she possessed, apart from her new red dress, *without* matching shoes), lifted the handle and pulled it to the door.

"Bye then Em, I'll see you next week."

Emma smiled and nodded then they gave each other bestie-hugs just as Pete turned up in his car. Emma watched Ruby, her favourite little geek, depart and then she returned indoors, feeling slightly lonely and forlorn. Everyone was leaving to go and join their families for the festive season and although Emma was going away too (although not very far – in fact, just to the other side of town) it didn't quite feel as exciting as previous years. Emma was sure that meeting Andrew and the time she had spent with him had a lot to do with it – everything else could only be an anticlimax after her fleeting affair with him.

"Hi Mum, sorry I'm late!" called Emma from the front porch as Misty smothered her in sloppy tongue kisses. Laden with bags full of presents and her weekend holdall, she stepped through to the lounge where her dad sat flicking through the TV channels.

"Alright trouble," he said without turning to look at her. Dropping her bags on the floor, Emma looked around the room and smiled to herself.

"I see Grandma's been round then."

"Naturally," replied Emma's dad, still flicking through channels, looking for a decent programme that didn't have anything to do with the festive season. He was very much like the old *Grinch* – a movie character from her childhood and her dad had grown worse, the older he got.

"Where's Mum?"

"I'm here!" called her mum, from upstairs, "Hello darling, are you ok?" she asked as she floated down the stairs like an angel.

"Sorry I'm late. Have I missed tea?"

"No not at all, kept it warm for you. We haven't eaten yet, your Grandma's been round this afternoon," said her mum as she entered the living room, pecked Emma on the cheek and stood behind the reclining chair, where Emma's dad sat. "Grandad's not well again."

"Oh dear, will he still be coming tomorrow?"

"Hope so, Grandma's going to call in the morning. Your dad will pick them up – won't you Grant?" she said, poking him in the back.

"Yeah, of course I will."

Sadly, Emma's dad and Grandma didn't quite see eye to eye. They hadn't done for many years and Emma could recall the accusations that had flown around at the time, about her dad throwing her grandma into the lake at the local park. Grandma had never really forgiven him, although he was adamant that it had all been a terrible accident at the time and he had not pushed her in.

"What time will Joe be here?" asked Emma, excitedly. She hadn't seen her brother for a year, not since last Christmas in fact; when he proudly announced that he had a girlfriend. She was probably not his first one but certainly the first one he had ever mentioned to his family. This year he was going to bring Tiffany along to meet the whole family, so Emma guessed it was pretty serious stuff.

"About 8.30," replied her dad, stretching out in his old recliner, "Is the dinner ready Alex, I'm starving?"

"Get off your bum and go and check," said Emma's mum jovially, patting him on the top of his thinning head.

"Your stew is the best in the world," said Emma, wiping her lips with her sleeve, "I'm stuffed."

"There's more if you want it honey."

Emma's mum had made stew on a regular basis as all the children were growing up, she said it was quick, easy and healthy. Emma used to hate it and had a slight grudge, every other Sunday that she was made to eat it. She smiled as she remembered spending two hours most alternate Sunday evenings, pushing peas and carrots around her bowl until everyone had left the room and forgotten about her still sitting there, still eating. Then she would quickly rush through the archway to the kitchen, open the lid of the bin and sit back down quickly before anyone noticed. Making a game out of her meal, she would play toss the carrot or pea into the bin from the dining room and see how many times her aim was accurate. Now and again she would have to stop and pretend to be eating when anyone passed by. Emma recalled how she became an expert veggie-tosser during her childhood and along with her cleverly clandestine disposal of salmon paste sandwiches to the cats next door, she was an all round wafer thin child until she hit puberty. However the neighbour's two scavenging cats grew fatter and greedier as they reached old age and usually smelt very strongly of fish paste.

"No, honestly Mum, I'm full to the brim." Strangely, since leaving the maternal home, Emma had developed a taste for her mum's stew and even began to enjoy the *odd* salmon paste sandwich... *odd* as in maybe only one or two a year.

I'm here, but wish I was there with you. Andy xx

I've arrived at Mum's ok, have a lovely Xmas. Love from Ruby xxxxxxxx

Every time her mobile tinkled Emma's heart raced in anticipation – she couldn't quite get to it fast enough. It was always buried deep inside her oversized bag, at the very bottom, even though she swore she had put it on the top.

"It's nice to see that you've grown out of keeping your phone tucked in your bra love," said Emma's mum with a big smile on her face.

"Hardly anyone calls me these days Mum, but I might go back to that now," Emma grinned slyly.

"I call you."

"Yes I know Mum, I mean apart from you. Oh and Grandma – she calls or texts me nearly every day."

"Who's that then?" she enquired, trying to sound like she was not prying.

"I met a man the other night at the work's Christmas do."

"Oh? What's his name?"

"Andrew," said Emma, trying to talk and text at the same time.

"Andrew what?"

"Um, don't know... just Andrew." Suddenly realising she didn't even know his last name, Emma convinced herself that it didn't really matter, well not at the moment anyway.

"Just Andrew? That's a funny name," said her mum, smiling at her beloved one and only daughter. "Are you seeing him again?"

"Yes, next week. I'm going out on New Year's Eve with him. He's very nice Mum."

"Ah, lovely. It's about time you met someone nice."

"Who's she met?" roared Emma's dad, entering the kitchen and putting his arms over both Emma and her mum's shoulders and grinning.

"No one Dad, just a man I met the other night."

"Bring him round here so I can check him out. You know, give him the third degree about his intentions, ensure he's able to support you etc."

"Dad, shut up you wally." Punching her dad gently in the side of his ribs, Emma moved away, still clutching her phone in her hand and a half written text message, waiting to be sent.

You too Ruby, love ya! xxx

Hi Andrew, at my mum's just had a huge amount of stew, yummy. Wish you were here too ☺ xxx

Pressing the send button, Emma automatically slid the mobile into her bra strap and made sure it was securely tucked in. "There, you can't teach an old dog new tricks," she said, beaming at her parents.

"Joe's here!" hollered Grant from the front porch.

"Coming," called Alex, as she busily wrapped the last minute Christmas presents in her bedroom, "Emma, Joe's here!"

Stretched out across her old bed, Emma looked up at the ceiling and smiled to herself. Her room had never really changed much since she'd left home. Apart from some decorating and new matching quilt cover and curtains, the room was still hers. The cupboards still had some of her old school books and memorabilia stashed away at the back and her last school photograph, stood statically in its original frame on the bedside table. "Yes, I'll be down in a minute," she shouted. Jumping up, Emma checked herself in the mirror, practiced her 'hello' mouth movements to remind herself how not to talk in front of people, especially new people, for fear of exposing her receding gum line and spaced out pegs and went downstairs.

"Hello bruv," she said quickly as she tried to wrestle with Misty to get her out of the way. Emma gave a high-five to her brother, "Hi, nice to meet you Tiffany."

Standing, shyly behind Joe, Tiffany was not what Emma would have expected. Petite in every way, her long golden brown hair framed a tiny, pretty face with pixie-like features and large brown eyes. Misty circled the new guests, wagging her tail frantically and panting.

"Hello, nice to meet you too," she said in a gentle voice as she stretched out a hand to greet Emma in the traditional way.

"Come in, have a seat," said Grant, closing the porch door behind Tiffany and sending Misty off to her bed, "Make a cuppa Em. I'm sure everyone would like a cup of tea?" Aiming his offer towards Tiffany, rather than Joe, Grant gestured to her to sit down on the sofa.

Things never change, thought Emma as she went through to the kitchen to make the tea, leaving her mum and dad making polite conversation with Joe and his young lady. A vibration on her left breast made Emma jump momentarily, until she remembered her phone had been discreetly tucked away in her bra.

If I don't get a chance tomorrow, just want to wish you a very happy Xmas day again. Andy xx

Swooning over the kettle, Emma went into multi-task mode. Typing with one hand and popping tea bags into cups with the other, she reciprocated the message. *Ditto, enjoy yourself and don't drink too much lol ☺ xxx*

Living on planet Zog obviously, Emma listened to her family discuss the ups and downs of buying property. She'd been totally unaware that Joe and Tiff, as she preferred to be called, were actually going through the process of buying their first house together.

"I did mention it to you Em, probably not listening as usual," said her mum, raising her eyebrows and smiling, "When you came round with Pete, a few weeks ago. I'm sure I told you."

"How is your man Pete?" asked Joe, sarcastically.

"Don't know, haven't seen him too much and anyway, he's with Ruby now. He's not my man."

A communal, "What?" resonated around the room as they all looked at one another, apart from Tiffany who sat sweetly on the edge of the sofa, sipping a cup of tea politely.

"Ruby? But I thought he was obsessed with you," said Emma's mum. "Does that mean the dog walking will stop?"

"Suppose so, but I can still come over on my own, or maybe even with Andrew in the future."

"Who's Andrew?" asked Joe, inquisitively. He'd always looked out for Emma and she felt like he was her big, but maybe a bit weird, guardian angel brother.

"Just some bloke I met at the work Christmas do," Emma replied, awkwardly.

"How long have you been with him?"

"Err... since the work's Christmas do. Err... work it out big-boy-brains. *Christmas work do* on Saturday night!"

"Well how was I supposed to know that, you plonker," laughed Joe, "Going well then?" And then he burst into a raucous cackle.

"You'll get used to these two," said Grant, as Tiffany smiled and looked-on slightly confused by the siblings' weird interactions.

Although she'd been with Joe for over a year, they had only lived together for the last four months and Tiff was still discovering new things about him, almost weekly. He was indeed, unusual in many ways. His kind, caring heart made up for his few shortfalls in the tidiness department and his dry sense of humour compensated for his lack of memory when it came to cleaning their flat or cooking the tea, 'Oh, I completely forgot to do it,' he would always say. But no matter what Joe was or was not, Tiffany loved him dearly and that was plainly obvious.

The rest of the evening was filled with laughter, jokes, too many television repeats and lots of questions – mainly aimed at Joe and Tiff. At just before midnight, everyone decided to retire to their respective rooms and said their 'goodnights'.

Going to bed now so I won't frighten Santa and Rudolf off. Nite, nite Emma ☺ xxx Lying in her old bed, Emma waited hopefully for one last message from Andrew. It was difficult to think of anything else but him. The time they'd spent together seemed like a faraway dream now as she slowly drifted off in to another one of those restless sleeps.

***

Christmas morning had arrived. Opening her eyes and peering around the bedroom, Emma felt like an excited child again. She was actually looking forward to spending the day with her mum, dad, Joe, Tiffany (who was very nice, too nice for Joe, thought Emma) and her dear old Grandad. Oh, and Grandma.

Emma's heart fluttered as she picked up her phone from the side table and saw the envelope with a number two, displayed on the screen. Two messages, hopefully at least one of them would be from Andrew, she prayed as she opened the inbox.

You would stun them with your beautiful eyes, not frighten them away. Andy xx

Christmas couldn't be any more perfect, she thought as she hugged her phone to her chest. *Well, actually it could, we could be spending it together.*

Searching for the second message, Emma opened another one from him.

Good morning sexy, I hope you have a great day today. Merry Christmas. Andy xx

A thrill of excitement rushed through Emma's body, she desperately wanted him again. Sending a reply, she lay in bed and watched the phone confirm, 'message sent'. *Happy Xmas to you too. Em ☺ xxx*

"Morning love, happy Christmas," said Emma's mum, pecking her on the cheek as she went to fill the kettle, "Your dad's just gone. Did you sleep well?"

"Yes, too well. Why didn't you wake me earlier Mum?"

"I just thought you might need the sleep love." Flicking the kettle on, her mum took two cups from the cupboard, "Cup of tea?"

"Coffee please," replied Emma as the tinkle of her phone vibrated in her dressing gown pocket. "Where's Joe and Tiff?"

"Oh they were up early. They took Misty for a walk about half an hour ago."

Opening the inbox of her mobile, Emma smiled as she read yet another message from Andrew,

It's Christmas day and all I want to do is make love to you, Andy xx

Emma's face flushed as the heat of desire rushed through her again.

"Who's that love? Are you alright?" asked her mum, noting Emma's flushed appearance.

"Oh, it's just Andrew, wishing me a happy Christmas," she lied for the sake of respect for her mum.

"You must like him, blushing like that," she laughed.

"He's lovely Mum." Typing frantically again, Emma had to send a reply and put her phone away before she was overcome by an emotional love rush. *Ditto, OMG that would make my Xmas!* ☺ *xxx*

Alex was in control, the sprouts were bobbing around in a pan of boiling water, the potatoes were starting to roast and brown and the turkey was resting gracefully on the kitchen top. Grandma and Grandad had arrived, laden with extra little gifts (although Grandma had already filled the house with presents over the previous six weeks). Joe was watching an old film, *The Gladiator*, on *Sky* movies (very un-Christmassy) with his dad and Grandad, while Emma and Tiff stood together in the kitchen making small talk.

"Do you want any help out there with that dinner?" called Grant, from his recliner.

"No, it won't be long." Alex shouted back from the kitchen.

"Ah, she's always kept us waiting, our Alex," said Grandad, "Right from birth you know." Grandad paused and thought for a moment, "Did you know that the nurses in the maternity unit had to shave our poor old Dot twice – our Alex took so long to be born?"

Grant and Joe looked at each other in horrified shock and didn't quite know whether to laugh or cringe and then they both burst into laughter simultaneously. Grandad's random remarks were always either cringe-worthy, hilarious or both and no one really knew how to take his odd comments. He didn't make them often but when he did they were real classics.

"What was that you said Charlie?" asked Grandma, popping her head around the doorway and giving Grandad a hard stare.

"You really don't want to know Grandma!" squealed Joe.

Grandad sat quietly and didn't look up. His pale complexion was a visible sign of his failing health but his mind was still fully alert and active, even in his later years, but he knew when to keep quiet.

"Men!" Grandma huffed and returned to the kitchen.

Tiffany stood in the kitchen offering endless amounts of unwanted help while Grandma tried to quiz her about every aspect of her life. Emma finished laying the table with her mum's finest cutlery and place mats and then joined Tiffany in a vain attempt to rescue the poor girl from her Grandma's incessant questioning.

"Anything else we can do Mum?" Emma asked, smiling and slyly winking at Tiff.

"No thanks love, everything's under control. We'd better get some of the presents done before dinner."

Once again Christmas day was filled with countless, unwanted presents from Grandma and lots of smiles and nods to show gratification (albeit false). Aaron's (another of Emma's brothers) pile of unopened presents lay under the tree waiting for his return from Wales, after the New Year.

"I haven't seen Aaron for a long time," said Grandma, sitting with a hoard of smelly gifts on her lap and gazing at the neatly wrapped, strangely shaped (and probably unwanted) hoard of gifts for Aaron.

"He's very busy these days with his new job. I think he's met someone too," smiled Alex.

"About time as well, he'll be thirty soon. I was beginning to worry about that boy." Grandma heaved herself up from the chair and headed for the bubbling sound of sprouts in the kitchen, hobbling as she went. "Are we going to get this dinner ready now Alex?" she called, over her shoulder.

"Yes Mother... coming!" said Alex, winking at Emma and rolling her eyes, "Could you clear up the rubbish Em, thanks darling."

"Sure," she replied just as her phone tinkled yet again. *Just about to sink my teeth in to a Xmas dinner, wish it was you I had on my plate instead. Andy xx*

Never been eaten off a plate before! Lol, Emma xxx Emma replied quickly and felt a warm glow inside her as she then began to clear the mounds of wrapping paper from the floor.

Must try it, first time for everything ☺ Andy xx

Grandad had been quiet during dinner, more so than usual. He often kept his mouth shut due to his wife's incessant talking and overbearing personality but today he was definitely not himself. "Are you alright Dad?" asked Alex, as she watched him pick at his mostly uneaten meal.

"He's not feeling well again. I told him to get back to the doctors but you know what your father's like." Grandma butted in before Grandad could even part his lips.

Tutting, Grandad leaned over and whispered, "I'm fine. Your mother worries too much." Both Alex and Emma weren't sure that he was fine; they'd seen how he was just before the last time he was rushed into hospital with an ever present, heart problem.

In to his late eighties, Emma's grandad was still a very distinguished character, tall in posture and remarkably agile for his years. But his heart wasn't up to scratch and sadly, it was failing him in his later years. However, he'd never stopped tinkering and toiling in his beloved 'work-room' to create masterpiece after masterpiece of finely crafted, working models of ships, trains, planes and other types of transportation of a bygone era. It was his life's work and something he was very proud of and probably his only escape from the jaws of his wife.

"I'm stuffed," said Grant, leaning back in his chair and patting his swollen stomach.

"Christmas pudding?" asked Alex, scanning the table of over-fed, sleepy-eyed diners, for any willing participants.

A unanimous 'No thank-you!' resounded around the long dining table as practically everyone stretched back and mimicked Grant's belly rubbing, apart from Grandad, who had given up pushing sprouts around his plate and sat quietly watching everyone else over the rims of his well-worn glasses.

Retiring to the living room once again, Grant, Joe and Grandad slumped down on the comfy seats and prepared for the traditional, annual snoring contest. In the dining room, Emma remained at the table with her mum, Grandma and Tiff.

"Have you been to the dentist yet Emma?" asked her grandma, peering closely at Emma's partially opened mouth.

"No. Why do you ask that?"

"Mother, do we have to have this conversation now?" Alex asked rhetorically, throwing a menacing glare at Grandma, "She'll do it in her own time, leave her alone."

"Well I just thought…"

"Well, just leave it please Mother." Alex's tone of voice was enough to stop Grandma in her tracks.

Looking like someone that was listening in on a private and sensitive conversation, Tiff shuffled uncomfortably on her chair while her eyes stayed firmly fixed on a spoon on the table.

Emma's emotions had blown sky high in a matter of seconds, for some unknown reason and she desperately tried to contain the welling tears by rolling her eyes and staring at the ceiling.

"You alright love?"

"Yes, I'm going after Christmas anyway," replied Emma, cringing at what she thought Tiffany must be thinking of her.

"They're not going to get any better Emma," snapped Grandma as she swiftly caught Alex's evil glare again.

"I don't like the dentist," said Tiff quietly, feeling rather awkward having to listen to what seemed to be a tetchy family affair and not one that she really wanted to be involved in. "I haven't been for about two years."

"Well, Emma hasn't been for years and years," said Grandma, shaking her head, "She needs to. She's got problems with her…"

"Tea anyone?" asked Emma, standing up sharply as her anger began to rise. Silence filled the room as she walked towards the kitchen, slicing her way through the atmosphere that hung in the air. Following after her, Emma's mum joined her by the kettle.

"Try and forget it, love. You know what your grandma's like, she means no harm and she just doesn't know when to stop does she?"

The tears fell and Emma couldn't stop them this time. "Well she's right, they are getting worse and I'm terrified of going."

"I know you are love. I did say I'd come with you if you want me to." Emma's mum spoke in a whispered voice, "Come on, let's try and forget it for now. Your grandma has probably moved on to something new or someone else by now and poor Tiffany will be getting it all."

"They've noticed at work," said Emma, wiping her eyes and trying to gain some composure before Tiffany, or more worryingly, her grandma entered the room.

"How do you know that?"

"Because I got two horribly cruel secret Santa presents from someone in the office," said Emma, feeling the anger begin to rise again. Shaking her head in disgust, Emma's mum put her arm around Emma's shoulder and pulled her in.

"What were they?" she whispered.

"A pair of wind-up chattering teeth and an electric toothbrush," said Emma angrily.

"Oh no, who would do something like that?"

"I don't know but I'm going to find out." Grabbing the kettle, Emma filled it with water and then replaced it on its base.

"What are you going to do if and when you find out who it was Em?" Her mum looked worried.

"I don't know, but I'll think of something. If any one of those men has got something to say to me... well, they can say it to my face. Not insult me by giving me stupid, secret presents as a hint!"

"Come on, calm down Em. Don't let this spoil our Christmas love." Rubbing Emma's back affectionately, her mum said, "Make an appointment in the New Year and I'll go with you. Let's get this over with, once and for all."

Poor Tiffany had spent the whole afternoon under Grandma's torturous spell of idle gossip. She looked weary as she politely nodded and agreeably shook her head at all the appropriate moments. Now and again she would look through the door into the living room to see Joe sprawled out on the sofa, next to his grandad, snoring in unison and creating the backing track for Grant's spectacularly snorting snooze. Emma and Alex cleared away the turkey infested mess in the kitchen and began to prepare some nibbles and sausage rolls for the evening buffet.

"Your dad wants to get home, I knew he wasn't well," grumbled Grandma, appearing at the archway.

"Aren't you stopping for tea then?" asked Alex, concerned that her earlier assumptions had been correct and her father really was quite poorly again.

"No and Grant's awake now as well, so if you both don't mind, we'll be going home soon. I will get the doctor out if he feels no better this evening." Grandma's face was ashen, she'd seen her husband become very ill once before and her fears were rising again. Grandad never complained about anything (unlike his wife), but she knew when he wasn't right, however hard he tried to conceal it and brush it aside as 'just a dodgy spell'.

The evening was noticeably relaxed and entertaining once Grant returned from his tour of duty, dropping the in-laws home. Grandad had decided to go straight to bed to 'sleep it off', when they arrived home, leaving Grandma to entertain herself all evening with the television remote control firmly tucked in her lap. She was content.

Secretly relieved, Grant could now indulge in a couple of drinks with his family and not worry that he had to drive anyone home.

The buffet offerings were hardly touched as everyone picked at the tins of chocolates, nuts and nibbles, scattered around the living room on the occasional tables and Misty was stretched out in front of the fire, contentedly gnawing on her new bone.

"Well, you got through it babe. You met Grandma... and survived to tell the tale," laughed Joe.

Curled up next to him, Tiff smiled and rolled her eyes, "I think she's quite sweet really," she said, but nobody believed her and everyone knew that Tiff just hadn't had a long enough experience of Grandma.

Grandma Dot (as most people called her) was a very opinionated, meddlesome woman. Most of the family didn't particularly wish to get too involved with her (although they all cared about her), purely because of her uncanny way of upsetting or frustrating people over the slightest of things. She had most definitely worsened with age.

Oh dear, I so want you. Andy xx

The drinks cabinet had been opened and every conceivable alcoholic beverage, anyone could imagine, was on display. Grant had taken to making cocktails some years ago and even went on a short course to learn how to concoct the very best of them. When everyone had settled down with their favourite tipple, the games began. The old Trivial Pursuit board game had been updated and replaced for a new quiz game, played on the TV. Grant was always the winner in the trivia games, but this year he had a worthy contender in Tiffany. Her quiet disposition disguised a cunningly, clever and witty mind.

Ditto...RIGHT NOW! Em xxx and then Emma typed; *I'm drunk on Dad's cocktails but still want to desperately shag your brains out. Em xxx*

As the raucous laughter and disorganized gaming continued, Emma sat back with her phone poised in one hand and a third cocktail in the other. Although she loved her family dearly and enjoyed being with them at Christmas time, this year felt so very different, this year she wanted to be with a man she'd only just met and she wanted to be alone with him too.

Can't wait until next week. You are seriously going to get a piece of me. Andy xx

"Come on, wakey wakey, it's your turn fone-freak!" called Emma's dad. Startled, she looked up from her secret world of sexually explicit suggestions and tucked her precious phone back into her bra, just as it vibrated once again.

"Last go Dad, I'm shattered. I might have to go to bed soon," said Emma, knocking back the *Brain Haemorrhage* cocktail. "Woo," she spluttered, shaking her head as the potent liquid slid down her throat.

"Want another one of those, before you go Em?" Emma's dad loved to create miniature works of art in a glass and her favourite drink had been turned into one of the most beautiful looking cocktails she'd seen. Made from *Peach Schnapps, Bailey's Irish Cream* and *Grenadine*, the *Brain Haemorrhage* was far too drinkable and far too potent to have any more than...

"Go on then, just one more then I'm definitely going to bed," she said, reaching back into her bra for another Andy-fix.

That sounded violent but don't worry it will be anything but that. The words slowly, sensually, seductively, steamily and seriously are more appropriate. Andy xx

Bring it on. Miss you madly and this is crazy! Em xxx

As the frivolity abated and everyone sat mindlessly watching an ancient film, *'Back to the Future II'*, while sipping or knocking back cocktails, Emma got up from her chair, gathered her bundle of presents from under the coffee table and said goodnight. Four beautiful drinks had gone straight to her head and now she felt incredibly tired but deliriously happy at the same time. Past caring about her gappy teeth, Emma had to admit that she'd enjoyed her Christmas day (even seeing Grandma) but was now ready to get the rest of the festive season out of the way. She couldn't wait to meet up with Andrew again for the New Year, make a resolution at midnight and then get her darned teeth sorted out at the dentists – Pronto! She finally had everything sorted out in her mind and some clear goals for the future – although they weren't perfectly clear at the moment, due to the amount of alcohol she'd consumed. But they were clear enough. Her more than slightly, inebriated mind was made up for sure – she had to do something about her demons in order to comfortably and confidently enjoy a potentially, heavily sexed relationship with Andy. It was as simple as that.

Going to bed now, I'm a bit drunk. I wish you were here so that I could molest you, in the most passionate way possible of course. Em xxx

Goodnight Emma, it seems I'm falling for you already. Ridiculous, I know. I'm sure I'm not that drunk that I don't know what I'm saying. Sorry if it's a bit OTT. Sweet dreams, Andy xx

Chapter 10

The last text message on Christmas day had really thrown Emma and resulted in a restless, sleepless night once again. She hadn't replied to him, not knowing quite what to say in response to his unexpected and rather rash revelation. Dragging herself out of bed, she slipped on her new, fluffy dressing gown and pulled on the matching slipper booties while wondering whether to take his message seriously. Was Andrew more drunk than he thought last night? Would he remember what he'd sent? Time would tell and in the mean time Emma was hungry and the aroma of sizzling bacon and sausages seeping under the door of her bedroom, made her tummy rumble loudly.

Surprisingly she did not have a hangover, as she would have expected after drinking four of her dad's cocktails, on top of the wine she'd had at dinner time and most of the afternoon. But even if she had had a splitting headache, today would be a quiet day with her parents once Joe and Tiffany had left for her parents. Then it was back to work tomorrow, Emma recalled suddenly and a sinking feeling washed over her. Still, at least there were only two working days left before the weekend came round again and then she could count down to the moment she met up with Andrew on New Year's Eve. A rush of excitement powered through her sending the 'back to work blues' away.

"Morning love, you having a fry-up?" asked Emma's mum, turning the sausages over in the pan while Misty hovered around her legs, just in case a one came flying her way.

"Yeah, please Mum."

"Your grandma's been on the phone..."

"Oh, surprise surprise," said Emma sarcastically as she flicked the kettle on.

"No listen Em, she's getting the doctor out. Grandad is not well at all." The look on her mum's face said it all. She was really worried about Grandad.

"Oh dear," said Emma, feeling slightly guilty by her quick judgement, "Maybe he'll be alright once the doctor gives him something."

"Hope so. Grilled tomatoes?"

"Yes please," bellowed Joe, walking into the kitchen, already fully dressed, "Gonna miss me Sis? We're going this morning." Wrapping his strong arm around Emma's shoulder, Joe winked at her.

"Yeah... like a hole in the head." Emma grinned just as Tiffany's head peeped around the archway.

Softly, she said "Good morning," to everyone.

The tinkle and vibration of Emma's phone teased and tormented her, deep within the oversized pocket of her new dressing gown. She put her hand inside the fluff filled pocket and held on to it, desperately wishing she could read the message.

"You gonna answer it then?" mocked Joe, "Is it your new boyfriend?"

"Might be. Sod off, it's none of your business anyway," she snapped as she pulled the mobile from her pocket and walked out of the room.

Morning sexy, happy Boxing Day. Andy xx

Good morning, how are you today? Em xxx

Missing you still. Andy xx

Only 6 days (including today) then I'll see you again. How sad is that? I'm counting down the days. ☺ xxx

Not sad. Maybe you feel the same as I do? Andy xx

"Breakfast's ready!" called Emma's mum. Her dad flew down the stairs with his silky black dressing gown flowing behind him, looking like a *Dick Turpin* impersonator who'd lost his horse.

Really? Take it you meant wot u said last night then? Em xxx Emma's heart seemed to flutter like a caged butterfly as she sat down at the table.

"Have you turned back into a 'Texting Teenager Terror'? her dad asked, raising his eyebrows at Emma.

"Leave her alone, she's got a new boyfriend. I imagine that's him is it love?" asked her mum.

"Yes," said Emma, coyly, feeling slightly embarrassed as Tiffany sat down next to her dressed in a grey polo-neck jumper dress, thick black tights and knee high black boots. Emma wished she had got dressed first rather than sit at the table in a pink, spotty, fluffed up dressing gown. Her dad was the only other person not dressed for breakfast and there was a possibility that Emma's father wouldn't bother getting dressed all day if he didn't have to.

Itching to answer yet another vibrating message, Emma ate quickly.

"What's his name then?" asked Emma's dad, wrapping a piece of bacon in a slice of buttered bread.

"Andrew."

"Andrew what?"

"I don't know Dad. I only met him the other night," replied Emma, tetchily.

The teenage beast within her wanted to say that she'd only got as far as exploring his genitals – purely for the shock factor and to shut her dad up – but luckily Emma managed to control herself and decided to keep quiet. She didn't like being grilled by her dad at the best of times and certainly not in front of Tiffany. Her dad's intentions were always for the good of his children but he did go over the top sometimes and they all felt like they were getting the *Third Degree* when Dad started.

"What does he do?"

"Dad, I don't know much about him yet. We spent one evening together!"

"He sounds keen love, keeping on texting you all day long."

"Yeah," grinned Emma and raised her eyebrows at Tiffany who smiled back sweetly and quite innocently, Emma thought.

"I'll get it, it's probably Mother," said Emma's mum, getting up from the table and rushing to the phone. The distraction was a perfect time for Emma to slide the phone from her pocket and take a quick glance at the message, while keeping it hidden under the table.

Happy Christmas. Didn't get a chance to text you yesterday as I was trying to work out how to use this new phone. Hee Hee – present from my mum and dad! Did you have a nice day? Have you got Pete's mobile number? I'd like to wish him a happy Christmas too. Love from your best friend Ruby xxxxxxxxx.

Straightening herself in the chair, Emma looked up and felt more justified in the use of her mobile.

"Oh it's Ruby, she wants Pete's number."

"I can't believe those two are together," said Joe.

"Well it has only just started Joe, so early days yet but I do hope it works out for both of their sakes." Emma grinned again.

"Are you having a laugh? Ruby and Pete?" Joe shook his head, knowing both of them very well.

"Grandad's going in," spluttered Alex as she returned looking flustered and very upset.

"Hospital?" Grant's mouth fell open, "Today?"

"Yes, the ambulance is on its way." Pacing up and down, Alex began to gather the empty plates and cutlery in a robotic fashion, "We should go to the hospital Grant," she almost pleaded.

"Calm down babe, we can go now. Leave that mess, we'll get straight down there if you want to." Grant's harmonious voice did nothing to calm Alex as she continued to race around, back and forth to the kitchen, cluttering plates and pots around franticly. Misty pricked up her ears and sat patiently waiting, in case there was a chance that she was going out somewhere.

"Mum, text me later and let me know how Grandad is," said Joe, hugging her tightly. Nodding her head, his mum moved across to Tiffany and gave her a quick hug.

"It's been lovely to meet you properly Tiffany. Sorry things have turned out like this and we need to rush off."

"It's not a problem at all. I do hope your dad will be ok and thank you for having me Alex."

Grant and Alex swiftly left, leaving Joe and Tiffany to load their car up with their overnight bags and mounds of useless 'Grandma presents'.

Emma stood at the front door in a semi daze (still wearing her dressing gown), with an over-fed, sleepy Misty and watched her brother and Tiff prepare to leave.

"See you then Sis – come and stay once we get our new place sorted out. Well, that's if you want to." Joe rubbed the top of her head, messing up the mess that was already there.

"Yeah I will do thanks."

"Goodbye Emma, it's been lovely to meet you. Bring your new boyfriend too if you'd like." Tiffany smiled and pecked her on the cheek. Another rush of excitement surged as the word 'boyfriend', swam dizzily around in Emma's head.

Waving them off, Emma closed the door and suddenly realised she was on her own (if you didn't include Misty) and on Boxing Day too. An overwhelming feeling of missing Andrew bubbled up as she padded through to the kitchen and put the kettle on. Then she reached for her phone and sent a text message to Ruby, inserting Pete's phone number, thanking her for the lovely present (a gold bangle with a tiny, Chinese inscription that, according to Ruby's note inside the box, represented friendship) and wishing her lots of happiness.

Yes I did mean it (although I'd had a few) I know it sounds completely nuts! I just can't get you out of my head and it's doing me in! ☹ (sad face cos I can't see you) Andy xx

Four hours had gone by and still Emma's parents had not returned and not texted her either. Emma had spent the time getting dressed, texting Ruby a few times, clearing up, feeding Misty some more scraps and waiting patiently for the next text message from Andrew and of course, her mum.

Not having such a great day... sat here on my own. My Grandad has gone into hospital ☹ (sad face cos I need a cuddle) xxx.

When everyone has gone I'll give you a call if you'd like? Hopefully I might be able to cheer you up? Love Andy xx

'Love!' he hadn't written that before, Emma noted as the bubbly feelings resurfaced.

When the car pulled into the drive, Emma peered out of the window and watched her parents get out and approach the door. Getting up, she headed straight for the kitchen and turned the kettle on knowing full well that her dad, in particular, would need a cup of tea.

"Grandad is not good at all," said Emma's mum as she entered the kitchen. Her pale complexion and heavy eyes spoke louder than words, "We've left your grandma there Em. Would you go and visit after tea and bring her back here. She can stay the night." Emma's mum leaned against the worktop and rubbed her forehead. "She's in a right state and he's really not very well."

"What's wrong with him?" Emma poured the boiling water in to three mugs and made the tea.

"The doctors say he's got pneumonia."

"That's happened quickly!"

"Your grandad has always suffered silently Em. I expect he's been unwell for a while."

"Ok Mum, I'll go after tea. Let me sort something out for us to eat. Go and sit down."

They both carried the teas through to the living room and Emma passed one to her dad who had flicked the television over to the sports channel and looked just about ready to have a late afternoon snooze.

Going to the hospital this evening. Grandad very poorly ☹ We will have to talk later? Xxx

No problem. Hope he gets well soon ☺ Virtual cuddles to you. Love Andy xx

The festive goodies, sweets, nuts and nibbles had played havoc with Emma's teeth. Gazing in the mirror, she performed her daily ritual of smiling in varying degrees and then the exaggerated and rather ridiculous speech, *heelloooo...my...name...is...E...e...e...maa... ooh...aah...ee.*

One tooth in particular was even looser than normal and she suspected the previous night's alcohol had yet again, played a part in shrinking her gums back further. Her thoughts played ping-pong in her mind, backwards and forwards, should she be brave and go to the dentist or not? She was still undecided even though she had made a conscious effort on Christmas day to convince herself to go and see a dentist in the New Year. Feeling the usual anger rising and directed purely at her failings, Emma tied up her hair in a loose bun and went downstairs.

"I'm going to the hospital now Mum," she called, "I'll be back with Grandma about eight thirty."

His wrinkled, grey eyes had sunk deep into his face and Grandad looked nothing like he had the day before. Somehow he had aged another ten years overnight. Leaning over the bed Emma kissed his forehead and held his cold hand. His ashen face appeared smaller than normal and his chilled skin felt frail.

"Grandad, are you going to be alright?" Emma knew her question was futile as a sense of dread overwhelmed her. It was more than apparent that he was not well at all. Opening his heavy eyelids, he looked up and gently smiled at her.

"Of course I will be," he whispered in a wispy voice before closing his eyes again.

"He's eaten nothing today," said Grandma, peering up from the chair on the opposite side of the bed, "I told him he needs to eat something."

"He's probably getting everything he needs from that drip Grandma." Emma tried to comfort her with words, "They'll get him sorted out in here Grandma, try not to worry. He'll soon be home again. Grandad's made of tough stuff you know."

Change of plan, we're going over to a friend's for drinks tonight. Try to call you tomorrow. Andy xx

Back at work tomorrow ☹ (sad face, don't want to go). Get home at 6pm xxx

The nurse completed her observations, changed the drip bag and smiled at Emma and her grandma. "He should have a comfortable night. If you want to go home we can give you a call if anything changes."

Grandma nodded in agreement, grabbed her coat from the back of the chair and stood up. Both Emma and her grandma leaned over and kissed Grandad on the cheek – he looked peaceful and happy, Emma thought. Then they quietly left.

"Could we stop off at mine on the way home so I can pick up some bits please Emma?" Although it sounded like a question, it was more of a command. Grandma had been asked to stay with her family for the night so that she wouldn't sit at home alone, worrying about Grandad. She'd given the nurse her daughter's phone number before they left, explaining that she had been *ordered* to stay there for the night.

"Of course we can Grandma," said Emma as she pulled out of the empty car park and headed for the main road.

A frost was setting in over the windscreens and roofs of the parked cars along the road and everywhere was quiet and still. It was late evening on Boxing Day and Emma wondered if any other people were already feeling the anticlimax of Christmas and the low spirits of returning to work.

Mum, we're going to be back late cos Grandma wants to get some things from home xxx.

Emma pressed the send button and stood in the middle of the living room, gazing around at the faded pictures and the tall dresser unit filled with memorabilia, antiques and some of the smaller models from Grandad's younger years. Many of the objects in grandma's house gave Emma childhood memories of fun times, laughter and tree climbing with her brothers in the back garden. They'd spent many happy days in the school holidays, staying with Grandma and Grandad while their parents worked. They were the only grandparents she had and despite her Grandma's annoying habits and intrusive, overbearing personality, Emma and her brothers dearly loved her and they all worshipped Grandad.

"There, I just can't settle unless I've got my things with me," said Grandma as she appeared at the living room door. "I'm ready, shall we go?" Her tiny frame was lost behind the oversized patchwork bag she held as she tutted at Emma's reverie, "Well? Shall we go Emma?"

"Yes, sorry."

"I really should be getting home now," said Emma half heartedly, knowing she had to get up early in the morning, "I'll go and get my stuff together."

Leaving her mum, dad and grandma in the living room talking about Grandad's greatest achievements, his lifelong hobbies of building models and his reputation of being the

'Nutty Professor', Emma went upstairs and began to get her things together. Everyone had underlying fears about Grandad's wellbeing at such an old age yet no one seemed to want to mention it.

"We'll go over and see him in the morning Mother," said Emma's mum, smiling bravely, "They did say we could go outside of visiting hours."

Collecting her bags and Christmas presents together, Emma padded down the stairs and dropped it all off at the front porch, "I'll go over and see Grandad tomorrow night, after work if he's still in there," she said, upon her return to the living room, "You never know, he might be home by then."

"Ok love. I'll text you and let you know what's going on," said her mum, "It's been lovely having you here. Have a good day at work tomorrow honey and say hi to Ruby and Pete for us."

"I will Mum, bye Dad, goodbye Grandma." Emma went around and pecked cheeks before leaving her childhood home, always full of happy memories.

The flat was cold and eerily still. Although there were a few decorations in the living room it didn't feel at all festive and warm in her home. Emma felt like the only person in the world who was sat in a dull little flat – alone. She'd known all along that she would come home to an empty flat, as Ruby was away until the end of the week, but she felt oddly isolated.

Picking out her phone from her bag, she looked at the blank screen. The green light, which showed incoming messages, wasn't flashing and she wished it would – just once. Wondering what he was doing right now, her heart skipped a beat as she toyed with the idea of calling Andrew. At ten thirty in the evening she decided it probably wasn't a good idea. What would she say to him anyway? It felt like she hadn't heard from him for a long time but it was only a matter of hours and he had said he was having a drink with friends, so she wasn't even expecting to hear from him.

Trying to shake off her mood, Emma ran a bath and made a powdered milk coffee.

Hope it's not too late to say goodnight. Hope your Grandad is ok. Goodnight sexy love (Drunk) Andy xx

My grandad is really not so good. Just got in bed so not too late. Hope you had a nice evening ☺ Love from Em xxx
She'd done it and it made her feel so much better. A rush of excitement filled her as she sent the text... 'Love from Em xxx'. Checking her alarm, she switched the table lamp off and snuggled down happily.

Love from? Cute. ☺ Loads of sexy stuff from Andy who wants you really badly... even though he's very drunk. Very very drunk xx

The grotesque, *Gollum-like* creature crouched down by the side of the blood red river and dipped a gnarled hand into the malodorous flow. Slowly withdrawing a moistened palm, it then wiped it across its mouth. It grinned widely. Naked apart from a piece of tattered brown cloth, tied around its waist and concealing its groin, the freakish human shape twisted its tormented head around and glared. Jagged, rotting teeth dripped with liquefied, decaying flesh as it began to creep closer and closer to Emma. The rasping sound of its breath grew louder and louder... then the noise changed to a shrill, screeching sound...

Jolting awake, Emma realised that the sound she could hear in her dreams, was in fact the phone ringing. Jumping out of bed with a cold sweat she stumbled to the door, in the dark and headed down the hallway to the living room where she picked up the phone to silence it.

"Hello?" she said quietly, while gathering her scattered thoughts together.

"Emma... it's Mum."

Emma froze and looked up at the clock – 4.45am. Her heartbeat leapt into her throat. Somehow she knew what was coming next.

Chapter 11

So sorry Colin, I can't come in today. My Grandad has died.

Emma pressed the send button and began to get dressed absent mindedly. Everything was a blur, the world seemed so silent outside even though the early morning transit van rush was beginning. Traipsing to the bathroom, she stared into the mirror at her red, puffy eyes. Today her gums had taken second place and did not concern her enough to perform her usual pre-cleaning teeth routine. Tying her hair back in a ponytail, Emma washed her face, cleaned her aching teeth and sprayed deodorant underneath her top, then realised she'd done everything the wrong way round by getting dressed first, not that she cared. Hearing the tinkle of her phone from the bedroom, Emma returned to read a new message.

Very sorry to hear this Emma. Please take tomorrow off as well, we can manage at work. All being well we'll see you again in the New Year. Kind regards Colin and Rosie. p.s. Let me know if there is anything we can do Emma.

Tears began to roll down Emma's cheeks again. Sniffing and wiping her nose with a tissue, she then grabbed her old trainers and pulled them on.

The drive to her parent's house was slow and silent as she maneouvered the car through the growing traffic, on automatic pilot. Emma hadn't wanted to listen to the early morning radio show as she normally would have done on her way to work and so she had turned it off completely. Blinking away the tears she just managed to drive across the town to her parent's house, moments before her mum and grandma left to go to the hospital.

There were hugs and cuddles all round and tears flowed from both Emma and her mum. Grandma appeared cold and void of emotion, she was almost disbelieving of the situation, almost questioning the news and determined in her manner to seek out the truth for herself... or so it seemed.

"We'd better hurry up Alex, let's go," she demanded. Her hair looked un-brushed and smudges of yesterday's make-up remained under her eyes. Lopsided traces of lipstick, again from yesterday, remained around the outer edges of her lips and in the creased corners of her mouth.

"Can you make some phone calls while we're gone love? You know... Jo... Jack" Alex looked at Emma with pleading, blood shot eyes.

"Yes Mum," croaked Emma, before a stray tear welled in her eye again, "Don't worry I'll sort it out, you go." Emma realised she was crying more for her mum than anyone else. Her mum had lost her dad, her mum idolized her dad and her mum would be the one that would have to deal with all of this and mostly by herself. Emma's mum's resolve was something else but this could possibly push things a little too far.

Morning babe, have a good day at work, only 5 days until the New Year party. Can't wait to see you again sexy ☺ Love Andy xx. p.s. how's your grandad doing?

Wishing she hadn't read the message quickly, before her mum and grandma drove off, Emma gulped back the deluge and waved her elders off with a bowing of her fingers and a saddened expression.

My Grandad died this morning Andrew.

Oh no. I am so sorry Emma. I'll leave you alone, text me when you're ready. I really feel for you. Loving thoughts Andy xx

Emma's dad was searching through the address book at the dining table, as Emma returned indoors.

"Are you alright love?" he asked sympathetically.

"Yeah I think so. Mum wants me to call the boys." Emma still referred to her brothers as 'the boys', even though they were all older than her and certainly not boys anymore.

"I know, I'm just going to ring Jack now as it's getting on for eight o'clock in Germany," said her dad, checking the clock on the wall behind him, "Hopefully I'll catch him before work."

"Tea?" asked Emma forlornly from the kitchen as she automatically flicked the kettle on, she'd never known her dad to refuse one.

"Yes please love," he mumbled, holding the phone's receiver to his ear.

The day began to drift by slowly, emotionally and quietly. Grandma and Emma's mum returned from the hospital mid morning, looking rather subdued and shocked. While Emma's mum gazed mindlessly at the frosty garden, from the patio doors, Grandma took control of arranging the leftover food into some sort of buffet meal for everyone to pick at.

The phone was in constant use and between Emma and her dad the messages, condolences and enquiries were kindly accepted and dealt with.

Thank you xxx Emma replied to Andrew's text, not knowing what to say really but wanting to acknowledge his last message.

If there is anything I can do, please let me know. Andy xx
Cuddle me?
I really wish I could be there for you. Andy xx

Grandma had hardly sat down. It was obvious to everyone else that she hadn't acknowledged Grandad's death yet. She was keeping busy, looking after everyone else. Now and again she would stop in her tracks, look up to the ceiling like she'd just remembered something, pause, then carry on with what she was doing before.

"Mother will you sit down please," said Alex, exasperated by her mother's hustle and bustle behaviour.

"I don't want to sit down. I need to do things Alex."

"Ok, that's fine but I want you to stay here again tonight. Grant can take you back to pick up some more things. And you as well Emma, do you want to stay?" Alex's drawn face looked desperately at Emma.

"Yes, I'll stay here," said Emma knowing her mum needed her company and someone to talk to, who would actually listen with some empathy.

Just to let you know my Grandad died this morning. Emma knew she should have told Ruby earlier and hoped she hadn't heard it from anyone else, although she was still on holiday at her parents' house.

Emma, I am so very sorry to hear the sad news from Colin. We're all thinking of you. Please let me know if there is anything I can do to help. Pete x

Oh no, I'll come home early Emma. There must be something I can do to help. I'm very sorry this has happened. Ruby xxxxxxxxxxxxxxxxx

Emma marveled at the phenomenon of the human race to have an overwhelming desire to offer to 'help out' or 'do anything' when someone has died. The only way that anyone could 'help' Emma was by bringing her grandad back – and that was just *not* going to happen.

No Rue, please don't come home early, I'm staying at Mum's until the weekend. Xxx

Thank- you Pete.

***

The next few days went by in a blur. Grant went back to work on Friday, although it was just for one day but the urge to escape from the house was overwhelming. Grandma continued to busy herself with anything she could find to do and at one point she annoyed Alex by going in to the garden, in the freezing cold and proceeded to move the gnomes around, saying that they 'looked better over here' and 'fitted better over there'.

"Mother please leave them where they are. I can cut that bush back later and then we will see those ones again," said Alex feeling very peeved by her mother's meddling ways. "I'll sort it out in the spring."

"I just thought they would look nicer over there," replied Grandma, pointing to the rockery by the pond.

"There's too many over there." Alex had to contain her frustration, realising her mother was just trying to cope somehow. "I'll tidy it all up as soon as the weather is better. Come on in, it's freezing out there."

"I'm just trying to help out." Grandma huffed as she returned indoors and slumped down on a chair at the dining room table.

Jack, Emma's eldest brother, and Joe had been in contact by phone and they would be coming home for the funeral, as soon as there was a date set. Jack lived in Germany with his wife and two children and Emma hadn't seen him for over a year so the reunion, although a sad occasion, would also be a happy one.

Aaron was already on his way home from Wales, having decided that he should get back, although there wasn't much point and nothing he could do anyway. Aaron was the only one who still lived at home with their parents. Emma found it quite strange that he had never wanted to leave, or to buy his own place. He was loaded with money and worked six days a week when he could. Owning his own business, he'd never seemed to have much time for girls and their parents were beginning to worry that he might remain a bachelor for the rest of his life – until just very recently. Apparently, Emma's mum had said that he'd met a woman and appeared to be quite keen to get to know her more. He'd had the odd girlfriend in the past but each time it started to look like he was 'in a relationship' it would end, usually due to Aaron's excessively obsessive work commitments and reluctance to let anything stand in his way of success.

Emma's phone had been pretty quiet for a couple of days; it seemed that Andrew had indeed decided to leave her alone, which Emma didn't like at all. Holding the mobile in her hand, she willed it to tinkle, even just a tiny bit. She could send him a text message but she wasn't quite sure what to say as most of their messages had been very flirtatious and she realised now that she didn't really know him in any other way at all.

Hello, I just wondered if we were still going out on Monday night. Emma x Pressing the send button, a rush of heat swept across her face. Would he reply? What would he say? Had he forgotten about her? Had he moved on and found someone else? The latter was probably more likely as he was such a handsome and nice natured man (from what she knew of him so far). Sadly, Emma realised how pathetically needy and insecure she was but she just couldn't help herself.

Alex and Grandma had dragged the tins of old photographs out from under the stairs and were sifting through them trying to find the best ones of Grandad. Stopping once or twice to reminisce over the baby photos and the wedding photos, they began to gather a pile of old photographs of Grandad. Alex had always liked to have the 'physical copies' of photos, rather than store them digitally, much to the annoyance of her family, who had tried to convince her otherwise.

Tears of joy and sadness flowed freely as they sat at the dining table drinking tea and talking about 'the good old days'.

"Oh look, do you remember this one?" asked Alex, holding up a picture of a papier-mâché iceberg floating on a lake.

"Yes I do!" barked Grandma, snatching it from Alex's hand, "Your father always traumatised me with his nutty ideas. That was when your 'dearly beloved' knocked me over and in to the lake. How could I ever forget it?" Then Grandma burst into tears, "Oh I do miss him," she struggled to say while her hands covered her unmade, wrinkled face.

Alex rubbed her back gently and began to cry silent tears of her own. "I do too, but Grant didn't 'knock' you in to the lake. You slipped in... remember?"

"Hmm," replied Grandma and then wiped the wetness from her face and got up to look through the glass of the patio doors. "I do remember..."

So happy to hear from you. Feels like forever since I last spoke (text) to you. Silly and probably totally inappropriate question but how are things? Yes of course Monday is still on if you want to come (I would understand if you didn't want to but then we could arrange something else), I can't wait to see you again. Love Andy xx

With a fluttery sensation in the pit of her stomach, Emma eagerly replied, relieved that nothing had changed since their last bout of text messages. *Things ok-ish, can't wait to see you again. Still at mum's, going home on Sunday. Love Em xxx*

"Emma." Her mum's sweet and soft voice whispered, "Are you ok?"

Coming to her senses, Emma opened one eye and could just make out the figure of her mum, crouched down at the side of the bed. Her blurred vision made worse by the tears, Emma wiped her eyes and was surprised to feel just how much dampness there was on her cheeks.

"I think you must have been dreaming. You were crying out loud, I thought something was terribly wrong."

"Oh no, I keep having these horrible dreams Mum," said Emma, propping herself up in the bed. "It's nearly every night now."

"Dreams? About what?"

"Well, they're nightmares really. Stupid nightmares about monsters with rotten teeth. My gums are getting worse every day and I can't bring myself to do anything about it. Mum, I'm scared." Glancing at the clock, Emma could see that it was 3.26am, "What are you doing up at this time anyway?"

"Oh, I couldn't sleep. I think you need to get your teeth sorted out very soon, don't you?" Gently rubbing the side of Emma's arm, her mum continued, "I'll definitely be coming with you. You shouldn't have let it get this bad. I can see it's really getting you down Emma."

Emma nodded, "I know, it's stupid, I'm pathetic. I know they're going to fall out soon and then no one will like me."

"Don't be silly, I'm sure the dentist can sort them out." Emma cringed at the word 'dentist', she hated them that much. "Let me make an appointment for you at my dentist. They're very good you know." Emma couldn't believe she was sitting in her old bed, in the early hours of the morning, in the darkness, nodding her head in agreement.

"Yes, ok. Make an appointment then and Mum..."

"Yes..."

"Thank you."

Pulling the covers up to her nose, Emma watched her mum tiptoe out of the room and close the door quietly behind her. Emma felt like a small child again, having just had a nightmare and her mummy coming to the rescue, it was just like the old days. Her mum always rescued everything and everyone.

***

Sunday morning arrived and the continuing blurry atmosphere was pulling everyone down. The phone didn't stop ringing. Messages of sympathy, enquiries as to when the funeral might be and genuine offers of help in any way, kept coming. Grant tried to stay out of the way as best he could by tinkering in his frosty shed or trawling through paperwork piled high in his office. Grandma hadn't gone home yet, except to pick up some more things and check for mail. The thought of returning to her empty house was not a pleasant one and Alex had decided that she wasn't ready for it yet. "Maybe after the funeral," she'd said to Grant who just nodded in agreement, knowing that any other response would not go down too well. "I just don't think she's ready yet," added Alex.

Today Emma was getting ready to go back to her flat to try and restore some normality back into her life. Christmas had seemed to be one big cloud of gloom and she couldn't wait to put it behind her, although she also realised that Christmas would never be the same again as the anniversary of her grandad's death came around each year. The seven days she'd spent at her parent's house had all rolled into that big gloomy cloud. Feeling like she had hardly spoken to anyone, let alone seen anyone (apart from her immediate family); Emma felt it was time to go.

Having promised to make an appointment the following week for Emma to visit the dentist, her mum had said she would make sure she got an emergency one. That way Emma could be seen quickly and probably not have to pay any money for the initial appointment. Trying to brush the worry from her mind, Emma packed her things together and stuffed them in her bag.

Tomorrow night she would see Andrew again and every time she thought about it a feeling of guilty excitement fluttered through her. She was nervous about seeing him and could only vaguely picture his facial features. She knew she fancied him like crazy but just couldn't seem to produce a clear picture of him in her mind. The tinkle of her mobile quickly snatched Emma from her reverie and she picked it up from the side table.

Are you home yet? I could give you a call if you'd like. I'm home now Andy xx

Having lunch at Mum's then I'll be home later this afternoon. I'll text you when I get back. Em xxx

Are you busy tonight? Would love to see you again over a coffee maybe? At mine? Andy xx

Emma's heart raced and her palms perspired as she replied, *Yes, I would really like that. Text you when I'm home. Emma xxx*

Itching to get away as quickly as possible, Emma gulped her turkey sandwich down and then offered to help clear up the kitchen. "No that's fine love. If you want to get home, you go," said her mum.

"Thanks Mum, I'll come back New Year's Day and have dinner with you all, as long as I'm not too hung-over." She laughed and once again felt guilty for doing so as Grandma peered at her over the thin rimmed glasses sitting on her nose.

"Well have a good time and try not to worry about things Emma. I'll make that appointment for you next Wednesday just as soon as we've got the date for Grandad's... well, you know."

Emma knew her mum found it difficult to say the word 'funeral', it made it all too real. She was keeping herself busy just as much as Emma's grandma was. Every day at some point, everyone had cried (apart from Emma's dad) and then put on a brave face for the rest of the day.

Picking her bag up, Emma slung it over her shoulder and kissed her mum and dad on the cheek. She waved to her grandma who had just answered the phone to her late friend, Evelyn's son.

Evelyn's son, Gordon, was going to attend the funeral. His mum had passed away four years ago but he had stayed closely in touch with the family and that's just how his mum, Evelyn would have liked it. However, most of the family, well all of the family (except for Grandma) had been somewhat relieved when Evelyn's life came to a timely end. Evelyn was Grandma Dot's counterpart in all matters of interference and meddlesome interaction and between them both they caused quite a lot of problems for Emma's dad in particular, in the past.

But that's another story.

The frosty afternoon air caught her breath as Emma jumped in her car and reversed out of the drive. Pink, snow-filled clouds hung gloomily in the sky, waiting to burst their contents on to the icy land below as she headed home feeling rather excited about her guilty pleasure amid the sorrow and grief in her family.

Chapter 12

Throwing on her best jeans and a very old blouse, which she'd had since her late teens, Emma sat on the edge of her bed and carefully applied some make-up. She wanted to look her very best, she wanted to look sexy without looking too sexy and she wanted him to fancy her just as much as he had done the night they met.

Nervously, Emma waited at the front door of the old Victorian building. The red intercom light flickered as if it was in rhythm with the beat of her heart. "Hello." The sound of a familiar deep, scratchy voice came from inside the small box.
"Hi, it's Emma," she said with a slight tremble.
"Come on in." Andrew's voice sounded cheery, "I'll meet you at the top."
The wide, black door clicked and Emma pushed it open. A familiar smell of polish and some sort of cleaning fluid sent her into a reverie. Lustful passion in the form of Andrew had been at the top of the two flights of stairs the first time she was here, and the clean smells reminded her of it.
It was highly likely that the aroma of household cleaning products may never be the same again and she could possibly end up in a heightened emotional state every time

she tried to do some housework in the future. She smiled to herself before taking in a deep breath of the scented air. With her heart beating fast, Emma climbed the stairs slowly and quietly.

"Hello, how are you?" asked Andrew as she reached the top.

Coyly, she replied, "I'm fine thanks. I forgot how many stairs there were."

Andrew laughed and stretched out a hand as she took the last step up. Still holding her hand, he leaned over and kissed her softly on the lips, "Good to see you again, and the last time you ascended these stairs, I'd imagine that you were not completely aware," he whispered. Emma's face flushed and then a rush of anticipation tingled through the rest of her body. "Come in, do you want a coffee?"

Emma nodded and smiled as she followed him into the flat. It smelt clean and fresh inside the flat too, there was absolutely no hope of her ever doing housework again, she mused. The flat appeared larger than it had the first time she was here. Maybe the last chink of daylight that filtered in through the small kitchen window made it look different, or perhaps being sober had something to do with it.

"How are things with your family?" Andrew asked sensitively as he poured the percolated coffee into two mugs.

"Mum and Grandma are getting through it all right I suppose." Emma shifted uncomfortably, "There's just so much to sort out."

"I can imagine that there is. I'm here to listen if you want to talk about it." Passing a mug to Emma, Andrew invited her to follow him through to the lounge with a roll of his big brown eyes.

Placing her mug on the coffee table, Emma sat down on the sofa and Andrew sat next to her. "I can't believe how much I've missed you. I didn't even know you before last week."

"I know, it's silly isn't it," she replied, her heart had slowed down just a few minutes ago and now it was beginning to dance around in her chest again. As soon as she had set eyes on him at the top of the stairs she'd remembered his face and his amazing physique. The muscular figure of this fine looking man was now sitting close to her again and his eyes stared intently into hers. As he reached over and gently pulled her long hair away from her neck, a shiver surged through Emma's body. Then he kissed her tenderly.

Passion and desire overcame them both. Andrew stood up and held his hand out to her – she grasped it and followed him through to the bedroom. The fading light outside cast grey shadows across the bed as Andrew pinned Emma against the wardrobe doors and proceeded to undress her.

Their love making was long lasting, emotionally charged and all consuming as they moved together in unison. Heavy breaths and perspiring silhouettes filled the air with a sexual scent as they gasped and moaned, succumbed by pleasure. And then the end came – forceful and strong, Andrew and Emma fused together in an embrace filled with the deepest of thrills and elation.

Stunned into a beautiful silence, Emma lay resting her head on Andrew's chest, watching it rise and fall with each recovering breath. There were no words to follow what had just happened so she rested contentedly and peacefully in his arms as the darkness of the night crept into the room.

Some four hours after she had arrived, Emma looked over to the bedside clock, 8.15pm. Andrew slept tranquilly alongside her, his warm and taut body sprawled out across the bed. Lying on his front, Andrew's peachy coloured skin was flawless, Emma noted as she studied his form, barely covered by the quilt. He was the most gorgeous man she had ever met, perfect in every single detail.

Tiptoeing from the room, she walked through to the kitchen with her shoes in her hand and reheated the coffee in the percolator jug. When it was hot enough she made another mug of coffee and went through to the lounge. Andrew's suitcase was still on the table – he'd travelled home this morning and was obviously very tired after his journey. Not knowing quite what to do now, Emma sipped her drink and made up her mind to leave. Scanning the room for a pen or pencil and a piece of paper, she found a note stack and matching pen pot next to the phone, behind his suitcase. Before she began to write a note, Emma went back through to the bedroom, pushed the door open slightly and checked that Andrew was still asleep.

Thought I would get back home as I have so much to do and sort out and you were sleeping so peacefully. Text me when you wake and let me know the arrangements for tomorrow night (if we're still going LOL). Thank you for a lovely evening, it was so nice to see you again. Love Emma xxx

Pulling the front door closed, she heard it click and knew it had locked safely. Then she left and made the short journey home to her own flat while large snowflakes splattered on the windscreen of her car and then melted into droplets of water before the wipers pushed them away.

Emma's mum wanted some 'nice' pictures of Grandad and Emma had promised she would have a look when she got home. It had been agreed that a slideshow should be made and then displayed on the television, at her parent's house, for the gathering after the funeral. Aaron didn't know it yet but he had a job to do on his computer and it would have to take priority over everything else that he had going on in his busy life.

Sifting through her memory box, full of old photographs of family, friends and memorable occasions; she found the one she had been looking for. Her grandad was standing tall and proud by the side of a glass case which housed his most precious of models, a replica of the *Titanic*. With a huge beam on his face, one hand rested on the top of the case, proudly.

Emma recalled the tales she had been told about how her grandma had ended up in the lake, which stretched out in the background, in the picture, but she was also told never to mention it in front of her grandma, for fear of upsetting her. She smiled to herself and the tears began to fill her eyes once again. He was gone now and she still couldn't believe it had happened so quickly. The only thing left of her grandad, apart from the memories, was his beautiful ship which had rested for many years in the local museum. *I'll take Andrew there one day, to see my grandad's magnificent model*, she thought and then smiled again as the tears continued to fall.

Hello babe, are you still awake? Just read your note, sorry I fell asleep like that. I was so tired after the long journey home. And then you finished me off completely! Love Andy xx

Sill awake, been sorting out photos of my grandad for my mum. Need to clean up the mess in my flat tomorrow too, baah! What time tomorrow night? Em xxx

Placing her milky coffee mug on the sink, Emma studied the red shoes, filled with soil, which stood proudly on the windowsill. She still couldn't believe that Ruby had done such a crazy thing but then she supposed Ruby was very drunk at the time and if that was the extent of her misbehaving, then it really wasn't so bad at all. She missed her friend and was looking forward to her return home on New Year's Day. They would probably spend most of their time at work on Wednesday catching up with their latest news and Emma desperately wanted to hear whether there had been any developments in the 'Ruby loves Pete' department.

Do you want to stay here tomorrow night? Come round whenever you want to. We can leave about 8pm. Pub is only round the corner. Andy xx

Emma shuffled through to her bedroom, the phone clutched tightly in her hand, slipped off her dressing gown and got into bed.

Ok, yes I would love to stay. I'll come round about 7.30, that way I can get things tied up here, ready for work on Wednesday☺. At Mum's for dinner New Year's Day (if I'm not completely wrecked!). Love Em xxx

Great! See you then. Need to try and get some sleep now but still can't get you out of my head. You are driving me crazy! Love Andy xx

Ditto. Em xxx Switching the bedside lamp off, Emma snuggled down and drifted off in to another one of those restless nights.

Emma woke up wondering who on earth was texting her at this unearthly time of the morning and was then very surprised to see that it was almost nine o'clock.

Gosh, I'm not going to see you until next year, hee hee. Be home about 9pm tomorrow night. Missed you. Hope you and all of your family are ok, considering your terrible loss. Thinking of you as always, lots of love Ruby x

Smiling to herself, Emma suddenly felt full of mixed emotions. She felt excited that it was New Year's Eve and she would be spending more time with Andrew and probably enjoying lots more delicious sex with him, but she was also terribly upset and still could not believe that her dear old grandad had gone. Pleased that Ruby would be home tomorrow, the downside was that it meant she would be returning to work on Wednesday and trying to catch up with her usual workload. Terrified that her mum would make an appointment at the dentist for her (and she knew her mum wouldn't forget that), she also felt... in pain. In pain again. The festive drinking binges and wine at almost every meal at her parent's house had played havoc with her gums and as she lay in her bed, she felt the familiar throb of new beginnings... another abscess would be on its way very soon.

Standing in the bathroom, she stared hard into the mirror as she went through the usual over-expressed routine. She had to get her mouth sorted out before anyone really noticed... before Andrew noticed. Well someone had noticed already at work and that's why she'd received such a rotten secret Santa present, she reminded herself and suddenly felt the familiar rise of anger. She still hadn't found out who it was but that could wait until she returned to work. She wondered how they knew but then realised that she was far more relaxed at work and had probably let her guard down on more than one occasion, more so than when she was out in the general public, or most certainly when she was with Andrew. So that was why they had obviously noticed in the office, she decided.

When she was with Andrew, she cleverly disguised her gappy teeth by choosing her words carefully, smiling tightly and generally keeping her mouth shut. Kissing him had not seemed to be a problem at all and she just hoped that it wasn't for him either. *Well...he always came back for more*, she thought, *so it can't be that bad*. Oral hygiene was always the top of her agenda and her problem probably wasn't noticeable to those who didn't know, like Andrew.

The throb continued, even after two *Paracetamol*, and Emma knew it would only get worse as time went on. She knew how it worked, she understood what the next stage would be, she was fully aware that by tomorrow she would be feeling rough and another tooth would have turned numb and be starting to loosen.

Emma stared at the mounds of clothes lying on the bed – she'd practically emptied her wardrobe. What was she going to wear tonight? It was a pub party, a live band (friends of Andrews') would be playing and it was New Year's Eve – what could/should she wear? Feeling hot and sweaty from her marathon-trying-on-clothes feat, she decided to make herself another coffee, take some more pain killers and have a think about it.

Hi babe, can't wait to see you later. Don't wear too much tonight cos I feel like ripping it all off you and shagging you senseless. Sorry about that, lol, love Andy xx The message sent a new surge of excitement through her as Emma began to reply.

Ditto, yes please, that would be very nice. Can't decide what to wear, but will try to keep it to a slip-on (off) number! Lol Em xxx

Actually my last message sounded terrible, sorry, don't usually talk like that. I'll rephrase it...I want to make mad passionate love to you again! Andy xxx

Is that what you've been doing then? Em xxx
What? x
Making mad passionate love to me...
Yes, what about you?
Yes. Em xxx Now Emma really felt emotionally charged, excited to the extreme – in love maybe? Ridiculous, she'd only known him a week!

Peering in to the full length mirror, Emma was pleased with the way she looked. It had taken some time, several cups of coffee, a few hair pulling moments, some cursing and lots of dressing and undressing. But now she was ready and she looked pretty hot, by her own standards.

Wearing a black pencil skirt, just above her knees, black stockings (of course), a sparkly red, low cut top that she'd had for so many years she didn't care to remember, but it always looked great on the appropriate occasions, and three inch, black patent shoes. She hoped and prayed it wouldn't be too icy outside, especially as they were walking to Andrew's local pub. Pulling on the matching black jacket, she took one last look and smiled to herself. She looked pretty sensational, she decided, knowing deep down that the ugly truth was well hidden. Her dark hair fell over her shoulders in twists and curls and just for a moment she thought she looked a bit like her teenage idol, *Tulisa* – in her younger days as a pop star.

Have a nice evening darling. Dinner at 2pm tomorrow (if you are in a conscious state to make it) ☺ Mum x

Emma dialed the number for the taxi, there was no way she was going to risk driving home in the morning, still intoxicated.

Locking her front door, she jumped in the taxi and left with the familiar flutter in her stomach and hope for the best evening of her life, ever.

Chapter 13

He smelt so delicious and the crisp white shirt reminded Emma of the first night they'd met. "You look stunning. Are you really all mine?" he whispered, softly touching her lips with his.

"Yes," she replied, leaning back over the kitchen worktop and responding to his lips. They spoke through joined, partially open mouths, "Are you all mine as well?" she asked, breathing heavily.

"All of me... every inch of me," Andrew said as the sexually charged exchange became more fervent. "I want you so much," he whispered, holding her around the waist with one arm. His dark eyes of desire burned into hers.

Emma couldn't resist... it was impossible... she kissed him softly. She reached down to his crotch, unzipped his trousers and took hold of him.

Carefully sliding her knickers down over her stockings, she leaned right back on the work top and waited for him.

Fully dressed, the lovers frantically expressed their desire for each other. Fast and reckless the moment was over quickly and they both sighed and shuddered as the ultimate ending came.

Returning from the bedroom Andrew had changed his ruined trousers. "How's that?" Standing in the kitchen doorway with his arms outstretched half-mast he also wore a smirk on his face.

"Very handsome," she replied and then smiled. "Do I look ok?" she asked, brushing her hair down with her hands.

"Beautiful," said Andrew, as he poured two glasses of wine. "We'll have these and get going shall we?" His face was still slightly flushed from their energetic, intense burst of fornication against the cupboards, in the kitchen. Emma nodded and smiled, she was totally obsessed with this man. He was compelling and full of passion like no one she'd ever known.

Their short walk to the pub was relatively silent, apart from the ever-increasing whisper of the strengthening wind. Emma held on to Andrew's hand the whole way in a heavenly dreaminess. It was bitingly cold so Andrew lifted his collar up around his neck and sped up the pace. Now and again he gently squeezed Emma's hand, looked down at her and winked.

As they approached the large public house, situated on the corner of a crossroad, Andrew stopped and said, "Right, let me warn you before we go in..." Emma's eyes widened, "Dean and the boys are quite boisterous. They'll all fall in love with you and they'll probably try to chat you up. That's what they're like, so just ignore them ok." Andrew leaned over and kissed her, "Don't worry, they just go over the top sometimes but I'll keep an eye on them." Emma felt slightly uneasy but nodded and smiled just the same. "They're bloody good though. Hope you'll enjoy it."

It was ten to nine and the pub was heaving with mainly young people, dressed in sparkly and glittery clothing. The ambient warmth, the buzzing, jolly atmosphere and low lighting made it feel welcoming as Emma followed Andrew, still holding his hand, to the crowded bar.

Over on the far right, the band were tweaking their instruments and checking their equipment under the spotlights. Andrew pointed to a man leaning over a huge speaker, "That's Dean, bending over," he said, "They kick off at nine o'clock – we're just in time. What would you like to drink?" Andrew had pushed forward to the bar and the barmaid looked up and flicked her head and eyebrows upwards slightly as if to say what do you want?

"A *Baileys* please." Emma smiled as Andrew let go of her hand to reach in to his pocket for his wallet.

Collecting the change from the barmaid, Andrew tossed it in to his pocket, along with his padded-out wallet, which Emma had noticed earlier, during the throes of passion over the kitchen worktop. She guessed that he wasn't short of money – not that that had any bearing on their budding relationship. Emma wasn't a gold digger and would much prefer to be penniless and in love, than rich, sick and tired.

"Let's go over and I'll introduce you quickly, before they start," said Andrew, pulling her out from the crowds and the bustle by the bar. A throng of spectators had already begun to mingle around the small, step-up stage. "That's Frodo, on the drums," said Andrew, pointing again as they drew closer.

"Frodo? That's a funny name."

A short, dumpy man with tight brown curls teetering on the top of his head could just be seen climbing over all of the electrical wires on the stage before he almost disappeared behind a huge set of drums, centre stage. "Oh," Emma giggled, "I can see why he's called Frodo now." The man, now peering over the top of the smaller drum on one side, did indeed look remarkably like he had just stepped out of, *The Lord of the Rings*. "What's his real name?"

"Lee." Andrew almost shouted over the increasing noise of people talking, the juke-box music playing on the far side of the lounge bar and the general sounds of glasses chinking and jangling in a very busy pub. As they reached the front of the stage, Frodo caught sight of Andrew and put his thumb up in acknowledgement. The two guitarists had strapped themselves to their electric guitars and plugged them in when Dean looked up and noticed Andrew, standing tall, amongst the spectators.

'Hello mate!' he mouthed, from the stage. Andrew raised a hand and moved closer to the step, with Emma in tow. After a quick exchange of greetings and handshakes, Andrew put his arm around Emma's shoulder.

"This is Emma," he said proudly, smiling up at Dean. The electric guitars started to screech and ping as the two men on either side of Dean tested the volumes and their equipment. Dean leaned over the stage and held a hand out to Emma. Reaching up, she smiled and shook his hand and then he leaned over further and kissed it. Emma smiled again and laughed off her shyness. Then Dean crouched down and spoke in to her ear, over the loud noises coming from behind him.

"'Old on to yer teef luv," he shouted and then laughed out loud, "Got yerself a gud man there." Then he stood back up and grabbed the microphone, "Are... you... ready?" he shouted to the crowd before winking at Andrew.

Cheers and roars echoed around the lounge while Emma stood motionless, gawping into the distance, stunned into silence, as the room seemed to close in on her and vanish. The distant, faint hum of the lively band could just be heard as she sank deeper and deeper inside herself. Andrew stood by her side and eagerly started to jigger up and down as the band began to play. Unable to move her eyes from Dean's face, for fear of a tear welling and falling, she was frozen to the spot and the lump in her throat started to swell. *What did he just say... about my teeth?* She questioned herself, she questioned her hearing. Jolting from her moment of self-torment, she realised she'd been standing there like one of the Queen's Guardsmen, perfectly still and vacant looking. Everyone around her was moving, dancing and swaying. Andrew was oblivious to her sudden predicament as he twisted his feet in rhythm with the music.

Tapping him on the arm, Emma shouted, "I'm just going to the ladies, I'll be back in a minute." She forced a smile and turned around to fight her way through the growing, writhing crowd of merry people as she headed for the toilet sign which she could just see over in the far corner.

Luckily, Andrew hadn't heard what Dean had said but Emma could still not believe her own ears. What did he mean? Had he instantly noticed the poor condition of her gums and her loose teeth? He couldn't have... or was this just one of those horrible nightmares and she would wake up in a minute? Maybe, from the top of the stage, he had a bird's eye view of the inside of her mouth as she smiled and laughed at him.

Rushing past the now almost empty bar, Emma had to get to the toilets quickly and have a look in the mirror. She hoped and prayed there would be one in there and as she opened the door, she saw that there was and breathed a huge sigh of relief. Two women stood by the double sink unit, chatting, laughing and generally preening themselves in the long, rectangular mirror. Emma briefly smiled as she walked over to the first toilet cubicle. Once inside, she closed the door behind her and then looked up to the ceiling, blinking away her tears while she waited for the women to leave. She couldn't cry – not now – Andrew might notice and then it would all come flooding out – her big secret about her failing gums would be exposed, in more ways than one.

Regaining some composure and having checked the way she looked (which turned out to be just the same as she had when she left home), Emma headed out of the toilet before it became obvious that she'd been missing for a while. She'd obviously misconstrued the comment made by Dean, turning it into a demon's taunt, made up by her own insecurities. She needed another drink to wash away the constant nag in her mind that was turning her in to an anxious and uptight mess. "Want another drink babe?" Andrew's calming voice brought Emma to her senses. "Thought you'd left," he laughed as he joined her and slipped his arm around her waist again, directing her back to the bar.

"Let me get these," she said, shakily.

"Wouldn't dream of it. I'm taking *you* out remember." Andrew pulled a twenty pound note from his wallet and waved it over the bar. "Are you ok? You look like you've just seen a ghost." He smiled and squeezed her in a one-armed hug.

"Yes, I'm fine," she said, forcing a smile. She really wanted to smile at him; he really did make her feel better. Toying with the idea of telling Andrew what Dean had said, Emma knew that it could highlight her issue if she brought the subject up. It could make things a lot worse for her or it could make Andrew realise (if he hadn't yet), that she had such a big problem with her self-image. Emma imagined that she would be a toothless old lady by the time she was thirty and that probably wasn't a good advertisement to start off a beautiful new relationship.

"Are you sure you're ok?" Andrew was slightly puzzled by Emma's vacant look. "Oh no... I'm sorry, I didn't mean what I just said... I mean about..." Andrew hesitated for a moment, "I mean the bit about you just seeing... a ghost. I mean, what with your grandad. What an idiot I am."

"Oh no, I'm fine honestly. I'm sorry. I suppose I was just daydreaming a bit. Come on," she said, smiling genuinely as she squeezed his bottom, took hold of his hand and pulled him away from the bar with a sexy glint in her eye. She had to get over this blip – she'd probably misheard what Dean had said and she had to believe in that thought. It was New Year's Eve and she *was* going to enjoy herself with the most handsome man in the building, if it was the last thing she did.

Returning to the gathering of merry party-goers, Emma held on tightly to Andrew's hand as they moved around to the side of the stage. The band played on loudly and vigorously. They jumped around on the spot and with all the equipment on stage there was absolutely no room for error or any wrong footing. Emma watched intently as Dean sang with so much fervency, that it sent shivers through her.

"That's John," shouted Andrew, pointing to the guitarist on the left, "And Terry." He pointed to the other man, strumming his instrument like some sort of mad man. Emma tried to appear pleased to see them. Terry continued to strum violently, shaking his head around and bending his knees and then flicking his head back and looking up to the ceiling.

An hour of music, the odd 'bad' joke and three quick drink breaks later, the band paused for an intermission. Sweaty and thirsty, they headed off to the bar for a much needed glass of *Coke*. Andrew took Emma's hand and pulled her over to the bar, "Come and meet them all. Want another drink?"

Terrified by the thought of Dean's words or anything the other three might say to her, she reluctantly trailed behind Andrew nervously. She really needed another drink and if this was all going to go 'tits-up', she would rather be drunk when it all came out. She could always walk out of the pub and hail a taxi home if things really got too much.

"John, Terry... Frodo. This is Emma," said Andrew, placing a comforting arm around her shoulder. The trio nodded and smiled as each one greeted her (politely) and raised their eyes at Andrew. Dean hadn't turned around from the bar and was busy chatting to the young girl who was serving him.

"How the hell did you manage to pull a gorgeous chick like her?" asked Frodo, looking Emma up and down and grinning.

"Well you know how it is Baggins, you've either got it or you haven't, and in your case, you haven't." The men laughed and teased Frodo as Andrew, once again, gave Emma a reassuring smile.

"I'll be back in a minute," said Emma shyly, "Just nipping back to the ladies." She had to escape, she had to check her appearance again (she was becoming obsessed) and she needed the toilet anyway. Andrew gave her a puzzled look but nodded to her and then turned back to his friends, so Emma scurried away as fast as her heels and the alcohol would allow.

The evening wore on. The drinks ran out on several occasions but each time their glasses were topped up, either by Andrew's wealthy wallet or by the compliments of the band's running tab behind the bar. The men in the band re-enacted their hectic routine of jumping about like children on pogo sticks and Emma drank, then drank some more.

The short conversation with the band men earlier had been menial but luckily Emma hadn't been the topic of their conversation as first feared. Even Dean had not said anything else to her but she did notice him staring at her chest at one point, which made her feel very uncomfortable. It was plainly obvious by listening to them, that the band members clearly loved to talk about themselves, all of the time. Only once had she managed to buy the drinks, much to Andrew's protests. "It's only fair," she'd insisted, but it was purely a means of escape for Emma and another chance to check the mirror in the ladies toilets, before going over to the bar. She was well aware that she had a huge problem and her crazy mirror-obsession was taking over. She had to stop it and soon.

At one point Andrew had dragged two bar stools around to the side of the stage so they could sit and watch the band. A makeshift dance floor had been created by a semi-circle of people dancing around the stage. Several of the women were dancing awkwardly in a very drunken state. Emma jumped off her stool as the band began to play one of her old, favourite songs. "Shall we dance?" she asked, feeling her inhibitions beginning to melt away. Andrew obliged with a wide grin and took her hand.

How is it possible to dance with someone and feel like you've just had sex with them? And in public, thought Emma as they returned to the one stool that hadn't been taken up by somebody else. Their dancing, at the back of the crowd, had been sensual to say the least. Admirers watched on the sides as Andrew held Emma in one arm and they writhed and twisted and twirled in perfect formation to the bands version of, *'Crazy' by Gnarls Barkley*. Andrew's kiss, at the end of the song was sexy and long but perfectly polite in public. An elderly man, who was sitting over in the corner, began to clap his hands together as Andrew slowly pulled away from their kiss and stared deeply into Emma's eyes. She was sure that some of the other, elderly spectators might have given a round of applause too, by the pleased looks on their faces – but they just smiled and nodded instead.

The time was ticking ever closer to midnight and the band were drawing to a close. It was approaching 11.30pm and the buzzing hype in the lounge was growing. "Shall we have one more drink before the clock strikes," said Andrew, clearly tipsy by the way his eyes were glazed and weary, "They've got *Buck's Fizz* on the house at 12."

"Yes, sounds like a plan," slurred Emma, feeling quite drunk as well. Dean's words of earlier had become a distant memory and one that Emma really didn't care much about anymore, now that the alcohol had warmed and numbed her.

Sitting down at a small oval table, Emma noticed a full bowl of chili peanuts. Most of the other snack bowls, spread around the pub, were empty. The public house had been very generous in providing nuts and nibbles and a celebratory midnight drink but Emma guessed, by the amount of custom they'd had, that it had been a small price to pay for the constantly pinging tills that collected the money all evening.

Hungry and slightly too drunk to make any sensible decisions, let alone any meaningful advances on Andrew later (which had been on her mind earlier), Emma grabbed a handful of nuts and proceeded to devour them. She'd hardly eaten all day and decided that the nuts should be enough to 'soak-up' the alcohol, swishing around inside her tummy.

The band stopped playing and a rapturous applause filled the pub. After lapping up the accolade Dean and the other band members began the arduous task of dismantling their equipment.

"Where do you know them from?" asked Emma, realising they still knew practically nothing about each other.

"Oh Dean and I go way back... school days." Andrew leaned back on the seat, "He was a total idiot then too." Andrew grinned, then sipped his beer, "The rest of them..." he wiped his mouth, "Well, I've been to a lot of their gigs and I just got to know them over the years."

"How many girls have you introduced to them in the past then?" Emma laughed, trying to appear nonchalant as she popped another chili peanut in her mouth.

"None – believe it or not. I don't think the boys knew quite what to say when they saw you, they were so shocked." Andrew laughed.

"Shocked? Why?"

"Because you are so gorgeous..."

Emma laughed and shrugged it off, cramming more nuts in to her mouth.

'CRUNCH!'

Emma froze. The pain filled her already full mouth and her eyes began to water.

"You ok?"

"Um...bit...ma...tung," said Emma in a muffled voice as she held her hand to her mouth. The searing pain spread rapidly into her lower jaw and chin as the sobering reality kicked in. She hadn't bitten her tongue at all and as she tried to swallow the half chewed nuts, she knew there was a tooth hanging by a thread, at the front, on the bottom row. Why had she been eating bloody nuts? She knew the damage they did to her teeth and when she wasn't under the influence of alcohol, she wouldn't have normally touched them. It was just too painful to eat nuts or crisps and the little bits always got stuck in the voids between each tooth, no doubt causing the abscesses. However, this time was different, this time she knew that far more damage had been done. "Goin...toilut," she said, still guarding her mouth. "Bleedin."

"Are you going to be ok?" Andrew looked at her with a deadpan expression, "Try not to be too long, it's nearly midnight. We don't want to miss it do we?" He wasn't fazed by her predicament at all and why would he be, after all she'd only bit her tongue.

Sitting in the cubicle, Emma took the small vanity mirror from her bag, she had just remembered it was there. The last minute rush for the toilets meant that she was unable to have a good look in the mirror with so many women milling about by the wash basins and she did not want to cause a scene by spitting blood into the sinks. The self-inflicted tooth injury was serious. Although it appeared to look normal, the small front tooth was sat in its socket, held in by what must have been only threads. Emma could move it around, push it in and out and then wedge it back between the teeth on either side, with her tongue. The bleeding was beginning to stop but a dull throb in her lower jaw suggested that she would feel the pain much more in the morning when she'd sobered up. Her face burned with the embarrassment of her predicament. What should she do? Go to a dentist and bloody well quick – that's what she should do. Except it was almost midnight on New Year's Eve and she was with a most charming man who she really liked. The tooth would have to wait... somehow.

Ensuring the little tooth was wedged firmly between the others, Emma practiced her usual routine, staring into the little hand mirror, which made it all the more difficult to see the full picture. The initial pain had subsided and the dull throb was starting to lessen but Emma guessed that her drunkenness had a part to play in her quick recovery.

"Hurry up Jill, we've got 5 minutes." A woman's voice shouted across the toilets. Emma looked at her watch, there was indeed just 5 minutes left before midnight struck, she had to get back to Andrew. One last look in the mirror above the wash basins and Emma felt satisfied that she looked the same as before, even when she smiled – tightly.

"Are you all right babe?" said Andrew, standing up to meet her.

"Um, got a swollen tongue," she said, discreetly placing her fingers across her lips.

Andrew shook his head and pecked her on the forehead lovingly. "You numpty," he said and grinned down at her.

Two huge television screens had been switched on, one at either end of the pub's lounge bar. The same TV programme was displayed at each end, showing a countdown clock in one corner of the screen. 4 minutes and 25 seconds remaining. *What an ending to a year this is going to be*, thought Emma as Andrew grabbed her by the hand and tugged her gently.

"Come on, everyone's going outside in a minute," he said excitedly, pulling her towards the doors.

The icy cold air outside sent shivers through her and Emma began to feel very drunk, more so than she had before. The car park was filling with New Year well wishers as the minutes and seconds ticked away. The volume of the televisions inside the pub had been turned right up so they could be easily heard through the open double doors.

"10...9...8...7..." Andrew pulled Emma closely to his chest and wrapped his arms around her tightly, "6...5..." she felt warm, "4..." and loved, "3...2...1... HAPPY NEW YEAR!"

The cheering of the crowd resonated around the privet bushes, lining the car park's perimeter. Party poppers began to 'pop' and people started to sing *'Auld Lang Syne'*, quite badly.

"Happy New Year Emma. This is going to be the best year of my life," said Andrew before leaning over and kissing her fully on closed lips, and then he pulled back momentarily before returning with several short, soft and gentle kisses, while cupping her face in his hands. "I'm falling for you," he whispered softly.

"Ditto," she whispered drunkenly, trying to savour every nanosecond of the moment while worrying how she could ever kiss Andrew properly again.

The *Buck's Fizz* was enough to render Emma useless and careless as she fell into a loved-up stupor, gazing into Andrew's eyes while resting her elbows on the table. The menacing chili peanuts sat in the bowl in front of her but Emma couldn't even bring herself to look at them, let alone pick one up and suck it. Could Andrew really feel the same as she did or was it just the drink talking? She smiled softly at him and watched him drink the small glass of *Buck's Fizz*, whist all around them, chilled party-goers celebrated and hugged each other. Emma wondered if it was madness to feel so strongly about him, after all she hardly knew him apart from their mutually clear and sensuous understanding of each other in the bedroom... or the kitchen... or maybe anywhere else in the future. Maybe even before they made it back to the flat, Emma shivered, no it was far too cold for that.

The instruments were fully dismantled and the band members were now ready to leave. The earlier thrills of the approaching New Year had lulled into a subdued atmosphere of drunken and overly tired well-wishers. Dean and the others headed over to the table, shook Andrew's hand or patted him on the back and Frodo leaned over and kissed Emma's hand. "Nice to meet you luv," he said, winking up at Andrew. Dean nodded his head at Emma and rubbed the top of Andrew's head as they parted with all of their belongings.

"Shall we go?" asked Andrew, rubbing his forehead and squinting. Emma got up and pulled her jacket on.

"Headache?" she asked.

"No, I feel shattered."

The frosty night had progressed into an icy early morning, so the lovers walked home quickly and unsteadily, hand in hand. "Did you have a good time?" asked Andrew, half way along the road.
"Yes, lovely."
"How's your tongue." He smiled at her cheekily.
"Bit sore," she lied, "Why?" Emma laughed, realising just what he was insinuating by the cheeky smirk on his face. "I thought you said you were shattered, she teased and smacked his behind. Then she placed her hand back in his and they hurried home as fast as their slightly uncoordinated legs would carry them, while the icy air bit in to their cheeks.

The warmth in the flat was comforting. Skipping the weak suggestion of coffee, Emma followed Andrew to the bedroom, kicking her shoes off as she arrived at the top end of the bed. Undressing on opposite sides, their eyes were fixed on each other in the gloomy light that filtered in through the gap in the curtains. Climbing into bed, clothed only in their underwear, they met in the middle and held each other in a warm embrace.
Their love making was purposely perdurable and powerful. And they were truly in love for that moment in time.

Chapter 14

Somehow Grandad was there. He'd been there all the time but she hadn't noticed him before. Sat at the end of the stage making a miniature sized model of a ship, Grandad looked happy. A cork lay resting on the stage floor, waiting to be pushed in to the bottle, once the ship had been placed very carefully inside. Looking up, Emma's grandad saw her and grinned.

Dean sat on a stool in the centre of the stage, playing soft, magical music on a magnificent woodwind instrument. Lips poised around the mouthpiece, he smiled from the outer edges of his filled mouth. The pub was still and abandoned, only the sound of fine musical notes filled the empty void.

All of a sudden the music stopped and Dean slowly pulled the instrument away from his mouth. Fear struck in her throat as Emma gasped and gulped. Rotting teeth had left Dean's mouth, along with the mouthpiece and were still firmly attached to it, dripping in putrid ooze and glistening under the bright stage lights. He laughed, loudly. Blood and drool dripped from his gaping, toothless mouth.

Then Grandad shrieked and began to convulse as he spat his own teeth out on the floor. He bent over, picked them up one by one and popped them in to the ship's bottle. He glared at Emma, shaking the contents of the bottle and beckoning for her to come closer – Emma screamed as her heart skipped a beat.

Opening her eyes wide, Emma flicked a glare around the room and remembered where she was and then sighed – another horrible dream. A tear welled up, tipped over the edge of her eye and began to roll down the side of her face. Aware that Andrew's warm body lay next to her, she turned to see him still sleeping. Climbing out of bed, she reached for his dressing gown hanging on the back of the door and went through to the kitchen. Her head was beginning to pound as she moved. Her jaw was aching slightly and then she remembered the chili peanuts. Her tooth – it was still hanging on for dear life. Moving her tongue around, she could feel just how loose it was. She could twist it right around, almost the other way and move it backwards and forwards. The hot flush of fear encompassed her again and she pushed it back in to place, wedged in between the adjacent ones. She was too afraid to touch it.

A hot, sweet coffee would be just what Andrew needed, thought Emma as she gently stroked his shoulder to wake him. "I'm going to have to go soon," she said down-heartedly. She really didn't want to leave him and wished she could take him to her parent's house for dinner but she realised it wasn't a good time for her family to be meeting her new boyfriend and particularly on New Year's Day without Grandad, when there were bound to be lots of tears. Andrew squeezed his temples and scrunched up his eyes in the bright light pouring in to the room from the window.
"God, I feel rough," he said quietly.
"Hang over?"

Andrew nodded and squeezed the sides of his head again.

"Want some pain killers? I've got some in my bag."

"Yeah... please."

"Wish I didn't have to go and leave you like this," said Emma, standing in the foyer waiting for the taxi. Andrew squinted at her through eyes full of pain and attempted a half smile. Standing barefoot in his dressing gown, he looked like a little lost boy. "What are you doing today?"

"Bed... sleep... and then think about you a lot, once I find my brain."

Emma laughed, he was so sweet. "Do you want me to give you a call later tonight, when I get home?"

Nodding his head just slightly, Andrew pulled her to him and kissed her, "I meant what I said last night. Do you remember?"

"Which bit?" she asked coyly.

"The bit about how I feel about you."

"Yes, I remember and do you remember what I said?"

"Yes." Then they stood in an embrace in the foyer, until the taxi arrived.

Showered, changed and teeth cleaned extremely cautiously, Emma was ready to go to her parent's house. The time had reached 1.30pm so she left quickly, knowing she might be late for dinner if she didn't hurry up. She jumped in her car and set off. Her mobile had been tinkling all morning with wishes for a happy new year, but there had been nothing from Andrew since she'd left him 3 hours ago. Still it was only 3 hours, Emma thought, knowing he'd probably gone back to bed to sleep off his hang-over. She smiled to herself as she became lost in her lush reverie of last night.

Dinner was a solemn affair. It was usually an annual celebratory New Year dinner at mum's but the atmosphere was understandably lifeless and dull today. Emma's grandma had stayed with her parents (much to her dad's disappointment), since Grandad's death, not wanting to face the reality of an empty home. Emma's parents were munching their way through the turkey roast dinner on auto-pilot and Grandma just pushed peas around the plate. Now and again, she would attack half of a roast potato and stuff it in her mouth and then huff rather loudly.

Emma felt hungry. She'd eaten practically nothing in the last two days, apart from the dreaded nuts and some tablets. Her stomach was tied up in knots and the slightly dazed feeling of a mild hang-over lingered, along with the pain in her mouth. Eating her food tentatively, she maneouvered each mouthful to the good side and chewed carefully, taking much longer to eat her meal than normal.

"Aren't you hungry Emma?" asked Grandma, stuffing another potato into her mouth.

"Yes I am. Just feeling a bit rough, that's all."

"Drunk last night was you?" said Grandma, with a full mouth.

"Yes, I suppose I was a bit, I had a really good night though."

"Hmm," mumbled her grandma, through mashed up potato teeth.

"You went out with your new boyfriend didn't you?" Emma's mum butted in thankfully. Emma knew her grandma wouldn't see the nice side of going out with a man and getting drunk and would be more likely to frown upon the damaging alcohol consumption aspect.

"Yes, we went..."

'CRUNCH! CLICK!'

The pain surged through Emma's gum. She'd done it again and the taste of blood seeped through her mouth and mingled with the half chewed turkey. Angry with herself, Emma knew she shouldn't have tried to eat and talk at the same time. Clutching her hand to her mouth, she got up as she realised there was something else in her mouth apart from the blood and turkey – something hard.

"What's up love?" asked her mum, "Emma?" Jumping up, her mum quickly followed her up to the bathroom. "Emma, are you all right?" she said as Emma closed the bathroom door behind her.

"I'll be back down in a minute, I'm ok Mum," Emma replied, with a muffled voice.

Spitting the small piece of blood-stained turkey in to her hand, she noticed a long white object alongside it – her tooth – long because it was the whole tooth, including the root. A perfectly formed, beautifully white tooth, it had come out of its socket completely.

Staring horrified in to the mirror, Emma's heart raced and a cold sweat dampened her brow. She opened her mouth and there it was – a big black hole, slightly off centre on the bottom row. Tears poured from her eyes as she threw the meat down the toilet and began to frantically wash the tooth under the tap. She had to put it back in. Hysterically she tried.

Distressed by her bizarre behaviour, she believed that she was possibly going mad. It would not go back in. It was too sore to try and push the tooth deep enough to wedge it back in to place. Emma stepped back and sat down on the edge of the bath, feeling faint. Devastated and worried beyond belief, she never really thought it would happen – she couldn't believe it had. She'd lived in denial all this time and now it was real. She really was losing her teeth.

"Emma?" Her mum knocked on the door twice, "Emma... let me in." Emma unlocked the door and beckoned to her mum to enter. "Emma, what's the matter love?" Putting her arms around Emma's shoulder, she hugged her.

"Mum, my teeth are falling out!" Again, Emma burst in to tears and slumped back down on the edge of the bath and held out her hand, containing the tooth.

"Oh my goodness. How has that happened?" Her mum looked horrified as she peered deep in to Emma's reddened, tear-stained eyes. "Oh, Emma," she said as she knelt down in front of her." I really *must* make that emergency appointment tomorrow." Emma nodded and cried some more.

"What about Andrew? I won't be able to see him again. Oh no mum, I've ruined everything," she sobbed.

"Of course you will. Let me see." Emma partially opened her mouth. "It's hardly noticeable Emma," said her mum, unconvincingly.

"I can't see him, not like this, I look... I look like a monster," she cried.

"Come on, you're getting yourself in a right state darling. You do not look anything like a monster."

"He's so perfect Mum, you haven't met him... I'm not good enough for him... look at me!"

"You look the same Emma, you can hardly notice it." Wiping away Emma's tears, her mum stood up, "Come on, why don't you go and have a lie down. I'll tell your dad and Grandma you're not feeling too well." Emma nodded in agreement; she was so exhausted from the shock and the tears. "Your grandma won't even notice it and I'll talk to your dad later. Try not to worry about it love, we'll sort it out tomorrow."

Emma stood up and went to her old room where she climbed in to her old bed, hid under her old duvet clutching her little tooth and fell in to a peaceful sleep... for once.

Several hours later, Emma was aware of the bedroom door opening slightly. Peering over the duvet, she could see her mum peeping round the door. "Are you ok love?" Emma's mum asked in a soft voice.

"Yeah," said Emma, feeling like a young child again as she glanced around the room.

"I told your grandma you'd been sick so you went to sleep it off. I'm afraid you might get a lecture about drinking alcohol, but at least that's better than the alternative."

Emma smiled – she loved her mum so much and knew she could always count on her to make everything right. She just wasn't sure how her mum would manage to put this latest dilemma right – unless she had a magic wand that could bring the tooth fairies back with all her baby teeth. At least that way, she could find one that would fit in the hole her tongue was now playing with.

Emma sat up and stretched, she'd been more tired than she thought and the sleep had made her feel so much better, but only in the sense of her hang-over earlier. Emotionally, she was a ticking time-bomb and now her new appearance was going to add to her already mounting pile of insecurities, loss (loss of both her grandad and her tooth) and worries.

"Your phone has been making funny noises in your bag all afternoon as well."

"I'll get up and come down now. Where's Grandma?"

"She's asleep in the living room."

"Good," said Emma, climbing out of bed.

"Coffee?"

"Yes please Mum. Oh and thank you Mum."

"Don't mention it and don't worry. We'll sort it out, first thing tomorrow."

Emma's parents were great but she'd always known that really. Sadly, she always took them for granted, until it came to a crisis and then they were always there, always supportive. After a lengthy discussion, once Grandma had gone to bed at 7.45pm, it was agreed that Emma should stay overnight and not go to work tomorrow. It was easier to take a 'sickie' rather than go to work and have to explain (lie) her way through the day and try to get time off to visit a dentist (secretly), should she be lucky enough to get an appointment. The butterflies fluttered frantically in Emma's stomach at the thought or mention of the dentist but she now knew there was no other option.

Four unread messages waited in Emma's inbox and she flicked through to find out who they were from. One was from Andrew (of course), Ruby, Colin and then Andrew again. She opened the one from Ruby, *I'm home early. What time will you be home? Love from Ruby x*

Long story but not home tonight. Not too well. Call you later and explain. Em xxx

Hello Emma, best wishes for the New Year, although it must be very difficult for you at this time. See you tomorrow, all being well. Regards Colin and Rosie.

Thanks Colin, I'm really sorry but I won't be in again tomorrow, really not very well.

No problem, totally understand. Take care of yourself and get better soon.

Ok, hope you're all right. Love from Ruby x

Emma's heart began to race as she opened Andrew's first message, *Hi babe, can't believe I slept all afternoon! How did the meal go? :(Love Andy xx*

Then she opened the second. *Been awake an hour and missing you like crazy! I really should get a grip of myself (but NOT how you would be thinking... LOL). Are you home yet? Love Andy xx*

Hi, I'm not going home tonight, staying at Mum's. I've been feeling ill since dinner – think my mum tried to poison me. LOL xx. She hated lying to him but she couldn't let Andrew find out the truth.

"Emma!" called her mum from down stairs, "Ruby's on the phone." Rushing down, Emma took the phone and then went back up to her room.

"Ruby hi," she said with a lump in her throat. She'd missed her dearest friend and knew she could safely talk to her about her terrible situation without it going any further. "How was your Christmas?"

"Oh, it was nice. I'm so sorry yours wasn't good. I just thought I'd call to give my condolences to your mum and then I could speak to you as well. I need a bath but I thought I'd call you beforehand. Are you all right?"

"Yes... ish. I'm going to the dentist tomorrow, if mum can get me an appointment. I've texted Colin to say I won't be in work because I'm ill. I told him a little white lie." Emma waited for the shock-horror response but unusually, it didn't come.

"Have you got another abscess?"

"Yeah, but not a big one. The thing is... I've lost a tooth as well, right at the front, that really wobbly one. Please don't say anything to anyone."

"Oh dear, you know I won't tell anyone. Oh gosh, I'm so sorry Emma. We knew this would happen sooner or later. I just don't know what to say Emma."

"There's nothing to say, it's my fault entirely. I know I've been really stupid but my fear of the dentist has been so great, as you know Rue."

"Honestly, it won't be as bad as you're thinking Emma." Ruby sounded concerned.

"Anyway, how have you been?" Emma hesitated, "Have you heard from Pete at all?"

"Yes... Pete texted me 3 times over Christmas and phoned me this morning to wish me a happy New Year." Ruby's tone of voice lifted. "We're going out for a meal on Saturday night. I'm really scared – so that's two of us." She giggled, "I'm probably nearly as terrified as you are of going to the dentist."

"Yes, you're probably right, but what are you frightened of really?" Emma could just imagine what Ruby would be like come Saturday.

"I don't know, it's just that... well... I was drunk the last time I saw him."

"So what."

"Well I think he may like me a little bit now. I mean... he does seem keen to see me."

"Well that's good isn't it? I'm sure he liked you before 'now'."

"Um."

"You'll be fine Rue. Just have a few drinks, maybe even a couple before you go out, then you'll relax and it'll be fun."

"Um."

"So I guess that means you're going on a date then?"

"Um... yes I guess it does. I wish you were here, I'm really nervous about going to work tomorrow."

"I expect he is too. Just act normal... well no actually, don't act normal. You need to be a little more adventurous and say good morning with a smile and even give him a wink if you can muster one up."

"I can't do that!" screeched Ruby.

Emma laughed at her friend; she felt so much better just talking to Ruby on the phone. If everyone lived in Ruby's world, it would be a beautiful, happy place (boring – but beautiful and happy).

"Yes you can. After seeing you at the Christmas party, you can do anything Rue. Go for it. Fill your boots – to match your shoes." Emma roared with laughter down the phone.

"Oh my goodness, those shoes are ruined. I am so sorry Emma."

"They'll be ok, just rinse them out – unless you really do want to plant flowers in them."

"Um, anyway, will you let me know how you get on tomorrow? Are you sure you'll get an appointment? Do you know when your grandad's funeral is?"

"Yes... no... no" replied Emma. "I'll text you or call tomorrow night or I might even be home. Mum and Grandma are sorting the funeral out tomorrow, so I'll let you know as soon as."

"Ok, well I'd better go and have a bath, ready for work tomorrow. I do hope everything goes all right for you Emma."

"So do I, talk tomorrow. Bye."

I forgot to ask you if you'd heard from that man (Andrew) again. Sorry Em I felt so sad about your bad Christmas and then I was wrapped up in my own worries... how selfish of me. Love from Ruby xxxxxxxxxx

Hope you feel better soon babe. Would you like to meet next weekend? I'd really like to get to know you better. If we meet in a public place, we might get a chance to talk more and we could get past the temptation of the underwear-removal bit (although I love that bit a lot!). LOL. How about going out for the day on Saturday – ploughman's lunch in a country pub? Dinner in a nice restaurant in the evening? And then back to the underwear-removals! Love Andy xx

Have I heard from him Ruby? Seen him, heard from him almost every day and been shagged senseless by him a couple of times too! LOL.

Oh gosh! Love from Ruby xxxxxx ☺

That sounds lovely. I'll have to let you know nearer the time as it'll depend on when the funeral is and when my family arrive. Em xxx

Emma cringed as she sent the message. She really wanted to spend the whole day with him and couldn't care less if her family (namely Jack – her eldest brother) might be here at the weekend, depending on when the funeral was. But how could she see him if she had a tooth missing?

Ok, I understand. Let me know as soon as you can or maybe we could do Sunday? If it's easier we could just meet up in an evening, although you would be in danger of me ripping your clothes off. Really want to see you again soon, love Andy xx

Ditto xxx

Chapter 15

Morning, hope you're feeling better. Just off to work 😞 don't know how the day will pan out with visions of you in my head all of the time. Andy xxx

Sent at 7.50am, noted Emma. She looked at the time on her phone, 10 minutes to 9 – damn. He was probably working by now. What did he do? Where did he work? Stupidly, she didn't even know that. She still didn't know his last name either. What did she know about him? Nothing it seemed – except that she was crazy about him.

Sorry, only just got up. Didn't go to work today, still feel rough. Hope your day's ok wherever you are. I don't even know what you do for a living, LOL. Love Emma xx

"Mum can I have a quick bath please?" Emma called from the top of the stairs.

"Of course you can love," she replied.

Just as Emma was about to turn around on the landing she heard her grandma down stairs.

"Why hasn't she gone to work today? Is she still poorly?"

"Yes, she's not right and hopefully she's going to the dentist today as well."

"Oh I see, that will be alcohol poisoning. If she's not careful it will rot all of her teeth away. What time are we going... out... you know... to sort everything?"

"Ten o'clock, I did say that last night."

"Just checking," said Grandma, pompously.

Pouring bubble bath under the flowing taps, Emma mused over the possibility of an appointment at her mum's dentists while she waited for another message from Andrew. Mum had assured her they were very nice people and they wouldn't actually do anything if she did get an appointment today. They would just have a look and tell her what needed to be done.

The frothy bubbles looked inviting so Emma slipped off her mum's old dressing gown and then reached across to grab her phone from the windowsill above the bath – one last check before she jumped in.

Plop! The phone had slipped right out of her hand...

Emma watched her mobile phone sink through the bubbles, leaving a little pathway behind it and then it sank to the bottom of the bath. It was like watching a horror film in slow motion as Emma froze and stared into the hot water. "Oh shit," she muttered under her breath and plunged her hand in. "Argh!" the water was far too hot. She turned on the cold tap to full flow and hesitantly dipped her hand in and out quickly to mix the scalding water around at one end until it was cool enough that she could stir it around at the other end of the bath. Then she fumbled around in the bubbly water and managed to retrieve the phone. Quickly, she reached for a towel, wrapped it up and started to pat it dry. It was dead.

"Dry it right out first and then try and turn it on," her mum said. Emma nodded and placed it on the kitchen windowsill, wrapped in paper towel. She couldn't bear the thought of not having her phone. It just had to start working somehow.

"I've managed to get you an emergency appointment, it's at 5.15 this evening Emma."

"Oh, really?" said Emma suddenly realising it was inevitable and beginning to feel sick with fear. "Are you coming with me Mum?"

"Yes of course I will, I did say I would. I told them you've got a really bad toothache, so they said they'll squeeze you in."

"Well I have got a sore tooth where the small abscess is so you weren't lying."

"Oh my goodness, what a mess you are Emma." Her mum tutted and turned to walk away, "It's just gone too far hasn't it? An abscess as well?" she added, looking back over her shoulder, before she disappeared in to the kitchen.

Still dead – great. How was she going to contact Andrew if she couldn't get her phone working? She didn't know his number. Emma pulled the back off the phone, took another piece of paper towel and began dabbing the insides again. Her mum and grandma had gone to the funeral directors and she was hoping to take the opportunity to catch up with Aaron, if he ever woke up. He'd arrived home very late last night – in fact it was very early this morning, so her mum had told her. But Aaron had never been good at getting out of bed, particularly if he didn't have to go to work.

The funeral date had been set and Emma's mum and grandma returned, ashen faced and full of emotions again. "I'll call Jack and let him know when it is," said her mum, wiping away the tears. Grandma sat down in the dining room and stared out of the patio doors once again, absent mindedly.

"Is there anything I can do Grandma?" asked Emma, tentatively.

"No love, thank you." she said, without taking her eyes from the view in the garden, "You just get yourself sorted out. I know those teeth of yours have become a real problem for you." Emma nodded and turned down her mouth in agreement. What could she say to that?

It was only a short drive to the dentists. The private practice was run from an old Victorian house, just outside of town and funnily enough, very close to Emma and Ruby's flat. The long gravelled driveway comfortably housed eight cars, diagonally parked on either side. As her mum pulled in to the drive, Emma noticed there was only one other car in the visitor's bay, therefore she assumed they may not be very busy and she might be seen quite quickly. A signpost pointed to the staff car park, located behind the once four-bedroom mansion. There were at least 6 cars there that Emma could see. "Oh no Mum, I feel sick," she said, holding her hand to her mouth. A vision of many dentists peering inside her mouth, while she laid back on the patient's chair, filled her head with dread.

"You'll be all right love. Come on, nothing is going to happen. They'll just have a look today."

Climbing out of the car with leaden legs, Emma's heart raced and a cold sweat broke out on the palms of her hands. The queasiness and fluttery tummy far outweighed her painful tooth and the abscess. But for once, the fear didn't outweigh the toothless gap in her mouth. Emma had to get through this somehow, no matter how terrifying it felt.

"Not sure I can do this Mum," she said in a splutter as her eyes filled with tears, "I feel like crying. I know it's really stupid of me."

"Emma, calm down. Take a few deep breaths and then we'll go in. Pacing around the car park, with her hands on her hips, Emma breathed in and out slowly. In... out... in... out...

The smell sent another surge of terror through Emma's veins. A clean, clinical scent (unlike the fresh smell in the foyer of Andrew's place) wafted around the empty waiting room. Her mum was at the reception desk explaining that 'her daughter was literally terrified' and 'in a bit of a state'.
"Did you have to over-emphasise the fact that I'm nervous Mum?" whispered Emma when her mum sat down.
"They totally understand how you're feeling Emma. Stop worrying. I'd say you're a bit more than nervous love. You look like a prisoner on death row who's just about to sit in the electric chair."
"Mum do you have to say things like that? Honestly." Emma gulped and felt terribly sick again.
Five minutes later Emma's name was called by a young dental nurse standing at the entrance door to the treatment rooms. The words felt like they punched Emma straight in the stomach as she froze momentarily.
"Emma?" said the nurse, looking directly at her (she was obviously Emma as there was no one else in the room). She stood up, smiled shakily and moved her heavy legs in the direction of the nurses pointed finger.
The torture room (as Emma imagined it to be) was quite small with a large window at one end which looked out of place in comparison to the size of the room. In the middle sat the patient's chair, modern and fresh looking, in light blue and white. There were lots of nasty looking tools and equipment on both sides and Emma stared in horror as she was ushered to the chair by the nurse.

Sitting on a swivel stool, a petite woman with jet black hair tied in a bun was typing on a computer behind her as Emma perched on the bottom edge of the chair, clasping her hands together tightly.

"Seet back," said the lady with a Chinese accent, behind her, "Come." Waving her hand, she gestured to Emma to lie back. "You have pain, yes?" she asked sternly.

"Hmm." Emma nodded her head while keeping her lips firmly closed, she was sure that her heart was going to jump right out of her mouth if she opened it. Her mum smiled down at her and then took a step back to sit in a chair at the side of the room. Emma gripped her hands tighter together as she was slowly lowered to a horizontal position. The beaming light above her glared straight in to her eyes, until the woman moved it slightly. Then the petite Chinese lady swivelled around on her chair to one side of Emma's head. She peered down at Emma through large, orange eye shields; the expression on her face was lifeless.

"Open," she barked, while holding a small hooked tool in her hand which Emma could just see from the corner of her eye. Emma opened her mouth and screwed her eyes tightly shut. "Open," repeated the dentist. "Wide please. Much wide now."

"Argh," cried Emma as the metal hook touched one of her teeth on the bottom row. Opening her eyes, Emma looked up in desperation at the Chinese ladies piercing, dark eyes.

"Not gud," she said, shaking her head from side to side as she moved the tool around the inside of Emma's mouth. Emma's whole body was rigid with fear and her feet were clenched together at the other end of the chair.

"Argh." The pain sent an electric shock through her gums and Emma attempted to snap her mouth closed.

"Open. You have pain?"

No it's just the way I freaking well sing! Emma wanted to say but nodded her head desperately, instead. Tears lay on the surface of her eyes and she continued to grip her hands together so tightly that her knuckles turned white.

"Ah yes, I see periodontitis. Not gud... yes?" The dentist mumbled and looked up to the nurse standing on the opposite side of the chair. "You smoke, yes?" Emma shook her head. "You drink lot of alco-whole?" Emma shook her head again, desperately trying to understand what the young, stern-faced woman was trying to say. The dentist reeled off a complicated dialogue of numbers, letters and unrecognizable words to the nurse opposite, who scribbled things on to a form.

"Argh...urgh," shouted Emma, "'Hat 'urts."

"Yes, yes" the dentist nodded slowly and almost sadistically, thought Emma, as the woman grinned to herself. "You clean teeth all time yes?"

Emma nodded again, *what did this stupid bloody woman think she was... a dirty skank that never brushed her teeth?*

"Ah." Withdrawing the hooked probe, the dentist moved the patient chair and Emma to an upright, seated position. "You are final stage periodontitis. Not gud."

"What does she need to do?" asked Emma's mum, standing up and rubbing Emma's trembling, right leg.

"Err.. Final stage? Month and month treat...ment, long time. Some you lose, some stay with treat...ment." The woman was shaking her head all of the time that she spoke and her wrinkled up nose gave the impression that she was disgusted.

Emma moved to the edge of the chair again and hung her head like a naughty school-girl.

"We give anti-biotic," said the dentist, "You come back. We start treat...ment?" The nurse was still frantically scribbling things down on to the clipboard. Emma couldn't look up and remained seated with her head held down, she was ashamed, she was hot with anger, she was totally embarrassed by the dentist's remarks – she hated herself and she hated this demon of a dentist woman.

"So how much could this cost?" Emma's mum asked.

"Err... many treat...ment. Come many time. Small price for gud teeth. Yes? Smile impor...tant for young lady. Err... can be some thousands pound. We know more when x-ray and treat...ment start."

"Ok, thank you." Emma's mum nodded and smiled.

"You go, make point-ment one week – we can start?"

"Yes," said Emma, nodding as she stood up and began to edge towards the door.

"Thank-you. Gud-bye," mumbled the little Chinese lady, with her back turned. She was already looking at her computer and searching through files.

"I'm not going back there," said Emma, holding a prescription in her hand, as they quickly walked back to the car. "I'll cancel the appointment tomorrow, sorry Mum."

"But you've got to get your teeth sorted out Emma."

"She was horrible Mum!" Emma climbed in to the passenger seat. "She looked at me like I was some sort of filthy tramp."

"She wasn't that bad. You need to do this or you're going to lose all of your teeth and then what will you do?"

Emma shrugged, "Don't know. Can't we find a nicer one?"

"A 'nicer' one will say the same thing Emma. You're losing your teeth!"

"I know, I just didn't like her at all. I'm not going back there Mum. I'm sorry but I'll find another one myself if I have to."

The mobile phone lit up briefly and then turned straight off again. 'Damn', mumbled Emma and threw it in to her bag in frustration. "Right, I'm going home now," she called through to the living room. Giving everyone a peck goodbye (including Aaron who'd only been awake for an hour and had noticed her missing tooth already and laughed his tatty head off, much to the annoyance of Mum), Emma walked to the front door.

"I'll ring you in the morning if I manage to get you in at the medical centre. I'll talk to my friend Carol, there – and make sure you pick up your tablets. You need to get rid of that abscess pretty quick Emma. They can be very dangerous things."

"Ok Mum. Don't worry about me, I'll be fine, Bye." *Bless her*, thought Emma as she drove away, waving goodbye. Her mum always sorted everything out for absolutely everyone. Although Emma didn't want to face the situation, she knew she had to and maybe the *NHS* Medical Centre would be a nicer place with much nicer dentists. At least her mum was going to explain more clearly, how terribly nervous she was, and that she *really* needed to see a *very* sympathetic dentist that would understand her fears.

Hugging your best friend can be the best thing in the world sometimes, thought Emma as she squeezed Ruby tightly. "I've really missed you Rue."

Recovering from almost being crushed, Ruby shuffled through to the kitchen in her fluffy booties and flicked the kettle on. "I'll make some hot chocolate and you can tell me everything, if you want to, that is."

"I need to contact Colin first. I'm not going back in this week – how can I?" said Emma, removing her coat and throwing it on the table. "Could I borrow your mobile, and that's another story."

Colin my phone is broken, had to borrow Ruby's. Went to doctors today, still feeling ill. Got anti-biotic, so won't be back this week. Also the funeral is next Monday, really sorry for all the inconvenience. Hope to be back next Tuesday. Emma.

"What's happened to your phone?" asked Ruby, taking her mobile as Emma handed it back.

"It went for a swim in the bath. Now I can't contact Andrew as I don't know what his number is." Emma sighed.

"Do you know where he lives?"

"Yes but I'm not going round there Rue, he can't see me like this," said Emma, pointing to the gap in her mouth.

"You can't see it that much," said Ruby, squinting at Emma's mouth.

"But you can see it a bit and that 'bit' is enough to keep me from going round to see him."

"I'm sure he'd understand Emma. Why don't you just tell him? You always say that if someone doesn't like you as you are then they can clear off."

"Yeah but this is different, I don't want him to clear off."

"Oh, I see," said Ruby, raising her eyebrows. "I've still got my old mobile if you'd like to borrow it."

"Have you?" Emma's eyes lit up. "If I could borrow it, I could drop a note through his door and give him the number. Where is it?"

"It's at my parent's house. I left it when my new one was delivered there. Mum was going to use it but she ended up buying herself a new one, like mine." Emma frowned at her, "I'll go over there tomorrow after work and pick it up."

Emma smiled. "Thank you. You're a real treasure Ruby, I owe you one." Ruby smiled and handed a mug of hot chocolate to her.

"Let's sit down and you can tell me all about Andrew and everything else," said Ruby, suddenly sounding quite dominant – which really wasn't like Ruby at all.

Maybe she was one of those people who suddenly became the strong leader in a crisis – but only in a crisis, thought Emma. Maybe she didn't know the real Ruby at all and just assumed she was a bookworm who lived in her own little world because that's all Emma ever saw.

An hour and a half later and several deep inhales of breath during her incessant talking, Emma reflected on the countless facial expressions, displaying every emotion conceivable, that Ruby had made as Emma went in to great detail about her experiences with Andrew, the devil-dentist and her grandad's sudden death.

Curled up in the chair, Ruby looked very weary, "So you'll definitely go through with it if your mum gets you an appointment at the Medical Centre then?"

"Yep," said Emma trying to sound confident but looking like she'd seen a ghost, "I've got to haven't I?"

"Um," replied Ruby, rubbing her red eyes. "I'm really going to have to go to bed Emma, I'm sorry. I've got to get up early in the morning."

"Before you go, what did they say at work today?"

"Oh, Colin and Jeff didn't say anything. Dave said you probably had a week-long hangover but he also said to say sorry about your grandad. And Pete just asked how you were."

"Ok, so they don't think anything dodgy is going on."

"No, not at all."

"How was it when you saw Pete again?"

Ruby smiled, "He said good morning and then made a herbal tea for me. We were the first ones there. Then he sat at my desk for a few minutes and said he was looking forward to going out on Saturday." Ruby's smile turned in to a big cheesy grin, "I went really red and he said I looked sweet when I blushed." And then Ruby blushed as if she was giving Emma a demonstration.

"Ah, I'm so pleased that you two have got it together Rue," said Emma, giving her a gappy-grin, "You just need to give him one now."

"One what?"

"You know... sleep with him."

"I slept on the sofa all night with him last week." Ruby stood up and wrapped her gown tightly around her.

"Ah you know what I mean," said Emma, raising her eyebrows.

"Um, I'm going to bed now. Night, night Em."

"Goodnight Rue and remember, I'm ill. This has nothing to do with my teeth, if anyone asks at work. And can you still try and find out who gave me that present – I really need to know what I'm up against here."

Ruby nodded her head and yawned. "I'll try. Honestly I'll try Emma. Night, night."

Chapter 16

It had only been 24 hours but it felt like a lot longer. Emma missed Andrew's text messages terribly, in fact she missed *him* even more and what must he be thinking? He would have received her last message yesterday morning, probably replied to it (maybe at lunchtime – but almost certainly by the evening) and then not heard anything back from her. She had to get in contact with him soon in case he decided to turn up at her flat to see why she hadn't replied to his messages. Lying in her bed musing, Emma suddenly heard the phone ringing. It couldn't be Andrew, he didn't have her home phone number and at this time of the morning he would surely be at work.

"Hello," she said hesitantly.

"Emma, I've made you an appointment for tomorrow afternoon at 3.15. Is that all right love?"

"Oh yes, thanks Mum, can you come with me again?" Emma felt a bit silly at her age, asking her mum to go with her.

"Of course I will love. I'm going in to work in the morning but I'll come over about two o'clock. Is that ok?"

"Yeah, thanks Mum, love you."

"Love you too honey. See you tomorrow."

"Bye."

The long day dragged by and Emma tried to busy herself with menial chores around the flat, once she'd been to collect her prescription of anti-biotic tablets. Now and again she went in to the bathroom and spoke to the mirror – and the gap was slightly visible every time. She thought about filling it with chewing-gum, a mint *Tic Tac* or maybe even the old tooth if she could somehow saw off the root and just wedge it in. She knew she was being absolutely ridiculous and if anyone could tell what she was thinking, she was sure she'd be put in a mental institute. Pacing up and down the flat, which seemed to be shrinking with every step, Emma looked for things to do and waited for Ruby to come home from work.

"Sorry I'm so late Em," said Ruby, taking her coat off and neatly hanging it on a coat hook by the door, "Mum insisted I stay for a bit of tea."
"That's ok, did you get it?"
"Yes, here – it needs charging." Ruby passed the antique mobile phone to Emma, "I think there's still some credit on it," she said as she took her lunchbox from her bag and went to wash it up, ready for re-filling in the morning.
"How's everyone at work?" asked Emma, plugging the charger in to a socket.
"Ok. Colin asked what was wrong with you today."
"And what did you say?" Emma knew Ruby would be no use at lying to anyone.
"I said you were very poorly, that's all."
"Ah, well done – you lied! Didn't he question it?"
"No, he just said ok and walked off. It was only a little white lie, after all you are poorly in a way," Ruby said in her defence.

"Are the other's all right?" Emma plugged the charger in to the phone and it lit up with a battery display showing that it was charging.

"Yes. Although it's been a short week, I think everyone is looking forward to the weekend. Mr Kibble has been on the phone again today as well," she giggled.

Ruby had definitely changed, thought Emma. She seemed to be more alert, more switched on to what was happening around her. "Oh dear, I bet Jeff was pleased about that. What did he want this time?"

"A snow-shovel."

"Are we expecting snow then?"

Ruby giggled, "I don't think so but he didn't want it for the snow anyway..." she paused and turned around from the sink. "He's going to remove the handle and make a small canopy, from the 'shovel' part and fix it above the new cat-flap he's just put in."

"Oh dear!" Emma burst into laughter and realised she hadn't laughed like this for some time. "And how's Pete?" she managed to splutter out.

Ruby smiled coyly, "He's fine. We went out at lunchtime for a coffee, well I had a *Liptons Iced Tea*."

"Ah, that's sweet Rue." Emma smiled. She missed everyone at work, even Pete, and she honestly never thought she would ever think like that. Leaning against the kitchen worktop, waiting for any signs of life from the mobile phone, Emma asked, "Do you know what the number is?"

"No, I can't remember. I've never been any good at remembering phone numbers, even when it's my own, sorry Em."

"Why are you leaving it so late?" asked Ruby, tucking in to a large baked potato with coleslaw piled on the top.

"I want to make sure he's in bed and won't see me. I can't risk it Rue. Hopefully he might notice he has mail before he goes to work in the morning and then he can text me."

"How do you know he'll be in bed at eleven o'clock?"

"Well I might just leave it later than that then."

"What are you going to do Em? Surely you can't avoid him for too long."

"I really don't know. I'm going to see another dentist tomorrow so I'll see what they say. They might even be able to put a temporary tooth in or something." Emma couldn't bear to think what might really happen. *Ignorance is bliss*, she kept thinking to herself, foolishly.

Ruby had shuffled off to bed over an hour ago and Emma sat in the living room with a pen poised on the notepad, trying to think what to write.

Dear Andrew,

This is my new... She tore the piece of paper from the pad and scrunched it up, her handwriting wasn't neat enough.

Dear Andrew,

Here is my new mobile number because the other one drowned in the bath sadly, before I could dive in (naked of course) and rescue it... Again, she ripped the paper away from its binding, screwed it up and fired it in to the waste paper bin – *sounds too childish*, she thought.

Hi Andy,

I've got a new number, sorry if you've tried to contact me. My old phone died after a watery accident so I've had to borrow one from Ruby (my flat-mate). I couldn't contact you because I didn't know your number. Anyway, hope to hear from you soon.

Love from Emma xxx

Tel: 079495797...

She read it once, folded it in half and pushed it in to an envelope. Then she pretended to be Andrew, pulled the letter out and read it again, trying to imagine what he would think. *Did it sound ok?* She wondered. Why was she being so over-sensitive about the content and quality of a hand-written note for goodness sake? Leaving it on the arm of the sofa, she went through to the kitchen and made a coffee, she'd go after she had finished it. It would then be approaching midnight by the time she arrived at Andrew's place and hopefully he would be asleep.

I'll just read it one more time and then seal the envelope, she decided. Contented that the note had no underlying tones of anything, except the simple message she wanted Andrew to perceive, she tucked it back in the envelope, licked it and stuck it down. Then she rubbed the back repeatedly to ensure it was stuck down properly. Neatly writing his name on the front of the envelope, it dawned on her that she still didn't know his last name – how stupid. She made it clear (she hoped) by writing 'Andrew- flat number 3' and then sighed as she gazed at it, pondering over whether it looked ok or not. Then she left home in the middle of the night.

***

48 hours was an even longer time to not hear from the person that Emma had become so close to in the course of just two weeks. She padded in to the kitchen, turned the kettle on and began to tidy up. The red suede shoes were still on the windowsill but at least Ruby had emptied the dirt from them at some point. Emma decided that she would clean them (the best she could, bearing in mind they were stained inside from the soil and they were suede) this morning while she waited: a – To hear from Andrew and b – To go to the dentists. She'd

almost forgotten about the dentist because she'd been so wrapped up with thoughts of Andrew.

The morning dragged by seemingly endless as she scrubbed Ruby's shoes, checked her mobile 14 times to make sure it was working properly and paced the carpets. She dreaded what the next dentist would say to her and what he/she would be like. If there was another petite woman with jet black hair sitting behind the patient's chair, she had already decided that she was going to walk straight back out again.

Then she began to worry whether Andrew would get the letter? How long would she give him to contact her? A day? Two days? The weekend? What if she'd heard nothing by Monday? Then she made another decision. She'd wait until Sunday night and then drop another letter round, asking if he'd received the first one and if he had received the first one could he kindly let her know, one way or another, what his intentions were (even if it was bad news).

Chapter 17

The Medical Centre was right in the heart of town. A modern looking structure with two broad, domed turrets at either end, the building was three storeys high and each level had an identical row of small windows dotted along its length. As they pulled in to the car park, Emma could see that the main entrance was entirely made of smoked glass. A giant canopy which was attached from the top of the building by long, white poles, stretched all the way down to just above the sliding, glass double doors. It almost looked like a cross-section of a witch's hat.

Emma shuddered. It appeared to be a very professional place – a place where lots of people came for treatment by one of the two practices residing there – a place where lots of people possibly had painful procedures done.

"Come on love, you'll be ok." Emma's mum threw her arm around her shoulder as they walked towards the building of doom, as Emma saw it.

"No don't Mum, you'll make me cry," whispered Emma as she scuttled out from under her arm. Just like the last visit to the dentist, Emma felt extremely emotional and over-sensitive and more so this time. She had visions in her head of walking in to the room and bursting in to tears and just having that image in her mind was enough to make her want to cry.

"You'll be ok love." Her mum tried to reassure her, but it wasn't working.

The waiting room was full of patiently waiting patients. It consisted mainly of elderly people and young women with prams and tear-away toddlers. As they walked through the waiting room, towards the reception area on the right, Emma studied the woman sitting behind the counter who was having a jolly conversation with a little old lady. She laughed, smiled, chatted and then smiled again. She looked like she was a very nice person – but then she wouldn't be peering in to Emma's mouth.

"Hello, err, my daughter Emma Frey. She has an appointment," said Emma's mum, gesticulating and pointing to Emma, who was less than a metre behind her.

The woman looked down at the open book in front of her, "Ah yes. Hello Emma, are you feeling all right?" she almost whispered. "We have a very nice dentist that will see you today. He deals with all of our nervous patients." Emma smiled tightly. Although she was in the right place for it, she didn't want this nice woman to see her gap-toothed grin. "Take a seat," said the woman and gave a smile that Emma thought looked quite genuinely sympathetic.

"She seems nice. Carol did say that they were very good here with people like you."

"Shush Mum, keep your voice down, I don't want everyone knowing I'm petrified," whispered Emma.

"Sorry love," her mum whispered back, "I think it will be all right here, don't you?"

Emma shrugged her shoulders and then began to watch the comings and goings of so many different people – each with their own affliction or ailment – each with a different story to tell.

"Emma Frey," a loud voice behind them startled Emma and brought her back from her thoughts. A nurse stood in the passageway looking around the room. She beamed as Emma walked towards her, "Emma?" Emma nodded and then she followed the portly nurse along the corridor, closely followed by her mum.

The third door on the right was slightly ajar and the nurse stopped outside then pushed it open, while ushering Emma and her mum to go in. Hesitantly, Emma walked in to the bright, fresh-looking room. The dentist sat on a swivel stool behind the patient's chair, typing away at a computer, just like the little Chinese lady of the last time. *Do all dentists do this*, wondered Emma as she slowly edged closer as if it was an electric chair she was going to sit in, having just been given her last rites. The man looked quite young from behind, with his cropped brown hair and the arms of a pair of glasses curling around the back of each ear.

"Hey, Emma isn't it?" the dentist drawled as he turned around and propped his glasses on to the top of his head. His American accent was smooth and calming, "Okay, we're not going to do anything today Emma. I wanna take a look if you're happy for me to do that."

Emma nodded and half-smiled, she felt comfortable-ish and so far this dentist scored 10 out of 10 for 'niceness' and he hadn't done anything yet. Her mum sat down in the visitors chair at the side of the room while Emma took the one, centre-stage.

"Okay, now then Emma, I can explain everything to you step by step if you're happy for me to take that look inside your mouth. Anytime you want me to stop just put your hand up, okay?"

"Ok," said Emma, her heart pounding in her throat.

"I'm going to tilt you backwards now Emma, just so that I can see up your nose, okay? Oh no... hey there's no teeth up there Emma. Guess I'll have to take a look in your mouth instead. Would that be all right?" Emma giggled and nodded. "Now I've got a small probe here," he said, holding it in front of Emma's eyes. "Would you like to feel it? The point on the end is not sharp. Here give me your finger." Emma nodded again and held up her index finger. The instrument touched the tip of her finger in a very nondescript way. "Okay, are you ready to open wide?" Emma glanced across at her mum, smiled and then opened her mouth wide. Her hands gripped together like a vice.

Apart from one brief moment of sensitivity-shock when Emma wanted to cling to the ceiling by her fingernails, the examination was relatively pain-free and very informative at every stage. Emma actually liked this man and couldn't believe she would ever have said that because he was one of those dreaded dentists. Raising the patient chair back up, he then swivelled on his stool, around to the right side and looked at her.

"Okay, so you know it's not great news Emma. The options are limited. I take it, by the look on your face earlier that you really don't want to go through with a long treatment programme." Emma shook her head. "How about taking this one step at a time and seeing how it goes Emma? As you know, there's no guarantee that we can save them all and you may end up having to have a partial plate of false teeth."

Although she liked this man quite a lot and trusted him, she was still terrified of having anything done. No matter how nice he was or how many injections he might be able to give her – and that was even if she could face having any injections, she still couldn't imagine going through any treatment at all.

"Okay, here's what I would like you to do Emma. Make an appointment to come in next week for some x-rays. I would like to check the abscess then to make sure it's clearing up satisfactorily. Does that sound okay?"

"So there's nothing you can do to temporarily fill this gap," asked Emma, pointing to her mouth.

"I'm afraid there isn't. You have a pretty serious condition going on here from what I can see and sadly, the lost tooth is the least of your problems." Emma looked on, horrified and truly devastated. "We'll know more when you've had the x-ray but it's not looking good, I have to say."

"Ok," said Emma, deflated and weary. Her mum stood up and thanked the dentist for his kind patience and understanding. Emma slid off the chair and smiled tightly, "Thank you," she said to the American man and couldn't quite believe she had thanked him as she noticed his name badge. It appeared that Dr Will Davey DDS-MDSc must be a very professional and well respected man in dentistry, judging by the amount of letters after his name. "Thank you Mr Davey," she said before walking out of the room, feeling very brave indeed.

"Well, what did you think?"

"I've made another appointment, for next Tuesday haven't I?" Emma snapped back.

"Look Emma, you knew it wasn't going to be good news. And I didn't for one minute think you would be able to get that missing tooth sorted out. He was a very nice man though."

"Hmm," Emma harrumphed, "Well, if Mr or Dr Davey, whoever he is, is that nice then I'll ask him if I can be put to sleep and have them all taken out and get false ones."

"Well they won't do that by next week either and that's a ridiculous idea for heaven's sake Emma, you're only 26!"

"Actually, that's the answer Mum! I hate my teeth, I hate dentists – except, maybe Dr Davey, and I hate having bad dreams all the time, so if I get false ones then I'll never have to worry about any of it again." Pulling the phone from her pocket, Emma turned it back on and waited...

But there were still no messages.

Ruby had just got in when Emma arrived home, "Ooh, you've cleaned my shoes Emma. Thank you so much."

"You're welcome. They're a bit stained inside but I thought that once you put your feet in them no one will notice that they had once been plant pots."

Ruby giggled. "Have you heard from Andrew yet?"

"Nope," replied Emma, suddenly feeling sad again. "I expect he's been at work all day." She desperately hoped this was true and he just hadn't had the time to text her yet.

"What does he do?" Ruby sipped her herbal tea and tucked her legs up under her, on the sofa.

"You know what? I don't even know what he does for a living. I don't know his last name. I don't know much about him at all. I'm not even sure why I don't know that much. I think we've been so wrapped up in each other that we haven't managed to get past the lust stage yet." Emma smiled and felt happy again as flashing images flickered around in her mind. "He's so sexy Rue – I can't keep my hands off him when I see him." Ruby smiled coyly and lowered her head to gaze into her mug of herbal tea.

"It will be nice to meet him again."

"When you're sober do you mean?" Emma smirked, "Do you even remember what he looks like?"

"Vaguely…" Ruby lifted her nose from the mug, "He's tall and he's got dark hair. Is that right?"

"Yes, tall, dark and very handsome." Emma looked up to the ceiling and sighed. "I really don't know what to do about this though Rue," she said, pointing to her partially opened mouth, "I just can't see him again, like this can I?"

"Emma it really doesn't look that bad. Did you go to the dentist today?"

"Yep and I've made another appointment for next week." Ruby's jaw dropped slightly as she stared, wide-eyed.

"Really?"

"Really," said Emma as she sat down and very proudly, proceeded to tell her best friend all about her experience with Dr Will Davey – the American dentist.

***

Ok, so almost 72 hours is really getting to be an awful long time, thought Emma as she stared at the kitchen clock, despondently.

The morning was icy cold and the pathetic heating system chugged its heart out desperately, as it fought against the elements to warm the flat. Peering out of the window, Emma could see icicles hanging from the bird table, in the communal garden, making it look very picturesque. Smiling to herself, she remembered how excited Ruby had been when she brought the bird feeder from their DIY store and rushed home to fill it with nuts and seeds, last summer. She was not only a bookworm but also a keen bird watcher. Ruby knew the names of practically every type of bird that came into the garden and would often study them for hours through her cheap, seaside-purchase, binoculars.

Flicking the kettle on, Emma pulled the phone from her dressing gown pocket and checked again for any signs of life. There was nothing. She was far too obsessed.

Fiddling with the chattering, wind-up teeth in her hands, Emma looked down at them and pondered. They did look quite real. They were of a similar size to her teeth. Ok, they were a lot whiter than her ones, but would anyone notice that? Maybe she could discolour them, leave them soaking in a cup of black tea, overnight. How was she going to extract just one tooth from the plastic mould though? How was she going to fix a tooth into the gap in her mouth, even if she did manage to break just one of the plastic teeth off? How totally insane and haunted had she become? *Superglue?* How would she remove it again, even if she could do it with *Superglue*, before her trip to the dentist next week? What on earth would Dr Davey think of her if he knew what she was contemplating?

While all of the crazy thoughts were whirling around in Emma's head, Ruby entered the room, wearing a towel turban and her new Dalmatian-dog onesie.

"What are you doing with those?" she said, looking horrified. Emma wondered, just for a moment, if Ruby could read her mind and grinned suspiciously.

"Just wondering who it was," she said, holding the teeth in the air and studying them. "Have you any idea yet?"

"No, I'd forgotten about it to be honest, sorry Em."

"It still pisses me off when I think about it Rue. And now I'm really going to be the laughing stock when I go back to work. I've got to do something." Emma jumped up from the sofa and headed towards the bathroom, "Where are the nail clippers?" she called.

"What do you want them for?" Ruby's worried voice replied.

"Found them," Emma shouted, "Hammer?" She knew they had one in their cute little, pink tool box which had some very basic tools for those little odd jobs, that never got done.

"Emma, what are you doing?" Ruby followed her to the cupboard in the hallway.

"I've got an idea... wait and see." An annoyingly, corny ringtone could be heard in the living room as Emma searched in the bottom of the rather over-filled cupboard.

"That's my old phone – you've got a message Em." Emma froze and stared up at Ruby from inside the cupboard. Then she raced through to the lounge and picked up the old mobile. Holding it in her hand, her heart thumped and she almost dared not look to see if it was Andrew because if it wasn't, she would be truly gutted.

Bloody hell, I have just found your letter in the foyer. When did you post that? I was going to come round to your flat if I hadn't heard from you by today. Andy xx

Emma's blood ran cold. Today? He could not come round today; she had an important job to do.

I'm so sorry Andy. I dropped that note round to you, two nights ago. Are you ok? Emma xxx

Missing you but apart from that I'm ok. When can I see you? Can I call you?

Lost my voice, can't talk. Emma had to think quickly. *I really want to see you but all the family are coming tomorrow and I'm still not well. I was going to take it easy, so that I'm better for tomorrow. Could we wait until next week? Xxx*

Emma hated lying but she feared talking to him in case he heard the slight whistle in her voice. She feared hearing his deep, sexy voice trying to persuade her to meet up. She feared her own sexual desire which could possibly take over her rational mind and lead her to him. She feared seeing him. She feared him seeing her... For heaven's sake!

Yes of course we can. I understand you want to see your family. Are you ok though? xx

Ditto. Sorry Andy, yes I'm ok, just a really sore throat and sniffles. ☺ Miss you too xxx

"Is everything all right?" asked Ruby, hovering over Emma, who was sat on the floor, leaning back on the base of the sofa.

"Yeah. He wants to see me but there is no way that I can let him see me like this, at least not until I've sorted something out."

Grabbing the hammer, Emma lifted it just enough to bring it back down with a soft blow on to the chattering teeth that she had placed on the floor, in front of her. The plastic toy bounced up and away under the force of the hammer, but remained intact. Again, Emma pounded the teeth but this time a little harder. *Ping!* The spring loaded dentures separated and the small, wind-up mechanism disintegrated into little bits, scattering across the floor.

"What are you doing?" said Ruby, utterly horrified. She began to worry about firstly, Emma's violent act and secondly, why she might be doing it. "Why are you doing that Emma?"

"You'll see..."

Could I perhaps call you tomorrow? Love Andy xx

I'll text you when I get home from my mum's. Things will be a bit better after the funeral. Lots of love and cuddles Emma xxx.

Examining the two rows of teeth, Emma decided that the teeth in the top row looked nearer the size of her own, as she held them against her exaggerated smile in the bathroom mirror.

Ruby flapped around in a disheveled state just outside the door. "You're not going to do anything stupid are you Emma?"

"Like what?"

"Like... well... like pull all your teeth out and put those ones in their place." Ruby gulped and removed the almost dried out towel from her head.

"No, don't be daft. Oh my Goodness Rue, I think you'd better wet your hair down again."

Ruby stepped into the bathroom, stood alongside Emma and then peered into the mirror. They both looked straight ahead at themselves, then they stared at Ruby's wildly, over-grown spiked hair, sticking out of the top of her black and white spotted onesie, then glanced at Emma's toothless gap and then simultaneously they gawped at the dentures, held up between their faces. Suddenly they both fell about laughing hysterically.

Ok, keep in touch and don't scare me like that again. Love Andy xx p.s. Write my number down on a separate sheet of paper Lol xx

The nail clippers were useless. The hammer was too efficient at smashing bits off of the plastic molded teeth and Emma had already caught her thumb nail under the wickedly sharp chisel as it shattered the teeth into pieces, under the force of the hammer. "Argh!" she grunted, tossing the chisel aside. "How am I going to get just one tooth off?"

"I don't think it would work anyway Emma. I mean, how are you going to fix it in?" Ruby had dampened her hair down and sat curled up with a mug of herbal tea and her latest *Mills & Boon* novel on her lap.

"Well, I've got to try." Emma had managed to break away several parts of the plastic, leaving a set of just four little teeth. One of the middle ones looked like a perfect fit for her gap.

"Em, don't you think this is a bit..."

"A bit what?" snapped Emma.

"Well, you know... a bit crazy," Ruby sighed, "Aren't you getting a bit obsessed Emma?"

"Sandpaper – that's what I need!" she said while ignoring Ruby's last comments. Emma jumped up and went back to the cupboard to root around in the depths of what could have been mistaken as the wardrobe in the *Chronicles of Narnia* film, it stretched back so far.

She'd spent 2 hours on the damned thing and then thrown it across the bathroom in rage. The little, single tooth looked totally ridiculous wedged in between her own teeth. It stood out worse than the actual gap itself. The colour did not match at all and the plastic replica was far too small. *What a frigging waste of a Saturday*, she thought to herself and stomped into her bedroom and threw herself on the bed.

Ruby was next door in her room, getting ready for her night out with Pete. She'd spent the afternoon pacing up and down the hallway, talking to herself, patting her hair down and studying her fingernails before devouring them.

"Do you think these will be ok?" she asked, peering around the bedroom door, clutching a pair of old jeans in her hand.

"They're a bit tatty Rue. I suppose it depends on what you're going to wear with them," said Emma, slightly bitterly. She should have been going out with Andrew tonight.

"Trainers... or these?" Ruby asked, holding up her black *Hush Puppies* used mainly for work.

"Neither!" Emma picked herself up from the bed and padded through to Ruby's room. "Boots, you haven't got any have you?"

"I've got my grey snow boots."

"No, you can't wear them. If you're wearing old jeans you need to tart them up with a nice top and some high-heeled boots!"

It was a good job that Emma was the same shoe size as Ruby, "Here try these," she said, throwing her black, knee high boots on to Ruby's bed. A few minutes later Emma returned from her room, laden with different tops and blouses. "And this would look lovely on you." Dropping the other tops on the floor, she held up a low-cut blouse with pale blue, silky flowers embroidered down each side of the button edge. "Try it on."

Emma walked back out of the room, noted the time on her new cheap-looking, digital watch (a Christmas tree present from Grandma and Grandad – but most definitely purchased by Grandma) and went into the lounge to check the phone. No messages. Good. She'd felt a little on edge all day, fearing that Andrew might just turn up unexpectedly. Now and again she would go to the window and peer outside to check he wasn't coming along the road or parked up outside the flat. Quite what she would have done if he had turned up, she really had no idea – unless the spare cupboard really was the way to *Narnia* and she could disappear in to it. Teeth and all.

"Do I look all right?" asked Ruby, hobbling in to the lounge wearing Emma's boots.

"Gorgeous – Ruby Winters, are you wearing make-up?" Emma looked surprised.

"Just a tiny bit. I bought a brown mascara from the chemist yesterday lunch time."

"Good for you Rue," said Emma, even more surprised that her geeky little friend had actually been to the shop and bought herself some make-up (even if it was only one item) and more astonished that she'd managed to apply it herself.

"Does it look ok?" asked Ruby, moving closer and thrusting her face forward, almost nose to nose, into Emma's face for a closer inspection.

"Yes, you've done well. I'm amazed at the way you've changed Rue." Emma had to admit that Ruby was naturally good looking and didn't really need any make-up at all. The most beautiful thing about Ruby was the fact that she didn't know how beautiful she was. "I'll hide in my bedroom when Pete turns up. I really don't want to see him, or anyone else for that matter. Tell him I'm in bed if he asks." Ruby nodded and smiled. "I hope you have a lovely time tonight Rue."

"Thank you," she said sweetly. "We're going to see an old movie at the cinema, not sure what it's called but I'm so excited. Then we're going to the *Waterhouse* for an all-you-can-eat Chinese meal."

"That's nice. Bet you'll have a lovely time with Pete. You're made for each other." Emma really meant what she said but she just couldn't help feeling slightly jealous. Not jealous that Ruby was seeing Pete but jealous that Ruby was going out, having fun, spending time with a man and all with her teeth fully intact.

Once she was sure they'd left, Emma vacated her bedroom, went in to the lounge and put the television on before picking up her phone to read the message. She'd heard it play the antique notification tune before Pete and Ruby left and had to sit and wait patiently before she could read it.

Hi babe, hope you're feeling a bit better. I'm looking forward to seeing you really soon. Love Andy xx

Ditto. Feeling rough still and throat is killing. Can't wait to see you after the funeral stuff is all over and done with. Em xxx

Cringing through the lies, Emma placed the phone on the side table and flicked through the channels, it was going to be a very long night and she still had to fathom out how to fill the gap.

Chapter 18

Morning again, hope you're feeling better and enjoy seeing your family today, although for a very sad occasion. Andy xx

Feeling a bit better, still can't talk (probably a blessing for Ruby). Hope you have a good day. Miss you too Em xxx

Placing the phone on to her bedside table, Emma stretched and yawned and then snapped her jaws together quickly to listen to the noise outside of her room. Muffled voices and footsteps drifted away, along the hallway, and into the living room. It must be Ruby – and Pete! Had he stayed overnight again? Emma couldn't imagine Ruby inviting Pete to stay the night, especially if she was sober. Would she? Had they slept together? Surely not.

Listening through the opened crack of the door, Emma's thoughts were confirmed, it was definitely Pete. "I'll just have a quick one then I had better go," said Pete in a low, hushed voice but just loud enough that Emma could make out what he was saying.

The sound of cups being placed on the worktop and the kettle revving up could be heard, then Emma closed the door and went back to sit on her bed. Damn – she'd have to wait until he'd left before she could get up. There was no way she was going to see Pete, unless she could keep her lips sealed and that would look very odd if she said nothing, apart from 'Um'. There were enough 'Um's' in the flat from Ruby, let alone Emma taking on the trait too.

Emma buried her head in her hands. What the hell was she going to do? She needed to get to the bathroom mirror and check that she didn't look like the lagoon monster, permanently imprinted on her mind. She picked up the magnifying hand mirror on the dressing table and stared hard into it. It always made her face look horribly porous and downy as the 10x magnifier blew everything out of proportion – including the now, gigantic gap!

Tossing the mirror on to the bed, Emma slumped down and then began to think about the coming couple of days: Jack coming home, the funeral and all the people that would attend (at least it wouldn't be an occasion to smile all day), the dentist on Tuesday, back to work and seeing Andrew. She had to face up to the fact that she couldn't hide away forever. Maybe she could say that she fell down the stairs and hit her mouth on the banister. That wouldn't work because she had no bruising around her mouth and they also had no stairs. Emma was lost in her thoughts, until the moment she heard the front door close.

Tiptoeing down the hallway, Emma listened carefully for any signs that someone else was in the living room. "Morning Emma," said Ruby, from behind her.

"Oh God – you made me jump!" Emma slapped her hand on her chest, "Has Pete gone?"

"Yes, I hope you don't mind that he stayed last night," said Ruby, clutching a mug of her usual morning tea. Her hair could only be described as the after effects of a hurricane-blown bird's nest as she smiled sweetly, while waiting for a response.

"No, not at all. You could do with sorting your hair out though," laughed Emma, "Did you have a good night?"

Ruby looked down at her slippers, "Um... yes." Then she smiled, coyly.

"Did you sleep with him?"

"Yes, it was a bit of a squash though."

"No, I mean did you s...l...e...e...p with him?" Emma was itching to know and by the look on Ruby's face she was guessing that maybe she had.

"Um," replied Ruby and scuttled away in to the living room.

Emma followed her. "Well?"

"Well what?" Ruby curled up on the sofa, gripping her mug like it was her last ever cup of herbal tea.

"Well, how was it?" Emma thought for a moment, "I mean, did you have a nice time?"

"Um," replied Ruby, unable to look Emma in the face. "The meal was lovely."

"No, I mean when you got home. Bedtime... you know what I mean."

"Um..."

"So you've had sex with him?"

"Um." Ruby suddenly began to cry softly. The tiny tears welled up in her eyes and plopped over the edge on to her soft, rosy cheeks.

"Rue, what's the matter?" asked Emma, sitting down next to her and placing an arm around her shoulder.

"I don't know," she said, sniffing and wiping her eyes. "I really like Pete."

"Well that's good isn't it?" Emma was puzzled. "So why are you crying? I don't get it."

"It was a lovely evening and I like him a lot. I think I'm just really happy," sobbed Ruby.

"Oh, come here you daft lemon." Emma pulled Ruby closer to her and hugged her tightly. "I'm so happy for you

Rue. You make a lovely couple, and you've had SEX!" Ruby gave a quivering smile and wiped away another tear. "You're officially a non-virgin Rue! Oh my Goodness, I can't believe it."

"Please don't tell anyone."

"Of course I won't. This is your private life, no one else's. I'm hardly going to write a book about it, am I?" Ruby laughed and Emma decided not to press for any more details about Ruby's budding sex-life – that could come later.

"I'm leaving now Rue. I'll see you tomorrow night, all being well."

"Ok, send my love to everyone, especially your mum and grandma." Ruby walked through the hall to the front door and held the door open. "Goodbye," she said, pecking Emma on the cheek.

"Have fun tonight with Pete and make sure you keep off my bed if you start tearing each other's clothes off and having sex all over the flat."

Ruby breathed a sharp intake of breath, "Emma – I'm not going to do that!" Her face looked horrified again. "He's only coming round for a coffee. We've got work tomorrow."

"Ah well, once it's started Rue, it won't stop. You'll soon be humping like randy rabbits."

Ruby laughed as her face glowed a crimson red, flushed with embarrassment. "Goodbye Emma," she said pushing her best friend out of the door, "I'll be thinking of you tomorrow."

The urge to jump on Jack's back was still overwhelming after all these years but Emma managed to control herself, hugged him tightly and pecked him on the cheek. Misty ran around in circles, at their feet. She had already sensed that something was going on in the Frey household and she kept collecting bones and balls from her toy box and depositing them at the feet of anyone who showed an interest in her.

"Allo Sis. Good to see yer." He smiled and then studied Emma's face with a puzzled look on his. Jack's accent had changed over the years whilst living in Germany and funnily enough, he sounded more like a cockney than anything else now and more so since he'd learned to speak fluent German, which didn't make any sense at all.

"Lost one," said Emma, pulling her bottom lip down and smiling.

"Bloody hell, how d'ya do that?" Jack frowned, while trying to get Misty to sit down by his side. "You been in a fight?"

"No, it just fell out." Emma rolled her bottom lip and gave a 'puppy-dog' look with her big brown eyes.

She always felt like the baby whenever she saw Jack. He was the eldest of her three brothers and 8 years her senior. The family had always joked about the fact that Emma's parents had needed to take a 5 year break after Jack was born, as the shock of raising a child was just too much for them, before they had the other 3 children, who then came along, one straight after another.

Emma sat down and quietly explained her whole predicament to Jack, knowing he would understand her problems and worries. Her other two brothers had far less empathy and would have told her just to get to the dentist and 'man-up', or in her case 'woman-up' and if her boyfriend didn't like her anymore, just because she had a tooth missing, then he wasn't worth bothering about. Only Jack understood her real insecurities and fears. It was a great shame that he lived out in Germany with his wife and 2 children and Emma often wished he would just come back to the UK where he belonged.

Jack had done his time in the Army and then he left and became a heavy-goods lorry driver. He'd met his wife who was half German, half English while still serving in the Army and shortly after leaving the forces they'd married and had 2 beautiful boys. They ventured over to the UK about once every year, usually in the summer time, to see Jack's family and Emma always missed them terribly when they went home after their 2 week stay. She begged them to move over to England every time they came. For this occasion, Jack had come over alone. He had 3 days leave from his job to attend the funeral and would have to return to Germany on Tuesday.

"I would have come with you on Tuesday, if I hadn't had to get back Sis," said Jack, staring at Emma's mouth.

"I know you would have. Mum's coming with me though, so it'll be ok," said Emma.

Jack grinned and winked at her before returning to the dining room where everyone was sitting around the table, drinking tea and talking, mainly about Grandad.

Alex and Grandma flapped around most of the day, worrying about this and fretting about that. Was there going to be enough food for the buffet? How many people would come back after the funeral? Was the house tidy enough? Where was the dog going to go? Grandma did not want Misty disrespecting Grandad's wake by going around sniffing everyone's bottom – and rightly so, everyone had agreed. And then there were all of the other things to worry about, like were the two toilets clean and did Alex have enough plates and cups?

Jack and Aaron played about upstairs, in Aaron's bedroom, with the photo streaming film that would be played on the television during the wake. Everyone had rallied round and collected as many photos as they could of Grandad, so

Jack and Aaron could put them into some kind of order to tell the story of his life.

Grant was at work but would be taking the day off tomorrow and Joe and Tiffany would be arriving early in the morning.

The phone didn't stop. Great Aunts and Uncles, Cousins from near and far, old friends and even older work colleagues, called all day to finalise the arrangements and times for Grandad's funeral.

The house was full of hustle and bustle, which was just what Emma needed to keep her mind off her own problems. She'd worked out how to speak without the gap showing too much as she knew she would have to talk to a lot of people tomorrow. She could talk clearly while sucking in and holding her bottom lip firmly against the bottom row of teeth, aided by her tongue at the back. She looked a little odd, as if she'd had a facelift on her jaw line, which pulled and stretched her bottom lip backwards, towards her ears but she had decided that her appearance looked far better this way than the one of a 7 year old child, having lost her first tooth.

By the evening the sausage rolls were cooked and everything else was prepared and ready to go. Jack and Aaron returned from the Chinese take-away, carrying bags of chicken fried rice, chicken balls and chips.

Grant was slumped on the sofa after a long day at work and Grandma and Alex pottered around in the kitchen, unable to sit still for 5 minutes. Soon enough, everyone sat down at the dining table and quietly nibbled their way through the mountains of food as Grandad's funeral loomed.

Back in her old bedroom, Emma lay on the bed staring at the ceiling with a very full and gurgling tummy. She'd eaten nothing all day and then over-indulged on the Chinese meal. Looking around the room she felt like a young girl again, except she was minus her dear old grandad. Christmas had come and gone in a blur and Emma had spent more time in her childhood bedroom, these last couple of weeks, than anywhere else. She was nervous and felt over-emotional about tomorrow's events – she almost wished she was a child again, things were easier then.

Ruby's antique phone trembled on the bedside table and Emma knew it would be Andrew. Strangely, she hadn't thought about him quite so much today.

Hi Emma, just to let you know that I will be thinking of you tomorrow. Missing you madly. Andy xx

Thanks Andy. It's been like a beehive here today. Dreading tomorrow – but then I suppose that is to be expected. Em xxx Smiling to herself, Emma replaced the mobile on the table and went to take a shower and practice new verbal skill. A skill that was not quite good enough however, for her to confidently see Andrew again.

Chapter 19

Everyone was rushing around, in and out of the bathroom, up and down the stairs, answering phone calls, eating breakfast, ironing, dressing, either flapping and fretting or brooding and grieving. Grandma paced around, not quite sure what to do and followed instructions automatically as Alex gave them. Alex generally sorted everyone else out too. She'd always been the same – disorder, disloyalty or disempowerment were not words in her vocabulary. A strong-willed woman, Alex happily welcomed and would use the threatening words – dismember or dissect – should anyone get in her way.

Joe and Tiffany arrived, dressed very smartly in a black suit, purple shirt and tie and a navy blue skirt suit and white blouse, respectively. Tiffany sat on the edge of the sofa, looking uncomfortable and watching everyone, to-ing and fro-ing, she smiled sweetly, but awkwardly, here and there.

The three brothers, Jack, Aaron and Joe, clumped together, fully dressed in their smart suits, talking quietly in the far corner of the dining room. Discreetly laughing now and again, they tried to suppress any outbursts as a mark of respect for their Grandad's funeral day and for Grandma's sake as she tottered around the house aimlessly.

"I hope you'll all be ready soon," shouted Alex, "We all need to be over at Grandma's house promptly at 10.15."

An eerie silence fell on Dot Stern's house as the time approached 10.45. Everyone knew it was coming and the atmosphere in Grandma's living room turned icy cold like the wintery air outside. Watching from the window, Emma's mum sighed and gulped back the rising flood of emotions. The hearse was coming.

Beautifully coloured wreaths lay on each side of the coffin. One of the largest ones formed the word, *'DAD'* and on the top of the coffin sat the small shape of a ship, intricately made from the tiniest of red and white flowers. Emma looked at the ship and swallowed hard as she linked arms with her mum and grandma.

Trailing behind them, Jack, Aaron, Joe and their dad walked quietly to the second funeral car as a few neighbours stood out on the pavement, wrapped in heavy coats, acknowledging them in a respectful manner.

Tiffany was the last to leave Grandma's house with strict instructions to lock the front door behind her. She did so with her head bowed all of the time. Then she slipped the key in to her pocket and walked silently away.

Leading her mum and grandma to the first car, Emma nodded her head to her grandma's neighbours and then guided her elders in to the back of the black limousine.

"Are you ok Grandma," whispered Emma softly. Grandma nodded her head and looked out of the side window at the group of mourning spectators on the side of the road.

Emma's mum held on to Grandma's hand, patting it gently with her other hand and then looked to Emma and half smiled through watery eyes. "Are you all right?" she mouthed to Emma.

"Yeah," Emma mouthed back as the limo slowly and silently pulled away, following closely, behind the hearse.

Tiffany followed the funeral procession in her own car. She was going to help escort people back to Alex's house for the wake. Grandma Dot had not wanted to have the wake at her own house. She'd hardly been at home since losing her husband, the one and only love of her life. She couldn't face being at home. The emptiness and the bleak winter days made it almost unbearable to stay in the small bungalow alone, staring at the four walls that were filled with memories of him. Alex had offered to have the wake in her home, which was far bigger and much better equipped for functions of any kind, than Grandma's was. Alex liked to take control of things and insisted in providing the buffet to relieve her mother of some of the stress. It also kept her mind focused on something else as well. Alex would grieve privately for her dad, when the time was right for her but until then she needed to look after everyone else – as was usual.

There were far more people than Emma would have ever expected, waiting outside the chapel of the crematorium. She didn't know what she had expected when they arrived but the sheer volume of people, quietly standing at a respectful distance away from the driveway into the chapel's porch, was touching and emotional. Emma gulped and held back the tears as she helped her grandma out of the car.

The second car soon followed and Emma's dad and her brothers got out, pulled their suit jackets down by the hem and adjusted their ties as if they had all practiced to do it together in unison. Looking around at the crowd of reverently silent mourners, they all nodded their acknowledgements and then joined the others. Moments later, Tiffany arrived, sullen faced and with her head still bowed.

A member of the clergy stood waiting by the chapel doors, hands clasped together across his bulging midriff. Several other attendees from the crematorium and the funeral directors hovered around, tacitly respectful and standing with their hands clasped together, one hand over the top of the other, in front of them. Emma marveled at their duteous stance and dress code and the fact that this was only a job to them yet they did it superbly.

Grant and the three siblings were instructed to move towards the hearse in preparation for the removal and lift of the coffin. They would then carry it into the chapel.

Emma looked at Aaron and noted he was gulping. She guessed he would be anxious so she moved towards him and rubbed him gently on the shoulder, "Are you ok?" she whispered. Aaron nodded and half smiled. Stepping back out of the way, Emma returned to her grandma and mum and they all quietly watched, while the coffin was lifted, put into a secure position on everyone's shoulders and then slowly carried into the chapel.

It was terribly solemn and silent.

Emma and her mum linked arms with Grandma and followed behind as Tiffany and the other mourners, courteously left a short distance between themselves and the immediate family, before they too entered the chapel.

The service was relatively short and simple but then Grandad's brother, Great Uncle Norman to Emma, got up and made an emotional speech about some of his own memories of his elder brother and their years of growing up together. He spoke about Grandad's lifelong hobby of model making and his greatest achievement, the scaled replica of the *Titanic*, which he built for the 100th year remembrance day, way back in 2012. He told the tale of how Grandad managed to create some hype in the papers and local television as he launched his most prized model into a lake to coincide with the real *Titanic's* one and only voyage. Much to the disgust of Grandma, he also told the story of her misadventure, when she fell in to the lake and prematurely sent the *Titanic* on its maiden voyage. He told everyone how amused Grandad had been by it all when he phoned Norman to tell him about it. Great Uncle Norman's tales gave everyone in the chapel, a reason to smile in Grandad's memory, apart from Grandma who cried or scowled or both at the same time incredibly.

A few sobs were heard coming from around the over filled chapel and Emma guessed that there had to be about 40 people present, which she felt was a fitting tribute to her grandad's final day. Then the tears began to prick her eyes and her lip trembled as she repeatedly gulped and sniffed, trying to suppress them for her mum and for her grandma's sake too.

As the curtains began to close and the CD player played Grandad's favourite song by *Celine Dion - My Heart Will Go On*, the sobs turned to obvious cries and anguished tones of grief. Emma couldn't stop it, the tears came copiously and she shuddered as she realised she was crying, not only for her dear old grandad, but she was crying for her own personal loss too and for the total mess she was in.

Slowly the mourners turned up in over-filled (to the point of being of illegal carrying capacity) cars and glided along Pinewood Avenue, trying to find spaces to park. Luckily about half of the residents in the avenue were working families and had left home for the day.

The Frey's and Grandma had all been escorted home, at an extra cost, by the funeral director's minibus and were waiting with bated breath for everyone else to arrive.

An eerie, hushed silence hung in the air as everyone filtered in through the open front door, greeted and hugged the widow and her family, and then hung around in the kitchen or dining room, either staring at the spread of food laid out on the table or talking in hushed voices to each other.

Misty barked and yapped at the patio doors, wanting to be let in as everyone arrived.

Tiffany had brought a car load of people back with her. She had then rushed through to the kitchen (still with her head bowed) and busied herself by making cups of tea and coffee. She politely made her way through the gatherings to hand out hot drinks and then she asked the new visitors what drinks they would like and started all over again. She looked very at home in her new, albeit temporary, role as a waitress and gently nodded and smiled at everyone as she took their orders.

Eventually, after many stops to greet and acknowledge her extended family members, Emma reached the kitchen which was just as packed as anywhere else and squeezed into a corner away from the kettle. She did not want to steal Tiffany's job or assist in the distribution of beverages, as she felt that Tiff was doing a fine job on her own. She reached into her small black bag and grabbed her phone. No messages. She hadn't heard from Andrew since last night but she assumed it was because he was so good natured and well mannered that he would probably be showing his respect today by not texting her at all. *Shame,* she thought and threw it back into the bag.

Misty came bounding in to the kitchen and then out again, having just been let indoors by Emma's mum. Misty didn't know where to go or what to do as she sniffed at the multitude of legs filling every room. She didn't have enough bones or balls to give every single person a token gift so she gave up and squeezed herself underneath the dining table, waiting patiently for any misplaced tidbits that might reach the floor.

Aunt Josie had finally made it to the funeral, along with Emma's cousin Daniel and his wife, Ali. They had been a little late and had to sneak in at the back of the chapel discreetly. Emma couldn't stand Ali's snooty air of importance and she was sure that her aunt Josie couldn't either.

"Emma's en hair Joosie," said Ali, pointing a down turned finger in Emma's direction. Aunt Josie sidestepped into the kitchen, walked straight over to Emma and flung her big arms around her neck.

"Hello honey, how are you?" she asked in a reserved kind of way... a very reserved way for Aunt Josie. She was normally a bouncy bubble of buffoonery and at 52 years old, she seemed all the more funny as she told her tales of dark comedy and impersonated practically everyone to the point of ridicule. Today, Aunt Josie was on her very best behaviour and very respectful of the mourners and her brother Grant's, family.

Daniel had already disappeared and was talking to Aaron, Jack and Joe, by the front door. The cousins hadn't been together like this for years and it was such a shame that they had all been brought together on such cheerless terms today.

In the kitchen, Ali smirked slyly at Emma and made her way over to Tiffany who was decidedly short, in comparison to Ali whose legs were up to her armpits. Her blonde hair was so long that she could sit on it. "Would yoou leke a han weth thoose?" she asked in her strong Welsh accent.

Tiffany looked up and smiled at her sweetly. As a fairly new member of the family she was quite unsure who was who and therefore she felt she should be very polite to everyone and oblige.

"Thank you, that's very kind of you. That gentleman over there would like a coffee," she said nervously, pointing in the direction of two elderly men standing at the end of the dining table. Tiffany handed the cup to Ali and watched her saunter off, flicking her blonde hair back as she went.

"Yes I'm ok, thank you. How are you doing?" asked Emma quietly, smiling at her beloved aunt. Her childhood memories of Aunt Josie were filled with happy thoughts of laughter, silliness and generally, lots of clowning around.

"I'm good, sometimes." Josie winked and smiled, "How's your mum and grandma coping? I haven't really spoken to them yet."

"Bearing up I suppose, considering." Emma shrugged. "How's Jacob?"

"Oh you know my Jacob, always covered in bruises. I keep telling him he's getting too old to be throwing himself on the ground all of the time." Josie shrugged, "He's stuck out in Paris at the moment, some big rugby tournament for the under 16's."

"Oh, I see. Is that why he couldn't come then?"

"Yes, well you know what he's like Emma. His teaching always has to come first."

Emma sensed the annoyance in Aunt Josie's tone of voice and tried to think of how to change the subject momentarily.

"Honey, what happened to your tooth?"

Instantly Emma's face flushed a deep burning red and she sucked her bottom lip in tightly.

"Lost it," she mumbled disconcertingly. "It fell out." Emma cringed as she realised that she had dropped her guard during the day and probably everyone had noticed her missing tooth – even possibly, perfect, pompous Ali.

"Ah, my love, come here." Josie pulled Emma to her and gave her another hug, "Have you got problems with them honey?"

Emma nodded like a little girl and looked in to her aunt's eyes as if she was pleading for help.

"It happened to me, you know. I was about your age, well, maybe a little older. Terrified I was. No, I was petrified in fact."

Emma's face lit up instantly – she had someone she could really talk to, someone that understood how frightened she was, and best of all it was her dear Aunt Josie, whom she loved and respected dearly.

"These are falsies," she said pointing to a forced grin. Emma stared hard, disbelieving that her aunt had false teeth.

"Really? I... I never knew."

"Suppose I kept it pretty quiet. I didn't want to scream and shout from the rooftops about the fact that I was terrified of the dentist and my teeth were starting to fall out. I had periodontitis."

Emma gasped, "Oh my Goodness, so have I." Looking around the crowded room, Emma could see that everyone else was wrapped up in their own conversations and mostly on the topic of Grandad, which made Emma feel a little guilty that she was having this self-indulgent conversation with her aunt. However, it was a deeply needed chat on Emma's part and one that she now had to have in order to gain as much information as she could.

"I told them to whip them all out," whispered Josie as she used her hand in a flicking motion across her mouth.

"Oh gosh, really? They don't even look false, I just... well, I never knew." whispered Emma, still shocked from her aunt's revelation.

Josie winked again and then accepted a cup of coffee from Tiffany as she approached her from behind. "Thank you darling. It's nice to see you again, although under very tragic circumstances."

Tiffany nodded, pulled the corners of her mouth down and then turned around and headed back over to the kettle and her new acquaintance, Ali, the sleek super-model.

"No, they're pretty real looking these days, aren't they?" Aunt Josie forced another exaggerated grin. "Are you going to have treatment?"

"No I'd much rather do the same as you. I'm scared of my own teeth, I know it sounds ridiculous."

"No, it doesn't sound ridiculous Em. I know exactly what you mean honey. I used to have terrible nightmares about mine." Emma's jaw dropped again and she stared hard at her aunt without blinking her eyes as she began to register her words.

"Oh gosh, so do I. I can't believe it." Suddenly Emma wished her aunt didn't live so far away, in the thick of Wales. She needed her here. She needed her understanding and support.

"Honey, I understand that they're worrying you a lot and you're very scared but I advise you to think long and hard about having them all removed." Aunt Josie looked very serious, which was always such a shock to see as she was usually the most un-serious person anyone could meet. "Think very long and very hard, Emma. It's not an easy option and it takes a while to learn to live with them, but it was the right choice for me. You're still very young though honey, you need to make sure that you are making the right decision, for you."

It didn't matter what Aunt Josie said now, Emma's mind was definitely made up. She did not want her own teeth anymore – there was no way she could handle all of the treatment required to correct and save her own. At least she would be put to sleep to have every one of her teeth removed – she knew that much.

"Thank you Josie, you've really helped me out a lot today. I still can't believe that I didn't know anything about your teeth though."

"Give us a hug," said Josie, pulling her niece towards her. "Just don't rush in to anything Emma – get some proper advice please." Josie winked at her, "Now I'm going to find your mum and dad, and your dear old grandmother."

Aunt Josie waddled away and left Emma standing in the corner of the kitchen, gazing into the middle-distance, unsure whether she wanted to laugh or cry or both.

By five o'clock, almost everyone had left. Aunt Josie, Daniel and Ali sat on the sofa together, waiting for the last few people to leave. They had a long journey back to Wales but it was one they had to make as Josie had young children to care for tomorrow morning, in her role as a child-minder. She had spent most of her life either bringing up her own two boys or looking after other people's children. Sadly, she had never re-married after her first husband left her and had spent her life on her own. She was content though and probably one of the happiest, go-lucky people that Emma knew. In fact, the whole Frey family hoped that her bubbly personality was not just on the surface – secretly hiding an inner and lonely existence – and that she truly was a happy person.

"Right, we'll be getting along now then," said Josie, standing up and tugging her tunic down, over her bottom. Daniel stood up and then turned to pull Ali out of the seat.

"Come on you two," said Josie, eyeing Ali with what Emma thought was contempt. Ali stood up and forced a sarcastic smile at both her husband and Josie. "Right," said Josie, clapping her hands together, "It's been good to see you all again, I'm just so sorry that it has been under very sad circumstances."

"Yes it is but thank you so much for coming Josie. You've travelled such a long way today," replied Alex as Grant slipped his arm around her waist. "And you two, of course," she said, smiling at Daniel and Ali. "Drive carefully and please text me when you get home."

"Sure will," said Josie before doing the rounds of cuddles and pecks of cheeks to every member of the Frey family who was standing in the room, waiting to wave her off. Daniel walked to the door first, shoved along by his dearly beloved, shifty looking, artful Ali. Josie followed behind them, turning and waving, several times, as she went. Then they were gone – as quickly as they had arrived.

Grandma had remained seated on the recliner chair, teetering on the edge and looking like she was about to fall off at any minute, as Josie and the others left. Absent minded and weary she looked up and smiled here and there (when she thought she ought to) but actually everyone had noticed that she wasn't really engaging with anything and her smiles were randomly misplaced. The pain and grief showed in her grey eyes and everyone felt quite worried about her ability to go back to her own home eventually, to continue her life alone as a widow.

The Frey household slowly started to return to some sort of normality. Joe and Tiffany left an hour or so after Josie. Jack went to pack up his things, ready for his return journey in the morning and Emma grabbed her overnight bag. She kissed everyone goodbye, cuddled Jack and then reminded her mum of their appointment at the dentist tomorrow.

"Oh yes, what time was it?" asked her mum, still somewhat subdued from the day's events.

"Err... in the afternoon. I'll ring you when I get back home and check the appointment card. You never told me Aunt Josie had false teeth," whispered Emma as they approached the porch.

"I didn't know she had!"

Emma eyed her mum suspiciously and then opened the front door. "Right I'm going now but don't tell Aunt Josie that I told you that. Ok?"

"Ok," said her mum, looking genuinely surprised, "See you tomorrow love."

Hi Colin, I won't be in tomorrow, have major toothache. I've managed to get an appointment for tomorrow afternoon. I'm really sorry to keep messing you around. I've been in the wars it seems, just lately. Emma ☹ She hesitated before pressing the send button, did it sound ok? Sighing, Emma held her thumb down and then watched the little envelope animation until the words, 'message sent' appeared. She knew she couldn't keep hiding away from everyone for ever – she had to return to work on Wednesday.

Lying in her bed, Emma listened to the faint noises coming from the bathroom. She'd hardly spoken to Ruby all evening, except for a short conversation about the funeral and how the day went, while Ruby sat pensively on the edge of the sofa, clasping her hands together as if she was praying and blinking away genuine tears of sympathy. The familiar sound of the toilet flushing and the ancient plumbing rattling and humming, throughout the flat, signaled Ruby's departure from the bathroom. Crossing paths in the hallway, they said goodnight, smiled and gave each other a 'high-five' as they went their separate ways.

Emma returned to her bedroom, turning the hall light off as she went. Slumping down onto her bed she picked up the old mobile and looked at it – she thought she'd heard it go off while she was in the bathroom.

Hello Emma, you have been in my thoughts today. I hope it went as well as it could. Andy xx

Thank you Andy, the service was a lovely tribute to my grandad. Em xxx

Let me know if and/or when you would feel ok to meet up again. Very vague text message but you know what I mean. Good night Emma, miss you a lot xx

Ditto xxx Emma cringed, maybe that wasn't a good enough reply, she thought to herself as she held the phone tightly and watched the screen. Before she knew it, Emma had slipped into a slumber where the creature from the murky lagoon was waiting for her, once again.

Chapter 20

Thanks for letting me know Emma. You've been through a tough time lately. Can you let me know tonight, if you're back tomorrow or not (we may need to get cover for you). Regards Colin.

Shit, thought Emma. She had been off work for a while now and the invoices and unpaid bills would be mounting up on her desk. She had to get back to work and deal with everything – including the possibility of ridicule that she might receive from the office staff (and in particular, Dave), when they noticed her missing tooth. There was no point in hiding away. There was nothing the dentist could do to temporarily 'fix' the gap anyway.

Also, if she didn't want to lose Andrew, she would have to see him sooner or later. Perhaps she could tell him that she'd had a fight with Ruby, just after the last time she saw him and her face was healing now. How absolutely ridiculous – Ruby wouldn't fight with a flea, even if her life depended on it. Emma tutted and rolled her eyes at how bloody pathetic she was being...

Trust you're back at work today? Just wanted to say good morning before I go off to work, talk later. Andy xx

Good morning, yes back at work today. Hope to see you soon. Love Em xxx p.s. where do you work lol? It felt so wrong to lie but Emma succumbed to her poised thumb and pressed 'send'.

It was busier than the last time she was here, Emma noticed as she waited in the small queue at the reception desk. The Medical Centre was filled with people of all ages. Some waited to see one of the six doctors on duty others were seated in the dentist area nearby. A stream of young mothers carrying babies in one arm while pushing buggies, laden with 'basic-baby-baggage', strolled into the *'Tuesday – Mother and Baby Group'* room on one side of the building.

"Emma Frey. I have an appointment," said Emma, swallowing the lump in her throat.

"Have a seat," smiled the receptionist, pointing to the few remaining chairs in the dentistry waiting area. Emma smiled back and just for a moment, thought that the woman looked oddly familiar. She wasn't the same receptionist as the last time Emma was here.

"Well done – see, you've done it yourself now. Next time you'll be able to do it all on your own," said Emma's mum.

"Mum, will you keep your voice down, I don't want everyone to hear you!" whispered Emma, frowning with annoyance at her mum's lack of discretion.

"Ok, I'm just saying"

"Yes I know – Ok!" Emma forced a tight lipped smile and then huffed as she folded her arms across her lap. She knew her mum was only trying to be supportive but Emma couldn't help feeling angst about the whole situation, what a great start to the new year this was turning out to be.

The dentist turned around and smiled and then he offered the chair to Emma, "Hello again. Okay Emma, today you'll be having an x-ray. Are you happy to go ahead?" Emma nodded and stared at her mum.

The nurse looked up from the notes she'd been scribbling, "Would you like to come through to the imaging room?" she said as she walked towards the door. Emma dragged herself back off the chair and followed her mum and the nurse. "Could you wait outside?" the nurse asked her mum as she steered Emma in through another door.

In the centre of the room stood an odd looking x-ray machine, hanging from the far wall. The nurse guided Emma towards the hood of the machine, "Ok, I need you to bite down on this," she said, pointing to a plastic piece, jutting out of the machine, "and rest your chin here." Once the necessary checks and procedures had been completed, the nurse began to walk out of the room, "You need to keep really still," she said before she disappeared. The machine began to whirr and slowly it moved around Emma's head as she stood perfectly still and gripped on to the plastic tube, in her mouth. Emma's nerves jangled as the large arm of the x-ray machine circled her head entirely but she tried to think about something else (Andrew) until it was over.

Returning to the dentist's room, Emma and her mum sat back down and waited for Dr Davey to turn around from his computer screen. Expeditiously he tapped away on the keyboard then he stopped, grabbed the mouse, guided the cursor around the screen and then he began to type again, while Emma watched him from behind. After a minute or so, she became bored and turned around to sit in the chair correctly, wondering just when he might be ready to see her.

Moments later, Emma's mum began frantically pointing in the direction of the computer screen, gesticulating to Emma to turn around and have another look.

The images on the screen were crystal clear and they clearly showed the x-ray pictures of Emma's teeth and her one gap. She strained to look closer, over the dentist's shoulder, as he leaned over his desk appearing to study the images intensely. Then he swivelled round on his stool and scooted over to Emma's right side. Reclining her chair, he peered over her, "Okay Emma, can I take another look?" he asked in a gentle tone. Using his gloved fingers the dentist wiggled each tooth in turn, while reeling off a list of dentistry terminology. Some of her teeth hurt as he pinched hold of each one and wiggled it slightly and some of them didn't, but Emma remained calmly seated in the chair, feeling rather brave.

"Okay, well, I'm afraid it's as we suspected Emma. You are in the final stage of periodontitis," he sighed and then continued. "This means you are losing your teeth. It will take extensive treatment to save them but I can't guarantee we can save them all. The disease has eaten away at your jaw bone. Here, take a look…" Dr Davey turned around and pointed to several areas on the image and Emma's mum stood up from her chair and stepped forward to take a closer look. "This is an area of great concern," he said, pointing to her lower jaw bone. "There are possibly 3 or 4mm of bone damage and loss here."

"Can I be put to sleep and have them all taken out?" asked Emma, speaking before she'd even thought about what she was saying. Her mum gasped and the dentist turned around and stared hard at her.

"I may have to remove some of them, like I said befo…"

"No – I mean take them *all* out."

"Emma! Dr Davey might be able to save most of them," her mum said, pointing to the dentist.

"No. I want them all taken out – I want to have false teeth. You don't understand what it's like Mum." Emma turned her head and stared pleadingly at the dentist.

"Emma, no," said her mum.

"Sit down Mum, please."

Emma's mum sat back in her chair and cupped her hands around her mouth, shaking her head as if she was saying 'No... no... no'.

"I want false teeth, can you sort it out?" Emma had suddenly become very determined and direct in her requests. She knew exactly what she wanted.

"Hey, that's a little drastic Emma. You have a very good set of teeth there," he said, pointing to her mouth, "Unfortunately you just don't have the anchors to keep them there."

"Exactly – so I want them gone altogether!"

"I can refer you to the hospital for an appointment to see a specialist to see what their opinion is," said Dr Davey, rubbing his brow and looking to the nurse who stood at the side, still scribbling things down onto a form. She nodded to him and picked up another sheet of paper.

"How long will it take?"

"They can see patients within 10 weeks of the referral..."

"Ten weeks! Could it not be done any sooner?" Emma's eyes opened wide and her mouth dropped open.

"Quite often it's sooner than that," said the nurse, "Most of our patients only wait about 6 weeks."

Emma stared into the middle-distance feeling like she had left the room in an out-of-body experience. Her mind wandered and images flickered through her mind of Andrew and her work colleagues.

"And if the specialist did agree that you should have them all removed, it would take a further 3 weekly appointments to make a set of dentures for you as well. That's once you had an appointment for the extractions." The nurse was clearly trying to be helpful and informative as she possibly could but Emma sat dazed and silent.

"Ok, thank you," said Emma's mum, standing up again. "Does Emma need to make another appointment?"

"Not at the present time if she is set on seeing a specialist, we'll get the referral sent off," said the dentist, "Emma you'll need to book another appointment with us once you have been to the hospital for your initial examination and have a date for your next appointment with them, okay?" Dr Davey looked rather despondent, "However, don't be surprised if the specialist recommends that you don't have dentures fitted for at least 9 months after the extractions."

"What?" Emma shrieked, "I'm not walking around for 9 months with no teeth!"

"It is usually their recommendation as problems can arise after having so many extractions but they have to deal with many people like yourself and would possibly fit your plates immediately for you, if you insisted. They just would not advise it."

"Oh good – I really couldn't be without teeth for that amount of time – certainly not in my job."

"Okay, so all you have to do now then, is wait for your appointment to come through." Dr Davey raised his eyebrows over the rim of his glasses and feigned a smile as Emma nodded and slid off the chair.

The nurse gave her some forms to complete and told her to pay her treatment bill at the reception desk, then she left the room, followed by Emma and her mum who both walked out in silence, after nodding and mouthing a 'thank you' to Dr Davey.

As they walked slowly along the corridor back to the reception desk, Emma cupped her hands to her face and began to cry.

"I'll go and pay the bill honey," said her mum, putting an arm around her shoulder, "Go straight out to the car and wait for me – here's the key."

Emma took the bunch of keys and stuffed them in to her pocket. Aware that someone was walking towards them, she shrugged her mum's arm from her shoulder and then looked up to see the figure of a tall man dressed in the usual blue dentist uniform, as she wiped the tears from her eyes.

Inhaling a sharp intake of breath that sent her head spinning and her stomach churning, Emma felt a veil of burning heat engulf her face, her ears, her eyes...

Her heart thumped frighteningly fast, deep within her chest and her legs became weak and useless as she held her breath and stared in disbelief...

Standing directly in front of her, looking rather shocked and worried by Emma's reaction was Andrew. He mouthed words to her that she could not hear or understand. As the strength returned to her legs, Emma pushed past him and hurried along the corridor, through the waiting area and out to the car park with her mum trailing behind.

"Emma, what the bloody hell is going on?" her mum said as she reached the car where Emma was crouched over, clutching her knees and breathing heavily.

"Let's go Mum, please. Now."

"I need to pay your bill Em..."

"Go then, hurry. I'll wait here," Emma opened the car door and slipped inside. Sliding down the seat, she felt like she was bursting as a sombre bubble of pent-up emotions popped and began to pour out and kept on pouring out. She hadn't cried like this since she was very young. Her worst nightmares were becoming real.

As her mum pulled out of the car park, Emma turned to look back at the entrance to see if Andrew was there but there was no sign of him. Tears fell from her cheeks and she sniffed hard as she reached for a tissue from the glove compartment. Her mind was numb from the frazzled fragments of thought that darted around. A thumping pain began to pound in her head and she stared out of the windscreen absent mindedly, while her mum's questions floated around in the air above her.
"Emma!" her mum shouted, "Will you tell me what the hell is wrong with you? Why did you run out like that?"
"Andrew..." Emma continued to gaze through the traffic ahead, "That was Andrew."
"Oh my goodness, was it really? I saw him looking around the waiting room and then a nurse called him back in to the treatment corridor."
Weaving the car through the two lanes of traffic, Emma's mum headed for her own home, "Come back to mine Em, we'll have a coffee and talk about this."

He was a dentist. How could he be a dentist? Surely he wasn't really a dentist... was he? Emma had spent the last 2 hours crying – crying about her teeth, sobbing over Andrew, grieving for her grandad and everything else that she could possibly think of to cry, sob or grieve about. Her puffy, red eyes and blotchy nose fitted well with her thumping muddled head and buzzing ears. He was a dentist.
Emma's phone had made a sound earlier but it remained deep inside her bag, unanswered. She guessed it would be Andrew, pleading to talk to her. Or worse still,

begging to see her after her strange reaction to his presence in the corridor earlier. He was a dentist. How could he be?

Grandma hadn't quite understood the absurdity of the whole situation and sat listening to the story, while mumbling and muttering about the youngsters of today and how they had things far too easy... and in her day, it was so much harder and how Emma should just deal with things one step at a time.

"You're really not being very helpful Mother. You can see how upset she is about this," said her mum.

But they just really didn't understand – either of them. He was a dentist. It was over. It was finished before it had really ever begun.

"Well I'd be more upset about my teeth than I would a man." Grandma had said.

"She is upset about her teeth, of course she is but she also likes Andrew, very much. You must understand how difficult it is for her, knowing he is a dentist and he works at the very practice that she now feels comfortable with."

Emma had sat with her head propped up in her hands while she listened to her mum and grandma battling it out as if she wasn't there.

"Look, I'm going home now," said Emma, sniffing as she stood up and tucked the chair under the dining table. "Thanks for coming with me today Mum. I'll sort this mess out for myself. I'll give you a call at the weekend – let you know how things are going." Grabbing her bag and coat, Emma kissed her grandma and mum and then hurried out of the door – she did not want to go through any of this again when her dad and Aaron arrived home from work.

"I tried to ring you earlier," said Ruby, as Emma walked through the door, "Andrew has been round asking to speak to you." Emma froze on the spot, ran the words past her numbed mind and slumped down on the sofa, next to Ruby.

"Oh no – really? What did he say?"

"He said he needed to talk to you urgently. He wants you to call him when you get in."

Emma sighed and cupped her hands over the top of her head, trying to squeeze the pain away.

"What's happened? He looked very worried Em."

"Oh Ruby," breathed Emma, "What a mess this is..."

"Why? What's happened?"

"He's a bloody dentist for heaven's sake."

Ruby stopped mid-chew of her apple and looked at Emma in amazement, "Oh!"

Emma stared at her despondently and nodded as her mouth took another downward turn.

"Is that good or bad?" asked Ruby, sensitively.

"Bad Ruby – he works at the same one that I went to today – he's going to know everything about me now." No sooner had Emma spoken, her phone began to ring. Frozen to the spot again, she stared at her bag and waited for the ringing to stop. Moments later the message notification tone came.

There were five missed calls, two from Ruby and three from Andrew along with two text messages.

Emma opened the first message, *Where are you Em? Andrew's just been round asking for you. I'm worried – what is going on? Love Ruby xxxxxxxxxxxxx*

Emma, I really need to talk to you. I know you were very shocked to see me today. Please can we talk about it? All my love Andy xx

Clutching the phone to her chest, Emma felt the burning sensation of tears again. How could she ever get out of this mess now? There was only one thing to do – she had to end their short but incredibly sweet relationship. But just the thought of doing it hurt so much.

I'm sorry Andrew. I think it is best that we don't talk about it. Emma

"What have you said to him?" asked Ruby, finishing the last mouthful of apple and placing the core neatly on top of a piece of pre-positioned paper towel, on the coffee table.

"I think I've just ended it," spluttered Emma before the tears flooded down her face again. Her mobile phone began to ring again and Emma and Ruby just stared at each other, transfixed by the jingly melody. Then it stopped.

"Oh Emma, think about this. Sleep on it and decide what to do in the morning." Ruby could be very wise at the most unexpected of times and this was one of those times. Then the phone started ringing again and the two girls held their breaths for the duration. "You can't let him go Emma, please answer it. He seems to care about you an awful lot," Ruby pleaded with her.

Please think about it. I'll contact you again tomorrow. I'm sorry if I have upset you in some way. Andy xx

It won't work. It can't work. I'm so sorry. Goodbye Andrew, it was lovely while it lasted. Emma. She burst in to tears again.

Colin, you'll be pleased to hear that I'll be back tomorrow. Emma.

Great news, your paperwork is piling up ☺ Colin.

Chapter 21

Morning Emma, I had to send you a message before I go to work, haven't slept all night, thinking about you. Please talk to me tonight, we CAN work this out, I just don't understand??? Andy xx

The warm water was comforting and Emma wished she could stay in the bath all morning to think everything through. But she had to go to work. With a dazed and muddled mind, she dragged herself from the bath and wrapped the warm towel around her. She felt angry to look into the mirror this morning. Annoyed that she had been so wrapped up in her own self pity and ignorance, and so consumed by the appearance of her teeth, she now realised that she had been incredibly foolish to allow it all to come to this.

"Have you nearly finished in there, Em?" Ruby's voice came from the other side of the door.

"Just coming..."

The journey to work was silent, neither of the girls knew what to say and Ruby's earlier attempt to start a light-hearted conversation at home had been flattened before it got going.

Emma steered through the traffic absent-mindedly, re-living the events of her chance encounter with Andrew, the dentist, frame by frame. What must he have thought about her strange reaction? Did he talk to Dr Davey to find out why she was there? She cringed at the thought of him finding out about her dreadful condition. Perhaps he didn't know yet. Maybe he would find out today and not bother contacting her again.

"Emma – where are we going?" asked Ruby as she pointed to *Webb's* car park, disappearing behind them.

"Oh shit, I'll turn at the next roundabout. I wasn't on planet Earth then."

"Are you going to be all right today? I mean, can you cope with all of this?" Ruby looked worried and sat staring wide-eyed at her troubled friend.

"I'll be ok. I wasn't thinking, that's all," said Emma, chewing her bottom lip and feeling quite anxious.

Everyone was going to notice her in the store, and more so because she'd been off for a while. But her missing tooth would give more opportunities for strange stares or whispering behind her back or even blatant ridicule from the office men. As she pulled in to the car park she heaved a sigh and parked in her usual place, at the rear of the building.

"Come on, I'll make you a nice mug of coffee," said Ruby, linking arms with Emma. "I'm sure everything will be fine. Once you've seen everyone you'll feel better." Emma smiled at her friend's kind-hearted words of encouragement and headed through the back door.

"Bloody hell, glad you could make an appearance, part-timer!" shouted Dave, "That was a long-winded hangover Em." Emma rolled her eyes at him and smirked sarcastically.

Laughing to himself, Dave brushed past the girls and whispered in Emma's ear, "Only joking hun, good to see you back," before he trotted off down the stairs.

A straggly piece of tinsel still hung from one of the light fittings but Emma thought how clean everything else looked. Hesitantly, she went over to her desk and found two new letter trays, still wrapped in cellophane, sitting on top of piles of paperwork. Someone had been tidying her desk, she noted, as she scanned the new office stationery items piled in one corner behind her desk. "Is this all for me?" she asked, noting that the other desks were looking well-organised and tidy with their new pen holders, racks and trays.

"Yes, nice isn't it. Jeff brought it all last week. I forgot to mention it to you," said Ruby as she busied herself making coffee and herbal tea.

"Good morning," called Pete, as he walked through the doorway, looking directly at Emma. Turning his head towards Ruby, who was pouring hot water into three mugs, he smiled and softly said, "Hi." Ruby reciprocated with a shy smile and then passed a steaming mug of coffee to him.

"Emma, how are you?" asked Pete, mouthing the words 'thank you' to Ruby as he popped the coffee on to his desk.

"I'm ok, thanks Pete."

"Good to have you back, there's a pile of paperwork for you to sort out there," he said, eyeing the mounds on her desk and smirking.

Somehow, Pete seemed to have changed, Emma thought as she smiled at him tight lipped, of course. He seemed to be more assertive and confident. She couldn't help wondering if sleeping with Ruby was his first time too. There was definitely a spark between them, which had become apparent within seconds of Pete walking into the office.

"Yeah, great," replied Emma, "Nothing's changed then."

The sound of Dave's feet, thumping up the stairs made Pete turn around and return to his desk. Ruby carried a hot mug of coffee across the room and carefully placed it on the new brown, leather coaster on Emma's desk. "Thanks Rue," said Emma as she removed her coat and placed it over the back of the chair.

"So, how ya been then Em?" Dave breezed around the room, looking more like a fairy than ever before, thought Emma as she watched his arms floating around in the air. "Oh shit, I've just remembered, your grandad... err... sorry Em. I'm so up my own arse sometimes I forget things."

"You can say that again," replied Emma, with a harrumph. Ruby sat down and buried her nose in the papers on her desk to avoid getting involved in a potentially crude conversation, while Pete sat across the other side of the room, watching her work.

"Don't worry about it Dave, I'm ok." Emma grinned.

Stopping dead in his tracks, Dave peered at Emma's mouth, "What's happened to your tooth?" he said, moving closer to her desk. Emma froze and stared in his direction, then flicked her eyes across to Ruby – then Pete, both of whom were looking directly at her.

"It fell out – ok. Any more questions?" snapped Emma, just as Colin and Jeff entered the room. Stunned by Emma's sharp reaction, Dave stepped back, held his hands up as if he was about to be shot, then walked backwards to his desk. "Look, I'm sorry Dave. I didn't mean to snap like that."

"Bloody hell, are you two arguing already? She's only been back 5 minutes," said Colin, staring hard at Dave. "What's going on?"

"It's my fault Colin," said Emma, standing up at her desk, "I've lost a tooth and I'm a bit over-sensitive about it at the moment – that's why I was at the dentist yesterday." Amazed by her own revelation, Emma perched on the edge of her desk and continued to blurt out everything. "I've got a major problem with my teeth and I need to have extensive treatment to put them right, but I'm sure you all, or at least one of you, knew that already, judging by the secret Santa present I received for Christmas." Unable to believe what she was saying, she continued anyway, "I do not wish to talk about it, be ridiculed about it or have you all stare at me in pity. I just want to come to work, do my job and then go home so don't even bother trying to talk about it – just leave me alone – all of you!"

The atmosphere in the room turned to ice, one swing of the ice-pick and it would shatter into a million pieces. Ruby looked almost close to tears as she held a sheet of paper in her hands, poised and ready to be thrown into the bin behind her. Pete's eyes darted across, from Ruby to Emma and then back again to Ruby, before he examined the reaction of every other member of the office. Dave stood beside his desk, transfixed on Emma's face. Jeff too, had halted mid-stride and looked anxiously around at his colleagues. Motionless, with his jaw hung slightly ajar, Colin looked at Emma with a glint of empathy in his eyes.

"Emma, get your coat, you're coming with me," he said, in his voice of authority, as he scooped up a folder from his desk and tucked it under his arm.

Emma did exactly as she was told, grabbed her coat and bag, mouthed a message to Ruby, 'I'm sorry Rue' and followed Colin out of the office, down the stairs and out of the back door of *Webb's DIY Store*.

"Where are we going?" asked Emma as they climbed in to Colin's top-of-the-range *BMW*.

"I've got a meeting in London, you can come with me and then I'm taking you to lunch," said Colin, firmly. Then he pulled away from the car park, smoothly and silently, and headed for the motorway.

"So..." Colin paused and looked right as he left the slip road and headed out to the central lane of the motorway, "What's been happening in your world Emma?" Colin wasted no time in always getting straight to the point of any subject. His quick thinking and expert, snap decisions had earned him the position he currently and rightfully held at *Webb's*. He was a kind and thoughtful man, who knew his staff well enough to know when something was wrong and he would be the first to show genuine concern for his workforce.

"I'm losing my teeth Colin, I'm losing everything. I've lost my grandad, I've lost a tooth, I've lost my phone and now I've lost my boyfriend... I've nearly lost the plot!" Emma couldn't believe she was blurting it all out. Tears welled in her eyes but she blinked them back.

"Calm yourself down Emma and tell me all about it – one thing at a time," said Colin, calmly.

"Ok," said Emma inhaling a deep breath, "Well, I've had a problem with my teeth for a long time but I'm so terrified of the dentist that I won't go – well not until recently when my teeth started to get really loose and I was so scared of them all falling out and I keep having horrible nightmares and some of those include everyone in the office and I was so upset about the present, but I'll find out which one of you did it and I know you must all be talking and laughing about me and my teeth, which makes it all worse and I keep getting really bad abscesses and I'm too scared so I don't go and get them sorted out, so I do it myself which I know is really bad for my health but my fear of the dentist has been much worse than the fear of a dangerous infection." Emma breathed in sharply, "I've looked it all up on the internet so I know all about it and there's no point in my family or friends saying to me, 'Ooh – why don't you just take some calming herbal tablets' and 'Aah – I felt like you but once I plucked up the courage to go, there was nothing to it' and then the other day one of my front teeth fell out and when I went to the dentist the worst thing ever happened, my boyfriend was a dentist and I then knew that my nightmares were turning into reality and..."

"Whoa! Slow down!" hollered Colin, "What do you do yourself? What nightmares? Nightmares don't become true Emma. What present? You're rambling and making no sense at all. Slow down, we've got all day!"

Emma sighed and turned to look out of the window at the frosty countryside passing by, as a single tear filled her eye and then plopped down to her cheek.

"Right, one thing at a time and slowly. You've had problems with your teeth for a long time..."

"I'm sorry Colin, I've been such a mess lately and that's without losing my grandad on top of everything else."

"Why didn't you come and talk to me Emma, before you got yourself in this mess. You know I'm always there to listen."

"I don't know... I guess I feel so ashamed and pathetic," said Emma, beginning to calm down again.

"It's not pathetic, I know how you feel Em... exactly how you feel." Colin turned his head sharply, stole a glance at Emma and then returned his gaze to the road.

"Why do you know *exactly* how I feel?" she asked, inquisitively.

"Because I'm petrified of the dentist as well..."

Silence fell in the car and the seconds turned into minutes as Emma peered out of the windscreen at the busy motorway and Colin rested his hands over the steering wheel and stared straight ahead.

The meeting was over quicker than Colin expected. Gathering up her scribbled, shorthand notes, Emma joined him at the double oak doors, smiling and nodding politely at the other members of the board as they slowly departed, one by one.

"You did a great job, they would never have guessed that you weren't my secretary," whispered Colin as they too, left the conference room and headed down the stairwell to the street below. "How about over there," he said, pointing to a Thai restaurant across the road, "Fancy that?" Emma nodded, walked towards the kerb and waited to cross the road with him.

The restaurant was relatively quiet for lunchtime in the heart of London. Colin secured a table for two and they followed the waiter to a small table by the front windows. "Perfect, thank you," said Colin, accepting a menu from the baby-faced man. The waiter scuffled around the table and pulled out a chair for Emma to sit down and then he stood by their side with a notepad and pen poised.

"You like drink sir? Madam?"

The next hour rushed by so quickly that Colin and Emma hadn't noticed the time ticking away as they chatted about Emma's major teeth issue, her grandad and her new or x-boyfriend, Andrew the dentist.

"Bloody hell, I can see why you've got yourself in such a state Em, what a mess. And it's pretty ironic that your new chap is a bloody dentist!"

Emma raised her eyebrows and nodded her head as she stuffed a forkful of noodles into her mouth. It was great to eat soft food and plenty of it. Emma didn't have to worry about crunching down on anything too hard that would cause her further problems with her delicate teeth.

"You're right about the calming tablets too, I'm sure they would probably be of no use to you now that you have got yourself in to such a state about this. However, I'm still not convinced you're making the right decision." Emma shrugged and continued to eat, "Having them all removed is pretty drastic Em."

"I know it is but it's the only option for me. I'm in a different place than you were Colin. You didn't require major work when you had to go, so calming tablets helped you out." Emma said, in her defence, "The dentist can't even guarantee that he can save them all anyway, so I might as well be done with them..." she paused and thought for a moment, "I would be so much happier if I didn't have teeth. I really, really don't want them anymore, however hard it might be to deal with. They consume my every waking thought Colin."

"Ok... I do understand. What are you going to do about your boyfriend though?" Emma shrugged again and felt a sudden pang of sadness fill her. "I think you should talk to him. At least give him a chance Emma – he's done nothing wrong here except gain a very good profession for himself."

"I know but I really can't see it working out now. How can it?"

"It can if you get your head sorted out. You've got the problem with this – not your boyfriend."

"Yeah, I know." Emma had to agree but it didn't make it any easier.

"And I can promise you sincerely that I did not buy your secret Santa present. Nobody has mentioned anything about it. I wasn't even aware of what it was – or anyone else's for that matter – apart from Dave's and I don't think anyone missed him cavorting around showing off his present." Colin smiled warmly.

"I didn't think for one minute that it would have been you. I suppose it doesn't matter that much. If I hadn't been so sensitive about my teeth, I might have seen the funny side of it. After all, look at Dave – he can take a personal joke can't he?"

Colin smiled and gesticulated that it was time to go by pulling his sleeve up and pointing to his watch. Holding his hand up to attract the attention of the bored waiter, propping himself up against a high marble counter, Colin beckoned for him to bring the bill over.

"Get yourself home. I'll send Ruby down and she can go early too, then you can have a 'girly' chat – that's what you girls do isn't it?" Colin laughed, "Wait in your car, I'll send her down in a minute and I'll see you tomorrow morning, bright and fresh!"

Smiling and contented, Emma climbed out of Colin's sleek company car and headed over to her own. Colin had been just what she needed to straighten everything out in her mind. The only thing she was still unsure about was Andrew. She wondered why he hadn't told her before now that he was a dentist, and could a relationship with him ever work out? She really couldn't see it happening.

It was almost 3.30pm and Emma could just see down the side of the building, to the warehouse at the end of the store. A delivery lorry was parked at an awkward angle to the entrance and Emma spotted Darren, manoeuvring his fork-lift truck in and out of the double doors, as he off-loaded the contents of the lorry. Smiling to herself, she wondered how well he had got on with Amanda at the Christmas party. She didn't care either way now, but thoughts of the party soon bought about a sense of sadness as she remembered the whirlwind romance she'd experienced with Andrew. Suddenly, she felt empty once again.

A few minutes later, Ruby arrived, looking slightly confused, "Hello is everything all right?" she asked, climbing into the passenger side. Emma smiled, engaged the gear lever and began to pull away. "Colin's in a good mood. I mean letting me go early. Where've you been all day?"

"He took me with him to London, for a meeting. Then we had lunch," said Emma with a cheesy grin on her face, "I've told him everything this morning. I'm so glad I did Rue, I feel so much better for it. What did the others say when we left?"

"Not much, they were a bit shocked by your sudden outburst."

"Did anyone admit to the present?" asked Emma, as a touch of anger surged through her briefly and then evaporated away, as quickly as it had appeared.

"No... well I didn't hear anything anyway. I think they all feel sorry for you Emma. They're not your enemies – they're your friends." Emma stared ahead at the shinning, frosty road and continued the rest of the journey in contemplative silence.

I haven't got anything to say really, I'm sorry Andrew, let's just leave it at that. Emma. Pressing the send button, Emma squeezed her phone tightly. She wished she wasn't so stubborn – so wrapped up in her own mess. Then she began to type another message. *Why didn't you tell me you were a dentist? Emma.*

"Do you mind if Pete comes round tonight?" asked Ruby, tentatively.

"No, it's fine." Emma's glum expression suggested that she was feeling completely miserable, "I'll stay in my bedroom, no offence Rue, I just don't feel like seeing anyone."

"I could put him off Em. I really don't mind, maybe you and I could have a nice evening together, chatting or something."

"No, I'm fine, tell Pete to come round. I've got no problem with it at all."

I don't normally meet someone and say, 'Oh! By the way I'm a dentist.' It hadn't occurred to me at all that you might have a problem with my profession Emma and why would it? To be honest, I hadn't thought about my job at all since I'd met you and been so swept off my feet! And I don't care if you think that last statement was cringe-worthy – because it's true! Please can we talk properly? Better still, can I see you? Andy xx

Emma's heart raced and her face flushed. She desperately wanted to see him but how could she? Did he know her full dental history yet? She felt too ashamed to see him... ever again.

I'm sorry Andy, it just won't work. I hate dentists and that's why I'm in such a mess. You probably already know that though. In fact you probably know everything by now. Emma.

She heard the front door close and the low murmur of Ruby and Pete's voices as they went through to the living room. Lying on her bed, she stared up at the ceiling and wondered what on earth she was going to do. She couldn't sulk about her self-inflicted teeth problems for ever.

I don't know anything... that's why I want to talk to you. At least let me understand why you don't want to see me anymore. Surely you at least owe me that. Andy.

Hmm, no kisses this time, thought Emma as she slung the phone down on the bed like a stroppy teenager. She remembered how she used to be quite good at acting like a misunderstood, hormonal teenager when she was younger. But she was an adult now and maybe it was about time that she started acting like one, rather than like a spoilt brat.

The phone vibrated first, before it began to ring. Emma picked it up and peered at the display screen, 'Andrew calling', she gulped and then pressed the 'End call' button. Again, the phone rang and she could hear a little voice in her head screaming, *pick it up, answer it* as she watched Andrew's name flashing again.

"Hello?"

"Emma... it's Andy." He hesitated and the moment felt like an age as Emma listened, not knowing what to say to this man who she'd been so close to physically, but who still remained a relative stranger to her. "Emma, please listen before you hang-up..."

"Ok," she whispered, her heart softening at the sound of his deep, calm voice. She'd almost forgotten how he spoke and what he sounded like. The tone of his voice was comforting and sent a shiver of remorse through her tense body and brought tears to her eyes.

"I don't know what is going on Emma. I understand that you don't like dentists but we are normal human beings. You think I know everything that went on when you saw my colleague Will – but I don't. I only know that it was you that saw him because I looked in the appointments book and I presume that your mum was with you. I have no wish to pry into your private business and ethically I would never dream of doing so. I could see from your reaction that you were horrified to see me." Andrew paused, "Emma I'm crazy about you, not your teeth." The phone went quiet and Emma held it to her ear, struggling to find words to say. "Emma, please say something."

"I'm sorry. I don't know what to say... you wouldn't understand. I'm completely screwed up. You'll be better off finding someone else. I'm really sorry Andrew... it was good while it lasted." Her thumb pressed the 'End call' button before Emma had even processed the thought of hanging up and the phone went silent. Bursting into tears she buried her face in her pillow and cried herself to sleep – disappearing deep inside her world of twisted and tormented creatures.

Chapter 22

I won't give up on you that easily. I want to see you at the weekend. PLEASE!! Andy xx

He was persistent – she'd give him that. Emma pondered as she began to get dressed in a pair of black trousers and pale pink blouse. She could hear Ruby pottering away in the kitchen, chopping up her usual vegetable delights, ready for lunch. The week had flown by, it was Thursday already so yet another weekend was just around the corner and the invite to see Andrew too, but could she bring herself to do it? She had to try and find some positivity amongst all of this chaos she'd created. The tearful night had done her some good however and she did feel slightly better this morning. Emma had to get through the next 2 days without getting over-emotional about anything, she needed to catch up with her work-load and re-affirm her professional status within the office, rather than acting like a complete and utter 'Dork'.

"Morning. Did you have a nice evening?"

"Um," replied Ruby as she plunged the small sharp knife into another unsuspecting baby beetroot.

"Everything all right?" said Emma, puzzled by the frown she could see on Ruby's face.

"Um."

"What's wrong, you don't look very happy..."

"I'm fine," snapped Ruby, before placing the knife down on the top, plonking the lid on the container and snapping the clip sides shut. Momentarily stunned by her dear friend's unusual show of emotion, Emma flicked the kettle on.

"Want a herbal tea before we go?"

"No, I'm ok thank you," replied Ruby, sharply, and plodded out of the kitchen and disappeared.

Emma stood gazing at the kettle, waiting for it to boil and wondered what on earth was wrong with Ruby. Had she had a row with Pete? No she'd probably be crying if she had. Yet Ruby seemed positively angry about something.

The ride to work was fragile as Ruby's angry expression had turned to one of pitiful sadness and she looked like she was about to burst into tears at any given moment. Maybe she'd had an argument with Pete. *Shame,* thought Emma, *and at such an early stage in their relationship – but who the hell was she to speak!*

"Rue, what's the matter? Is it Pete?"

"Oh goodness gracious me, please Emma, can we just leave it? I don't want to go into work in tears. They'll think you and I are completely weird."

"I'll pull over or we can sit in the car park... please tell me what's wrong."

"It's nothing, really. Please, let's just get to work," Ruby replied sternly.

"Ok, but I want to know later what is wrong with you. You don't normally get up in the morning looking like someone has just burnt your book collection Rue."

"Um," she replied, blinking away her watery eyes.

Before Colin, Jeff and Dave arrived Emma had noticed Ruby and Pete whispering at the top of the stairs as she sifted through countless bills on her desk. Then Pete walked into the room looking slightly pensive as he headed towards the tea urn.

"Morning Emma," he said without turning his head to look at her.

"Morning Pete, everything ok with you?"

"Yes... you?"

"I'm ok thanks," replied Emma just as Ruby walked back in and without looking up, headed straight to her desk and sat down behind it, burying her nose in a copy of the *Webb's* latest sales pamphlet.

"Are you two ok?" said Emma, "I mean, I don't want to pry but you look like a pair of criminals this morning." Pete and Ruby glanced quickly at each other but said nothing.

"Morning all," said Colin, entering the office and smiling when he saw Emma seated behind her desk. Everyone replied simultaneously with a chirp of 'morning' chorus, which Dave thought was a welcoming chant for him as he strolled in too.

"Morning peeps. It's good to see you Em," said Dave, sounding like he was actually being genuine for a change.

The day sped by quickly and smoothly and turned out to be very productive, especially for Emma. Jeff had taken the day off, complaining of a toothache and at one point during lunchtime, Emma had joked that maybe bad teeth were contagious. The rest of the office staff were unsure whether to laugh or not as she smiled and screwed up her nose.

Ruby and Pete had been decidedly shifty all day as they avoided joining in with any jokes flying around the office (usually made by Dave) and kept their heads buried underneath mounds of paperwork or hidden behind the pretence of the important phone calls they were either receiving or making. They were both unusually quiet but more so Pete – Ruby was renowned for being the quiet, focused type, but Emma just couldn't put her finger on what was wrong or what was going on with them both. They didn't appear to have fallen out because they went out together at lunch time to pick up a sandwich for Pete and a pot of fruit medley for Ruby, so it seemed that they were still an item or at least friendly towards each other. So what was bothering them both? Emma decided she would give Ruby the *third degree* when they got home and uncover the mystery lurking deep in both Pete and Ruby's eyes.

"So what's been going on between you and Pete today then?" asked Emma, point blankly, as she pulled away from *Webb's DIY Store*.

"Nothing, why?" Ruby still had that shifty look in her eyes and had spent most of the day avoiding eye-contact with Emma.

"Yes there is Rue – you've hardly looked at me all day, let alone talk to me." Emma was slightly annoyed by her best friend's nonchalance.

"It's nothing, honestly Emma... I... I'm just tired."

"Being tired does not mean that you avoid someone and spend all day in clandestine meetings with Pete."

"Um... I don't know, nothing's wrong."

"I don't believe you Ruby."

The rest of their journey home was quiet and thoughtful but the atmosphere was thick and heavy. Emma felt very uncomfortable – it was so unlike Ruby to be acting in this secretive, solemn way, she had to find out what was wrong.

Hello Emma, could we meet up at the weekend, even if it is just for a coffee in town and even if it is just to end it. If there's nothing else left, let's at least split up on a caffeine rush. PLEASE! Andy xx

Yes ok, Emma. She hesitated before sending the text. She did want to see him but she was scared, of what, she didn't really know. Even if it was just to end the relationship, it was still like living in her nightmares. She felt so ashamed of her own stupidity and the way she had let things get out of hand to this extent. She almost wished she could meet him somewhere where it was very dark and then at least she could smile at him and pretend everything was ok. Then they would fall in to each other's arms and everything would be good. But it wasn't going to happen like that and she knew it. Emma pressed 'send'.

Great, meet you at Jimbo's at say, 12.00pm on Saturday? Andy xx

Ok. See you then Em.

Popping the phone back into her bag, Emma strolled through to the kitchen where Ruby was busily scrubbing large potatoes, in preparation to throw them in the oven to bake for an hour. "I'm meeting up with Andrew on Saturday, just for a coffee." Emma smiled nervously, waiting for another snappy reaction from Ruby, which thankfully was not forthcoming this time.

"Oh that's good. You should really sort it out Em. I am so pleased to hear that." Ruby opened the oven door and tossed two potatoes onto the rack, before flipping the door up with her foot.

"What's been wrong with you today Rue? I don't like it when you're not happy, or dare I say it, angry?"

"I said before, it's nothing. I'm fine can we just leave it at that? Cheese?" said Ruby, holding a block of mature cheddar in her hand.

"How about cheesy beans, would you like that?"

Ruby nodded and then sliced through the block of cheese with a large knife.

"What are you doing at the weekend then? Are you seeing Pete?" Emma desperately tried to inject some pleasantries into the strained atmosphere which she thought might pop if Ruby lost control of the knife she was using to chop an innocent onion.

"Not sure..."

"Ruby, is everything all right between you and Pete?" Emma paused and thought for a moment, "You're not pregnant are you?"

"No I am not!"

"Ok, ok, I just thought I'd ask as you haven't been at all happy today. I'm getting a bit annoyed actually that you won't tell me anything Rue."

"Nothing to tell," she replied without looking up from the cherry tomatoes which were waiting for their moment of doom under the cutting edge of Ruby's knife.

"Well what's up with Pete then? It's either you or him. I saw the way you were both whispering in the office today..." Emma suddenly jumped from the sound of the knife that Ruby had been holding, hitting the worktop before it bounced off and went dangerously diving to the floor.

"Oh, I'm going to have a bath before dinner," squeaked Ruby as her eyes filled with tears and she ran off out of the kitchen.

Emma stood speechless, propped up by the sink and watched three cherry tomatoes roll off the edge of the kitchen worktop, one by one, *plop... plop... plop.*

Good. I can't wait to sort this out. Even if it's not good news at least you could tell me why. Until Saturday, Andy xx p.s. coffee and cakes (if you would like) are on me ok?

Ok, thanks. Em ☺

"Rue... the spuds are ready... come on." Emma called through the bathroom door, "Do you want mayo with yours?"

A muffled voice replied, "Yes please, I'll be out in a minute." Emma could tell by the slight quiver in Ruby's voice that she had been crying, just as Emma had suspected.

They ate dinner in silence, except for the television which twittered in the background. Now and again Ruby would sniff and brush the back of her hand under her nose.

"Ok, I can't bear this anymore," shouted Emma, plonking her knife and fork on to the plate with a loud clatter, "What the hell is going on Ruby?"

Ruby looked up, startled by the sudden outburst and tears began to pool around her eyes again as she gulped down a mouthful of food.

"Well? You need to tell me Ruby or we will fall out, big time!"

"Oh..." sobbed Ruby, "I can't te... tell you."

"Ruby! Yes you can – you can tell me anything." Emma tried to reassure her, "Come on, please."

"No... I... I can't," stuttered Ruby, before leaping up from the sofa and running off to her bedroom, crying her eyes out.

Emma followed after her and met with a slammed bedroom door in her face. Hesitating before she knocked, Emma wondered whether she should pursue her questioning or leave it for another time.

"Ruby, I won't come in but please remember that I'm always here for you. I'll stick by your side, whatever the problem is. I mean, look how supportive you are to me. Please let me help Rue." Emma listened intently through the door, "Ok, well could you just tell me one thing at least." She waited but no reply came, "It's nothing to do with Andrew is it? You haven't found out something else about him that you're not telling me, have you?"

"No," a shaky little voice replied from the other side of the door. "It's nothing to do with Andrew at all."

"Well, who is it to do with then?"

"No one... please leave me alone Em. I'm ok really. I've just got over emotional about everything that's been happening, like I always do."

Emma could totally understand and had to agree one hundred percent on that one. But this time she just had that feeling that there was something else as well. Something that Ruby was not telling her and possibly something that involved her, by the way Ruby had been acting towards her – and Pete for that matter.

"Ok, I'm going now, talk to me if and when you're ready Rue. I care about you and don't like to see you like this." Turning to walk away, Emma could hear the sniffles and sobs coming from Ruby's room and wondered what on earth could be so wrong with her best friend. The mystery was driving her crazy and momentarily, Emma was compelled to call Pete to find out what was going on, but then she decided against it, just in case it was nothing to do with him, which could possibly stir things up even more for Ruby. She resigned herself to the fact that she would just have to wait patiently before she could begin the slow process of draining every ounce of energy from Ruby, until she gave in and told all.

Just before she went to bed, Emma gently tapped on Ruby's bedroom door again, and waited... nothing. Ruby hadn't come out to get her dinner and said she had a bad headache when Emma told her that her baked potato was getting cold. With her heart pounding in her chest, as if she was an intruder in the house, Emma pushed the bedroom door open and saw Ruby tucked up in her bed, fast asleep. *Damn*, thought Emma, closing the door. It would have to wait until the morning now. Great! Another sleepless night lay ahead because she was so worried about Ruby. Emma only hoped there wouldn't be any nasty beings coming to visit her dreams again tonight or worse still, a devil-dentist in the form of Andrew.

***

"Morning, are you feeling any better?" said Emma, poking her head around Ruby's bedroom door.

"I've got a terrible headache, could you tell Colin I won't be in today," whispered Ruby.

Emma could just make out two little, blood-shot eyes peeping over the duvet, "Ruby, it's not like you to miss work. What is the matter?"

"I just don't feel very well... that's all. I'll be ok if I go back to sleep. Please apologise to Colin for me."

"And what about Pete?"

"Tell him I've got a migraine and hopefully I'll see him tomorrow." Ruby pulled the cover back over her head and curled into a ball under the quilt.

"Rue, I'm getting seriously worried about you. If you don't talk to me or tell me what's wrong... well... well, I'm going to speak to your parents."

"Promise I'll talk to you tonight. Sorry Em, my head is thumping."

"Ok, as long as you keep your promise. I've hardly slept all night, worrying about you."

"I will... pinky promise," said Ruby as she pushed her little finger out from under the quilt and held it up in the air.

"Ok, pinky promise." Deflated, Emma closed the bedroom door and headed to the kitchen to make a much needed large mug of coffee, before she went to work.

Her saving grace was that it was Friday and she'd managed to get through the week much easier than she initially thought. The one problem with it being Friday was that tomorrow would most definitely be Saturday – the day she was meeting Andrew. Emma squirmed at the thought of seeing him – what was he going to think of her? He was bound to notice her missing tooth before she even began to tell him about it and she knew she had to explain everything to him if they were to stand any chance of reconciliation.

Strangely, no-one else seemed to have noticed at work though (apart from the office staff obviously), or had they? Perhaps they were all being very polite down on the shop floor or maybe Colin had held a secret meeting to threaten all the staff of *Webb's DIY Store* not to mention Emma's tooth problem at all or they would be instantly dismissed from their posts.

Emma laughed to herself and padded through to the living room with her steaming mug of coffee, at least she could laugh about the problem now which she supposed was a step forward.

Darren had been up to the office once and had spent most of his time cracking jokes about the Christmas party and his blossoming relationship with Amanda, head of the 'giggle-girl' gang but Emma had noticed that he didn't look at her any differently. In fact, he had actually winked at her again (which did not have the same effect as the last time he had looked at her flirtatiously).

This morning, Emma seemed to have a renewed vigour and felt optimistic about her meeting with Andrew tomorrow. After all, what was the worst that could happen? They could both chose to go their own separate ways, after the coffee and cakes of course, and that was probably about as bad as it could get.

"Morning," said Emma as she walked in to the office past Pete, who was leaning over his desk, scribbling something on a piece of paper.

"Morning," he replied, without looking up.

"Ruby won't be in today, she's got a bad migraine."

"Not like her to be off," said Pete, still looking down at the paper on his desk, "A migraine?"

"Yes but I think it's been brought on by worry. She's not herself Pete."

"Why what's wrong with her?" Pete shot a glance at Emma and then turned away to the kettle and began making coffee for two.

"Don't know – she won't say. I thought you might know."

"Why would I know?" Pete snapped back. "Sorry Em but I don't know why she's got a migraine do I?"

"I'm sure you don't Pete. I just wondered if you knew why she's been so unhappy for the last day or so."

"Nope. Don't know why." Pete continued to stand with his back to Emma as he busied himself preparing mugs of coffee while he waited for the kettle to boil.

"Ok, what about you? Are you alright?"

"Yes, why do you ask that?" Pete turned around and eyed Emma suspiciously.

"I was just wondering Pete, that's all. You seem to be as bad as Ruby, what's wrong with the pair of you for heaven's sake?"

"Nothing, I'm fine... coffee?" Emma nodded and sighed as she slipped her coat off and hung it on a hook. "I'll call her tonight, check she's ok," said Pete, nonchalantly.

"Ok, I just thought..."

"I'll call her ok?" Pete scoffed.

Again Emma nodded and gave a half-hearted smile just as Dave appeared in the doorway, beaming as usual and looking around the office.

"No Ruby?" he asked, looking at both Pete and Emma.

"No..." Emma and Pete replied simultaneously and then continued to busy themselves, while Dave slipped off his jacket and looked around puzzled.

"Why's she not in then?" asked Dave, feeling the tension in the air.

"Headache" replied Emma without looking up from her desk.

"Blimey, what's wrong with you two this morning?"

"Nothing." Again, the same simultaneous response came.

Dave tutted and went to his desk to sit down, rather sulkily. His entrance this morning hadn't had the usual effect of being a big one – full of admirers and colleagues, speechless in awe of his presence. "Can see this is going to be a long day," he harrumphed and began to sieve through the papers on his desk.

Emma and Pete remained silent with their heads down and everyone sulked together – about what? They didn't really know.

Jeff was off again and Colin didn't arrive in the office until way past eleven o'clock. The other three had worked silently during the first part of the morning and had each taken a break at separate times. They made excuses to avoid sharing a break by making out that they 'just had this to finish', or they just had to 'tie up these loose ends', or they just had to 'nip down to the shop floor to sort something out'. All in all, Emma, Pete and Dave had pretty much ignored each other all morning and the atmosphere was like a sheet of thick, black smoke when Colin turned up.

"Morning," he said firmly, as he trudged over to his desk, next to Emma and plonked a briefcase on the top. "It's quiet in here this morning." No one said anything but they all looked up and gave him a half-hearted smile or nod. "You look like a bunch of concentration camp prisoners – has someone's cat died or something?" Colin cringed and realised his words may have been slightly inappropriate because Emma had just lost her grandad and because someone's cat may have just died, but then Colin couldn't think of anyone that might have a cat.

"You know Ruby's not in today don't you?" Emma broke the trio's silence. "Did you get my message?" Colin nodded and sat down, still wearing his overcoat on top of a dark grey suit.

"Not like her to have a headache or take a day off. In fact I think she's the only member of staff that has never had any time off – apart from holidays."

"She really wasn't good this morning," said Emma, looking over at Pete from the corner of her eye. Colin noticed Emma's sly glance and also peered over at Pete, who continued to work with his head down, ignoring everyone.

"She's not pregnant is she?" laughed Colin and then stopped abruptly as he realised he'd probably done it again when he saw Pete's horrified reaction.

Pete had raised his head and dropped his jaw, staring wide-eyed from Emma to Colin and back again, like his eyeballs were on a relay circuit.

"I'm sorry mate, only joking." Colin tried to retract the comment, "No, I hear she has a migraine. Not the same here without our Ruby, is it?" He looked down and picked up a pen and then began to drum it on the side of the mahogany desk.

"I'll be off out again in half an hour. I don't expect I'll be back today – more bloody meetings," said Colin, tutting and raising his eyebrows.

Emma smiled weakly and looked across to Pete, who had returned to studying the paperwork in front of him. Dave too, had steered clear of any involvement in the conversation and continued to sulk. He was probably *Webb's* sulkiest employee when he wanted to be and Emma had always thought that he should win an award for it.

Lunchtime arrived and everyone breathed a sigh of relief. The strained atmosphere of the morning had faded slightly but it still felt to Emma, like there had been many words un-said during the morning.

Colin had left the building a while ago and the three remaining office staff had quietly got on with their duties while the phone rang from time to time, only once had it been Mr Kibble at the end of the phone but Pete and Emma could tell by the way that Dave raised his eyebrows, slumped back in his chair and rubbed his forehead, that Mr Kibble had some new, strange requests for *Webb's DIY Store*.

Emma hesitated before leaving the office, in the hope that Dave would disappear and then she could talk to Pete again, undisturbed. "Anyone want anything from Halley's?" asked Dave, slipping his jacket on and checking his wallet. Both Emma and Pete shook their heads, mumbled an incoherent, 'no thanks' and smiled awkwardly.

"Ok Pete, I know something is going on between you and Ruby," said Emma, once she was absolutely sure she'd heard Dave stand on the squeaky step at the bottom of the stairs and then the sound of the back door closing. "I know there's something funny going on. Rue hasn't just got a headache."

"Told you... I don't know. I'm going shopping." Pete snatched his coat from the peg and hurried out of the door before Emma could reply.

Speechless and confused, Emma stood in the middle of the empty office and wanted to scream.

How are you feeling? Love Em xxx

Much better, I'm sorry Emma. Could you tell Colin I am so sorry for taking the day off and I'll do overtime to make up for the lost time today.

He's out of the office all day – just text him. See you tonight, hope we can have a chat ☺ love Em xxxxxxxxxxx

The afternoon was much the same as the morning had been – tetchy, tedious and glazed with a thorny hush. As the clock on the wall slowly moved around the hours, Emma sighed every once in a while. She mulled over the idea of standing up and bellowing out a statement of facts about the ridiculous situation she had come to find herself in with her two estranged colleagues and scowled across the room at them from time to time. However, her better judgement prevailed and she just sat quietly and got a surprising amount of work completed and tied up. Much to her relief, the minute hand finally made its way round to the number 12, while the little hand just about reached the 5 and that was it – time to go home.

"See you tomorrow," said Emma, grabbing her coat and slinging her bag over her shoulder. Both Pete and Dave mumbled, 'goodbye' as she left the room and headed for the top of the stairs, feeling annoyed. *Stupid bloody idiots,* she thought and trotted down the steps with a sudden 'Friday feeling' in her heart.

Sorry I've been a miserable person today Emma. Hope you have a good weekend. Pete.

Thank you and don't worry about it. I'm just worried that you and Ruby are upset with each other, or maybe even me? I just don't know? Em

It's not you, honestly. Talk to you on Monday Emma.

Ok, no worries. You're lucky that I like you both – have a good weekend. Will you be seeing Ruby over the weekend?

Yes – hope so ☺ Pete.

Me too ☺

Chapter 23

"You really shouldn't have done this Rue," said Emma, dragging out a chair from underneath the small, rectangular table in the kitchen. The table was set for two people and every effort had been made to present their best set of crockery on top of the white, lace tablecloth that Ruby's parents had donated as one of their house warming presents, when they moved into the flat. Ruby pottered around the kitchen, draining saucepans of water, stirring others and checking the contents of the oven.

"I wanted to apologise for last night and thought you might like this," Ruby replied.

Moving across to the fridge, she pulled out two pre-prepared, prawn cocktails, elegantly displayed on two white plates. She'd obviously gone to a lot of trouble with the way she presented the starters. Each one had a single, large leaf of lettuce laid out on the plate which was surrounded by blue coloured seafood sauce (Emma could only assume) which had also been carefully formed in to a wave pattern. Each lettuce leaf was filled with prawns in a pink sauce and one trimmed spring onion lay across the lettuce leaf, on each side, sticking out to the edge of the plate. To top it all, Ruby had placed a slice of (crust removed) white bread on the top via a cocktail stick. Her magnificent creations looked like little rowing boats on the sea, although they also had a sail, in the form of a single slice of bread, held up by the cocktail stick. But whatever they were, Emma decided that the duo-powered sea vessels were absolutely fabulous little works of art.

Placing them gently onto the table, Ruby smiled sweetly and then returned to the fridge to collect two side plates with buttered brown bread on them.

"Ah, this looks lovely Ruby. You really didn't have to go to all this trouble, especially if you weren't feeling well earlier."

"I wanted to Em. I felt so bad about everything... I'm really, really sorry."

"Oh, don't worry about it; just tell me what has been wrong. I've got a sneaky feeling it's something between you and Pete, as he has hardly said a word to me all day."

Ruby picked up her fork and began to gather up a prawn, dripping in seafood sauce, some lettuce and a piece of spring onion that she had chopped up.

"It didn't need to come to this. You know you can tell me anything Rue." Emma hadn't touched her starter and watched Ruby eating hers for a minute. Ruby's creative masterpieces looked too good to eat, Emma thought before picking up her fork and tucking right in.

"Let's enjoy this first and then we can talk afterwards." Ruby gave one of her melt-any-heart smiles and continued to tuck in to her beautifully-made, prawn cocktail.

"Ok," said Emma, resignedly. "What's for main?"

"You'll have to wait and see," said Ruby.

Looking forward to seeing you tomorrow at 12. Andy xx
Ditto. 12pm it is. Em.

Emma placed her phone on the side table and stretched her legs out along the two-seater sofa. She'd eaten far too much but the meal that Ruby had made was truly delicious. The main course had consisted of a mouth-watering mix of unusual vegetables (Ruby always liked to experiment with different and quite exotic vegetables, especially when they were available in the local supermarket), roasted potatoes and a meat and nut loaf, which Emma found to be surprisingly nice. She'd never liked the sound of Ruby's nut loaves before, but today she'd tried it out of politeness and was pleased that she had.

Dessert was something else – a 'Ruby creation', all of its own. Biscuit crumbs sat on the top of a bed of mixed berries in a fruity sauce and then a thin layer of sponge, soaked in brandy followed by a dollop of thick cream. On the very top, Ruby had drizzled toffee sauce and chocolate shavings.

"What is this, I've never seen anything like it before? It looks very yummy though," said Emma, politely.

"Upside-down dessert," replied Ruby with a squeaky giggle. "I thought I'd try something different. I did it all the wrong way round... sort of."

Now, Emma was so bloated, she could hardly move and the only comfortable way to sit on the sofa was to spread out along its whole length, while she waited for Ruby to bring two *Baileys* coffees through to the lounge.

"Washing-up all done," said Ruby as she entered the room, carrying the drinks.

"That was so nice of you to cook all of that food Rue. Thank you so much, I owe you one." Emma smiled and took the mug from Ruby.

"Oh, it was nothing. You're my best friend," said Ruby, curling up on the opposite sofa, "I wanted to do it for you. You've had a hard time lately and you deserved it."

Emma could sense that there was a 'but' or something more sinister coming. "Come on then, what was wrong with you yesterday?" Emma sipped the sweet, alcoholic beverage.

"I got so upset because I didn't know what to do Em."

"About what?" asked Emma, desperately trying not to burn her lips, but wanting to drink more of the coffee.

"About Pete."

"What's wrong with Pete, I knew it was to do with him. I hope he hasn't upset you Rue."

"No, it's not like that." Ruby hesitated as if she was deep in thought, "He's done something that I wasn't happy about."

"Oh no, another woman?" asked Emma, still sipping.

"No, not that," replied Ruby, coyly. "I don't know what to say. I don't know how to say it."

"Right, I'm totally intrigued now – tell me," Emma propped herself up further on the sofa, in case she slid off it completely.

Ruby peered down into her mug of coffee, like she was contemplating her next string of words carefully.

"It can't be that bad, surely," Emma added.

"It was the other day when you went out with Colin." Ruby began to sip her coffee too.

"After my explosion in the office – yes?"

"Yes."

"What happened then?" Emma was becoming more intrigued by the second, "So this is to do with me as well – is that why Pete has been a bit funny with me too? He sent me a text tonight to apologise for being 'off' with me."

Ruby sat motionless and looked quite petrified. Her big blue eyes stared ahead and appeared to gaze right through Emma, to the window behind her. So much so that Emma turned around to check that nothing was behind her – like a giant, black, house spider or something else, far more horrible and scary, maybe even something from her dreams.

"Um," said Ruby, absent-mindedly.

"Go on then, tell me," said Emma trying to hide the agitation building in her voice.

Ruby's eyes refocused and she appeared to snap back into the here and now. For a moment Emma thought that she was going to start crying again as her eyes looked very moist. Tilting her head questioningly, Emma waited for a response.

"Well we all had a talk after you left."

"Oh? About me I guess."

Ruby nodded, "Everyone was really concerned about you. They all care about you, you know."

"Yes, ok. Carry on..."

"Well, after the chat, Pete went very quiet and didn't seem to be himself," said Ruby, struggling to find the words to carry on.

"Yes?"

"We went out at lunch time together and that's when he told me. He feels so awful Emma. He doesn't know what to do. And then we had some more words that evening when he came round. He didn't want you to know but I disagreed with him."

"About what?" asked Emma, shifting further up on the sofa. Taking a large gulp of coffee, her eyes began to smart as the hot liquid slipped down her throat.

"It was Pete..." Ruby bowed her head as if in shame and gazed into her mug which was tightly gripped in the palms of her hands.

Emma briefly wondered how Ruby's hands were not burning. "What was Pete?"

"It was Pete who did it," Ruby paused, "Err... you know... Pete did it." Tears had actually welled in Ruby's eyes for sure this time as she peered across the room, on the brink of a watery explosion.

"Did what? I don't understand Ruby." Emma thought she sounded overly aggressive, "Come on Rue, spit it out – it's no big deal."

"Secret Santa..." Ruby set her mug of coffee on to the side table and padded into the kitchen to grab some kitchen roll. Returning to the lounge, she blew her nose and sat back down.

"What? So it was Pete that bought my presents?" Emma was amazed rather than angry, like she thought she might have been once she'd found out who it was that gave her such a cruel and insensitive present. "I can't believe it..."

"Um," replied Ruby, looking somewhat dumbfounded that Emma hadn't actually hit the roof with rage.

"I... I just can't believe it... is that why you've been acting like this?"

"Um," said Ruby, nodding her head in little movements while peering from underneath her fringe with watery, blue eyes.

"Oh Ruby, it didn't need to come to this. You could have told me sooner." Emma felt a strong urge to leap off the sofa and go and hug her friend tightly but she resisted. She didn't want Ruby mistaking her lunge towards her as an impending attack. "Is that why Pete has been a bit funny with me?"

"Um," said Ruby, "He feels terrible. I'm so sorry Emma"

"Why did he do it then? And you don't have to be sorry, you haven't done anything Rue!" Emma's emotions were beginning to swing towards disappointment and a slight agitation began to build inside her again. "Why did he do something like that if he was going to regret it?" The tone in her voice was beginning to change, "Do you want a drink?"

Ruby shook her head and picked up her half mug of coffee, gripping it tightly, with both of her trembling hands.

Emma jumped up off the sofa and headed for the kitchen – this news required another alcoholic drink to help her mull it over.

Returning with a large glass of *Baileys*, Emma sat down and gulped a substantial amount before placing it on the table beside her. "So, why did he do it if he felt so bad?"

"You don't understand Emma."

"Well explain it to me then," said Emma reaching for the glass again, "Come on, I'm not angry Rue. I'm completely amazed that Pete would do something like that. I didn't know he had a dark side to him."

"He hasn't Emma... that's just it. He's been so stupid and realises that now." Ruby took another gulp of her cooling coffee, "He meant no harm by it, honestly. I just couldn't believe it when he told me though. I said to him that we couldn't carry on seeing each other unless he told you that it was him that sent you the present." Hiding her face in the mug, Ruby then peeped over the rim again at Emma who was rolling her eyes up to the ceiling and shaking her head.

"You mean you've finished with Pete?" asked Emma, more astonished than before.

Ruby nodded, "He was so worried about you finding out and he didn't want me to tell you. I said that I couldn't live with secrets, when you had so desperately wanted to know who had done it."

"So you have really finished with him?"

"Um," replied Ruby.

"Why have you both been whispering in corners and going out at lunch together then?"

"Because he wants us to stay together. We've been sort of arguing about it all this time," said Ruby, sniffing and wiping a hand across her nose.

"Oh my God, I don't believe it – this is madness." Emma gulped another mouthful of *Baileys* and tucked the almost empty glass into her lap.

"He didn't mean to hurt you Emma..."

"What – so he just thought I'd laugh about it? He, like everyone else, had probably noticed my teeth were bad. I just don't get how he thought I would find it funny!" Emma gulped down the rest of her drink and suddenly felt the warmth of the alcohol inside her – it felt good. Jumping up, she went back to the kitchen and poured herself another large *Baileys*. "You want one?" she called through to Ruby.

"No thank you."

Ruby had finished her coffee and sat tightly curled-up on the sofa, when Emma returned, feeling flushed and slightly tipsy. The alcohol was, yet again, going to play havoc with her gums but she didn't care too much right now. "So, what now?" asked Emma.

"I need to let you know why he did it."

"Oh go on then." Emma laughed, "Not that it will make any difference – he still did it."

"It's not like that, he feels really stupid now and had no idea that you would see it differently," said Ruby, pulling herself upright on the sofa. "You had told him at some point when you were both out dog-walking, that you hated dentists."

"Did I? Don't remember that!"

"Well, he bought the electric toothbrush for you because he'd seen an advert about them and how they were supposed to be better for you than a traditional toothbrush." Emma laughed out loud and took another gulp from the glass in her hand. "He thought it would keep the dentist away if you had a really good toothbrush," added Ruby.

"Oh for goodness sake," said Emma, unsure about how she was feeling, now that the alcohol was beginning to set-in, "And the wind-up teeth?"

"Well, you know he used to have a thing for you..."

"Glad you said 'used'," replied Emma.

Ruby smiled sweetly. "Well, he gave you those as a sort of message really."

"A message? What sort of message?" Emma was feeling quite tipsy now and the whole evening was turning into an amusing night of revelations.

"It was meant to be taken as, 'fancy a chat' or something like that, maybe it was, 'wanna chat' or 'I love chatting to you'. I can't remember exactly," said Ruby, looking anxious as she waited for a response.

When Emma had finished laughing hysterically (almost spilling her drink) and holding her aching tummy, she took a deep breath and sighed. "Oh dear Rue, what a ridiculous state of affairs this has all been."

"Um," replied Ruby, looking nonchalant as she shrugged. "So you're not really angry then?"

"How can I be – it's ludicrous," she laughed. "Why don't you text or call him and tell him to come round then we can sort it all out?" said Emma, feeling more than slightly tipsy now. "You shouldn't finish with him Rue."

"Ok, but maybe you shouldn't give up on Andrew either..."

Pete looked pensive as he walked into the living room, biting his bottom lip and clutching his hands together in front of him. Following him in to the room, Ruby sat on the sofa with him. "Right, we... err... we need to get this all... err... out in the open... and err... and be done with it... don't we?" slurred Emma. "I obvi... ously took it all the wrong way, didn't I?"

Pete and Ruby sat motionless on the opposite sofa, looking uncomfortable, like a couple who had just come to visit an estranged great aunt, with a speech impediment.

"I'm really sorry Em, I just didn't see it the same way that you did. I had no idea about your teeth before... well, before the beginning of this week." Pete sounded like he was pleading for forgiveness and his words had the effect of making Emma burst into raucous laughter yet again, while the alcohol continued to muddle her mind and take over absolutely everything. Pete and Ruby just stared at her with dead-pan faces, unsure of what to do or say as their friend made a complete fool of herself by laughing so much that she rolled off the sofa and ended up flat on her face on the floor.

Less than an hour later and Emma had been carefully guided to her room under Ruby and Pete's supervision. Laying her down on the bed fully clothed, they tiptoed out, turned the light off and shut her bedroom door quietly. The night had become theirs alone and they could now rekindle their love affair without upsetting anyone.

Chapter 24

The crisp and frosty January morning lay under an oppressively gloomy, grey cloud cover, just outside Emma's bedroom window. She opened her eyes wide and strained to focus as her muddled mind tried to make sense of the day... the time... the previous evening. Turning her head to one side, her senses kicked in and the pain inside her head became prevalent – hangover. Emma rubbed her forehead and then moved her fingers over her eyebrows, trying to rub away the thumping pain that seemed to be beating in rhythm with her heart.

It was Saturday morning and as consciousness began to dawn, Emma abruptly stopped rubbing her aching head. *Shit – Saturday – Andrew!* Glancing over at the alarm clock on the bedside table, her eyes widened as she took in the red, illuminated numbers and the time of day began to compute. *Oh no – 10:36.* Jumping out of bed as if she'd been electrocuted by the mattress, Emma grabbed her dressing gown from its hook on the back of the door and headed to the kitchen and more importantly the kettle and the medicine drawer.

"Morning," Ruby mumbled, peering sleepily over the rim of her mug. Propped up by the kitchen cupboards, she had that usual, worried expression on her small-featured face. "It's just boiled," she said, indicating with a small pointed finger, towards the kettle. Emma smiled weakly, flicked it on and then proceeded to root around in the drawer for some pain killers. "Have you got a hangover?" whispered Ruby.

"Yeah, a bit of one," replied Emma, becoming frustrated when she found the foil packet of tablets, only to discover that there was only one left. "Guess that will have to do." Closing the drawer with a flick of her hip, Emma prepared a mug of coffee and momentarily puzzled over why Ruby was standing in the kitchen, mug clasped between her hands and watching Emma's every move. "Are you ok?" she asked.

Ruby nodded, "Yes I'm fine."

"What time did Pete leave? I don't even remember saying goodbye... or going to bed for that matter."

"About 20 minutes ago," said Ruby, peeping wide-eyed over the top of her mug of steaming coffee.

"Really? He stayed the night again then?"

"Um," mumbled Ruby. A smirk appeared on her face and she raised her eyebrows, "He'll be back later. We're going out tonight."

"Well I'm glad you've sorted everything out." Emma moved across the kitchen and began to leave the room, "It's just my warped world to sort out now then, one way or another," she said while looking back over her shoulder, before she disappeared into the lounge.

"Rue!" shouted Emma, "Rue... come in here quick!" Emma returned to the bathroom mirror and studied her reflection again.

"Are you all right in there?" asked Ruby from the other side of the partially opened door.

"Yeah – come in." Emma continued to stand at the sink examining her image, which presented itself with a ridiculously, over-exaggerated grin. "Look!" She pointed to the mirror, "It's going!"

"What's going?" Ruby leaned over and stared into the mirror too.

"The gap – look!" Emma pulled down her bottom lip and they both gazed at the small space in awe.

"Ooh, that's strange," whispered Ruby, turning to Emma and squinting straight into her opened mouth. "How has that happened?"

"I think they've all moved," said Emma, turning back to the mirror with a finger hooked over her bottom lip, pulling it downwards to the bottom of her chin.

"Ooh," breathed Ruby in astonishment. "How have they done that?"

"I don't know... I did think the other day that it looked a bit different but not as much as this."

"Perhaps it was all the *Baileys* you had last night," said Ruby, trying to sound light-hearted and 'jokey'.

"Exactly!" said Emma, letting go of her bottom lip creating a *'Pop'* as it sprang back into place.

"Really?" Ruby looked puzzled.

"Yes – really! Alcohol always makes my teeth loosen. They've all moved round and spread out." Emma was high-spirited, the big gap that she'd had before had now turned in to two smaller gaps. It appeared much more normal and far less noticeable. Her gums were slightly inflamed, but Emma couldn't care less how they felt today, as long as she looked reasonably ok. "It looks better doesn't it?" she asked, hooking her lip down again and thrusting her face closer to Ruby's.

"Yes... yes it does Em."

"They're really loose though," said Emma, wobbling three other teeth on the bottom row, with her tongue.

"Ugh – that's not good Emma." Ruby looked in disgust and then turned her head away. "You have got to get them sorted out otherwise they'll all drop out."

"I will, don't you worry. I've made my mind up, I'm having them all removed and that's my final decision." Emma grinned and turned back to the mirror to smile at herself and move her mouth around in lots of different ways. Ruby stood speechless in the bathroom, watching her friend go through her usual and rather absurd ritual, in a daze of despair and disbelief, for she knew how serious Emma really was.

Her headache had dulled slightly which made it easier for Emma to search fruitlessly through her wardrobe, trying to find something to wear. It had to be right. She had to look good. Although the sun had peeped through the ash-grey sky once or twice, it was still freezing outside. Emma's favourite, grey jumper-dress was too grey for a dull day like today and she felt that she needed to wear something bright to match her renewed mood. *That'll have to do,* she thought, reaching for a crumpled up, heavy-cotton, fitted dress. She'd have to run the iron over it but the well worn, red dress had always looked great when paired with her knee-length, high-heeled black boots and her black, suede jacket with a fake fur collar.

Peeping out of the bedroom window, Emma could just see that the conifer trees, over on the back road, were gently twitching in a slight breeze. She would leave her hair down in a tumble of waves and flicks cascading down her back like a lion's mane, as it wasn't too windy.

Hi Emma, are we still on for coffee? Andy x

Emma read the message twice, which sent shivers running through her. Nervous and worried, but strangely excited too, it felt like an age since she'd seen him or spoken to him but Emma's resolve was far more prepared for the possible onslaught of ridicule and rejection today.

Yes, I do hope to be there on time... running a little late at the moment though. See you soon. Em xx

"How do I look?" asked Emma, standing in the doorway of the lounge. Ruby looked up from her *Mills & Boon* as Emma twirled around, holding her arms out to the sides.

"Lovely," replied Ruby, smiling in admiration. "You look really nice."

Emma smiled back, slapped her hands down to her sides and then shrugged, Well if he doesn't like me anymore, because of my teeth, it's his loss," she stated firmly, with a stiff upper lip.

"He will... he does like you Emma, I'm sure. Just remember, he has wanted to see you all the time – it was you that called it all off."

"Yeah, I know." Shrugging her shoulders again in an exaggerated gesture of 'oh well, we'll see', Emma picked up her black bag, rummaged through to check she had everything and then left the flat.

The town centre was already buzzing with bargain hunters, looking to pick up a new outfit or some cheap shoes in the January sales. Large, red letters and numbers jumped out from every window display and nearly every single one showed a percentage sign reduction in varying degrees. Single people, couples, small groups and families all hurried from one shop to another, wearing cheesy grins at having bagged a bargain. They all held on to their branded carrier bags, proudly swinging them backwards and forwards, just to prove that they'd been in the best shops.

Emma nervously made her way through the precinct towards Jimbo's café, her dry mouth and rapidly beating heart made her feel even more worried about the pending rendezvous with the most handsome man she had ever met – even though he was a dentist. Trying to catch a glimpse of herself in the shop windows, she almost bumped in to several passers-by. Just up ahead, she could see the illuminated sign of the café and felt like her heart had rushed up to her throat to play music with her tonsils. She paused, looked around and then suddenly changed direction, heading straight for the *Littlewoods* store and more so, the shop's toilets to check herself in the mirror yet again.

Two elderly women were standing chatting at the sinks in the ladies room. Emma hesitated before turning right into a vacant cubicle, closing the door behind her. She didn't want to use the lavatory – she only wanted to check in the mirrors before she went into the café to meet Andrew. Her doubting fear had raised its ugly head yet again and the self-images flickering through her mind's eye were appalling.

Seated on the lid of the toilet, Emma waited until the two women had left the room before she flushed the toilet needlessly and exited the cubicle. Time was ticking by and Emma noted that it was 11.55am. Looking up from her wristwatch, she stared into the mirror – she had to hurry up. She looked fine, why had she worried so much? Why did she always have a grotesque image in her mind of how she must look to others? Her nightmares really did haunt her all of the time.

The café was packed full of hungry and thirsty shoppers. Emma peered around the edge of the window, scanning the circular tables, covered in red and white checked cloths. Then she scoured the two-deep queue at the serving hatches. No

Andrew. Casually, she strolled along the length of the four large paneled windows and door, to the other end, peering inside all of the time. Halting on the other corner, Emma turned around and surveyed the precinct, as far as she could see. No Andrew. *Maybe he is inside,* she thought as she began to feel a little embarrassed by her strange behaviour hovering outside of the café like she was stalking someone.

Again, Emma strolled back past the front windows, peering intently in to the café, searching... searching. Anger began to bubble away in her stomach as she realised how stupid she was probably beginning to look. Why hadn't she just gone inside and ordered a coffee? That way, she could have looked around and waited for him if need be, while looking totally normal, drinking coffee in a coffee shop.

Unable to bring herself to stop, turn and enter the café, Emma moved swiftly across the precinct to the *Specsavers* shop opposite and walked straight inside. Cursing under her breath, she stood by a rack of glasses frames and pretended to look at them while peering straight past them and out of the window towards the café.

"Hello, can I help you at all?" A man's voice made Emma jump and she turned around to face the scrawny looking, smartly dressed, young man.

"Err... no... thank you... I'm err... I'm just looking thanks," said Emma. She felt flustered and slightly pathetic. The young man smiled and stepped back, nodding his head in acknowledgement.

"Just let me know if I can help at all," he said, with a puzzled expression on his face. "We have got some good deals on those frames today." The young man pointed to the frame rack behind her.

"Oh ok... err... good... yes, thank you."

"May I ask? Do you currently wear glasses madam?"

"Err... no... no I don't."

"Ah, I see. We have some excellent offers for our first time customers. Would you like to book an eye test madam?"

"Err, no thank you... well not at the moment thanks. I would just like to look at these," said Emma, turning and pointing to the frames in the window display.

"Ok, that's fine madam. Please let me know if I can help at all."

Emma nodded her head and then grinned wryly, "Yes, thank you." Then she turned back to the frames rack.

Averting her eyes from the rows and rows of frames of all different colours and designs, she stared back out of the window and across the precinct to the café on the opposite side... and there he was. Andrew stood just in front of the doorway peering up and down the precinct in just a short sleeved, green checked shirt. He looked just as handsome as she'd remembered him and her heart fluttered in her chest as she turned around, smiled at the young, male assistant and left the opticians very quickly.

Chapter 25

"Hi," said Andrew, softly. Emma almost swooned at the tone of his voice – he sounded incredibly sexy. "Why did you go shooting off? I saw you walk past a minute ago and then you disappeared." He laughed and then hesitantly, leaned over to peck her on the cheek. Emma reciprocated with a twist of her lips onto the side of his face before pulling away coyly. "Come on – I've got a coffee in there," he said, indicating the café door with his eyes. Grabbing her hand, Andrew pulled her in to the café and they weaved through the tables, full of dining customers, to the far end where his padded jacket hung over one of two chairs at a small table tucked away in the corner.

He is a true gentleman, thought Emma as he pulled the opposite chair out and offered a seat to her.

"Coffee?" he asked with that same glint in his eye that always seemed to turn her to jelly.

"Yes please and sorry, I... I just panicked and ended up going in the opticians. Silly of me really," she replied quietly and smiled straight into his eyes. Andrew winked a lash-laden eye before he turned and walked over to the queue.

Emma watched his every move, his muscular build was appealing to most young women who caught a glance of him and likewise, the men too seemed to take a second look at his tall and strapping figure that stood out in the crowd. *He really does not look like a dentist*, thought Emma, or maybe she had a warped view of what dentists should look like. Perhaps her nightmarish image of a crouching *Gollum*-like figure, leaning over a murky pool of filth and dripping saliva from its rotted teeth was imprinted on her conscious mind and lived outside of her dreams as well as in them. But then, wasn't that hideous figure her subconscious portrayal of herself, not the dentist.

Emma shook her head to dispel the vision and pulled her arms from her coat and hung it over the back of the chair. Looking up she noted that Andrew was gazing across the café, in her direction. He smiled and Emma's heart skipped. Smiling back through tightly clamped lips, she shifted uncomfortably and realised that the awkward 'you never told me you were a dentist', conversation was inevitable.

"I wasn't sure if you would be here already so I just popped over to the opticians to have a look at their frames," said Emma, as Andrew placed 2 large mugs of frothy coffee on the table.

"Ah, I did wonder where you went off to, do you need an optician as well?" he laughed.

Emma froze unsure whether he was joking or whether the ridicule was just starting.

"Ok," he said shaking his head, "Maybe I shouldn't have said that – I am sorry."

"It's fine, don't be sorry."

"This is my second one," he said, raising his mug. "Wasn't sure if you would get here early or not and I had nothing else to do so I thought I would have one before you arrived."

"Oh, I see"

"I think we need to talk about things don't we?" The tone of Andrew's voice had lowered even more as he spoke.

Emma nodded her head and curved her mouth downwards, before reaching for the handle of the mug – she didn't want to drink it yet, it was far too hot but she needed something to hold on to.

"I had no idea Emma –it never occurred to me that you didn't know what I did for a living, I thought we had been through all of that at the Christmas do. I certainly would never have imagined that you might have a problem with it," Andrew half whispered, while leaning across the table.

Staring deep in to his eyes, Emma realised that he was absolutely right. How could he have known she was petrified of people in his profession?

"I got your text on the morning I bumped in to you... you know, the second one about what did I do for a living?" Emma nodded her head, remembering that she had sent it. "I was too busy to answer it and had decided to text you later that day. But then, obviously, it was too late and everything bad happened and it all went to rat shit." Andrew drew a breath and sighed. Gripping the hot mug, he looked deep in to Emma's eyes as if he was wondering what her response was going to be.

"I'm sorry, I know it all sounds... well, it sounds totally crazy but I really can't help it. I am sickeningly terrified by dentists and haunted by my own teeth." Emma pulled the mug to her lips and tried to hide behind the milky froth, precariously balancing around the rim.

A momentary silence fell upon them as Andrew followed suit, picking up his coffee mug and gently slurping the creamy froth from the top.

"I really didn't know Emma. I'm so sorry that we've ended up like this."

"So am I," whispered Emma, blinking away the prickling sensation that comes just before a teardrop. Although she felt like she just wanted to burst in to a flood of supersize tears and fall in to his embrace in a faint, like on the old black and white movies, she just couldn't let herself weaken in front of him. "It's not going to work is it?" Emma swiftly glanced at his surprised expression, "I mean... well, surely it can't. I am the one with a big problem here Andrew."

"I would like it to be my problem too."

That was it, there was no way Emma could stop the well of watery droplets that seeped onto the rims of her eyes. Blinking quickly, she looked across the café and noticed that everyone else was engaged in conversations, engrossed in eating their food or staring dreamily out of the large windows at the front, watching the busy shoppers rushing by. No one had actually noticed that Emma was having a major crisis right here, in the corner of the café. She was just a table number, another person sitting in a café on a Saturday afternoon, drinking coffee. She really wasn't the grotesque monster that she thought she was. Placing her mug back on the table, Emma looked in to his eyes – they were pleading eyes, seductive and loving.

"Please come back to my place when we've finished these," said Andrew, holding up his mug and eyeing it. "We could talk about it much easier there. No strings, I promise. If you really feel there is no future for us, I'll... well, I'll leave you to decide that but you are welcome to come back to mine even if it is just as a friend, for one last time."

"I can't... I'm different. I've changed."

"What do you mean, how have you changed?" asked Andrew, looking puzzled again. Emma pulled her bottom lip down, revealing the small gaps in between two of her teeth. "I hadn't even noticed Emma, so how have you changed?"

"I've lied to you Andrew. It just won't work – it can't work – one of my teeth fell out last week. I've been avoiding you and that was before I even knew that you were a dentist." Emma sighed, "I'm sorry, I've got too much of a hang-up Andrew. I can't even go back to that dentist now. I just don't know what to do anymore." Emma began to sip the hot drink hastily, burning her lips. If she was going to leave, it had to be very soon. Now or never...

"Look, we'll go back to mine and then you can start back at the beginning and tell me everything. What do you say?"

Emma gave in very easily and nodded her head while the rim of the mug remained attached to her lips. What else could she do? She didn't really – not for one minute – want to walk out of the café and never see Andrew again. She had to tell him every gory little detail about her secret fear and what it had done to the health of her mouth and teeth and her state of mind, if this was ever going to work.

Aware of Emma's anxiousness and sensitivity, Andrew reached across the table and took her hand in his, "I care enough about you to help you through this Emma. Please don't push me away when I can really help you."

"Ok," agreed Emma and pulled away from his hand to retrieve a tissue from her coat pocket, "I'll come to yours," she said, nervously. Andrew smiled, then cupped both of his hands around his mug and drank the sweet coffee, with a warm and sincere smile on his face.

Andrew was already indoors by the time Emma parked her car in front of his on the side road. Nausea had hit her as she drove to his flat. She was incredibly anxious and decided that she had spent most of the New Year feeling this way and more so during the short time that she had known the real Andrew – the dentist. As she stepped out on to the pavement, she inhaled a deep breath of crispy air in to her lungs and held it there, hoping the sickness would go when she let it out. It didn't.

The communal door had been left slightly ajar so Emma pushed it open and entered the building. The familiar smell of cleanliness helped to make her nausea disappear. Tentatively she began to climb the stairs to Andrew's flat, her heart pounding with every step.

"Come on in," called Andrew as Emma reached the open front door and hesitated, she was sure that her heart was beating in her throat. "I've just put the kettle on if you'd like another coffee."

Slowly, Emma inched her way through to the small kitchen and leaned against the fridge door, coat wrapped tightly around her with folded arms.

"Shall I take your coat?" he asked, holding out a hand.

Emma shook her head and pulled the coat even tighter, "No, it's fine. I'll keep it on for a minute thanks."

"Do you want another coffee? I've got some biscuits too; they're in that top cupboard behind you. Custard creams I think. I never did get around to buying you that cake that I promised you, did I?"

Emma smiled. "That's ok," she replied and then turned around to search for the custard creams in the cupboard. She was hungrier than she'd realised when she saw her favourite biscuits – she wondered if that was why she had felt sick, a few minutes ago. Passing the unopened packet to Andrew, she slowly removed her coat and hung it over the back of the chair. Her heart was galloping at a pace but she knew she had to go through with this revelation and the outcome would simply be a case of 'kill or cure', as far as their fragile relationship was concerned.

"So... start at the beginning," said Andrew, placing the cups on to two black, leather coasters, on the glass coffee table, "I want to know everything, that's if you're sure that you want to tell me everything." He looked at her and smiled warmly. "Or at least tell me enough, so that we can get over this and carry on seeing each other."

Emma sat and stared straight through him, wondering exactly where to start and what to say – it all seemed a bit silly now.

"I know one thing for sure," he smiled again and laughed, "After all the years of study and training, I can't possibly change my job."

Thankfully the awkward atmosphere had been broken and Emma laughed too.

The daylight was dimming so Andrew switched the table lamp on which cast a warm glow across the room. "Another one?" he asked, picking up Emma's cup. She smiled and nodded.

They had been talking for over two hours and Emma's mouth felt quite dry. Things really weren't as bad as Emma's warped mind had made them seem. Yes – she did have a big problem with her teeth, or as Andrew pointed out, her gums, not the actual teeth, and yes – it was not going to get any better unless she took action and yes – he completely agreed with her after much deliberation and offers of alternative treatments (such as, having her teeth removed and screwed back in, at a cost of around £10k) that if that was what she really wanted (to have all her teeth removed), then that was the right thing for her to do.

Andrew had worn his *'I am a dentist and our ethos is always to save your teeth'*, hat from time to time but realising the extent of Emma's fears, he backtracked slightly and eventually understood that she just couldn't go through any other type of treatment unless she was completely unconscious every time and that would not happen on a regular basis. He even offered to help speed up the process by contacting the right people and getting her seen as soon as possible at the local hospital, by an orthodontic surgeon. "If this is truly the route that you want to take Emma then I completely understand you, but it will not be an easy one," Andrew had said in a gentle and kind way.

"I know," she'd replied, suddenly realising just how real it all was.

Feeling warm and cosy, Emma pulled off her boots and curled up on the comfy sofa, while listening to the clattering of cups in the kitchen. She began to muse over their long conversation and wondered how their relationship actually stood at this present time. Were they still in a sexual relationship or had it become more of a friendship and supportive practitioner/patient bonding? Unlike any other time that Emma had been with Andrew, the lustful excitement and insatiable appetite to tear each other's clothes off hadn't been there over the last couple of hours. Maybe the subject of conversation wasn't exactly a turn-on. Or had it gone deeper than any of that?

Chapter 26

4am on Sunday morning – what was she doing wide awake at this time? Rubbing her forehead, Emma stared hard into the mirror. Tousled hair rested upon her shoulders and the previous day's make-up had smudged under her eyes giving her a look of someone that might have had a heavy night of alcohol or maybe even drugs. Her appearance was not at all appealing at such an early hour.

Emma shuffled silently in to the kitchen, wearing only a dressing gown and hesitated before filling the kettle with water. Would it be ok to help herself, she wondered as she turned the tap on to barely a dribble and held the spout underneath. She knew that coffee would just prolong her insomnia but she desperately needed a drink and a think – some time alone to ponder her next steps and get everything in to some sort of order.

Checking her mobile, Emma noted an unread message had been received around midnight. She opened it up and read it, in the comfort of the living room.

Glad to hear you're not coming home (without meaning to sound horrible...hee hee!). I guess that everything has worked out fine then. Happy for you, love from Rue xxxx p.s. if you come home early, hope you don't mind but Pete is going to stay here. Love from Rue (again...obviously!) xxxx.

Emma placed the phone on the arm rest and smiled, she couldn't reply at twenty past four in the morning, it could wake Ruby and Pete. Emma was sure they would be none too pleased by that.

Emma's thoughts wandered to the previous evening's chain of events. There had been a very long discussion... and then sex, somehow a different kind of sex. She shook her head at the craziness of her carnal contemplation. She'd worried earlier in the evening that possibly their relationship had changed due to her revelations, but now she knew that everything was just the same as it had been when they'd met previously – a torrid affair of lascivious, wanton need. Their minds had conversed without language, their bodies had exuded intense passion, their spirits had shared a mutual pleasure – they were one and the same. Feeling warm and content, Emma curled up on the sofa with a mug of coffee and listened to the wind battering at the window pane.

Everything was going to be ok.

"Good morning, well, only just," said Andrew, from the opposite end of the sofa, as Emma opened her eyes and adjusted to her blurred vision. "Couldn't sleep?" he said, eyeing the cold cup of coffee on the table.

"Hmm," replied Emma, dozily, "I woke up at about four."

"We couldn't have gone to sleep until two." Andrew laughed. "I'll make you another one."

"Thanks."

Making a quick escape to the bathroom, Emma checked her appearance in the mirror, splashed her face with warm water, dried it and then dragged her fingers through her hair, in an attempt to comb it. She looked a lot better. Brushing her teeth with toothpaste and a trusted finger, she felt ready to take on whatever might lay ahead. She had no plans for today so she would happily just go with the flow – whatever 'the flow' entailed.

Tip-toeing through to the bedroom, she dressed herself, tidied Andrew's bed covers and plumped the pillows. "You don't have to do that," said a voice behind her. Emma jumped and turned around. "Where are you rushing off to?"

"Nowhere, I just thought I'd help," Emma laughed.

"Do you fancy going to that café again, for breakfast?"

"Sure, why not," replied Emma, as she thought about the last time they'd had breakfast together and then spent the rest of the day having sex. Her mind made an instant decision – yes, she was willing for that to happen again.

"You know…" Andrew paused and moved towards her, "Emma, I still don't think that you realise…" Placing his big hand on the back of her head, he pulled her to him and brushed her lips with his. "You are so beautiful, inside and out – teeth or no teeth – it really wouldn't make any difference to me." Then he embraced her while Emma's head swam around in a dizzy spin.

Maybe it didn't matter anymore. Maybe dentists really were human beings with thoughts and emotions and empathy and sympathy…

Maybe Emma quite liked dentists, after all.

Epilogue

The buzzing inside her head grew louder and then changed – turning in to the fuzzy, distant sound of a woman's voice...

"Emma..."

"Um" Emma replied instinctively, from deep within her throat. Eyes closed tightly, she didn't dare lift her heavy eyelids – she was too terrified to move in any way. Every inch of her body, every muscle, every nerve ending, tingled and twitched, she was returning to a conscious state slowly but surely.

"Emma." The same voice again – close yet far away.

Emma felt something touch her gently on the shoulder, warmth penetrated her skin. The sensation of what Emma thought was a hand, nudged her and then lightly shook her.

"Emma... wake up Emma."

Her mind wandered through the past and in to the present trying to make sense of the strange situation she was in. Peeling her eyelids open, she viewed her surroundings... blurred, jumbled, bright lights and a figure in blue, leaning over her. She closed them again and let the tears seal her safely inside.

"Emma," the voice was louder and clearer, "I need you to wake up now... come on... open your eyes."

The hand took her by the shoulder and rocked her from side to side very gently. Emma felt agitated through the jumbled mess of her drug-addled mind. She wanted to stay safe, stay behind closed eyelids, stay inside herself. Then she wouldn't have to face what she had done.

Gagging, spluttering, dribbling and crying. Emma struggled as the suffocating feeling of being chocked by something large, stuffed into her mouth, consumed her.

"Deep breaths... take a few deep breaths Emma," the nurse, in blue advised. She brushed Emma's straggled, damp hair from her face, "Come on now calm down – breath through your nose. In... and out, there you go and again... in... and out." The plump nurse took a glass from the side table and filled it with water, "I want you to take a sip and have a swill round," she said, placing a cardboard dish in one of Emma's hands and the glass in the other. Emma did as she was told and sipped the cold water through her swollen, slightly grazed lips. Gagging again, Emma dribbled the contents in to the dish and stared at the bloody mess of gloopy saliva. This was no dream or nightmare – this was real.

The taste of metal filled her mouth, the bloody saliva pooled underneath the plastic plate fitted to her lower-jaw and more oozed from the upper one. The plates supported a full set of false teeth. Her own had gone. Her mouth was filled with what felt like giant sized teeth fixed on to hard plastic plates. The plates seemed to reach down the back of her throat, causing her to retch as her tongue tried to find a place to rest in the alien surroundings.

She could almost control the gagging reflex now as long as she concentrated hard, she was coming round – the anaesthetic was wearing off. The panic meant that she couldn't breathe easily, she couldn't smile, she couldn't speak... she couldn't do anything. Oh God, what had she done? How could she live like this? What did she even look like? She'd waited for this for 3 months – had she made a terrible mistake?

"I'm going to sit you up Emma, that will help," said the nurse as Emma began to gag once again. The bed slowly rose at one end and Emma moved to a half seated position. It did feel better... but oh, what had she done? She continued to worry, as she drifted in and out of consciousness.

Some forty five minutes later Emma was wheeled around on her bed, to a small ward where Andrew was waiting anxiously. "Hey, "he whispered, leaning over the bed and stroking her hair, "It's all done now." He kissed her gently on the forehead and gazed in to her sleepy eyes.

"Um," she replied – too scared to speak.

Another nurse came trotting in to the room, carrying a tray, "Hello Emma, you will need to have a drink and eat something before we can let you go home," she said, before placing the tray on the table beside the bed. "Here's a cup of tea, a strawberry yogurt and some ice-cream and jelly – eat it up now and then you will be able to go home." Emma stared at the little tubs of dessert and screwed her nose up at Andrew.

"Just eat a bit of it darling, then they'll let you go."

Emma sighed and reluctantly picked up the small cup of wishy-washy looking tea. She placed the rim on her lips (lips that felt like they belonged to someone else) and attempted to sip the tea. Instantly, the warm drink began to run down her chin and trickle further down her neck. She'd missed her mouth. "Can't", said Emma, from inside her closed mouth. She placed the tea cup back on the table despondently and looked desperately at Andrew.

"Try the ice-cream," he said, passing the small tub and a plastic spoon to her. "You've got to eat something or they'll keep you in overnight." Emma took the tub and spoon and proceeded to pick up a small lump of very frozen ice-cream, still covered in ice crystals. Forcing herself to open her mouth, just slightly, Emma placed the tip of the spoon on her bottom lip and then used her top lip to pull the cold dessert in. Where did it go? Momentarily, Emma was unaware that she had anything in her mouth – she couldn't feel anything – but then a cold burst of vanilla hit the back of her throat and she knew she had eaten it. She then understood. She had a long, long way to go.

***

1 Year Later

Time truly is a great healer in many ways – physically and mentally. Emma's gums had healed from the extraction of 28 teeth and 4 wisdoms. She learned to live with wearing dentures – she was happier and confident – she learned to talk, eat (after losing over a stone in weight) and most importantly, she learned to sleep with them in. She never wanted Andrew to see her without them. Although he obviously knew about them, if he didn't see, it was easier for him to forget, and he was forgetting.

Emma had slowly shifted from the soups and liquid stews and progressed to tackling mashed foods. It was a joyous day when she ate a single baked bean and she felt like telling the whole world, 'I can eat a baked bean now!'

There were so many things they hadn't told her about wearing dentures – like getting small pieces of food stuck underneath the plates in the middle of a restaurant and having to make excuses to go off to the toilets to remove and clean them and then end up getting herself in a sticky mess when she tried to fix them back in to place in a hurry.

In the early days soon after surgery and before she was allowed to wear a denture glue (before the stitches came out), no one told her that if she sneezed (and she was a horrendously big sneezer, but thankfully not often), she could fire her top plate across the room at a dangerously, fast speed. No one told her that if she laughed too much, her teeth would drop out into a mug of tea and splash everyone around her.

Emma had laughed her way through all of the mishaps and her famous last words were always, 'Well, it comes to nearly all of us – just wait until you've got them!' But Emma was happier; she didn't have to worry about getting abscesses anymore, she didn't stress over the fact that her teeth were getting wobblier by the day, she no longer obsessed over the bathroom mirror and the terrifying creatures of her nightmares had vanished back in to their own miserable existence completely.

***

For the sake of Emma's dignity and their relationship, both Andrew and Emma had decided that she should find another dental practice for her routine check-ups in the future. That way, they could disconnect themselves from her old hang-up and his job. It worked. They were truly in love.

One year down the line and Ruby and Pete were still going strong as well. Ruby had changed from the book-loving geek she once used to be and now would much rather enact the storylines from her *Mills & Boon* novels – much to the terrifying anticipation of Pete.

Emma spent much less time at home and could often be found pottering around or cleaning Andrew's flat when he was doing late shifts, while Pete spent more time at Ruby and Emma's flat.

The staff of *Webb's DIY Store* had been amazing. Emma had never realised just how sympathetic and supportive the men in the office could really be. They had helped her out wherever they could. They fetched, they carried and they would beg, borrow or steal if they had to. Most importantly – they really did care. The huge pile of paperwork on Emma's desk shrank daily and almost disappeared as she regained her confidence and focus. She was almost on a par with Ruby for desk tidiness.

Pete was now looking to move up to head office for two reasons. 1 – He wanted the promotion and 2 – he felt that his and Ruby's future would be even better if they worked in different offices. Emma and the others had to agree that a separation would do Pete the world of good as he often spent his hours in the office daydreaming in a very slushy way, whilst he gazed lovingly and lustfully at Ruby, who was still seated across the room from him. Everyone knew when he had partaken in sexual activity the previous night as the look on his face could only be described as that of a soppy, love-struck teenager.

"You'll be sat at your desk, dribbling all over your paperwork in a minute Pete," scoffed Dave, one day.

Ruby, on the other hand, had always remained calm and demure with her nose buried in her work – as was the norm for her.

Darren had split up with Amanda after just 11 weeks and had spent the next 8 months, working his way through the rest of the 'giggle-girls'. Emma felt somewhat relieved that she hadn't managed to hitch up with him at the work's party, two Christmases ago, as she now saw him in a completely new light. He was *Webb's* very own lothario. The girls on the shop floor all wanted and lusted after him and would actually *pay* to take him out for the night if they had to. Darren had them at his beck and call but Emma felt that the time would come when he would slip up and his ego would fall.

Emma's grandma was slowly learning to live without her beloved Charlie (Grandad), but everyone in the family kept a close and watchful eye over her. Emma's mum raced around from her home to her shop to Grandma's house and back again, in a never ending loop – throwing in a bit of cleaning, shopping and organising, here and there as well. As for Emma's dad... well, he just remained the same old dad, living on the outside edge of the eternal 'loop'.

***

It was a freezing cold February evening and Emma really didn't feel like going out with the group of girls from the shop floor and Ruby, but Amanda was having her 29th birthday bash in the city centre and everyone, who was anyone, just *'absolutely had to come!'* Emma really couldn't understand why everyone had to go on about Amanda's birthday so much – it wasn't exactly a big one like one of the big 0's. But Amanda was like that – she had to have everything big and it always had to be about her.

"Well I consider this to be my best birthday yet – it's my last twenty-something birthday and I need to celebrate its passing," she said, adamantly.

However, Emma would much rather have stayed indoors at Andrew's place and curled up on the sofa with a Chinese take-away and a bottle of white wine.

What time are you all going out tonight? Andy xx

About 8pm, they're all meeting here at 7pm. We've got a mini bus hired, can you believe it?! lol xxx Why?

Oh, I just wondered, hope you have a nice time. Love you xx

Love you more. Em xxx

Ruby and Emma tottered around the flat getting ready. Hair done, nails done, make-up done – Ruby was now an expert in turning herself in to a hot diva at every available opportunity and seemed to have a part-time personality to match her glamourous evening wear. She had grown her naturally platinum blonde hair to her shoulders and had it cut in to a beautiful looking, inverted *Bob*.

"The girls are here," Ruby squealed from the front door, as five young women piled in to the flat, reeking of too much perfume and heavy lipstick.

Emma downed a large glass of *Baileys* and adjusted her hair in the mirror. By the raucous sounds coming from the living room, Emma guessed that Amanda and the 'giggle-girls' were probably drunk already. She glanced in the mirror again. She looked great with her new teeth and the slinky little red dress that Andrew had persuaded her to buy for the last Christmas party.

Missing you. Andy xxx
Ditto but more xx
Have a good night baby. Love you xx
Love you too. See you tomorrow. Em xxx

"Em..." shrieked Ruby, already half drunk on one large glass of *Baileys*, "Someone's at the door for you..."

"What?" replied Emma, curious as to who would be here to see her at this time on a Saturday evening? Taking one last look in the mirror, she smiled and left the bathroom.

"In the living room Em." called Ruby.

Emma could hear a lot of noise and babble coming from their living room as she slowly pushed the door open.

Emma froze on the spot and gawped.

"What the hell are you doing here?" she muttered. Perplexed and motionless, she stared hard.

"I just thought I would pop round to make sure that you were dressed properly, before you go out," said Andrew, smiling beautifully at her.

Unusually for a Saturday, he was dressed in a smart pair of black trousers and she could just see a lilac shirt and purple tie underneath his jacket.

"What? I don't get it. What do you mean? Where are you going, all dressed up? I've just been texting you – I don't get it Andy." Emma felt extremely puzzled and slightly embarrassed by Andrew's unexpected appearance and his strange words.

The 'giggle-girls' looked in bewilderment from Andrew to Emma and back again.

"Oh, I'm not going anywhere, I... I've been out... err... anyway, look at you," said Andrew, rather shakily.

Emma just stared at him bewildered and speechless, had she not just been texting him or was she going insane?

"You can't go out looking like that?" Andrew said, quite seriously.

Emma wondered for a moment whether he had gone completely mad. How could he come round here, just before she was due to go out and tell her what he thought she looked like or that she couldn't go out because of what she was wearing?

Emma was rooted to the spot in the doorway, not knowing quite what to say. "Andrew, what's the matter? What's going on?" The other girls gawped, speechlessly at Emma and then they all turned around simultaneously to stare at Andrew.

Amanda appeared to be still holding her usual cool composure of loveliness and Ruby held her head down, staring at her feet, which was a normal trait for her when situations looked like they may be getting a little tricky.

"Andrew?" Emma said, darting her eyes around the room, "Are you ok?"

"You're not dressed properly. Quite blatantly, you are under-dressed!" Andrew smirked and stared straight in to Emma's eyes.

She felt her face flush as her mind spun in turmoil at the madness of the situation – what the hell had got in to him?

Ruby continued to focus, intensely on her feet and scuffed one shoe backwards and forwards across the carpet.

Amanda folded her arms and peered across the room as if she were bored and awaiting another onslaught of ridicule and embarrassing comments from Emma's one true love.

The girls continued to glare in Andrew's direction, disbelievingly.

Tugging at the hem of her short dress to try and pull it down towards her knees, Emma replied desperately, "I really don't understand what's going on Andy, why are you here?"

"To make sure you are dressed properly before you go out anywhere."

"Why? What's wrong?" asked Emma, peering down at her dress and then her shoes.

"Something's missing... you would look better if you were wearing more."

The young girls were not giggly anymore as they shuffled around uncomfortably where they stood. Amanda and Ruby looked across the room at each other dead-pan faced.

Emma could feel the acidic bubble of hurt beginning to rise from her chest as she tried to comprehend what Andrew was saying and why he was in her flat, uninvited, in front of her friends and work colleagues, trying to make her look stupid. He was also making himself seem like an obsessive, controlling boyfriend – which he wasn't.

"Come here," he said in his usual, gentle tone and smiled at her. Andrew held out a hand and beckoned her over.

Hesitantly, Emma stepped across the room, past Ruby and Amanda and took Andrew's outstretched hand. "What?" she muttered.

"If you'll take this from me..." he said, as he began to lower himself to one knee, "If you'll accept this..." Andrew pulled something from his pocket. "If you'll wear this..." He held up a small gold ring, encrusted with a very sizeable diamond proudly sitting in the clasp. "You will indeed, be dressed properly."

The seconds of time almost came to a stop and Emma was transfixed as bubbles of tears rose to her eyes.

"Will you marry me? And will you add this to your outfit tonight?"

One of the girls let out a cry, "Oh my – Oh how lovely."

Amanda looked across and smiled at Ruby who was actually crying and blubbering and soaking up the tears with a tissue before they could destroy her make-up. The other four girls began to whisper, sob and sigh.

Emma stood motionless, suspended in time, holding on to Andrew's hand as the seconds seemed to stop ticking. Their gaze was firmly and mutually fixed ... until Emma had to blink the first droplet from her eye. "Oh gosh," she whispered as Andrew prompted her by placing the ring at the tip of her finger, "Yes. Yes... I will."

The other six women in the room clapped and whooped, sighed loudly and then screeched, 'Congratulations!'

Andrew slid the ring along Emma's finger, which she was amazed to find, fitted perfectly. He then stood up and pulled her in to him and wrapped his big arms around her.

"I love you," he whispered in her ear but Emma only just heard him between her own sobs of happiness and the babble from the others. Pulling away, Andrew looked at her while the other girls swooned and bleated about what they had just witnessed. "I'm coming with you tonight," he said, before looking across to Ruby and then Amanda.

"Yeah – sorry Emma, we already knew about this," said Amanda, pointing to Ruby who was still sobbing.

The other girls looked up from their mass, slush-filled moment and stared at Amanda. "I knew he was coming with us, sorry I couldn't tell anyone," she exclaimed.

"Me too," spluttered Ruby before exiting the room with a damp tissue attached to her nose.

Emma looked down at the beautiful ring on her finger in disbelief. She was engaged to be married and she hadn't had a clue about it.

Ruby returned to the room carrying Emma's overnight bag. Emma had remained riveted to the spot – speechless.

"We're staying in a hotel tonight," said Andrew. Emma gazed at him and then peered around at Ruby who was holding on to her bag, still crying. Tears fell from Emma's cheeks – she'd been set up for this – she'd had no idea at all and it was totally amazing.

Still stunned and silent, Emma followed Andrew to his car while Ruby, Amanda and her tribe of chuckle heads climbed in to the minibus. They were going to follow the others to the meeting point, which Emma hadn't taken any notice of. She was running on automatic pilot as the emotions of the last half hour swirled around inside her like clouds of rainbow colours. She didn't care where she was going as long as she was with Andrew. Amanda's birthday bash had taken on a whole new meaning.

Just outside the city centre the minibus, followed by Andrew, took a sharp left turn and drove along a short road to what looked like a small community centre. "Where are we going?" asked Emma feeling dunk on love.

"Don't know, I'm just following the bus," replied Andrew, as he parked up alongside the minibus at the front of the building. "Come on – I think Amanda wants to go in there," he said, climbing out of the car.

The passengers from the minibus all piled out and stood waiting, silently. Andrew scooted around the front of the car and took hold of Emma's hand as she climbed out and then he led her to the double door entrance of the empty looking building.

It was dark inside and eerily quiet, Emma stalled before being pulled through the double doors to an interior door. Looking behind her she could see the others, led by Amanda, following them. *Where the hell are we going?* Emma wondered.

Andrew opened the smaller door and thrust his arm around Emma to pull her in to what she thought was a blacked-out hall.

Instantly the lights came on, dazzling Emma's eyes. She jumped and then computed the sea of heads and then faces and bodies.

The people standing in front of her bellowed out 'Con...grat...u...lations!'

Music started to play and filled the room with one of *Cliff Richard's* oldest songs, *'Congratulations'*, and the people cheered.

Emma was dumbfounded. There was her mum... her dad... her brothers Aaron and Joe. Colin and his wife Rosie, Dave... and Jeff and Pete and others from work – everyone! They all stood there smiling at her.

Turning to Andrew, Emma realised exactly what was going on. It was their engagement party. Andrew had arranged it all and she'd had no idea. The young girls, along with Amanda and Ruby, moved around them and stepped in to the hall to join the crowd of onlookers and well-wishers.

Ruby was the first to approach Emma, even though she had already congratulated them earlier (once the tears had subsided), "I am so happy for you Em, you're going to get married and... and live happily ever after... and... and one day you'll have children... and..." Ruby wiped her nose and sniffed, "And then you'll be a yummy-mummy... no I mean you'll be a gummy-yummy-mummy!"

Emma stared at her in amazement, her little geeky friend had really changed over the last year but the things that came out of her mouth could often be quite bizarre and sometimes even outright humiliating as Ruby's vain attempts to be trendy, failed miserably. But Emma loved her all the same.

Ruby grinned and leaned over to kiss Emma on the cheek, "I bet you would rather see a dentist now than give birth to an elephant," she whispered.

Dear Dentist

I only came to see you for a filling
One look inside my mouth – you asked – was I willing
To have some new teeth? Yes, I said through tears
My fear had made me stay away for years.

You promised me that pain I would not feel
That crowns and bridges would be part of the deal
You filed my teeth away for hours and hours
While I watched thro' your window the birds in the boughs

At last it seems the time has nearly come
To finish my treatment, it's excellent, second to none
I have a new mouth worth a thousand pounds, I'm told
Who's worried about the dentist now, I'm quite bold!

By Joan Stevens (1988)

Printed in Great Britain
by Amazon